IRREGULAR
SAFARI

IRREGULAR SAFARI

HUGH ALDERSEY

Cover Design by BookPOD
Cover images by iStockphoto
ISBN: 978-0-9944339-6-1

Fifth reprint 2019

Contents

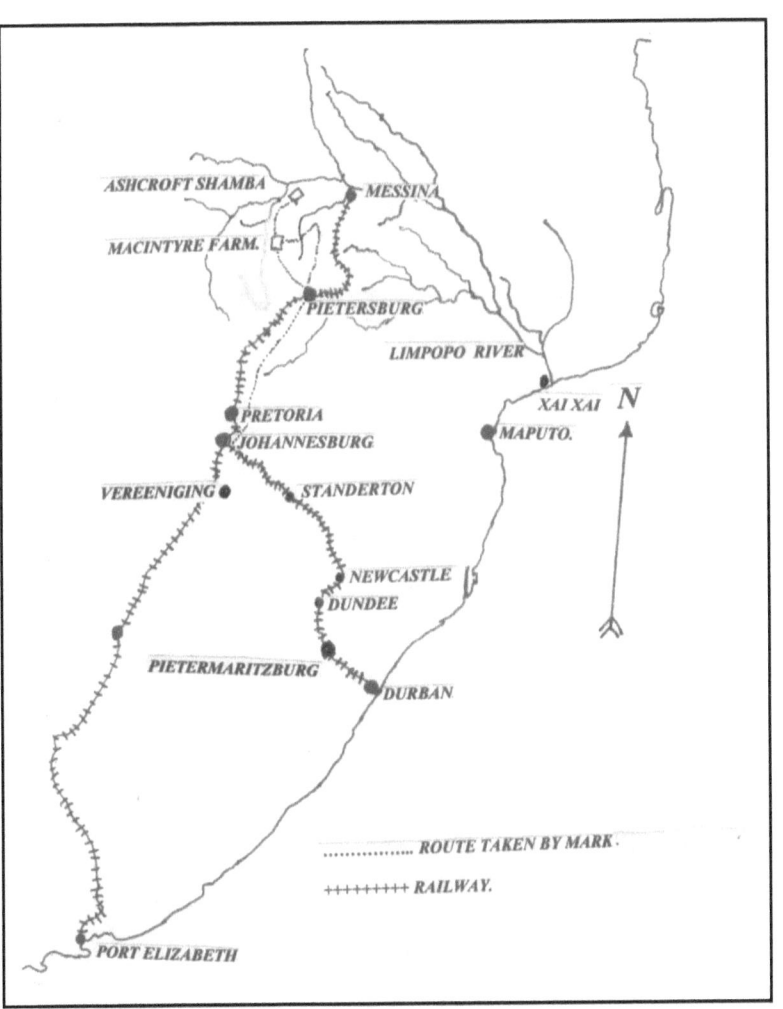

ASHCROFT SHAMBA

MACINTYRE FARM.

MESSINA

PIETERSBURG

LIMPOPO RIVER

XAI XAI

N

MAPUTO.

PRETORIA

JOHANNESBURG

VEREENIGING

STANDERTON

NEWCASTLE

DUNDEE

PIETERMARITZBURG

DURBAN

.... ROUTE TAKEN BY MARK.

+++++++++ RAILWAY.

PORT ELIZABETH

CHAPTER 1

SCOTLAND (1896)

The steam locomotive and its four bright red passenger coaches slowly wheezed and chuffed up the steep incline through the great wood while Mark Oakhill peered excitedly through the soot stained window. As the train topped the rise, Mark saw his father's groom, Phillips, driving the pony and trap down into the station yard.

At eighteen, Mark was already nearly six foot and well muscled. He could hardly wait for the train to screech to a halt before jumping onto the platform to start his summer holidays from college.

A porter soon had Mark's luggage trundled out on a trolley and loaded into the pony trap. As Mark took his seat beside Phillips he said, "Hello, what's happening at home?"

Phillips was a thick set man with bandy legs, from too much bare-back riding as a child, and a round friendly face. He lifted his cloth cap and scratched his head before answering.

"There is much preparation, for the master is all set to go to your uncle's estate in Scotland for some shooting on the moors."

"What, do you mean that father has accepted Uncle James' invitation to go to Glencairn again, who's going, how long for?"

"It looks as though you are all going, but I don't know how long for."

"That is super." Said Mark.

The sturdy pony tired as they started up the long drive between the avenue of chestnut trees leading up to Oakhill Hall. Mark's mother, Agnes, a tall, well built woman with light brown hair tied in a bun, came down the steps with Mark's sister, Anne, as the trap pulled up at the front door.

Mark gave each a quick kiss and followed them into the long dining room.

"I'm sure that you would like some tea dear?" "Yes please Mum, I'm starving."

While they sat at the long, solid oak table with Mark filling the void that had developed during the all day train journey, the conversation got round to the great news about the planned trip to Scotland, that had already been revealed by Phillips.

The 18 foot ceilings and full height windows gave a wonderful view of the slightly undulating park with its established oak trees, well cropped grass and herd of pedigree Hereford beef cattle. A lake with willow and poplar trees on the far side was situated on the lower slope in true 'Capability Brown' style.

"What is this super news about all of us going to Scotland Mum?"

"Oh, I suppose Phillips has already let the cat out of the bag and that you already know Dear. Well, your father has decided to go to Glencairn for some hill shooting and take us all this time. He says that it is time that you and your brother Hugh got some good Scottish air and spent some time with uncle James' Ghillie. Anne is coming as well so that we can have a proper family holiday." Anne was very excited and said. "I am really looking forward to seeing Scotland and all the places along the way."

Agnes said. "Don't forget that dinner is at eight, sharp, so Mark you had better go and have a bath and a rest."

Mark carried his luggage up to his room on the third floor, unpacked, and having decided to have a leisurely bath, he walked barefoot to the bathroom at the end of the passage with just a towel wrapped round his waist and ran a bath. He let the towel drop to the floor and had one leg over the edge of the bath when he heard the door open and close behind him. Looking round, he saw the eighteen year old, junior maid, Emily, standing by the door staring at him, while she clutched a towel and a change of clothes.

"Tis a fine strong man that you have grown into Mister Mark!"

"You gave me quite a surprise, Emily, but you have me at a disadvantage, I can't comment on your appearance because you are still fully dressed." Mark picked up the towel and while he was wrapping it round his waist Emily blushed and said. "Well, how much would you like to see?" "You could start by showing me those lovely long legs of yours."

"T'is a bit of a lad that you are. What if someone comes up here?"

"Nobody comes up here in the afternoon or evening and I am not expected till dinner time." Raising her skirt, Emily turned round and round exposing her shapely legs. Looking back at Mark she said. "How was that little peep show"?

"You certainly have lovely legs, but would you like to show me more?"

"What is that bulge pushing under your towel, it looks as though you are going camping.

Here, let me feel how hard you are? Oh my! You are like timber already."

Mark was becoming so excited that he said. "Let's have a bath together."

Emily said "Let's try undressing each other." Mark fumbled with Emily's dress, but she undid the buttons herself and after a few mock attempts to release the buttons and a lot of giggles, let the dress very slowly fall to the floor.

Mark was becoming totally aroused and studied every part of her shapely little body. Standing in just her underwear Emily looked very seductive and Mark came closer and tried to take off her brassiere but she removed it herself. She had well rounded breasts which Mark kissed at her invitation. Emily's hands caressed his back and then came forward, removed the towel and held him firmly. Then going down on her knees, she 'pleasured' him till he was moaning with desire. "Oh, Emily, where did you learn to do that?"

"The village boys often wanted just a kiss down there, but some wanted more."

"Now it is my turn to see you." When he removed her knickers, Mark was fascinated by the triangle of red curls that matched her red hair. Emily was now breathing heavily and her face was flushed with desire. "Quick, put him in, I can't wait any longer."

Mark was amazed at her sudden passion and how easily he penetrated her. He realized that she was definitely not a virgin. They both came to a quick climax and pulled apart with some feelings of guilt.

"Come on Emily we had better have a quick bath before anyone comes up here. That was my first time and it was so quick." While they sat in the bath washing each other, Emily said. "You were very good and fully satisfied me, even if it was your first time and you finished too quickly."

"You took me by surprise, and you just made it happen, but it was wonderful even if it was so naughty. I did not realize that girls are so passionate and enjoy it so much, you were absolutely amazing and the sight of your body made me wild with excitement."

While they sat in the bath, Mark found that Emily was 18 and had had several 'experiences'.

"The older boys are devils, they wait for us girls when we take a short cut through the great wood and then they get 'fresh.' At first I was scared, but then I found that it is so good to be with a boy, I always want more and when I saw you naked I wanted you immediately and had to have you.

I got excited and wet just at the thought of having you inside me."

After the bath, Mark went back to his room at the end of the passage and Emily went back to her bedroom in the attic which she shared with another maid.

Mark was very quiet at dinner and his mother said that he looked tired and that he had better not be too late going to bed. Exhaustion after the long journey home, and all the excitement in the bathroom, made Mark sleep deeply till the bird's dawn chorus had him awake at 6 o'clock and looking out of his bedroom window across the park where the herd of pedigree Hereford cattle munched their breakfast of grass.

Family breakfast was at seven sharp to ensure that everybody was ready to leave in time to catch the 9.30 train.

Brother Hugh had returned from preparatory school a day earlier and was already packed and ready to go. At thirteen, Anne was already quite mature for her age. She had long blond hair which was usually plaited into a pigtail. Agnes had decided to take her new maid, Emily, to help with the extra housework during their stay with her brother at Glencairn.

The journey northwards was exciting with all the new scenery and place names to absorb. Mark, Hugh and Anne were encouraged by their mother to each make a diary, but this soon deteriorated into the two boys doing the observing and shouting instructions to Anne on what to write in her diary. William Oakhill slept most of the way. Emily was reading a magazine but gave Mark the occasional sly wink.

It was well after midnight when Uncle James' carriage picked them up from the station and after 2 o'clock in the morning when they arrived at Glencairn on a dark and moonless night.

At first light the next morning, Mark, Hugh and Anne went to explore the house and grounds. The house was built from fully dressed, grey, local limestone and appeared to have been extended on several occasions. High, narrow windows were deeply recessed into the thick stone walls. The external doors were made from 2 inch thick oak planks and were hung on massive, ornate iron hinges. Neatly cut lawns sloped away from the house to end with a stone wall separating the park where sheep and cattle were grazing.

Having circumnavigated the house, the trio went through a wooden door into the farmyard. Smart new stone coach houses, stables and cow sheds made up the four sides of a large stone paved square. There were hay and grain storage lofts over all the buildings. A stone archway gave access to a driveway leading to the front of the house. The farm drive was lined with hay and machinery sheds. The quick tour of inspection gave the impression of a well organized and industrious business. All the horses and cattle looked in prime condition and the hay sheds were full of sweet-smelling clover hay.

Uncle James' only daughter, Elizabeth, a nineteen year old Oxford under graduate, came into the farmyard to tell them that breakfast was at eight, sharp, and was now ready, so they quickly followed her into the house while Elizabeth explained that she was due to go on a university holiday study tour later that day and then went to start packing as soon as she finished breakfast.

After breakfast Mark and Hugh were taken out to meet Ghillie and his black Labrador dog, Sam. Ghillie was a tall wirey man with large knobby knees and powerful legs showing under his kilt. Mark couldn't help noticing the large, strong hands with red hairs on the backs as his knuckles were held in a strong grip and accompanied by a friendly smile. Sam seemed to approve of the strangers and wagged his tail. As soon as the boys were alone in the gun room with Ghillie he said. "You will just refair to me as Ghillie and I will call you Mark and Hugh, we have a lot of ground to cover and only your holidays available."

Ghillie took some keys out of his sporran and opened a large gun cupboard on the wall. Inside there was an assortment of double barrel shotguns, hunting rifles, military rifles, a cross bow, small bore rifles and a rack of Webly Mk 1 revolvers. Ammunition was in a separate cupboard on the opposite wall. Gillie said. "We will start off with 0.22 rifles and then go to the latest 0.350 sporting rifles made by Rigby in London as well as 0.303 military rifles, then we can introduce revolvers."

"I was in the Army with your uncle James in India and was his sergeant major in the Highland Regiment' ye' ken. We had to look after each other in a 'few wee scraps' out there and developed an understanding, ye' ken."

Mark saw the two rows of medals mounted on velvet covered rails in the gun cupboard and realized that Ghillie had been sited for bravery along with Uncle James.

"Your father tells me that ye' have had some experience with a 20 bore shot gun and 0.22 rifles which is verra good, but we now have to make ye marksmen with a rifle and revolver as well as developing your bush craft and survival skills. There are many trouble spots around the world and we want ye' to be ready for whatever happens, ye' ken. Never forget ye' lads, 'a rifle is a man's best friend', especially when there is a wee bit o' trouble."

That profound statement was to prove to be very sound advice sooner than expected. Ghillie selected two 0.22 rifles, some paper targets and packets of ammunition before leading the two brothers past the farm buildings to the edge of a pine plantation, where a simple rifle range was set up. Some pine poles were embedded in the ground for mounting the targets in front of a sandy mound. Small posts were set out at 25, 50, and 100 yards with two sandbags by each post to be used as rifle rests. Sam knew the drill and lay down at the 50 yard post.

Ghillie taught the two boys basic range drill and safety rules and then showed them how to pin up the targets. "Lie down and fire a one round 'sighter' to the right of your targets."

Mark was keen to make every shot count, but in spite of taking careful aim his shot went low right of his aiming point. He realized that he had "snatched' the shot as he was not used to the trigger pressure required and Ghilie gave a detailed explanation. The training continued with ten round shoots before each target change and the accuracy slowly improved, with Ghillie's guidance, for the rest of the day. Once the boys got used to the rifles on the next day they were consistently scoring well. "Please Ghillie will you show us how you can shoot." Said Hugh.

"Ay, noo, just ten rounds then. Ghillie gave a whispered running commentary as he aimed and fired each shot. When the rifle had been cleared by Mark, Ghillie went and fetched his target which had a tattered hole half the size of a match box where all the bullets had passed through. "I saw that you used the rifle with the hair set trigger." Said Mark.

"Ay, that's the way I set up my weapons for the best performance every time. But it is different with a heavier rifle. I'll show you some time."

For the rest of the day Ghillie had them shooting from 50 and 100 yards till they were exhausted and hungry despite a sandwich lunch brought down by Ghillie's wife, Alice, a charming, motherly woman with her hair tied up in a bun.

On the following day Ghillie introduced the two brothers to the farm foreman and his forester, Archie MacLaggen. Archie already had a timber jinker harnessed up to six horses and loaded with saws, axes, mauls and wedges ready for a day felling timber high up the main valley. At first Archie had Mark and Hugh dressing off the branches and tops with axes and later they had to work one end of a cross-cut saw cutting up the already felled tree trunks into the required lengths for posts and rails. By evening, two very tired and dirty boys were glad to have a bath before the formal evening meal and bed.

Ghillie alternated forestry and rifle shooting on the range for the first week and for the second and third week forestry was replaced by long treks into the hills for rabbit shooting up on the moors. Each rabbit that was shot was immediately gutted under Ghillie's directions and later skinned back at the stable yard.

On the last Sunday of the holiday, Ghillie and Alice asked Mark, Hugh and Anne to have afternoon tea with them. Alice had made traditional Scottish oat cakes and scones which were washed down with hot, strong tea. By asking around, the boys had found that Alice could not have children but loved to have young people around the house.

"Now you practice every week till I see you at Christmas time." said Ghillie as they left to get packed for the journey home the next day. "Thank you for everything, you have been very patient with us." "And thank you for the tea." Added Anne.

For the last few weeks of the school holidays at home Mark took out a 0.22 rifle every day and culled the rabbit population by some 18 pairs, much to his father's delight. He wondered how he was going to keep up his practice during term time. His father was very serious about the training being given by

Ghillie. "You may need it before too long." but he would not elaborate. Back at college, Mark felt shut in and frustrated with classrooms, Latin, Maths, English and French, but at the end of the first week he saw a notice on the board asking for anyone interested to put their names down for the college shooting team. This was what he had been waiting for.

Elimination shoots were held each Saturday to select the first and second shooting teams.

Mark didn't like the clumsy college rifles and had great difficulty in obtaining a score good enough to qualify for the first shooting team. It took several attempts to persuade the master in charge to get the local gunsmith to reset the triggers and 'shoot in the sights'. Once this had been done Mark's scores steadily improved till he was equaling the scores obtained by the captain of shooting. By the end of term Mark was consistently getting the highest scores in practice as well as in matches against other colleges.

The Christmas holidays were to include 10 days in Scotland in January during the worst weather that Scotland could provide. Ghillie and Alice were delighted to see Mark, Hugh and Anne but the extreme cold was effecting Alice's health and she looked pale and was thinner.

In spite of a near blizzard, Ghillie and the boys set off for the range the next day "Just to see if you have been practicing." Mark scored well for the first 50 shots or so, then the extreme cold made his hands so numb that he started to lose accuracy.

On one particularly cold day with heavy snow falling, Ghillie said "How about some snap shooting in the loft?" The very thought of anywhere out of the freezing wind and snow drifts sounded like sheer bliss, so it was with much enthusiasm that they said. "Yes please Ghillie."

In a large loft over the stables and coach houses there was an access isle down the center with grain and chaff bins on each side and Ghillie had set up a snap shooting range with the targets raised and lowered by a system of cords operated by a large wheel beside the firing position. The end wall was protected by sand bags and logs. Before long Mark and Hugh were getting nearly perfect scores and Ghillie looked very pleased. The warmth generated by the horses below helped to keep the loft warm. "Up-two-three-down." said Ghillie as he turned the wheel to raise and lower the small targets giving just enough time to fire one shot, which had to be with pin point accuracy. The competition was so keen that the brothers soon had Ghillie, Uncle James and sometimes Anne, competing as well.

As Ghillie was to be away for the next few days to attend a highland gamekeepers' conference, he said. "Perhaps ye' can get Anne to work the snap shooting machine and get in some more practice while I'm away." Anne was pleased to help and even insisted on the boys doing the controlling while she had some fun at the snap shooting range herself.

When they were collecting the rifles and ammunition on the next morning, they saw Archie MacLaggen's son, James, furtively cross the yard and signal to someone to follow him. Much to their surprise, Emily quickly ran across the yard and hurried up the stairs to a hay loft after James. The trio entered another door to the hay loft and took up position to watch. As they watched, the kissing couple rolled about in the hay below them and then in a very confident manner started to fondle each other with Emily taking the lead. Emily then raised her skirt and James was penetrating her with great vigor while Emily moaned and called out with passion.

Anne said. "She is a little red headed raver. Who would have thought that our 'innocent' little Emily is like that.! She is so confident and knows just how to get what she wants."

Mark smiled to himself as he remembered the bathroom passion session.

The trio went quietly back to the snap shooting range and started shooting, with Anne working the snap shooting machine.

On one bitterly cold, February afternoon, Mark and Hugh were returning from an unsuccessful deer hunt, without Ghillie who was with Uncle James and their father on an adjoining property for the day, when Anne appeared. She was very out of breath from running up the rough track through the snowdrifts. "It's Daddy." she panted. "He's had a funny turn while out shooting over on the Archibald's moor." "Where is he now?" Asked Mark.

"Ghillie and Uncle James carried him to the crofter's cottage and he is still there, or so the crofter's wife told us when she arrived just after lunch. Mummy sent me out to look for you as I knew which track you had taken."

"Is there a short-cut across the moors to the Archibald's moor?" Mark said as they made a rough map scratched in the snow, but he was unsure if there was a way round a number of steep ridges. The 'map' confirmed that there were at least two steep ridges to cross, so with darkness closing in, the idea was abandoned as there was no immediate advantage in risking a cross-country trek in the dark and as it was only a doctor who could give medical attention anyway.

Back at Glencairn, the doctor had already been summoned and Archie MacLaggen had produced a wooden sledge from one of the farm buildings. The sledge could be hauled by a horse along the tracks or by men with long ropes up on the moor. The crofter's wife stayed over-night so that she could guide the rescue party, in the dark if necessary, on the next day. The plan was to set off on the three mile trek at 3. O'clock the next morning with the doctor and all his gear on the sledge hauled by horses for the first part along the tracks and then by relays of men on the steep section and arrive at the crofter's cottage at first light. The journey was a real test of endurance for Mark because of the blizzard which was raging and the extreme effort required to haul the sledge up the very steep parts.

Archie MacLaggen's man stayed with Hugh and the horses at the head of a valley and produced a bag of oats for the horses to eat while they rested and then lit a fire to keep warm.

The crofter's cottage was built of local stones with walls about three feet thick and had a low, thatched roof. Inside there were only two rooms, a kitchen / living room and a bedroom. William Oakhill was laid out on a large central table in front of the kitchen fireplace. His face was the colour of grey parchment and he was unable to speak. The wind howled and roared out side and snow continually blew under the door and then melted in puddles which the crofter's wife periodically mopped up. Uncle James had over stressed an old wound in one knee and it looked like a purple football. Ghillie was covered in blood from numerous falls in the frozen heather while supporting William Oakhill and latterly having to carry him to the cottage. A quick examination by the doctor confirmed that William Oakhill had had a severe stroke and that he may not live very long. The old crofter skillfully split some firewood logs to make splints for Uncle James' knee and his wife produced hot water to clean the cuts on Ghillie's legs and hands.

It took about an hour to get ready for the return journey with Mark's father and Uncle James well rugged up on the sledge and covered with a tarpaulin. Going downhill proved to be almost more difficult than coming up. Holding back on the fully laden sledge as it strained to break free and charge down out of control.

There was now a strange calm as the blizzard had suddenly abated. As they approached the head of the valley, a small column of steam rose up from where the horses were tethered in the lee of some gorse bushes.

The speed that weather conditions can change up in the mountains is a constant reminder of the power of the elements over the puny efforts of man, thought Mark, as they struggled back through the snow. The doctor was now complaining of the cold and the rough treatment his patients were getting on the sledge. He was very much out of condition and even walking and riding was an effort for him.

When the party reached Glencairn, Aunt Mary was the perfect nurse and had everything organised for Mark's father and Uncle James to be carried upstairs. The doctor stayed for about an hour with a promise to return the following morning and after a good stiff 'dram' for the road set of on horseback through the deep snow. Mark, Hugh and Anne took it in turns for the rest of the day to be with their father who slept fitfully and appeared to be in intense pain at times. Agnes sat up with her husband all night and was totally exhausted by the time the doctor arrived at noon the next day. Dr. Mackenzie gave William Oakhill another thorough examination and then took Agnes on one side and said "The end is very near. Ye' must be prepared. There is no more I can do for him. Now about your brother's old knee wound, there may be bits of shrapnel on the move again after all that exertion, but I canna' see to operate with all that swelling. Maybe in a week I can see where the trouble is and tak oot the hardware."

As predicted by the doctor, Mark's father died the next night having been unable to speak or even write anything. At times, his eyes spoke volumes and they had been able to 'communicate' by a sort of Morse code in long and short blinks in his more coherent moments. Funeral arrangements were quickly made and the simple service was held in the village church. Uncle James insisted on attending and had to be carried from the carriage to the church and back again. It was not till Mark returned to Oakhill Hall with the family that he realized that on his father's sudden death, under the traditional English inheritance system where the eldest son inherits the total estate, in order to keep it as a viable unit, that he had become the new master of the family estate and now had the responsibility of managing a large and complex business about which he knew very little.

Agnes Oakhill had not been given the opportunity to understand the details of her husband's business affairs, so Mark and Agnes had to piece together information gleaned from the agent, the bank manager and business associates.

It became apparent that the property was not as well run as Glencairn and that a large investment had been made in South Africa some ten years before. Returns from the South African Trading Company, (SATCO) had suddenly stopped during the previous year and there was a lot of correspondence demanding explanations from the SATCO. manager, Henk van de Brecht, but no meaningful answers had been given, other than. "There is much unrest in the Colony."

William Oakhill had kept putting off a visit due to bad health and the hope that Mark would soon be old enough to go and check out SATCO.

On the next morning while Mark and his mother walked slowly down to the lake in the bright winter sunshine over the frost covered grass, Agnes said. "Your father sold two farms about ten years ago and started SATCO. from scratch. After two visits all seemed to be going very well till just over a year ago when the returns stopped and your father was sure that the new manager had started some fraudulent scheme. We also found out later that the assistant manager appointed by van de Brecht had been in prison for causing some sort of uprising. SATCO. was providing one third of our income under the original manager before he became sick and had to retire early. We now have an urgent need to improve the home farm to compensate for the nil returns from SATCO, but we will need a large injection of cash to do that. Do you have any ideas Mark?"

"There must be some way we can raise the money without a mortgage. Is there something that we can sell to raise the cash? How about the timber in the great wood that runs along the railway, it is now fully mature and must be worth a fortune?"

"Your father often considered felling the great wood, but said that we do not have the skilled foresters to do the job properly and that it is much too far to the sawmill now that the sawmill at Brockington has closed down."

"How about me finishing at college and working here full time?"

"Oh no, you must finish and go on to university dear."

"But Mum, from the figures that the bank gave us the other day, the estate can't carry three sets of school fees on top of everything else now that SATCO has gone fut and we are in the red."

"Well there is truth in that, but do you feel ready to take the responsibility? You are still very young."

"I'm over eighteen and there is nothing like being chucked in at the deep end. What if I leave college now and work here for a while and then go and sort out that thief van de Brecht. But we must bear in mind that it may be necessary for me to stay on to train up a new manager or even sell the whole jolly show if it is as bad as van de Brecht says it is."

At this point Anne rode up to them and jumped down from her horse and started to walk along with Mark and his mother. The horse followed grazing from time to time. Mark noticed that his sister 'cut a bit of a dazzler' in her thigh-hugging riding breeches, well tailored tweed jacket and cap. "Some lucky blighter will get a bargain." Thought Mark.

"Mark and I were discussing the future of the estate and the possibility of him leaving college and starting to work on the estate. Have you got any ideas Dear?" "Well Mum, that is an alternative but shouldn't we have a proper manager now that we have lost Daddy."

"O Annie, trust you to squash the idea, but seriously, we are very pressed for the old 'luca' and saving school fees on one side of the equation and with someone to kick the backsides of the men here on the other to get some action, would be a great help."

Agnes said. "I have never mentioned it before, but Daddy knew that he had heart trouble and he had been taking things very quietly for the last few years and everyone had been taking advantage of him. That is why the place has gone back a little and the men have become lazy. Having a young, active member of the family at the helm would certainly spruce up the place and get things going again. There would be no need for you Anne to finish at college till you are 19 and then hopefully go on to university. By then Mark should have the estate much improved and running smoothly. He will also have to go out to South Africa and sort out SATCO pretty soon."

"I suppose that you are right Mum, but it seems a shame to have to leave college early and not have the chance to go to university, but if the devil drives, we must do whatever is necessary. What can I do to help; as you know I have started to do extra biology, perhaps that will be useful for the farm?" Agnes said. "Yes Dear, that is the best way that you can help. You continue your studies and learn as much as you can in biology and then perhaps you can go on to university and study agricultural science or something similar."

The trio was now at the gate into the stable yard, so Anne mounted her horse and rode off towards the stables while Agnes and Mark walked slowly up to the house.

Over dinner that evening, it was formerly decided that Agnes would write to Mark's head master advising that he would not be returning and that he would be taking up the duties as manager of the Oakhill family estate immediately.

At first, the men and the farm foreman resented being directed by someone as young as Mark, but then gradually accepted him as a competent leader. There were so many jobs that had been neglected that it was necessary to get their complete co-operation to fit each job into the busy program.

On one very cold day in February, Mark came back from a lengthy day of meetings with the bank manager and the agent in Chester to find that the men had only just finished mucking out the cow yards and had not got in a load of turnips or hay for the next day's fodder. It also appeared that they had just made work around the farm buildings and that there was no fodder for the ensuing week, with more snow expected. Mark called the foreman into the harness room, which doubled as a farm office, and asked for an explanation.

"Well, Master Mark, ye' see, it was too cold to go to the bottom barn to get the 'ay or turnips, the men wouldna' liked it, any road them cows is fat and they can chew a bit o' straw for a day or two." Mark was furious. "Firstly, you will not call me Master Mark, you will call me Mark or Mister Oakhill. Is that understood? Do you think I don't know how cold it was today, I left at seven in the open trap and was on the road for two hours each way. There is no excuse for not getting in the fodder, the men are well clothed and the work keeps you warm. I find your attitude decidedly Bolshie and I am warning you that any recurrence of this type or a lack of leadership will be your last. Now go to your men and ask for two volunteers to go with you to bring up a load of hay tonight." "B', b', but, it, is already dark, I can't."

"Get a hold of yourself man. Take a couple of lanterns. I will not listen to your feeble excuses while the stock go hungry. Can't you hear them bellowing? They are hungry because you failed to do a simple task, and just to prove that it is possible to bring up a load of hay in the dark I will join you as soon as I have changed." Reg. Maddocks went off to the cow sheds where the men were washing down after milking.

"The new boss, 'Mr. Oakhill', says we gotta' get a load of bleeding 'ay in the dark, NOW. With lanterns, he's daft, just because a few cows is blarting a bit with the cold. He wants two o' ye' to stay back and get the 'ay. Who's coming?"

"All rait Reg I will stay back." Said young Ken Phillips. "I need the money with the baby to feed." After some more banter another farm hand agreed to work back. They had a horse and dray harnessed up and rumbling down the icy track with a lantern swinging from each front corner in about ten minutes.

When Mark arrived they had quarter loaded the dray so Mark pitched in immediately and the load was ready for roping down in no time. The cattle smelt the load of clover hay from afar and started bellowing louder and louder as they approached the farm buildings. It was after eight o'clock when Mark took off his work clothes and went into the house to wash and change.

Over dinner Mark discussed the outcome of the meetings with the bank manager and the agent. Agnes, Mark, Hugh and Anne were all seated at the dining table and coffee was being served when Mark gave his report on the status of affairs.

"A nil return from SATCO again this month. The milk cheque was down again, and I'll bet that was because Reg. Maddocks has not been keeping up the feed to the milkers since they were brought inside for the winter, lazy bastard."

Agnes pretended to be shocked. "Mark you should not say that."

"But Mummy he is right." Said Hugh and Anne nodded in agreement.

"The last lot of steers we sent to market did not get our usual top of the market price, so I went and checked with the auctioneer and he confirmed that the Oakhill stock has not been up to our usual standard for the last year or so. Very disappointing after all the work father put in working up our herd over the years. Rent from the tenanted farms is lower than average for the district and there are two farms in areas, six months behind, one of them. The agent, Wickmass and Sons, are hopeless, just a fusty office full of dust, cigar smoke and stale fart with piles of papers everywhere. I am seriously thinking of sacking them and taking over rent collection and tenant agreements myself. I'm sure that I can make a better fist of it than that old whisky sot. I have been to Goldstien's the bookshop, and bought a couple of books. Farm Management, and Book Keeping Made Simple, I'm sure that we can sort out the estate and plan everything from here. We need a bigger office in the house with all the books kept up to date. We must not be dependent on some old dodderer in Chester who is six months late with everything. We are in the red and it looks like getting worse if we let things continue as they are at the moment.

Anne suggested. "Why don't we use one end of the library as the office rather than that pokey place father used?"

Agnes said. "Good idea Dear, we could move out the island book case and put in the desk, some more chairs and a table. It overlooks the stable yard and there is the side door for easy access from outside."

The office was set up in a few days, the agent sacked and stacks of musty papers taken to Oakhill Hall to be sifted through. A lot of the old records were burnt. Rents were increased to 4.5 % of the current value of each tenanted farm or cottage and those tenants overdue with their rent were called in for a meeting. Agnes proved to be a very tough negotiator in these meetings and very soon the back payments started to come in with the current month's rent. It was not till after Hugh and Anne had gone back for the Easter term that Mark discovered that his mother had written to her brother, Uncle James, asking if he could spare Archie MacLaggen, the forester, to supervise the felling of the great wood. Uncle James had replied by return mail offering not only the forester but Ghillie as well. His idea was that Ghillie could use his military experience in demolition to blow up the tree stumps and clear the land ready for replanting. Mark was delighted with the idea and asked Agnes to confirm the arrangements without any hesitation.

He then started feeling out the local larger timber merchants to put the best price on the logs. The best price came from Morgroves in Chester and Mr. Morgrove came out to inspect the stand of fine oaks. He liked to see the timber standing before confirming the final value and look for any rot caused by poor drainage. The great wood was on a steady slope with excellent drainage so the price per 'Super foot' was even higher than expected, but he would have preferred to have the logs 'broken down' by a local sawmill, if this had been available, to save cartage costs.

Mark saw Mr. Morgrove off in his trap and decided to walk back through the farm buildings and have a look at the stock. He was horrified to find a heifer down with a difficult calving and the men gone home. He quickly set up the local 'herdsman's windlass' by upturning a wheelbarrow against the heifer's buttocks, fastening a calving rope to the spokes of the wheel and securing the other end to the calf's' hind legs.

On turning the wheel, the rope was wound round the axle of the wheelbarrow thus becoming a very powerful windlass. Having soaped his arm and reached inside the heifer to ensure that the calf's position was as good as possible, Mark turned the wheel and applied tension. The heifer moaned and strained feebly, as she was very tired, and little by little the calf emerged as a breach birth. Ten minutes later the beautiful bull calf was being cleaned by its mother and Mark had a feeling of satisfaction having saved the life of the heifer and calf. He then realized that Reg. Maddocks must have known that the heifer was in trouble and needed help and he became very angry.

"That drunkard is unreliable and lazy." He fumed.

Reg. Maddocks was summoned into the office the next morning and Mark asked. "Did you know that the heifer was having trouble calving?"

"Oh 'ay, she bin down since dinner time but them young' uns have more push than an old cow, so she were alright."

"Oh no she wasn't, I had to pull the calf in a breech birth position. We would have lost them both. You were warned the other day over the fodder that I will not tolerate any more problems with the stock, you are fired as of now. Your pay will be made up and brought round to you tonight. You have a month to be out of the tied cottage."

Reg. Maddocks shuffled off without a word and went to find the other men.

"The bastard fired me. All because of that bloody heifer, who's he think he is? I'm going to the Bull's Head for a drink to steady me before I have to face the Misses."

After Maddocks had gone, Ken Phillips said. "He's been too bloody good at 'steadying himself to face the Misses' for a long time and wasn't in a fit state to do his job."

"Drunken sod was always half pissed." Said another man.

Over dinner that night that was exactly what Mark and Agnes were discussing. "He has been an alcoholic for years and couldn't control his men, I could never understand why my father put up with him for so long."

"Mark, your father was only tolerant because Maddocks had been in the Army, but I suspect that he was only a cook or a batman, but nevertheless a soldier of sorts."

"Anyway he's gone now and we must appoint a new foreman as soon as possible. How do you feel about Phillips, the groom, he has always been very loyal and he is very good with the horses and he keeps the equipment in perfect condition. He also manages the stable boys well and is good at delegation. I would like to consider making Phillips the overall foreman and giving the juniors a bit more responsibility." Said Mark.

Agnes agreed with Mark's suggestion to appoint Phillips and they then went on to plan the complete renovation of the cottage relinquished by Maddocks in readiness for the Phillips family to move in and take up their entitlement of the best cottage on the estate which was close by and complete with its own walled vegetable garden and all facilities.

A month later Ghillie, Alice, Archie MacLaggen and Sam arrived and moved into the cottage vacated by the Phillips family ready for the felling of the great wood. Archie MacLaggen made a complete study of the area and then to everyone's surprise said that he would like Mark to buy the sawmilling machinery from the old sawmill at Brockington. He proposed to set it up to saw the logs on site as required by Morgroves. Sawn timber would command a much better price and save freight costs. So as soon as this method of operation had been agreed upon, Archie carefully selected a team of strong local men to fell the great wood and operate the sawmill. The machinery was purchased at near to scrap value, repaired and transported to a level site near a stream at the lower edge of the great wood.

As soon as the machinery was installed, a flat roofed shed was erected over the top with a chimney for the boiler. Water for the boiler was piped from the stream. Ghillie made several trips into Chester to obtain his supplies to make the black powder for blasting out the stumps. His grin was like that of a small boy with his favourite toy. An ancient butter churn was commandeered for mixing the black powder. 75% potassium nitrate, 10% charcoal, and 15% sulpher, were carefully weighed out, mixed and filled into small cotton sacks ready for use.

Anne and Hugh were home for the Easter holidays when the operation started. Ghillie made sure that his expertise in demolition was passed on to Mark and Hugh. He skilfully set every charge with primer and fuse with just the right amount of powder to give the exact amount of 'lift' to blow each stump cleanly out of the ground. A few demonstration blasts were given when old dead trees were toppled in a predetermined direction. "Knocking the legs from under a bridge is much the same." Said Ghillie, with a knowing grin on his craggy face.

By midsummer the timber cheques were coming in regularly and the estate account was growing steadily. On one of Ted Morgrove's visits to check on the quality of the sawn timber, he brought his only daughter, Margaret, with him and late in the afternoon Agnes asked Ted and Margaret to join the family for dinner before returning to Chester. Mrs. Morgrove had died some years earlier and Ted always welcomed the opportunity of a little social life, so he accepted with pleasure. Dinner was a very happy occasion because the two age groups seemed to have much in common and the business venture was working well and profitably for all concerned.

After dinner, while they were relaxing in the beautifully furnished Victorian drawing room drinking coffee and port,

Ted Morgrove suggested that he could put Mark in touch with a contractor who had the very latest steam plowing engines which could haul away the stumps into windrows for burning and then cable plough the whole area ready for replanting. Mark was immediately very impressed with the idea and noted the details to follow up as soon as possible.

Margaret Morgrove now started to accompany her father on all his visits and soon the visits were extended into her staying for the weekends when Anne, Margaret, Mark and Hugh played tennis or went for long rides into the nearby hills. A close relationship started to develop between Margaret and Hugh in particular.

As Queen Victoria's Jubilee approached in 1897, Agnes started to make plans for the local celebrations. All the tenant farmers, employees and their families and friends were invited to an outdoor function with games and competitions for the children followed by a magnificent luncheon in a marquee with plenty of food, beer and spirits for all. Ghillie, Alice and Archie McLaggen were accepted as locals and joined in the festivities. During the evening, Ghillie played his bag pipes and there was much singing and dancing well into the night. The sound of Ghillie's pipes brought back memories for Agnes of her late husband and his military service and she had to make a show of blowing her nose to wipe away the tears. The following day the whole family went into Chester to see the unveiling of the new clock over the 'Eastgate' on the old Roman walls of the city. Even though the family arrived early, they had difficulty in getting the carriage into the Grosvener Hotel stables. Old Tom, the head groom at the hotel, suggested that for a good tip he could arrange for one of the reliable stable lads to feed and walk the horses, with the carriage, in a quiet street for the day.

When the mayor unveiled the new clock over the Eastgate to celebrate Queen Victoria's Diamond Jubilee, there was more of a gasp than a cheer because it was so modern and ugly.

There was much public speaking and celebrating for the rest of the day in the city and crowds of people thronged the narrow streets. It was quite impossible to get the family carriage back into the city till the throng had cleared, so Ted Morgrove invited the family to his house for dinner. Margaret proved to be a very capable hostess. During dinner the subject of South Africa was raised and Agnes gave a summary of the SATCO venture and its current problems with Henk van de Brecht, the manager, and his assistant Peer.

Ted had an agent in Durban who arranged shipments of mahogany timber for the furniture trade, so he said that he would arrange for his agent to make enquiries about SATCO and it's manager in Johannesburg.

It was after midnight when Ted and Margaret said goodnight to their departing guests by the light of a nearly full moon. The horses were tired after the long day, so Mark did not make them hurry as they travelled back to Oakhill Hall in the moonlight. Agnes and Anne slept inside the carriage while Mark and Hugh sat up on the driver's seat talking over the future plans for the family estate and their own personal plans and fantasies.

On the next visit by Ted and Margaret Morgrove, the quality of the timber was again being discussed when Agnes asked if a reply had been received from his Durban agent about SATCO. "I sent a cable last week to Gustav Petersen and will let you know as soon as I get a reply.

I was very fortunate to make contact with Gustav some years ago, because he has top quality African mahogany which makes the very best furniture in the world with teak it's only rival. In his earlier letters, Gustav says that even though the

Dutch Government, in their greed, sold the Cape Colony to Britain, the old, Dutch settlers, or Boers as they are called, won't let go and it may lead to war. The Boers have taken many of the government jobs and control many of the official services already."

Felling and milling the timber from the great wood continued and the monthly payments still continued to build a sizeable credit in the estate account. Arthur Phillips as foreman was proving his worth and the home farm returns steadily improved. Agnes said. "We must start the improvements to the buildings and farm cottages right away Mark."

"Yes Mum, I agree with you and I will put together a construction crew headed up by the estate carpenter and start work immediately. Extensions to the important farm buildings, new drains, piped water where possible, roof repairs, new stoves and hot water systems for most farms and cottages. I will get the carpenter to make up a list of what we need right away."

Now that the timber felling was well advanced, Mark engaged the steam ploughing contractor, recommended by Ted Morgrove, and Hough and Company duly arrived with all their latest equipment. Two Fowler cable ploughing engines, a special double sided four furrow plough, extra cables and a water cart puffed up to the great wood and set up camp close to the sawmill. The engines spent the first few weeks hauling the stumps into windrows ready for burning, then the ploughing started.

One engine stood at each end of a selected area and then winched the plough from one engine to the other and back again. Each time the plough changed direction, the engines moved four furrows width forward and as the plough tipped over, the four plough shears on the other side bit into the turf and four perfectly formed strips of turf were turned over without any apparent effort.

The power of steam is amazing, thought Mark. It required two teams of men to keep up supplies of dry wood for the furnaces and water for the boilers so that ploughing could continue all the daylight hours and often well into the night as well.

Ted Morgrove's agent in Durban, Gustav, Pedersen, of the Durban Forwarding Company had not been able to get any detailed information on SATCO or the manager. There appeared to be plenty of trade taking place with the Boer farmers, the mines and small traders but without access to the books it was impossible to tell why the operation had ceased to be profitable. Gustav supplied a lot of the imported goods and made periodic visits to his customer.

Pressure was building up for Mark to go to Johannesburg and find out for himself, but there was the logging, stump clearing, ploughing and replanting in full swing as well as the farm and herd improvements to supervise.

Archie MacLaggen had had to return to Glencairn because of forestry requirements there, but his background training as a ship's fourth engineer and experience with steam plant and machinery had been passed on to the men working the breaking down mill and the sawn timber continued to be loaded on to railway wagons each week with only minor problems. Ghillie and Alice were alternating between Glencairn and the Oakhill estate in two to three month stints as the work demanded. Mark did the blasting while Ghillie was away and was now using the new Dynamite rather than the old black powder. Huogh and Co. proved to be very reliable and was doing an excellent job of contour ploughing the hillside as the stumps were blasted out and hauled away.

Cable Plough

Steam traction engine with winch underneath

One Saturday, Mark and Anne rode over to where the cable ploughing was in progress and Harry Huogh came over to where they were standing. "Morning to yer' both." "Good morning Harry; do you think that you could plough the reedy and swampy area down by the pine plantation?"

"That'll depend on getting some firm ground for the engines, but if the distance is too great we can always use a longer cable to span a boggy area. Would you like me to have a look?"

All three rode down to the swampy area and Harry Hough checked out the bank of the brook and round the edge of the plantation.

"Reckon we could put in a channel and let it drain for a while and then plough it very deep to let it dry out and kill the reeds. But we would have to get someone to take the levels to do it proper."

Anne said. "If you mean use a theodolite, I can do that as we have learnt surveying at the university this year but we will have to buy or borrow an instrument from somewhere."

"How would you like to do that in your next vacation so that we can get this project started as soon as possible and then get this whole area into full production because it is beautiful, rich, black soil that should grow almost anything."

"You get the instrument and I will plan on starting at the beginning of next vacation, but I will have to work out the levels with Harry when I get started."

Harry nodded his approval and looked pleased at the prospect of an extended contract and working with such a good looking surveyor. He kept eyeing her shapely figure and smiling.

The next day being Sunday, was a welcome rest and the family was just sitting down to lunch when a messenger arrived with a letter from Ted Morgrove saying that another cable had come from Gustav Pedersen in Durban reporting that Henk van de Brecht had just vanished one day without any explanation and that Peer the assistant manager had also gone missing.

Mark now had to catch the very next steamer to Cape Town or Durban. He could not delay his visit to the dark continent any longer.

CHAPTER 2

SATCO

The ship was due to berth at Durban at 8 O'clock, so Mark was up early and packed by 6 O'clock and was leaning over the rail to see more of Africa. After the brief stop in Cape Town he would never forget the sight of the table mountain with it's mantle of cloud, just as he had heard it described by other travellers.

As the ship neared Durban, it rounded a headland and the strange smells of East Africa wafted across the water and Mark's excitement and apprehension mounted as the shoreline and port became more clearly defined.

As soon as the gangplank was lowered, a great bear of a man with a blond beard took up position on the quay. With his seaman's cap he looked like some maritime official as he prepared to scrutinize each passenger leaving the ship. Mark quickly returned to his cabin to collect his hand luggage in readiness to disembark.

Up on deck the heat of the day was mounting rapidly and he was glad that he was wearing his father's old open neck bush shirt and lightweight trousers. As he paused to get his bearings at the end of the gang plank a huge hand suddenly gripped his shoulder and spun him round.

He found himself looking up into the face of the man wearing the seaman's cap.

"You William Oakhill's son, ya?"

"Er, yes, I'm Mark Oakhill."

"Me thinking you having the same blue eyes, and maybe his shirt also?"

"Yes this was my father's shirt. Presumably you must be Mr. Gustav Pedersen?" "Ya, I'm Gustav Pedersen, welcome to Africa. My company did all the sheeping for SATCO, when your father first coming 'ere. I have not seen him for a long time and now Ted Morgrove is telling me he was sick and died. I am sorry for he was a very good man for this Africa, ya."

Mark had not expected to be met by Gustav, but it was reassuring to have a reliable contact who had been an associate of his father to show him the ropes in Durban. Gustav insisted that Mark stayed with his family for two days to get familiar with the lifestyle in Africa before going up to Johannesburg and arriving at SATCO. with all it's problems.

Mrs. Pedersen was a petite blond woman who was dwarfed by her husband and was a very busy and intelligent person. They had two very attractive girls of about ten and twelve with long, blond hair plaited into pigtails.

Gustav took Mark round Durban and showed him his warehouse down on the quay and his steam driven sawmill on the outskirts of town on the bank of the river where the barges and smaller ships could be unloaded. Mark was horrified by the old slavers camp and the 'barracoons' further up the river. "Do you mean to say that human beings were kept in those wooden cages, or barracoons, and then sold to the Americans?"

"Ya, that is so, the slavers were mostly Arab Muselmen, Moslems you are understanding and very cunning, they got selected African tribes to capture rival tribes and then marched the prisoners down to the coast in chains. Many died on the way or in the small ships on the way to Durban. The hyenas and sharks got very fat, ya.

When the American and Dutch slave ships came to Durban, the slaves were paraded naked on that platform over there by the Arab slavers and auctioned to the masters of the slave ships. The strong young men who could work hard in the cotton fields in America always made good prices. Also the healthy young girls with the big titties and broad hips for the good breeding of children were always making good prices. The ship's masters also looked for the slim virgins for making much jig y jig on the voyage, ya. The slavers made the young girls lie on that special bench over there so that two men could force their legs apart and demonstrate to the buyers that they were virgins, ja. We were always knowing when the slave ships were coming for you could smell them for ten miles over the sea. You never forget that terrible smell of the poor devils chained in little racks below decks on those terrible ships."

"I have read about the slave trade, but it is still a terrible shock to see where it actually took place."

"Many local Dutchmen and Arabs made very rich from the slave trade, so they were very angry when the British stopped the slave ships coming and made the slaves free. There still are many small Arab slavers, but they have much difficulty to trade with America so they only have the young girls with the beauty and the young boys for the houses of pleasure, ya.

I am from Sweden, ya, so these Dutchies are not liking me, so I am trading with the English and the export most times, but now there is a big trouble coming. I am thinking, there soon will be a very different trade, many soldiers to feed, and horses and army supplies needed."

On the third day the whole Pedersen family saw Mark off onto the train for Johannesburg. As Mark was about to board the train, Gustav shook his hand and offered every assistance and then Anna and the girls kissed him. The train rumbled out of the built up area and the expanse of Natal State spread out alongside the track for the first fifty miles or so. Mark felt very small and insignificant as the miles sped past the window and the heat increased as the morning progressed. By about ten o'clock the train began to climb up towards Pietermaritzburg. Mark was thinking about Gustav's background, brought up in a forested area and working his way up in the lumber camps till he was charged with negotiating the transport and sale of the timber to the masters of the freighters that plied the North Sea to England. The lore of the sea made him take a job as a deck hand on a freighter and start working his way up again till he was the mate on an ocean going cargo ship plying the London Tilbury docks, Africa, India route.

Engine trouble in Durban had caused a six month lay off for the crew, so Gustav had taken a temporary job in the local timber yards. He went back to his old skills learned in Sweden and soon became a respected employee working in the sawmill. During this time he met the owner's daughter, Anna, and they fell in love from the first meeting. Gustav continued the courtship for two more voyages till his contract had expired and then left the ship at Durban and married Anna shortly afterwards. Anna's father had died during an outbreak of diphtheria soon after the wedding and Gustav had taken over running the business. His trained eye for timber was soon adapted to the African species and he had then added the forwarding and trading part of the business, thus becoming; The Durban Forwarding Company.

At Pietermaritzburg, the other passengers got out of the carriage and a young English mining engineer and his wife got in and started up conversation. They were on their way to Johannesburg from Durban, but due to Heather being taken ill, had had to break the journey for a few days at Pietersmaritzburg. Heather certainly still looked very pale, but her husband, George, was a picture of health. They lived just out of Johannesburg and George had a consulting practice. What had started out as a quick visit to Durban for George to meet a client and a shopping trip for Heather had already taken over two weeks. Mark was delighted at the chance meeting and encouraged George to keep talking about the mining methods and the equipment used. George was a fund of information and had an excellent knowledge of the area.

As the train went up through Ladysmith, Dundee, Newcastle and Standerton, Mark recalled Gustav's comment about a steep climb and it being a bit cooler in Johannesburg. The journey from Peitermaritzburg to Johannesburg went quickly because of the company of George and Heather with their abundance of local information.

On arrival at Johannesburg, Mark booked into the Station Hotel for the night so that he would be fully rested for his first encounter with SATCO. He was not looking forward to the morrow and he had decided to arrive unannounced and have a quick 'recce' of the place before walking into the office, so he ordered a cab for 7 0'clock and got dropped off one street past the main entrance so that he could walk slowly back and see more of SATCO.

The size of the SATCO operation was very impressive. It occupied a whole outer suburban street block on the main road leading to Pretoria and Messina. A long clapboard building extended for most of the main street frontage with a cobbled entrance in the centre. Over the entrance, a timber archway carried the name; S.A.T.C.O. in letters two feet high. The archway extended for the full depth of the front building with the office door on the left and the general sales area on the right. Display windows faced the street on both sides of the entrance with the food section in front of the office. Four large corrugated iron warehouses could be seen in the centre of the SATCO compound and machinery sheds and workshops were located along the rear boundary. A large stone drinking trough for horses was prominent in front of the warehouses. Stables and fodder stores were on the right hand boundary with a smaller wrought iron gate leading into the side street. A very elaborate pair of wrought iron gates were folded back inside the main archway. Even at this early hour there was a lot of activity taking place. Several farmer's carts had gone in through the main entrance and were being loaded up by well built young Africans. A tall dignified man was walking round checking off the items being loaded. Having made a complete circuit of the compound, Mark braced himself and walked boldly in through the main entrance and into the office.

The first office alongside the cobbled entrance was deserted as was the second office but in the central general office area a bespecticled half cast clerk, probably Anglo-Indian, was writing up long bills of goods. He sat up and stared at Mark with disbelief and became very nervous. The other clerk just stared.

"Good morning, my name is Mark Oakhill and I have just come from England and I would like to see the man in charge." After some confused embarrassment the Anglo-Indian clerk said. "I was thinking at first that it was Mr. Willaim Oakhill, but he is dead, God rest his soul, but you will be his son, yes? I am Robert McKenzie, from India you know, but the manager, Mr. Van de Brecht he has gone a long time and also Peer his assistant so you can't see them. You will have to see Mr. Abdul Suliman, he is now in charge. Please wait in this office and I will ask Mr. Suliman to come to see you."

Mark waited in what had been Henk Van de Brecht's office and tried to study the man by what was left in the office. A large wall map with coloured pins dotted over it, a massive safe with the door open, a bookshelf that was nearly empty and some ledgers on a side table. The desk drawers were nearly empty and looked as though they had been cleaned out before the manager had departed. Peer's office told him even less as there was only the bare furniture left. A few minutes later Abdul walked in with his dignified manner and practically stood to attention as he very formally greeted Mark. "I am Abdul Suliman, who was chief clerk here till the managers left, and by very strict arrangement with Mr. Foster of the bank, you see, I am taking over as manager till you are coming. Please be very welcome and I will be pleased to be your obedient servant Mr. Oakhill." Whereupon Abdul very stiffly shook hands with Mark.

Mark said "I am very pleased to meet you Abdul and please call me Mark when we are in private. It was very good of you to step in and take charge. I can see that you are very busy so perhaps you can show me round quickly and then direct me to the bank and we can talk later." After a very quick tour of inspection, Abdul arranged for the senior stable boy, Raymond, to saddle up two horses and accompany Mark to the bank. After an hour with Mr. Foster, the bank manager, Mark started to get the drift of how van de Brecht and Peer had operated. All the transactions had started off as strictly normal but there was an increasing number of bad debts particularly with customers with Dutch sounding names and there was no record of any efforts to follow them up. These bad debts had been consistently negating any profit so that the Company was just hanging in limbo despite the successful efforts of Abdul and the staff to increase turnover. A very clever way of helping your friends and leaving the way open for graft and bribes. Mark made a mental note to follow up the bad debts as soon as possible. Mr. Foster was very keen to entertain Mark for lunch and or dinner but he declined as he needed a very clear head to maximize his time with Abdul over the next few days.

On leaving the bank, Mark got Raymond, to take him on a circular tour of the main business area before returning to SATCO for a one o'clock lunch. It appeared that SATCO was the largest of the merchant houses and had the potential to do a lot better than at present. He had to admire his father's judgment in setting up the company some twelve years ago. He remembered that some old army friend of his father's had done something similar in India a few years earlier and that it had been an immediate success.

Abdul sent for a sandwich lunch which was eaten in the office while Mark obtained more information from Abdul. The range of merchandise went from dry foods, kitchenware, blankets, bed linen, clothes, lamps, crockery, kitchenware, firearms, ammunition, harness, fodder, farm machinery and spares, fencing wire, pumps, hardware, tools, corrugated iron, sawn timber, mining supplies, explosives and they were also brokers for farm produce. A lot of the goods on display such as the dry foods and tinned foods were sold in case lots or in bulk direct from the warehouses in the centre of the compound.

Since Abdul had been in charge, the bad debts had mysteriously stopped and SATCO was about to show its first profit for two years. With an increase in custom, the whole operation could become highly successful. It was necessary for Mark to get right into the daily operation and get the feel of what brought the customers into town for supplies.

There was an attic over the office that was full of old ledgers and records so Mark decided to extend the attic and make some live in quarters for himself. It took six carpenters over three months to build a very comfortable suit of rooms with its own bathroom and kitchen.

This saved the cost of a hotel and also saved travelling time each night and morning. When Mark was ready to move into the new suit of rooms Abdul suggested that he could get a girl in from the mission school to do the cleaning and cooking each day. Mark agreed, and the next day Abdul returned with Sasha, a tall, dignified and very good looking girl and explained her duties. Mark was immediately attracted to this tall, very beautiful girl with long hair, light café au lait coloured skin and a wonderful smile. Sasha appeared to be from an educated family and was reserved and dignified. Mark was surprised that she also spoke French and English as well as the usual Swahili. How had such an amazing girl come from a mission school.?

Mark was sure that there had to be some way to improve sales to the farmers and miners and after some consultation with Abdul, he started to discreetly question some customers on their purchasing pattern. He also discretely 'tailed' some customers to see just where they shopped when they came to town. There was always a visit to the bakery for fresh bread. Then there was often a visit to a blacksmith to shoe a horse or repair a wheel or a broken implement, then they came to SATCO for general supplies and dry foods. But SATCO did not have a bakery or a blacksmith's shop, yet.

Across the side street opposite the stable entrance there was a jumble of run down shops owned by a retired English colonel who made his anti Dutch sentiments widely known. Behind the colonel's shops there were many acres of waste land partly covered with trees and scrub. If that land ever came on the market there was the opportunity to extend SATCO's operation into a bakery and a blacksmith's shop, as a draw card for the main store.

Mark moved into the 'quarters' on a Saturday and then helped Abdul pay the men and lock up at five o'clock before going to wash and change in readiness for going out to dinner with his friends from the train, George and Heather Bridgeman.

There was plenty of time so Mark decided to have a leisurely bath and contemplate the events at SATCO so far. His worst fears that SATCO was a 'fizzer' had not materialized, in fact, SATCO was a very successful operation with lots of potential to grow, if properly managed, the staff all seemed to be loyal and competent now that van de Brecht and Peer had gone.

Mark's thoughts drifted through his voyage, the time in Africa and at SATCO and the efforts of the day gradually took over and he drifted off to sleep in the bath.

FIRE! Suddenly he was awakened by someone screaming FIRE! FIRE! and by being choked by thick acrid smoke. There was also the ominous crackling sound of burning wood! Sasha was standing in the doorway shouting FIRE! and brandishing a bucket. Mark leapt out of the bath and quickly pulled on his recently discarded trousers and filled the bucket from the bath and stumbled down the stairs in the ever thickening pall of smoke which appeared to be coming from the cobbled entrance. There was fiercely burning material along the base of both walls and flames were leaping up to the timbers of the arch overhead and in another few minutes the fire would take hold of the whole structure. One bucket didn't make much difference, but Sasha had grabbed another bucket from the store and they both started to stumble through the smoke carrying buckets from the horse drinking trough in the yard. The office side was nearly out, but the other side was still burning fiercely. Some passers-by appeared at the locked gate so Mark let them in and the volunteers formed a bucket chain from the stone horse trough in the yard to Mark at the fire front.

After about ten minutes the fire at SATCO was out but the whole area was still filled with smoke and the cold winter sky was brightly lit by orange flames.

Up to this point Mark had been so intent on saving SATCO that he had not noticed that the Colonel's property across the side road had also been set on fire from the back of the complex and was now burning uncontrollably towards the road and would soon represent a threat to that end of the SATCO compound. The occupants of the accommodation above the Colonels shops just stood in the road looking helpless. More volunteers off the street with more buckets started to wet down the walls of the SATCO buildings facing the fire still raging in the Colonel's shops. The heat was too intense to get close enough to throw water onto the colonel's shops across the road.

A fire engine's bell could now be heard and the horse drawn engine appeared with the horses lathered in sweat. The engine slewed round at the intersection and stopped with it's rear facing the fire. Hoses were run out and men started to frantically work the see-saw handles of the pumps. Several bucket chains were needed to keep water up to the barrel built into the fire engine from which the pumps drew their supply of water. Jets of water shot across the road onto the fire and just turned into steam with the intense heat. Gradually the fire ran out of fuel and the fire died down but it had not been possible to stop most of the buildings being reduced to piles of char and rubble.

The man in charge of the fire unit sought out Mark and came over to determine the cause of the fires.

At this point Mark realised that it was Sasha's sudden appearance and his own presence in the quarters that had saved SATCO. This fact was not known by anyone outside the SATCO. office. Furthermore, Mark was not aware that anyone was still left on the premises when he had locked up. He would have to have a word to Sasha later and find out why she had stayed behind.

"How do you reckon she is starting?"

The accent told Mark that he was dealing with a Boer petty official. "Some sacks of straw, old rope and rubbish soaked in tar had been thrown over the locked gates and set on fire and this started the walls burning on each side of the entrance. It was deliberately lit."

"How do you know? You weren't here. Probably some cigarettes dropped in the office; here let me see."

Whereupon he pushed past Mark and went into the office. There was no internal damage so he went across the entrance and into the sales area. The base of the wall was partly destroyed but the fire had obviously come from the outside. "Some careless clerk with a cigarette, it happens all the time." "But can't you see the remains of the tar soaked sacks of straw and rope?"

"You should be more careful where you store things like that. I will report that it was started by some careless clerk dropping a cigarette in the office and that the sparks started the fire across the road. Very careless, you must have better discipline with your Kaffirs and foreign staff." Whereupon he stormed out before Mark could reply.

The ugly situation started to penetrate through the stress of the moment. SATCO and the colonel's shops had been singled out and 'Torched' by someone, and the official Boer report was that it was started by careless staff dropping a cigarette. Mark started to become furious but he could see the futility of trying to buck the entrenched Boer system of taking every opportunity to make difficulties and damage people or property that was not Boer owned and operated. Just as Gustav had warned him it would be.

There may be legal channels that he could explore later. There were still some thirty men and women in the yard who had given vital assistance and he felt that he owed them some form of thanks for their spontaneous efforts.

"Can I have your attention please."

They came round in a semi circle to where Mark was standing in the main entrance.

"Your spontaneous assistance is very much appreciated and I would like to repay you, so if you like to file into the office I will give each of you a 10 Pound voucher that you can use at SATCO any time during the next month."

Abdul appeared out of the crowd. "It is terrible, I am so angry, I was home with my family and a messenger came. Please may I help".

Abdul controlled the flow of volunteers and gave each one a firm handshake and a personal vote of thanks while Mark made out the vouchers on SATCO letterhead.

'Voucher for 10 pounds worth of goods re. help at fire 26th July 1899 Signed Mark Oakhill.

When everyone else had left, Abdul and Mark inspected the damage and checked that there was nothing left smouldering. During the tour of inspection Abdul was filled in on the events of the evening and the point was made that it was not known outside SATCO that anyone was living on the premises.

"This must remain a secret for the time being in case there is another attempt to burn down SATCO or make trouble in some other way." Said Mark.

Mark made a point of locking up and leaving with Abdul. When they were one block away, it was arranged that Abdul would call and give Mark's apology to George and Heather Bridgman and explain that he could not keep the dinner appointment. Mark would patrol the area from the outside and then when he was sure that all was quiet he would return to the quarters.

A huddle of people stayed for a while outside the colonel's shops, but soon after the colonel left in his pony and trap they started to drift away.

Mark stayed in the shadows for another half hour and got frozen in the chill night air and then cautiously let himself in through the main entrance and walked into the compound. There was still a strong acrid smell of burning and the walls of the main entrance were badly charred at the bottom with smoke stains up the walls to the ceiling overhead. Another few minutes would have let the fire get a firm hold on the timber building and at least the whole main building would have been destroyed. Mark had a lot to thank Sasha for. Not only for saving the building but possibly his own life as well.

A horse neighed as he walked past the moonlit stables and he looked in to see that all was well. The horses seemed very restless and he sensed that there was someone in the stable. Grabbing a pitchfork, he started moving slowly down the line of stalls. There seemed to be something wrong with one of the horse's legs! Then he realised that someone was walking behind a horse, stride for stride, with the horse. An old native trick that his father had talked about. Raising the pitchfork ready to strike, he rounded the horse's rump.

Sasha was standing there with her dress pulled up so that her bare legs would be hidden by the horse's legs. She looked terrible and was terrified.

"Sasha, whatever are you doing here?"

"Please do not be angry, I am having nowhere to go now that the mission has thrown me out." "Why did the mission throw you out?"

"They will not feed anyone who is working, so out you go, 'pacy pacy sana'. I am living in the loft, please don't throw me out because I am not having anywhere to go."

"Right now you need a bath and some new clothes and you are probably as hungry as I am. Select some good new clothes from the store and come up to the quarters and have a bath to wash off the soot and grime from the fire."

Sasha was waiting at the top of the stairs for his approval to use the bathroom.

"Of course you can use the bathroom and put on those new clothes to replace those that were damaged in the fire."

While Sasha was in the bathroom, Mark went down to his office and started to write to his mother for the first time since arriving in Johannesburg.

SATCO

Johannesburg.

Dear Mother,

Father has done an excellent job setting up SATCO and we are turning the corner already since the influence of van de Brecht and Peer has gone. They had been allowing their Boer friends to run up bad debts without any recourse and the SATCO. account was just hanging in limbo despite good trading. There is so much to be done that I have built quarters over the office so that I can spend more time at SATCO and get closer to the day to day operation.

In fact, living in the quarters saved our bacon tonight.

I was in the bath when we were 'torched' along with the English colonel's shops across the road. With the aid of Sasha, one of the girls on the staff, we were able to save SATCO but the colonel's shops were razed—a very close shave. The fires were deliberately lit, but the Boer fire chief has made out that it was caused by a cigarette dropped in the office—the liar. I will explore the insurance cover and any possible legal opportunity.

There is more trouble and ill feeling building up, as Gustav Pedersen has said, and we are going to have to take extra precautions from now on to protect SATCO.

Don't worry Mother, must away, will write again soon.

Please let me have your news from home.

Love Mark
P.S.

I met a very nice English couple on the train, George and Heather Bridgeman. George is a consulting /mining engineer and has been most helpful with local knowledge. Perhaps I can get the bank to send you a report on the SATCO account so that you can get the full picture of how van de Brecht was robbing us blind—there may be some political reasons.   M

Mark was addressing the envelope when Sasha came into the office and asked what he would like to eat for dinner. Sasha looked absolutely stunning in a new, light blue cotton dress with a full, pleated skirt which emphasized her well formed breasts and small waist. Her hair was brushed back and she had on red sandals.

"Let's go up to the kitchen and see what we have in the ice box." They chose some beef steaks and fresh vegetables from the ice box which Sasha expertly cooked on the small wood stove while Mark had a bath and put on some clean clothes. When he returned to the kitchen, Mark noticed that Sasha had some nasty looking burns on her legs and said.

"We must put something on those burns after dinner."

The meal was eaten in Mark's sitting room at the large table under the central lamp and they started to relax after the excitement of the day. Mark was fascinated by this exceedingly beautiful, uninhibited girl who seemed very capable for her 18 or 19 years and appeared to come from a different tribe or location because she spoke several languages and had very much lighter skin colouring than the locals. She also used an educated form of English and used some French words and expressions.

"Please tell me about yourself and your background." Said Mark.

"My mother was the daughter of an English geologist who had married a girl from the Southern Sudan and my father was a French engineer working for the Canal Suez Company.

We were living in portable housing moving along with the making of the canal and I had some very good schooling with the other senior staff children, which was provided by the company.

Suddenly there was a terrible argument over some missing money. My father was to be put in prison for making thief that he did not do, so we escaped into the desert and then the mountains that my mother knew and after a terrible year of travelling, we were living near Nairobi for a short time when the slavers came and we were captured and taken to Mombassa and then on a slave ship to Durban to be sold to the Americans with the big ships that smell so bad.

We were told later that one of the Canal Suez Company managers had made the false trouble about the money because he wanted to get my father out of the way so that he could force my mother to make mistress for him. He had come to our house many times in the middle of the day, when my father was working, and tried to, how do you say, 'mount' her, but my mother was very strong and stopped him, so he made very angry.

When the ship got to Durban we were put in wooden cages, I think they are calling them 'barracoons', n'est pas?

My father died very soon because of many beatings when he tried to stop the slave bosses hurting us. Mon pauvre Mamma was made to have jig y jig many times, cochons! Every day we were expecting the big American death ships, then suddenly very much noise and much excitement among the slaves, the slave bosses were running away very fast, much fighting and the English made us free, but nowhere to go and no food till the mission came and selected the young girls. I was forcefully taken from my mother by the fat priests from Johannesburg to learn school and cooking so that I could be sold to one of the big houses when I was old enough. At that time I was 12 years and had already had much school from the company and from my mother and father, but we only used the language of the Kenya people (Swahili) in case the Canal Suez Company found us because of French speaking.

We heard that the police had been told to look out for my father so he could be made to pay back the money and be put in prison. We also found that the Canal Suez Company manager paid many officials to believe his story about the missing money, that we think he had taken himself. We were still afraid of the old trouble about the money. Now I have been in the mission school for six years and I can read and write in English, sew, cook and work with numbers. I was told that the priests wanted to sell me for working in some big house, then Abdul came. The priests would not take any letters for my mother, I did not know if she was dead already, je ne sait pas. I did not have any money to go and see if she was still alive or find out how she was making healthy, but now I am told that she has died a long time ago. I only had the old clothes that had been given to the priests, other than the schooling, my living was not much better than the barracoons in Durban. Working for SATCO is the first work that I have had with proper wages."

Mark said "We must get a first aid kit from the store and put dressings on those burns."

So with the aid of a lantern they found a first aid kit and followed the instructions printed inside the lid. It was necessary for Sasha to sit in a chair with her dress pulled up to expose the burns on her legs while Mark applied the anti-septic jelly, gauze and bandages. Mark realised that he was becoming very aroused at the sight of Sasha's shapely thighs and had difficulty in concentrating on the job in hand.

"How did you plan on living in the loft over the stables without any running water, stove or food?"

"I had a few things that I had brought from the mission and one of the stable boys was getting me food and I knew it would be better soon."

After the meal they went round the compound again to check for any sparks or further damage, but all was quiet.

Sasha went quickly into the loft over the stables and returned with a small bundle of clothing, a tin mug, a plate and a few scraps of food.

"You had better sleep in the sitting room for tonight, and take care of those burns."

Sasha made up a bed on the sofa in the sitting room and Mark went out for a final check round the compound. Standing in the shadow inside the stable gates he saw two figures of European appearance moving in the still smouldering ruins of the colonel's shops and putting the odd item into a sack. Looters, I wonder if they will try to come in here? He watched them for an hour or so and realised that he was going have to take the law into his own hands to defend his property.

Moving silently, he went back to the quarters, and without using a lamp started looking for the trunk which contained his Rigby hunting rifle. The click of the locks awoke Sasha and she came over to investigate. Sasha volunteered to sit up in the landing at the top of the stairs inside a small window overlooking the entrance yard and part of the compound and watch out for any trouble.

Mark took the rifle with some ammunition to a position just inside the stable gate. The two men finished picking over the debris across the road and came over with their sack. One man tried the stable gate and then went round to the main gate and found that it was also securely locked. Mark took up a new position behind the large horse drinking trough which was in line with the main gate. He saw the two men move off down the street so he let himself out of the front gate and followed at a discreet distance in the shadows. The men had a horse and cart in a side street about a quarter mile away and there was a strong smell of tar coming from a small barrel in the cart. The men drank from a stone jar and moved off in a Northerly direction.

There was no point in trying to follow them so Mark went back to the quarters. Sasha was still sitting up at the window and had seen him go out and follow the two men and was visibly relieved to see him return unharmed.

At first light Mark was in the side street where the men had left their cart the night before and took plaster casts of the horse's hoof prints and the men's boots from the dusty road. Mark returned with the plaster casts in a carton. Sasha skilfully laid out the casts on the table just as they had been imprinted in the dust.

"I will know these evil men if they ever come back, as my mother's people can read the signs of the bush, so I can now read the signs of these evil men."

Abdul was shocked at the thought of Sasha spending the night in the quarters and was all for sending her back to the mission. He finally conceded defeat because she had saved the day by alerting Mark when the fire started and so it was arranged that another suit of rooms would be built for Sasha and any other female staff who needed accommodation. In the meantime Sasha used a camp bed in Mark's sitting room. Cleaning up and repairs were in full swing by nine o'clock on the Monday morning and customers started pouring in for fire sale bargains. Mark and Abdul decided to maximize on the situation and offered a 10% fire sale discount on everything for a month. The fire sale was an immediate success. George and Heather Bridgeman arrived at noon and Mark took them to survey the damage. They were appalled to think that the Boers would stoop to that level to avenge their leaders for selling the Cape Colony to the British.

"When your father built SATCO he did not have to worry about fire, it is a pity that he did not use brick or stone for the outside walls and make it more like a fortress."

"I suppose there's no way that we could build a stone or brick outer wall without too much cost?" "Sorry Mark, it would cost a fortune and take years but how about good old corrugated iron and a coat of paint? It would look the same but couldn't be set on fire from the outside."

"That sounds like a very good idea. Would you take an assignment to fix up SATCO and supervise the contractors if the prices are reasonable? Abdul has already turned SATCO round and we are in credit at the bank."

"I am very busy at the moment, but how about a few sketch plans and I will give you a list of reliable contractors."

"How soon can you do the plans George?"

"Give me till next Saturday and I will have it all ready for you to start the men."

George was as good as his word and came round with a roll of drawings on the Friday. He had detailed the corrugated iron cladding, added 2 inch thick timber shutters to all windows, extended the gates and added extra rooms over the main entrance with separate stairs. Mark was in agreement and the men were summoned for an estimates meeting on the Saturday. The costs were totalled and found to be reasonable, so work was scheduled to start on the Monday.

Mark had been successful in getting a settlement from the insurance company but the company lawyer was sure that it was no use going to the police with information about the arsonists.

"You will just get more of the 'official Boer bullshit' and may even be charged with starting your own fire and causing the fire across the road in the colonel's shops. Forget it for now but let me know if your native trackers find any more tangible evidence."

"Are you telling me that the Boers have infiltrated the government services to the stage when they can distort the facts and ride roughshod over whoever they please?"

"Yes, they are gaining strength and it will lead to war if events continue the way they are heading now. Just how long it will take the British Government to pull its lordly fingers out and take action remains to be seen."

After the meeting with the lawyer an intense sense of urgency gripped Mark and he had more carpenters added to the workforce and drove them from dawn till dusk for the next two months. The only way to preserve SATCO was to make it into a low key fortress and keep a guard on duty at night. Abdul kept on improving daily trading figures and ordered in more and more stock to keep up with the nervous stockpiling by the local people because of the threat of war. By nine weeks after the fire, the workmen had finished what they thought was the new look SATCO image, shown on George's drawings. It was now necessary to keep everything very low key and engage two guards to patrol the whole area at night. Mark asked Abdul for his suggestions.

"Askari, pacy pacy sana."(Soldiers, quickly—very)

"You use the same words as Sasha, why is that?"

"Though I came from Cairo, where I worked in my father's business, I was captured while on business in Nairobi and put into the slave camps where I learnt the language of the Kenya people, till I was able to escape and come to Johannesburg. I would like to go to Durban and get two good men who have army training and are not known here."

"Go as soon as you like Abdul and see Gustav Pedersen. You can tell him everything as we have a good understanding. In his last letter Gustav said that the Boers are keeping out of Durban because it is so cosmopolitan and they have little support there. Arrange with Gustav to hold our shipments coming into Durban and send up small quantities on each train so that if we are raided there will only be a few days supply on hand at any one time, for the fast moving lines anyway."

That evening Abdul stayed back when the store was closed and went into Mark's office.

"Your father's plans for this building are in the safe, I found them the other day and thought that we should look at them together." He spread out the drawings on the table and ran his finger over the elevation of the main office building. There was a large cellar shown under where they were sitting. "The cellar has never been used and I don't think van de Brecht knew of its existence because he was only here for about two years and the drawings were stored away with the accounts for the original building contract."

They took some measurements and located the trap door and stairs leading down to the cellar. It was necessary to move some heavy shelving to get to the trap door and when this was done the trap door opened easily and they went down. A musty smell and a skuttle of cockroaches greeted them as they used a lamp to explore the cellar. Stone blocks had been used to pave the floor and form the walls and a row of stone pillars supported the beams overhead. The racks and shelving were empty.

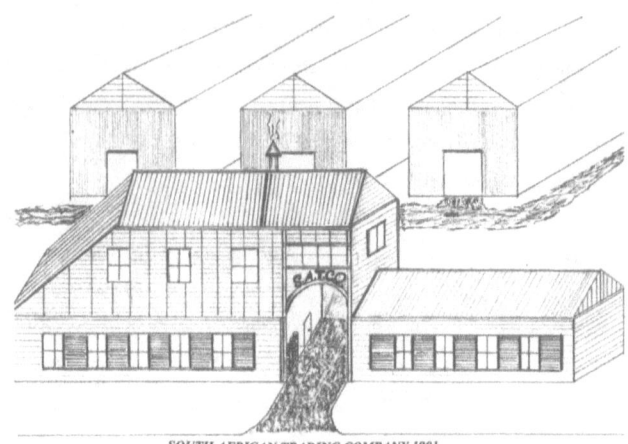

SOUTH AFRICAN TRADING COMPANY 1901

Mark decided to have the stock of selected items moved into the cellar while Abdul was in Durban. A letter from Mark's mother arrived the next day, which had apparently crossed his letter in the mail.

Oakhill Hall
Cheshire.

My Dear Mark,

I do so hope that you are well and that you are coping alright with the problems at SATCO.

Hugh and Anne are both well and we are having a good season. The beef herd continues to prosper and the last sales in Chester market fetched excellent prices. Felling in the great wood has nearly finished and Archie Mac Laggen is well advanced with the replanting. The ploughing is due to start in the low fields in about two weeks time and I have engaged an experienced man to grow vegetables. I am very pleased with Arthur Phillips as the new foreman and he has everything running smoothly now. The dairy herd is giving much better milk yields now with better feeding. Overall we are in very good shape but now there is the threat of foot and mouth disease spreading Northwards. It has already reached parts of Shropshire.

Everyone is talking about selling stock down South and we plan to sell off all but our very best breeding stock next week. We will have to sell off all the cattle except those we can keep fed in the farm buildings for six months. We will keep two bulls and up to ten of the best cows.

The farm improvements are well in hand and we are planning improvements to the cottages for next year. We see more and more of Margaret Moregrove and there is quite a romance budding with Hugh and Margaret which pleases me as they are well suited to each other.

We read of more trouble with the Boers and the Government is threatening all out war. I do so hope that you do not get mixed up in any trouble.

Young James Mac Laggen, Archie's eldest, has had to marry Emily as she is already expecting her second child. She was only eighteen when she had the first dear little blond headed boy and needs all the help that we can give her, so we have fixed up the cottage in the spring lane for them. Emily is still so young to be raising a family. We have employed James as a farm hand at the home farm.

Let me know what you have found and if it is worth keeping SATCO any longer.

Don't worry if SATCO is a lost cause, we can just write it off, particularly if staying on will put you at risk. We look forward to your letters and news.

Your loving Mother,
Agnes.

Mark was still rereading the last few paragraphs when Robert McKenzie brought a customer into his office.

"Please Mr. Oakhill, this gentleman, he is insisting that he sees you immediately. He is most upset, you see, we have no ammunition for his 0.577 Rigby express rifle, they seem to have all gone."

"Alright McKenzie, thank you, can you ask Sasha to bring some tea right away."

Mark introduced himself, and the suntanned stranger introduced himself as Major John Ashcroft.

"Your man tells me that he can't find any 0.577 ammunition for my express rifle."

"If you can wait a moment, I am sure that we can find some, it has just been relocated for security reasons."

"I can't hang around because we have to get our gear over to the station in time for the train to Pietersburg. I used to be in the Indian Army, major in the medics, you know, retired and came out here. I took up guiding hunting parties in the Northern Transvaal and over the Limpopo River into Bechuanaland. I don't take hunting parties out any more because I am tied of fat, wealthy industrialists from the cities blazing away at anything that moves and then we have to deal with the wounded animals that they leave, but they still want their photographs taken 'to show the folks back home'. Your man MacKenzie, tells me that you are a crack shot so I would be pleased to take you out any time."

Taking a pencil he started to draw a crude map.

"You take the train to Pietersburg and go North West till you hit the small river, follow the small river downstream to the Junction with the Limpopo river, go downstream for about half a day and the Shamba is alongside another small river soon after you climb onto a plateau."

"Yes I would like to accept your kind offer as soon as possible, thank you. I will get the cartridges myself and see that your stores are being loaded quickly."

Mark met Sasha in the passage and asked her to look after the major for a while and gave her a big wink.

John Ashcroft was delighted that he had got all his stores, including the 0.577" cartridges for his Rigby express rifle, which he used for very large game such as elephant and buffalo, and made some new friends, so he said with a twinkle in his eye.

"Very fine girl you have there, she is highly intelligent and speaks French, Swahili as well as English and has her eye on you. I am married to a local girl now, I can't speak highly enough of them, wonderful people, but damned city people are prudes and cut you off from society.

Many of the most vocal prudes do a bit of 'black birding' on the sly, bloody hypocrites. In the bush we just accept people as they are and no nonsense."

John said good-by and hurried out to take his stores to the train. Due to a feeling of the need for some company that evening, Mark asked Sasha to join him for dinner in the quarters after the other staff had gone home.

The mission, and more probably Sasha's mother, had done a very good job of teaching Sasha to run a household. This had all been superimposed by Catholic dogma at the mission, which had been totally rejected, Mark discovered at the meal table.

"The priests and nuns were very quick to throw me out as soon as I got a job at SATCO because I would not accept their preaching. Many of the priests are 'cochons'.

How can they be men of any God? They keep their 'flock' in a state of fear and poverty so that the priests can have 'beaucoup de vin et beaucoup de jeune fills. (Plenty of wine and young girls.)

You see, my father's family were Protestant Huguenots in France, they were persecuted and many were murdered by the Papal Armies, so many of them fled overseas. Some were lucky and escaped to England, but my father's ancestors escaped to North Africa and made their way to Cairo where my father went to the university to make civil engineer and then he got a very good job for the Canal Suez Company."

"That piece of history, about the Huguenots, is something I was totally unaware of. It must have been very hard for your father's family."

Sasha was almost in tears with the memory of her father telling the sad piece of family history so Mark changed the subject.

"O yes, Sasha, have you seen any evidence of the evil men again?"

"No, they have not been again."

Some time later when they had finished the meal, Mark saw that Sasha was becoming aroused and was looking into his very blue eyes with burning desire. While pouring the coffee she rested her hand on his shoulder and he felt the closeness of her body behind him, her firm breasts pressed against his back With mounting desire, Mark said.

"Would you like me to look at your burns and see how they are healing?"

"The burns are much better thank you, look."

Whereupon she sat on a chair and lifted her dress so that Mark could lift the dressings one at a time. The burns were certainly much better, but there were still some painful looking scars, she had very shapely legs. Mark started to slide his hand over the soft, cool, cafe au lait coloured skin of Sasha's thigh and she started moaning with excitement "Ooh, ah, c'est magnifique, il est tres bon, ne s'arret pas."

'CRASH' The noise came from the yard below. 'CRASH', again. Mark grabbed his rifle from the cupboard, loaded it, and ran to the rooms over the arch in time to see two men lighting fire sticks and throwing them into the cobbled area underneath the archway by the office door. Mark waited for a fire stick to flare up and then followed Ghillie's training and aimed at the heel of the boot of the man throwing the fire sticks. BOOM, the noise of the shot was magnified by the surrounding buildings. The man appeared to leap into the air and then collapsed with a howl of pain while his friend with the matches bolted as fast as his short legs could carry him.

Mark became aware of Sasha at his side. "Il est mort, oui?"

"Oh no, just gave him Ghillie's treatment for rioters and looters."

"What is a Ghillie treatment please?"

"Just an old army method of stopping people instantly and giving them enough of a shock to stop them causing any more trouble for a while."

After a few minutes, the tall man was slowly trying to sit up, he looked at his now sole-less boot and nursed his foot. He then very carefully stood up and limped away into the darkness.

Mark and Sasha ran down the stairs to the entrance yard and saw three or four fiercely burning fire sticks lying against the iron clad building. A shovel from the stable enabled Mark to scoop up the fire sticks one at a time and dunk them in the big horse drinking trough.

Other than smoke stains on the wall there was no damage thanks to George's good old iron cladding. Mark and Sasha took the rifle, a lantern and some matches and quietly slipped out of the main entrance, locked the gate, and started to follow the two men. A few blood spots told Mark that his aim had been a bit too high! Two blocks away they turned out the lantern before rounding a corner and then saw the now soleless man being helped by his little friend towards the same side street as before. The two men then quickly drove off in their cart in a Northerly direction. As soon as the cart was out of sight Sasha lit the lantern and looked carefully at the tracks in the dusty road surface. "The same evil men but the horse is different, only two of the iron feet were here before."

Mark laughed.

"It must have had two new iron feet since it was here last time. At least we now know that it was the same men trying to burn down SATCO, but why risk being caught? They must have some special reason. Why go for the office? Why not the warehouses where all the valuable goods are stored? There must be something in the office that they do not want us to have. I wonder if Henk left something that he does not want us to see, we must look carefully tomorrow."

Back at the quarters Sasha made more coffee and as they sat in the sitting room Sasha said.

"You are very good to me and I do not like to see you being robbed by Maria, the Irish woman in the household section, she has become an evil woman."

"What do you mean Sasha?"

"I am watching her when she can't see me and she is serving her Dutch friends. They come in and buy something small and pay for it but Maria makes up a big parcel for them to take home."

"Maria has always been the mainstay of that section and we have had no reason to doubt her honesty up to now, what has changed?"

"I can feel the evil ones so I am watching her, she seems very distressed when she is doing these things. I will show you tomorrow. Also I see her in your office when nobody is looking."

"Thank you for telling me Sasha, you are proving to be very good for SATCO as well as for me, good night." He kissed her and was amazed at how soft and cool her lips felt.

What was he doing letting himself become infatuated with this beautiful, exciting girl? Sasha was becoming a very important part of his daily life.

Abdul returned on the train the next day with his two Askari and found them lodgings nearby. They were employed as 'stable hands' but their main duty was patrolling the compound at night. They also helped with feeding the horses when necessary. The observant Abdul noticed the interest building up between Mark and Sasha and brought forward his suggestion that Mark 'did the rounds' of the customers as his father had done when SATCO was first started.

Abdul was in Mark's office the next morning when he pointed to the wall map and said. "Your father planned his rounds as shown by those red pins and red crayon lines. He did three one week trips based on here and then took the train to Pietersburg and radiated out from there. Van de Brecht only went once but he used to have a lot of the Boers in his office late at night. The same stable boy, Raymond, who went with your father is still with us, so he can show you the way round and save time."

"I can see the value of meeting our customers on their own land and negotiating more business and some produce broking as well. I would like to start as soon as possible. Can we get some catalogues printed that I can distribute on the way round?"

Abdul delegated the catalogues to Robert Mackenzie.

"Oh yes Abdul, Sasha tells me in confidence that Maria is cheating us by packing up more goods than have been paid for and that she is very interested in something in my office, the safe perhaps."

"I am shocked, she has always been such a reliable employee, are you sure?"

"Yes, I saw her charge two pounds for a small item and then pack up about ten pounds worth of goods into the same parcel. She may have been threatened by the Boers because her husband is Irish and has anti British sentiments. I think the Boers are trying to continue the thieving where van de Brecht left off. I will not stand for any thieving from SATCO, she must go immediately. Will you please dismiss her and pay her up right away."

Abdul called Maria into his office and challenged her. At first she denied the allegations, but then broke down in a flood of tears.

"I didn't mean to do it, but they threatened to harm my children if I didn't do as they said."

"Who are 'they'?"

"I must not say anything or I fear for my children and even my own life, you must forgive me, I have worked here for ten years."

"We understand the pressure that you have had applied on you and therefore we are not taking any legal action. You have been seen on at least two occasions making up parcels of goods that have not been fully paid for and you have been seen acting suspiciously near the safe, this means that you can't be trusted as an employee any longer and you must leave immediately.

Here is your pay which includes an extra month's wages as a gesture."

Maria departed with more sobs and left Mark and Abdul feeling sorry for the action that they had been forced to take. The Boers had become so powerful that they were manipulating innocent people to act as their agents. By closing time it was apparent that a replacement had to be found for Maria to service the household goods area. Abdul proposed that Sasha be made the supervisor of that area and that another girl be obtained from the mission to take over the cleaning and cooking and live in with Sasha in the other suit of rooms. Mark agreed and the following day Abdul collected Mjuba from the mission and she took up residence with Sasha.

Preparations for doing the rounds kept Mark fully occupied for the next three days. There were numerous bad debts to follow up, sisal crops to negotiate, new business to promote and machinery orders to follow up. Mark decided to travel with pack horses, as his father had, because of the bad roads and river crossings. Robert MacKenzie had excelled himself and produced a most elaborate catalogue. A bundle of 500 was so heavy that other items had to be left out of the saddle bags on the pack horses. With the Boer trouble brewing, Mark decided to take his high power hunting rifle and a Webley Mk 1 revolver for himself, and another revolver for Raymond together with plenty of ammunition.

By the Saturday night, all was packed and ready to load up on Monday morning. Mark had accepted an invitation to visit George and Heather on the Sunday for lunch. George announced that Heather was expecting a baby in about seven months time, much to Heather's embarrassment. It came out in conversation that the broken journey back from Durban had been necessary because of 'woman's problems' caused by the stress of the journey. A leisurely lunch followed by a stroll in a nearby park and afternoon tea made for a very relaxing time and Mark didn't leave till around five o'clock.

Mark was surprised to find Sasha working in the office because she had planned to visit one of her friends from the mission who was now working in Johannesburg. "I thought that you were going to visit a friend." "Yes that was the plan but my friend is sick so I didn't stay long. When I am coming here today I think that there is something that makes the evil men want to burn the office so I am remembering what Maria was looking at when she was in your office. She was by the safe but was looking up at the wall."

They went into Mark's office, stood by the safe and looked up at the wall. They both realised that it was the wall map that was the likely subject of Maria's attention. Mark had spent many hours with Abdul and Raymond planning the trips and he knew most of the planned trips off by heart. A few pins had been added to represent new customers but he was not aware of any being removed, but there were several places where pins had been put in and taken out. The patterns of holes appeared around the towns of Bloomfontein, Kimberly, Pietersburg and Messina, always along the railways. The map had been used to plan 'some other activity', like sabotaging the railways, perhaps. Further searching for possible items of interest to the 'evil men' didn't produce anything at all. As a precaution the map was put in the cellar.

A very early start was planned for the next day, so Mark asked Sasha to join him for an early evening meal. Mjuba had cooked a simple roast dinner which Sasha served in the sitting room. During the meal Mark said.

"I hear that one of the Boer bullock team drivers who was in the yard the other day tried to make off with you and that you fight like a hellcat and soon had him nursing his paternal prospects. Where did you learn to fight like that?"

"When I was at the catholic mission school the priests used to make us work in the vegetable garden or the farmyard for what they said was punishment for our sins. When I was alone they would come and try to take my clothes off for jig y jig, but my mother had told me how to make the priest or slave boss think that they are master and then attack pacy pacy sana. When you kick them 'there' it makes them turn green and cry out with pain for a long time, so I am running away."

"By what Raymond tells me, that bullock team driver won't be any good for a long time."

When they had finished the meal and were relaxing in the comfortable arm chairs, Mark became aware that Sasha was looking at him very intently and that her voice was becoming husky. Mark could see that Sasha was becoming aroused which had the same effect on him.

From where Mark was sitting he could see a large expanse of Sasha's thighs and while he stared with increasing arousal, Sasha smiled and slowly raised the hem of her skirt till he could see that she was wearing the very latest French satin knickers. Mark got up from his chair and kissed Sasha firmly on the mouth, she responded by opening her lips and probing his mouth with the tip of her tongue.

This was a new experience for Mark and he felt that he was loosing control, Sasha was such a beautiful, wonderful girl and he could not stop. Kneeling in front of Sasha, Mark started to kiss the beautiful pointed breasts and erect nipples that Sasha now offered to him over the top of her unbuttoned dress. Sasha's breasts were perfectly formed and he kissed and squeezed them while she stroked the back of his head and ran her strong fingers over his muscular chest and then sunk her nails into his back along his spine. Gradually Mark started caressing her buttocks and then the inside of her thighs. He could see that the crotch of her knickers was already wet and his desire was mounting to breaking point. As he touched Sasha in her most sensitive place, she started convulsing with excitement and cried out.

"C'est bon, magnifique, plus, plus, vite, vite." Sasha then pulled his face down between her thighs and said; "Kiss me there."

Mark responded to another new experience for a few minutes and then Sasha got up and said. "Fuata"(Follow) and led the way to the bedroom. They slowly undressed each other and explored their bodies all over before lying on the bed in each other's arms. Sasha enjoyed Mark's muscular young body and the faint man smell as she kissed and caressed him all over.

Mark explored Sasha's beautiful body with kisses. She had such soft, cool skin and now that she was fully aroused the smell of her body sent him wild. As Mark penetrated Sasha, he realized that it was the first time for her but she was past caring about any temporary pain and bleeding. They finally came to a shattering climax together and then lay entwined and slept for a while, till Sasha wanted a repeat performance. The second time was better because Mark was able to hold off for longer and enjoy the intimate contact inside Sasha. The aroma of Sasha's body lingered in his nostrils for hours afterwards. They slept the sleep of a couple with satisfied bodies in complete harmony.

Mark awoke just before dawn and looked down at the shadowy form of the beautiful girl still sleeping in his bed. How had he come to love this beautiful half French part Sudanese part English girl? Sasha seemed to understand all his needs and desires intuitively despite their different backgrounds and she was becoming the most important part of his life. The problem was that Victorian society did not accept marriages between different races, which was what John Ashcroft had said, but Sasha was part English and part French and only one quarter Sudanese and had a lovely skin colour like a healthy sun tan.

His mother always advised 'to take it slowly, don't rush into something which you might regret later'. But with a wonderful, beautiful girl like Sasha that advice was very hard to follow.

For the next three weeks Mark and Raymond travelled hundreds of miles visiting customers on their farms or business premises. They slept where they were at nightfall and Mark was able to shoot some game in the early mornings for fresh meat and to trade with the natives in return for supplies and assistance with river crossings as well as keeping up with the local gossip. Raymond was well accepted by the locals and the gifts of fresh meat spoke louder than words. This ensured that they had a safe passage even in the very remote areas. Mark had decided not to return to SATCO at the week ends as his father had done, and kept moving and visited more of the very remote properties.

There were some ugly scenes when they visited some of van de Brecht's Boer friends to ask for settlement of long overdue accounts. In most cases the Boer customers just denied ever having had the goods and that the invoices were wrong.

At one farm where this excuse was given, the item in question, a sisal processing machine, was clearly visible in an open sided shed. Mark pushed the point and threatened to reposes the machine if payment was not made within a month. A stream of abuse and a rusty old shotgun were directed at Mark to send him on his way, but Mark vowed to call back if payment was not made within the month. The three weeks planned for the trip came and went very quickly and it was over five weeks before Mark and Raymond rode into the SATCO yard, very tired and hungry but very fit from long hours in the saddle and being largely self sufficient. Mark had a note book full of orders and contracts to factor crops for the farmers which pleased Abdul very much.

The imminent threat of war was making everyone stockpile essential foods and farm supplies which nearly doubled sales each week in spite of the fact that most of the Boer activity was hundreds of miles further South round Kimberly and Bloemfontain.

On Mark's return, Sasha moved into the quarters and they spent two wonderful nights together and they became a lot closer to each other. The parting was a terrible wrench when it was time to go again. There was no point in waiting round Johannesburg for war to start so Mark and Raymond took off complete with their horses on the train for the 180 mile journey Northwards to Pietersburg on the Monday morning.

SATCO acted as wholesaler for a number of smaller stores in and around Pietersburg all of which ordered well. The orders were posted back to SATCO before they headed off into the more remote areas further North in the Zoutpansburg hill country. Mark enjoyed the outdoor life with plenty of 'nyama' (game) for the pot and for trading with the natives. Most of the farmers in the remote areas were pleased to see someone from SATCO and offered food and lodgings as a matter of course.

When they were some two weeks out of Pietersburg word got through that war had been declared and that there was fighting South of Kimberly. Mark wrote up all the contracts and orders and posted them to SATCO as soon as possible before starting to head for home. He had planned on going right up to the Limpopo River and not returning till just before Christmas, but declaration of war meant that they must get back to SATCO before the fighting came closer to Johannesburg.

CHAPTER 3

'WAR'

Back at SATCO, Abdul was becoming increasingly worried by the number of Boer soldiers moving along the roads. Late in November several Boer officers arrived and checked out the colonel's land and burnt out shops as well as the scrub behind. It appeared that they were the advance party for a much larger contingent that was due to arrive in a few days time.

Mark's emergency plan was fine tuned, some more stock was put into the cellar. Sasha and Mjuba were to hide in the cellar when there were any soldiers around. All records, books, firearms and ammunition were to be put in the cellar. Resistance was only to be given if there was attempted looting by one or two Boers, but if there was a large number, every attempt was to be made to prevent their entry or looting but there was no point in being heroic. Two days later a convoy of wagons streamed onto the colonel's land and a rough assortment of tents sprang up. There was no attempt to disrupt SATCO till noon the next day when two officers walked into the office and stated that they were commandeering all the food, clothing, horse shoe nails, horse shoes, and fodder available. After a brief discussion Abdul conceded defeat on the understanding that all the goods were itemized and signed for. The Boer officers agreed but obviously had no intention of making any payment.

The SATCO staff were told to assist the Boers loading their wagons as this would result in less damage and looting of other items. A cable was sent to Gustav in Durban to stop sending any goods on the train. Once the Boers saw that they had cleaned out SATCO of all the items of value to them they lost interest and started looking elsewhere for supplies and loot. Trade nearly stopped because of a lack of stock and the reluctance of the customers to venture out so close to a Boer camp. The Askari prevented individual looters from stealing and the staff used the time to plan the delivery of the orders sent back by Mark as soon as the war was over.

On a trip to the bank Abdul was told by Mr. Foster that the Boers had murdered the colonel and his wife and burnt down their home. George and Heather Bridgeman had escaped and gone into hiding just before the Boers had arrived. The quarters at SATCO were searched again and again and Abdul was repeatedly questioned about Mark's whereabouts. "He has gone away on business." They were told but were not satisfied and kept searching the office and threatening Abdul. Abdul was very relieved that all the valuables and the girls were hidden in the cellar.

By early January the Boers started sending off small relief squads to Kimberly and Bloomfontain. Then word came through that Kimberly had been recaptured by the British and that the 'Front' was coming Northwards towards Johannesburg. The British advanced quickly along the railways at first but then enteric fever and lame horses slowed down the advance in the open country. This situation was exploited by the Boers by making 'hit and run' or 'commando' raids on the stalled British columns and sabotaging the railways. Colonial forces from Australia and New Zealand then joined the battle.

These Colonial troops came with fitter men and horses used to bush life but their greatest advantage was that they were not burdened down with too much equipment and could travel huge distances without their horses going lame. Very soon the advance started Northwards again towards Johannesburg. One day the Boers were in camp and the next they just panicked and fled abandoning half of their equipment. They went to Pretoria to regroup and make a 'last ditch stand.' The British units then started to arrive and Johannesburg was recaptured without much fighting. SATCO went back into full swing with all possible supplies called up from Gustav and other sources. A British camp was set up on the colonel's land and SATCO became a major supplier of food, equipment and horses. Abdul had not been able to get word through to Mark because the Boers had control of all the railways to the North and he presumed that Mark was unable to return or write due to the Boers being in control South of his last known position. The Boers held out in Pretoria till June 1902 when the British High Command moved in and the war was supposed to be over and the Treaty of Vereeniging was signed.

But the Boers were by no means defeated and a dirty phase of the war started with patrols and commando raids for supplies. Boer leaders names such as Smuts, Botha, Steyn, De Wet and De la Rey became known through the scant coverage of the raids in the newspapers. The British set up road blocks and patrolled the railways but the Boers blew up the track and derailed trains almost at will. This prevented a concerted push further North to Pietersburg and Messina because of the lack of mobility of the Allied forces without a complete railway system and active Boar units still on the loose.

The 'dirty phase of the war' had reached a stalemate. Small specialized Colonial units, such as the Bush Velt Carbineers, or BVC, were formed by Kitchener's commanders with the idea that they would 'Flush out' the last remaining Boers and that the dirty war would soon be over, but this all took time because of the huge distances and virtually no communications. Even though President Kruger, the Boer commander had fled through Portugese East Africa to Holland, there was still a very strong determination amongst the Boers to fight on in the land that they knew so well, even though they were so short of supplies. This shortage led to the pillaging of farms and homesteads for food and fresh horses. This was usually followed by the poisoning of the wells and water holes to impede any possible followers.

The Boars also captured British patrols, stripped them of their uniforms and left the naked soldiers without water or food in the bush to die. This practice was called 'Uitshudden' by the Boers which literally means 'a reduction' and is against all conventions of war. Many Allied lives were lost due to mistaken identity with the Boers dressed up in the British uniforms. The Allied troops were tricked into thinking that an advancing unit was British and were just murdered at point blank range by the Boer uitshudden practice. General Kitchener issued an order through his staff officer, Colonel Hamilton, that any Boers found in British uniforms were to be shot, but this was not always carried out because this usually led to further Boer reprisals on helpless civilians. There were also Dutch and German sympathizers who collaborated with the Boers and provided food and shelter for the Boar commando units thus adding to the difficulties of ending the dirty phase of the war.

A few days after receiving the news about the outbreak of war down South, Mark and Raymond turned back towards Pietersburg from the large farm where they had spent the previous night. They soon had the feeling that they were being followed and this was confirmed by the sunlight flashing off the lenses of binoculars being used by their pursuers. Raymond slipped off his horse and disappeared round a thorn thicket while Mark rode on at a steady pace with the four horses. After about half an hour Raymond returned at a run and between gasps for breath, said that there was a party of about 12 Boers on horseback following in their tracks. Mark and Raymond were in a more open part of the veldt now, but there was no sign of their followers who must have been hanging back in some cover. As they were obviously outnumbered, Mark and Raymond rode on at a steady pace till they were in cover of some light scrub and quickly lit a fire which they heaped with green leaves and grass so that a large column of thick smoke rose into the air. Raymond then found a selected route for Mark to lead away the horses while he followed, covering their tracks as best he could for some minutes, and then mounted his horse and they both rode Westwards as fast as possible with the protesting pack horses dragging along behind. Two rifle shots rang out, but it appeared that they were signal shots indicating that their tracks had been found, not shots aimed in their direction, yet. Raymond was leading them to some higher ground which slowed down the pack horses, so Mark finally decided to strip the essentials from the pack horses such as food, water, ammunition and the two revolvers and turn the pack horses loose in the scrub.

The pack horses may even act as a decoy and give them more time to slip away. The essentials were quickly put into rucksacks and shouldered ready for the steep climb ahead. The hot noon sun blazed down and the sweat rolled off Mark and Raymond, but the threat of being caught on the partly exposed hillside gave them the incentive to spur on their panting and sweat lathered horses. The horses started to tire as the slope got steeper so Mark and Raymond dismounted and scrambled up on foot till they reached the ridge which was strewn with small boulders. A valley ran away to the West of the ridge and in the far distance there appeared to be some sort of cultivation or a farm, but that was many miles away across open veldt. Raymond moved along just on the West side of the ridge so that they could periodically stop and cautiously look back to the East side to check on their pursuers between the boulders. Discovery of the pack horses seemed to be causing some confusion on the lower slope. On the third stop to peer over the ridge, Mark saw two groups of Boers coming up the slope towards the ridge. If they headed off down the valley towards the farm to the West they would be out in the open without any cover, so they could only stay in the cover of the boulders on the ridge, till after dark anyway. Mark called to Raymond and they had a brief council of war.

"Bwana Mark I am sure that one of those men is Messa Vandebrik and that he is coming with the same evil men that came to burn SATCO at night."

"So it is Henk that has been following us, but why? We must be prepared to take cover and fight it out up here, there is no other chance. We must quickly find the best natural place to defend ourselves. How about that depression over there to tether the horses and then put a few more essential supplies from the saddlebags into our rucksacks."

The horses were left hobbled and still saddled in the depression with Raymond between two boulders with a view over the ridge. Mark took his rucksack and set up his position among some boulders on higher ground some fifty yards along the ridge where he had a view of the horses in the depression and a limited view down the slope that the Boers were climbing. There was a long wait with only the occasional sound of boots against rock. Mark crept forward taking care to be silent and not to present a silhouette against the skyline. No Boers were in sight, so that could only mean that both groups had reached the ridge, one on each side of them, and that they could expect a pincer attack along the ridge at any moment.

After about half an hour Mark heard a rifle shot and a bullet hit rock and went whining away close to where Raymond was stationed. Then Raymond's revolver fired three evenly spaced shots, silence. A volley of shots then a short scream and the two horses crumpled and fell to the ground.

So they are removing our only means of escape before the 'coup de grace' thought Mark. A series of raised voices and among them Raymond protesting loudly.

"Messa Vandenbrink, you bastard you will pay for making this trouble."

Another shot and Raymond's voice became muffled and trailed away. A man's head appeared over a rock where Raymond had been positioned, he was giving orders in Afrikaans. Mark took aim and was about to fire when a thousand thoughts flashed through his mind. He had never aimed to kill a man before, he must not hesitate now, it was their only chance. Ghillie's training told him "when it is him or you who dies make sure that it is him and no fancy trick shots, aim to kill with a well placed shot and keep your cover because the enemy may see where the shot came from." Mark aimed for the top of the man's chest and fired. He worked the bolt automatically while the sound of the shot was still reverberating between the boulders. The man fell back out of sight and a yell came from behind Mark. Rolling over, Mark was just in time to see two men moving among the boulders to his left. It was necessary to crawl round a boulder and take up a new position in the shadow before he could shoot to his left and there was just enough time to reposition himself when two men started moving again between the boulders. Ghillie's snap shooting training flooded through Mark's mind as he aimed and squeezed off a quick shot. The first man dropped his rifle with a clatter, clutched his chest and collapsed. His accomplice hesitated and stooped to check his comrade which gave Mark enough time to get off another quick shot as the man panicked and started to run for cover, but this time the man jerked and stumbled, then limped away among the boulders. Another man appeared close to the dead horses and Mark was able to shoot him as he stooped over the saddle bags. Bullets were striking all round him so Mark started moving his position so that he could keep watch on both groups of Boers. It appeared that the Boers had either killed, or mortally wounded Raymond, the horses had been shot, and if Raymond's revolver shots had been effective he may have downed one or two Boers. So with his own score there were at least three and a half less which meant that there were still about eight to his one. Not a healthy situation. There was enough food and water for one or two days at the most and about 50 rounds of ammunition left. At nearly twenty, Mark was in a life or death situation that he had never experienced before. His thoughts flashed back to some of his experiences since his father had died. On each occasion he had been free to make his own decisions that often involved other people's behaviour and livelihood, but now it was suddenly different.

Current decisions only affected his chances of survival and other people were not influenced by his decisions and kept up their relentless objective of trying to kill him. There was still some inexplicable cause for this vendetta against SATCO, and now against Mark. His only chance of survival was to reduce their numbers whenever possible and try to hold out till nightfall. The day wore on and Mark got thirsty and hungry so he consumed an estimated quarter of his food and water and then put the rest back in his pack. Flies buzzed round his face and crawled round his eyes and nose, but he just had to put up with the discomfort for fear of any quick movement attracting attention. By sunset, the Boers must have also had the need of food and water because they sent two men down the slope for supplies, to where they had tethered their horses. Mark calculated that it was better to let the men go down and have a shot at them when they were burdened down on the return up the slope, but the light was begriming to fade. It seemed an age before Mark's keen eyesight spotted the two figures struggling back up the slope with water bottles and canvas bags of food. The men were unsure of where they should be heading and stopped periodically to try to pick out a landmark. A match flared momentarily over to Mark's left and the two men started off again with more confidence. Ghillie's training told Mark that in the rapidly fading light he must wait till the men were very close and that he must be prepared for them to 'just melt into the ground' after his first shot.

A series of stones each side of Mark's proposed line of fire was arranged, with great difficulty, to try to conceal the muzzle flash from his rifle. The men were now only 60 or 70 yards away. Mark was getting comfortable for the necessary quick shots at 50 yards when he heard movement in the depression where the dead horses lay. This was not in his plans. The Boers must be looking for food and water in the saddle bags. They would be disappointed, but their position imposed a new and unexpected threat to his planned escape route after dealing with the men coming up the slope. There would not be time to reload the rifle quickly enough so he drew his revolver, cocked it and placed it ready to fire to his rear. The two men were only 40 or 50 yards away and were silhouetted against the sky now that they were so close to the ridge. Not an easy shot but it was now or never. The first shot downed the first man and he fell with a clatter of water bottles against the rocks. The second man paused just long enough for Mark to reload and in his panic dropped his sacks of food and tried to bolt for the cover of the boulders along the ridge. The second shot was aimed at a scrambling, stumbling figure that jerked and bobbed about like a demented puppet. The puppet screamed and clutched it's shoulder, but slowly kept on stumbling towards the ridge. Mark grabbed his revolver and fired two shots at the dark mass in the depression. The bullets hit rock and whined off into the distance but this seemed to have the desired effect because the dark mass moved and he heard boots scraping on rock in that direction.

The last dim light was rapidly disappearing and Mark expected a surprise attack at any moment. So after reloading his rifle and revolver he put on his pack and moved his position 20 or 30 yards towards the valley. He had only just taken up his new position, standing between two boulders, when he heard footsteps and muffled voices coming from where he had fired his last shots. They must have got a line on his position from the muzzle flashes. Perhaps he could stir them up a bit, he dropped his pack and started lobbing some small stones between his former position and the depression. Two rifle shots rang out, bullets whined away off rock and a stream of very angry Africaans words were shouted from the direction of the depression. They were mistakenly shooting at each other in the dark.

CHAPTER 4

ESCAPE

Now was a perfect opportunity to get away with the search concentrated behind him, but how was he going to move silently enough to slip away without attracting their attention? Strips cut from the towel in his pack wrapped round his boots could possibly muffle any sounds if he moved very carefully, but there was then the chance of being seen once he left the cover of the boulders. Again, there was likely to only be one chance, so he quickly cut strips of towelling and muffled his boots and moved off very cautiously down the slope and along the cover of the boulders. After ten minutes or so, he was rounding a boulder when a cigarette glowed in the dark just ten feet away. Mark froze and tried to melt into the surface of the boulder. The man was side on, and was sitting on a stone and was looking intently down the valley. A cigarette was stuck out of the side of his mouth and when he drew on it the red glow lit up his features and the rifle on his lap. When the cigarette was reduced to a stub, the man used the stub to light another and still sat there looking down the valley. Two cigarettes later the man threw the packet away with a muttered curse and started to savour the last one. Finally when the smokes were all gone he got up and relieved himself and went back to sit on his stone and appeared to be going to sleep.

Mark was getting very stiff and tired but forced himself to remain motionless, just waiting for any opportunity. The lone sentry became restless after a while, fidgeted and then started pacing up and down, presumably to keep himself awake. While the sentry was at the far end of his beat, Mark drew his revolver and grasped it by the barrel. The sentry's beat was a bit erratic and there was a chance that he would get too close to Mark's boulder for his health. Mark was coiled up like a spring and his hands were sweating profusely which made it very difficult to keep a proper grip on the smooth barrel of the revolver. Much to Mark's horror the sentry's beat fell short of striking distance for what seemed like an eternity.

Then it happened. Fatigue had taken over and the sentry came and leant against Mark's boulder about six feet away. His head lolled and sleep was not far away. Two quick steps and the butt of Mark's revolver slammed into the side of the sentry's head. For fear of any noise, Mark cupped his free hand over the sentry's mouth and then gently lowered him to the ground. To his horror and amazement Mark realized that the revolver's butt had completely penetrated the man's temple. There was no doubt that he was dead. Speed was now the most important factor in his chances of survival, so Mark removed the bolt from the sentry's rifle and put it in his pocket before starting off down the slope into the valley to the West.

Mark wondered how long it would be before the dead sentry was discovered and his most likely escape route was assumed by the Boers. Distance now appeared to be the best chance of remaining undetected. He must reach that cultivation in the distance and find water and food before sun rise, which meant four or five hours of difficult walking in the dark over strange country. In his exhausted state, Mark tried to take his bearings by the stars and set off with his still muffled boots. When he was sure that he was out of earshot, Mark took off the towelling from his boots and hid it under a rock together with the bolt from the sentry's rifle. After another drink and some food he was ready to start walking in earnest for the next four or five hours.

The first flush of dawn found Mark still far short of his objective and stumbling along in an exhausted and dazed state. The light was still not good enough to see clearly and most of the stars had disappeared anyway, he was hopelessly lost. He was practically asleep walking along and he knew that if he lay down that he would fall asleep instantly, so he had to keep moving. After a while the dawn became sufficiently well defined to determine where was East, so by keeping the dawn directly behind him he must be heading in approximately the right direction. He crossed a small, tree lined river which had not been visible from the ridge. Looking back at the ridge it was not possible to pick out any boulders against the dawn sky at that distance, so he decided that he would remain undetected for a while yet. The dawn came very quickly and within a few minutes the whole valley was bathed in shafts of golden light. Trying to memorize the scene from the previous day, he realized that the cultivation was away to his right so he headed for some higher ground to take his bearings to find that he had nearly overshot the cultivation in the dark and still needed to go about a mile in a more Northerly direction. His legs ached, his feet were sore and the pack felt like a ton weight, but he must hurry now and find food, water and shelter from the noon sun while he rested.

The farmhouse and barn were built from local stone and looked very English. The house had an iron roof and the barn was thatched. There were some small fenced paddocks round the barn. Mark crept cautiously round the buildings and then up towards a kopje on a small hill where there was very lush growth indicating a spring or creek nearby. Now totally exhausted, Mark staggered on into the cover of some trees and rocks looking for any signs of water. A half buried pipeline ran from a small spring fed pool down towards the house and the irrigated fields below. The cool, clear water from the pool tasted so good and refreshing that Mark started to relax and he found himself falling asleep while he filled his water bottles. Shaking his head, Mark pulled himself together and looked around for a suitable hiding place. There was no sign of life round the house and barn which was ominous, so he decided to hide in the kopje overlooking the pool till he was sure that it was safe to check out the house for food. Some 50 yards behind the pool there was a rocky ledge which had a commanding view of the house, pool and the track leading down to the irrigation, so Mark selected a position between a tree and a large rock and waited.

Sleep must have taken over as soon as he lay down and it was around noon when a horse neighing awoke him with a start. The Boers had arrived and their horses were drinking at the pool. Another party of three Boers was riding up from the house and it was the arrival of these strange horses that had caused one of the horses at the pool to neigh and awake Mark. One of the new arrivals was making a show of being an expert tracker and was taking an unhealthy interest in the damp earth at the side of the pool where Mark had filled his water bottles. Mark cursed his own stupidity to leave tracks while in his exhausted state. "Some one has been here in the night."

"There is no one in the house, we fucked the wife till she was no good then shot her and we shot the man in the barn, the Kaffirs were either shot or ran away, and the girls fucked till they were no good, so it must be Oakhills that was here in the night."

"Can he have travelled so far on foot, it is many miles in the dark?"

"It is his boot marks that I see in the mud, watch out for his good shooting. Set a guard while we drink."

Even though Mark did not fully understand Afrikaans, he understood enough to realise that it was only a matter of time before he was found so he might as well live up to their expectations and keep reducing their numbers at every opportunity. When the Boers had finished watering their horses and filling their water bottles they dispersed and started a systematic search round the house, then the barn, then up to the pool and then into the cover where Mark was hiding. Mark decided to let them get to within an easy revolver shot and then take some longer shots with the rifle. Within a few minutes two Boers were getting very close and Mark kept his fire till he was able to shoot them at practically point blank range. Dropping his revolver into it's holster he took up the rifle and searched for another target. Echoes of the revolver shots off hard rock appeared to have confused some of the Boers as to where the sound had come from and he saw two Boers move round a rock looking in quite the wrong direction. A well placed rifle shot downed the first man but the other rolled away to safety before Mark could reload. More men were now moving round behind him and the odds were stacking against him. Click! Just behind him, a quick revolver shot dropped the first man but the second man fired and Mark felt the bullet strike his right leg and tear up into to his ribs. He was immobilized with pain and shock, but just enough of Ghillie's training told him to 'feign being dead'. Very soon this became natural because he had passed out.

Sudden jabs of pain and a sense of drowning came into Mark's half conscious state. I was lying doggo, they have dragged me to the pool and some bastard is kicking me in the ribs, I must make them believe that I am dead. I must have air, I am drowning. At the next kick Mark was able to take a gulp of air.

He found himself praying for another kick so that he could get some more air.

"The bastard has died on us. Henk will never get the information he wants about his precious bloody operations map now."

One more massive kick and another gulp of air and Mark heard the men moving away. Imperceptibly raising his head above the water level, Mark was able to breath freely at last but this hurt his rib cage so much that he was on the point of passing out again. With a superhuman effort Mark moved sideways so that his head rested on a stone. He then passed out again with pain from the exertion and loss of blood. All sense of time was lost to Mark in his weakened state.

Sounds of splashing water and horses hooves on rock brought Mark to semi-consciousness. Some one was wading into the pool and putting a rope onto the corpses that had been thrown there to foul the water, as was the Boer custom, and with the aid of a horse was pulling the bodies onto a lower slope for the jackals and vultures. After three trips it was Mark's turn to be dragged out with the rope.

He had planned to lie doggo, but the sudden pain made him cry out. A youthful voice told the horse to "woo" and the pain subsided a little as the rope slackened and the jolting stopped. Mark was clear of the pool and a youth was standing over him with his revolver drawn The youth was tall and skinny and was wearing baggy clothes designed for a much larger man and had crossed bandoliers on his chest like a Mexican bandit.

"Who are you? What is your name? Answer me or I will shoot you."

There was some thing wrong. The accent was not Africaans, it was familiar though. At last Mark's semi-conscious mind registered that the accent was Scottish.

"Mark—M-Mark Oakhill." He managed to croak.

The youth came closer with his revolver still drawn and looked him over closely.

"Are you the chap that the Boers have been hunting for weeks?"

"So it would appear."

"Are you English and which side are you on?"

"Yes English my own side—Who are you?"

"I live here, this is my parent's farm. Promise me you won't try any tricks and I'll try to patch you up a bit."

The youth was not strong enough to lift him, so he had to use his good leg to stand on till the horse was brought closer and he could lean against the saddle. As Mark was passing out again with the pain, the youth lashed him to the saddle and half dragged; half carried him to the barn and laid him out on a work bench.

Mark awoke some twenty four hours later with his leg bound up and his ribs in a great plaster cast. There was nobody around and he was in terrible pain and his mouth felt like coarse sand paper. He dozed off again to be awakened by some one who gave him some gruel through a straw.

The next few days were taken up with long periods of being unconscious, terrible pain, feverish heat and some ministering angle who bathed and fed him at regular intervals. After about four days, Mark's periods of waking were becoming longer and it did not hurt to open his eyes any more. He became aware of long, strong, brown hands bathing his face and torso and the face of a girl with her hair up in a bun, leaning over him. Whilst being fed through a straw he thought there was something familiar about the accent. Yes it was the soft Scottish accent that he remembered from when he was being dragged from the pool. She was speaking again.

"How are you feeling? Would you like another drink?"

Words would not come at first, then he croaked. "Enough for now thanks."

"I have taken the liberty of going through your pack and have read your note book. You appear to be Mark Oakhill of SATCO. down in Johannesburg, is that correct?"

"Yes."

"Why were the Boers hunting you down with such vengeance?"

"I don't really know, but there was some comment about the wall map from my office being of importance to a Boer major, Henk van de Brecht who was the manager at SATCO, working for my late father, till he defected a few months ago."

Pain and exhaustion set in again and Mark went back into a feverish sleep. It was in the middle of the day when he came to again and the strong sunlight lit up the area round his improvised bed in the hay at the back of the barn. The girl was moving round and appeared to be preparing a meal on a primus stove. She was tall and well built and looked desirable in riding breeches and a loose fitting blouse. The boots looked familiar. Weren't they the boots that had stood beside him when he was dragged from the pool? After a while the soup was cooked and cooled for Mark. As the girl came up to him Mark said.

"Do you have a brother with boots like yours?"

"Not any more, the Boers shot him nearly a month ago. Why do you ask?"

"Some one with boots like yours fished me out of the pool."

"Oh, that was me in my boy's garb, Mother made me wear it when the Boers were around, she said that I wouldn't get raped in that outfit, just shot at."

"I overheard one of the Boers talking about what they had done to your parents and from my limited understanding it appears that you are very lucky to have escaped. How did you do it?" "Father had a plan for when the Boers were around. I put on my boy's garb and rode off to a small depression out in the veldt where there is a spring and we had buried some iron rations. You can't be seen unless some one virtually stumbles over you. I had been in the depression for a few days when I heard one shot then a little later two more. I was sure that Mum and Dad were in trouble and came back at night to check on them. Then a few days later there was a lot of shooting up by the pool and a party of ten or twelve more Boers arrived. They then looted the house again and rode off in a great hurry. When all was quiet, I came out of hiding and went back to the house and found Mum, it was horrible what they had done to her, you can't even call them animals because animals are noble and don't do that sort of thing. Then I found Dad beside the barn. They are buried together in the garden, just deep enough to spare them from the jackals and vultures. When I went up to check on our water supply to the house and irrigation I saw that the Boers had dumped some bodies in our water supply pool to foul the water.

Dad had said that they usually poisoned or fouled the water when they pillaged a farm. You cried out when I pulled you out with my horse. You nearly got shot, but your clothes were different and there was not much fight left in you. Can you remember how you were shot?"

"I was lying down facing the pool and I think I got about three of them, then two came up behind me, I got the first one but the second man shot me with his Mauser rifle, the bullet hit my right leg, then seemed to go into my ribs."

"Well that explains the rather odd wounds that you have. There is a deep furrow up your shin and there is a penetration of the abdomen at a very obtuse angle with the bullet lodged under your ribs. Mum was a nursing sister and patched up the locals for miles around and I learnt a lot from her, emergency operations, child birth, calving cows, spear wounds among the blacks and wounded from the war. Fortunately the Boers did not take Mum's medicine chest. Just threw the contents all over the kitchen. I have sewn up your leg wound, and it is healing nicely but the bullet is still under your ribs and it must be removed as soon as you are strong enough to get to help. You lost a lot of blood and it will be at least a week before your body has made up what you have lost." "Thank you, you have saved my life and have been a beautiful ministering angel but I don't even know your name?"

She blushed and said. "My name is Jean Macintyre and I was happy to save your life but if I can't get you to help very soon, that bullet will fester and it will all have been to no avail."

"How long can we stay here before the Boers come back?"

"They can come back at any time; that is why I have left the house more or less as it was when it was ransacked and taken what we need into the barn. We are very short of food so I must go down to the irrigation and get some vegetables, fruit and native mealy corn or we will starve."

Having checked that Mark was alright for an hour or so, Jean left with a small sack over her shoulder. Jean did not take her horse because she did not want to leave any fresh tracks in the soft sandy soil along the track. Walking carefully on the grass at the edges of the track leading down to the irrigation, she kept a keen look out for any movement across the veldt. All appeared deserted. There was a 'header' channel across the top of the irrigation which supplied all the smaller channels between the rows. A simple bridge spanned the header channel and as Jean approached the bridge, a weak voice cried. "Missy Jean." Suspecting a trap, Jean drew her revolver and called "Sikia sana." Very slowly Tsandra crawled from under the bridge and blinked owlishly in the bright sunlight. "Jussa Tsandra, Missy Jean."

Tsandra started chaffing her body which was purple and wrinkled from lying in the shallow water for so long. "How long have you been hiding there."

"Many days, jussa eating mealy corn nighttime."

"Fuata" (Follow) Jean led Tsandra up and down the rows till they had a sack full of produce and then they carried it back towards the barn. Jean's father had told her that he had seen the Boers raping the black women and girls a few weeks earlier, before the shamba was burnt down, and Jean was amazed that Tsandra had been able to hide. She was only about sixteen and would have been a prime target for the Boers to gang rape and murder. There was no sign of any other life around where the shamba had been. The corpses had been taken by the jackals, or other predators, and most of the natives would have been able to flee into the bush till it was safe for them to return and rebuild their shamba, and be happy working the irrigation again, their needs were simple and their lives were uncomplicated till the white man's war came and spoilt it all.

Mark could hear voices and drew his revolver, which Jean had been able to find near his vantage point above the pool.

Two shadows came up to the open door and Mark could hear the two girls talking in broken English and Swahili as they entered the barn. The sack of fruit and vegetables was placed on the work bench and Jean brought Tsandra over to meet Mark.

"It is alright you can put your revolver away, it is only me and Tsandra who lived in the shamba and was able to hide from the Boers till now."

Tsandra came forward very shyly and said. "Pleesa meetya Bwana Mark."

"Jambo, habari Tsandra." (Hello, how are you, Tsandra.)

"Missouri, santa, sana. (Good, thank you, very.)" said Tsandra.".

Tsandra blushed at the usual Swahili greeting coming from a stranger. Mark was fascinated by Tsandra's shapely little body with her well formed, pointed, naked breasts. Her narrow hips were scantily clad in a short skirt made from some sort of grass or reeds. Mark's mind went back to that last night at SATCO with Sasha, oh how wonderful it had been and he longed to be with her again and wondered how she was fairing now that there was a war on, hopefully she is being well looked after by Abdul and the other staff.

Jean noticed the long gaze that took in all of the exposed parts of Tsandra and mentally undressed the rest, and felt a pang of jealousy, for she had had the opportunity to 'get to know' Mark rather well while she was nursing him at the height of the fever. Jean explained to Tsandra that Mark was being hunted by the Boers and that after a battle at the pool had been left for dead in the water to go rotten and foul the water. She explained that she had been able to save his life and stitch up his leg but that he still had a bullet under his rib cage, which was festering.

"Him plenty sick, kwenda doktari Bwana mkubwa pacey pacey sana."

Jean had to agree that he needed to go to the big chief medicine man very quickly, or he might die. Jean showed Tsandra where to hide the contents of the sack and where the primus stove and utensils were hidden. She then started to prepare the evening meal. Mark then realised that if Jean had been able to find his revolver that there was a chance that other items of equipment may still be up at the pool, or even in it. At his suggestion, Jean sent Tsandra to search in and around the shallow pool to collect anything of value, boots, clothing, weapons, water bottles, etc. but to be careful not to leave any foot prints in the soft ground.

"Walk on the stones or grass if you can." She said.

Tsandra returned by sunset with a sack full of odd items and tipped them on the work bench. Mark was delighted to see his beloved rifle, even if it was covered in mud and rust. The rest of the contents included his ammunition pouch together with some spent cartridge cases, a water bottle, two and a half jackal chewed boots, a belt, and a few shreds of clothing.

"Jean, do you have any gun oil or Rangoon oil please? I must carefully clean my rifle immediately or the main spring will rust away and the other parts will be useless."

"Father had all that sort of thing in a special gun cupboard beside the fireplace in the house, I'll go and see what I can find for you."

While Jean was away Mark forced himself into a sitting position and asked Tsandra to bring over the rifle and some rags torn from the clothing that she had collected. Jean returned with a small bottle of Rangoon gun oil, a pull through, some flannelette squares and a leather roll of tools. Mark went to work stripping his rifle while Jean cooked the meal. Tsandra alternated between Jean and Mark giving assistance as required. When the meal was nearly ready, Mark got Tsandra to lay out all the now cleaned and oiled parts of the rifle ready for assembly.

"Better have a look out across the veldt before we eat." Said Mark.

Jean and Tsandra climbed up to a small hay loft and looked out of the opening. All appeared deserted except for the usual scavengers looking for food.

Part of Ghillie's training came back to Mark. "You always clean your rifle first, then you can feed your men, feed yourself, then you can sleep after you have set a guard."

"Please can you help me assemble my rifle before we eat." Jean was angry and said. "The meal will spoil, Can't it wait?"

"No it can't, we are helpless without it and it will be dark in a few minutes."

Reluctantly, Jean helped Mark to assemble the rifle and reload the five round magazine.

The boiled vegetables and boiled salt beef made a filling meal and together with the exertions of the day, Mark just healed over and went to sleep before the girls had finished their food. Tsandra made up a bed in the hay loft so that she could keep a look out at first light without disturbing the others.

Mark awoke while it was still dark in intense pain. The fever was building up again and making the sweat roll off him. Jean heard his movement and muffled cry of pain and turned over to touch his hand. It was hot and sweaty so she got up and fetched some water to sponge him down. Mark felt Jean roll back the sheet and start sponging his heavily sweating body. It felt good to have her soft, cool hands moving him to sponge each area. She was an excellent nurse and he enjoyed the intimacy. "Do you feel that you need some laudanum to kill the pain? I still have some left in Mum's medicine chest."

"No thank you, the 'bird bath' has made me feel much better."

Jean came and lay beside him and held his hand while they slept. Soon after first light, Tsandra came down to report that all was quiet and then went to start preparing breakfast, which was mealy corn porridge cooked on the primus stove on the bench. The morning chores completed, Jean went to check on her horse in the small house paddock, he was restive and had his ears cocked listening. Sensing trouble, Jean hurried back to the barn and quickly hid the utensils and then hid herself and Tsandra in the small hay loft. Marks bed was covered with hay and he was left sitting up so that he could use the rifle resting on an old box. Nothing happened for an age and then the girls saw two men approaching very cautiously. First they went into the house and later appeared carrying something that they had looted and put it into a saddlebag. Then they came across to the barn and started searching among the tools and harness, and did not find anything of interest. Mark became alarmed when one man climbed the ladder up to the loft while his friend stayed at the bottom. When Mark tried to elevate the rifle in line with the top of the ladder, he found that in his weakened condition, he just could not support the weight, so he quickly changed his aim to the man at the base of the ladder and fired. The man at the top of the ladder quickly jumped onto the loft and crouched down peering over the edge at where his fallen comrade lay. Jean rose up out of the hay in the loft and took a two handed shot with her revolver at the man at the top of the ladder at very close range. He kept moving so she fired again and all was still. Jean calmly reloaded her revolver and came down the ladder. A terrified Tsandra was told to keep a good look out while Jean used her horse to pull the bodies into a thicket several hundred yards away for the jackals to find. When the drag marks and blood stains had been brushed or washed away, Jean brought a sack of the items collected from the two men into the barn for Mark to check over. There was a German Mauser 7mm rifle, two water bottles, some iron rations, a message pouch and a hunting knife. There were also two horses and their saddles. The message pouch contained some crude maps and some orders in Africaans. The latest message was dated only two days earlier and Jean's translation was; "Proceed to the Macintyre farm where Oakhills was shot and carefully search the whole area again for the missing operations map. It may have been hidden in the house or the farm buildings or even be in his pack. Have your report ready for me when I return in about a week with the rest of 'B' company. If you have time, you could also check the area where we shot and wounded the kaffir who was allowed to escape. If you can catch the black, he will talk when suitably 'persuaded'. See you back at camp by the end of the month. Henk."

"So, Henk was definitely in the Boer army all the time that he was working at SATCO and employed by my father, robbing us blind and helping his pals in the Boer army before he just abandoned his position and vanished soon after my father died. There was also an assistant manager, Peer something, who also vanished shortly afterwards. Fortunately we had a very reliable chief clerk, Abdul Suliman, who just stepped in and took over in a very competent manner till I arrived.

He is running the show while I am away on this sales trip to the outlying areas. Going by that order from Henk, we can expect him here with about thirty men in about two days time. We must leave immediately. That is very good that Raymond was not killed, as I thought, and was able to escape, even if he is wounded."

"You are in no fit state to leave in a hurry, you are so weak that you would be dead in a few days at the most, blood loss has made you very weak and not fit to travel. No, we must just hide everything and take our chances."

"Where do you propose to hide three people and three horses?"

"Tsandra can take the three horses to the depression and stay there till I signal her with the heliograph to return. We can hide in the pocket in the thatch which Hamish and I made when we used to play out here as children."

The girls worked feverishly all day, preparing food, covering tracks with dust and removing all traces of habitation around the barn. The horses were then loaded up with food, fodder and essentials for Tsandra. It then came time to move Mark into the pocket in the thatched roof over the loft. It took both girls and all the strength that Mark could muster to get up to the loft and then into the pocket in the thatched roof. As soon as Mark was in position, Tsandra was sent off to the depression with detailed instructions about the heliograph signals to return. Jean then brushed out the horse hoof prints round the barn as soon as Tsandra had left and then took up position in the loft to wait. Mark was in great pain and the added discomfort of being wedged between two layers of thatch at an angle of about 45 degrees made it much worse. They could not risk having to get Mark concealed without Tsandra's help, so he just had to literally sweat it out and suffer in silence. Jean tensed about an hour after sunset and came back to the pocket where Mark was concealed.

"I can hear a large number of men on horseback riding in from the South, they are making a lot of noise so they must feel very confident that they are the only people around. Are you alright to stay here for however long they stay around?"

"I hope they don't stay too long, it is hell in here."

A few minutes later, the officer in charge walked into the barn and started giving orders for the men to feed the horses, set up lanterns, and cook the evening meal. A detail of about ten men was told to help him search the house again, they then left with some lanterns to return about an hour later. When they returned, the meal had been cooked in a large dixie over an open fire in the middle of the yard. The officer, whom the men called Henk, was very annoyed that they had found nothing and that the advance party was missing. A complete search of the whole area was to be made at day break. Some large wooden boxes were then unloaded from the pack horses and dumped in the barn. The men were so exhausted that they just dossed down wherever they could and fell asleep almost instantly. No guard was posted but the fire was built up to last till morning.

Jean moved over close to Mark so that she could whisper an interpretation of what she had heard into Mark's ear. When Jean had finished bringing him up to date she kissed him on the cheek. They slept fitfully and were often awakened by the men below snoring and stumbling around to go and relieve themselves. The Boer horses had been turned loose in the house paddock and became restive because they had finished the hay that had been put out for them and were hungry in the early hours. Jean kept very close to Mark and tried to comfort him when he awoke in pain. At long last, the first glimmer of dawn filtered across the veldt from the East, but it was well and truly daylight before the Boers came to life and cooked their breakfast.

Henk Van de Brecht was in a foul mood, and stormed out of the house with his NCO and tried to organize search parties for each area, the house again, the barn, the irrigation and burnt out shamba site, the pool and kopje. The search parties were to return by noon with their findings. The four men who were detailed to search the barn were very disinterested and only made a show of activity when their officer was in sight. Having clambered up to the loft and made a show of stabbing the edge of the pile of hay systematically with a pitch fork they went below and gave the other piles of hay the same treatment before going into the yard to scrounge some more coffee from the cook.

The NCO came bustling into the barn and looked at the piles of hay and then went and fetched his officer into the barn.

"We should burn down this barn and the house so that it is not a refuge for the bloody Englisher, or anyone else." The faces of the four men who had searched the barn lit up with broad grins and then they started putting small piles of hay along the walls ready for the big conflagration. Jean's grip tightened on Mark's arm as she translated in a whisper what she had heard.

"What can we do when they set fire to the barn, it will burn very fiercely and be destroyed in a few minutes?"

"I have run out of ideas other than giving ourselves up, but that would be terrible for you with all those men. May be we just go up with it; at least we have put up a fight so far."

Henk was standing in the yard talking to two older men who were obviously farmers turned soldiers. One of the farmers bent down and took up a handful of soil and sniffed it and let it fall through his fingers into his other hand as he was speaking to Henk. The other farmer was nodding in agreement. Henk came into the barn and called over the NCO.

"I have decided to keep this farm for myself, do not burn anything and tell the men to leave everything just as it is. Is that understood?" "Ja."

Jean leaned forward and gave Mark the translation and then gave him a hug and sighed with relief. The hug made Mark wince with pain. They were over another hurdle but still had the crisis of Mark's urgent need of surgery.

A group of men staggered into the barn carrying the half eaten remains of the advance party which they had found in a thicket on the way down to the irrigation. Signs of the advance party having been dragged into the thicket were also found and Van de Brecht went to see the location for himself, accompanied by some other men. Seething with rage, Henk returned to finish checking over the grizley find which was now in the barn. The NCO. found a neat hole in one man's chest, made by Mark's rifle shot, and there were two holes in the other man's head, made by Jean's revolver. Henk said "A man can't come back from the dead to shoot two of my men. Where is the idiot who claims to have shot that bloody Englander?"

The unfortunate man was fetched from the pool area and told to explain himself. "All the bodies that were thrown into the pool to foul the water have been moved, we can't even find their equipment."

"What did you do with Oakhill's rifle?" "It was thrown into the water and now I can't find it."

"Sergeant, take some men and search the pool area again."

Turning to the man who claimed to have shot Mark, Henk said. "What made you think that Oakhills was dead?"

"He was shot in the leg and through the chest and had lost a lot of blood. I held him under water and kicked him, but there was no response, he was dead alright."

After a while the search party returned from the pool and said that they had formed a chain of men to walk slowly through the pool and found nothing, not even a boot. Henk's temper flared again and he threatened to "shoot the man who claimed to have shot that bloody Englisher and assumed that he was dead."

"You are an army of gypsies who can't be trusted to do anything. Oakhills has shot your commander, eight of my men and now rises up from the 'dead' and shoots two more of my men and gets clean away. Just a bloody Englisher hardly out of school, a 'soutpiel,'(wanker) and you idiots go to piss and can't even beat him in your own country. We have our orders to go to the railway and put the master plan into action which must take priority over this fiasco. Sergeant, tell the men that we will have tiffin and head for the railway as soon as possible."

Henk personally supervised the loading of the boxes onto the pack horses while tiffin was being prepared. Jean whispered the translation into Mark's ear and then said. "Only about two hours more before they move out. Would you like a drink?" "Yes please" Jean gave him a drink from the water bottle at her elbow and then took a sip herself. "We will soon be able to get down and dress your wounds. I am bursting for a pee, it is very difficult for a girl at this angle."

The Boers seemed to take an age to finish loading their equipment before having tiffin while Mark and Jean continued to hide in the thatch, which was now like an oven in the hot midday sun.

Mark passed out and Jean was afraid that he would cry out with pain if he came to, so she held a handkerchief in one hand ready to muffle any sound that he might make. Henk sent off a detachment of about ten men to call at every farm in the area to see if 'that bloody Englisher' was hiding anywhere and seeking help with his wounds. "I want him alive so that he can be questioned."

After a quick check round the barn, they finally moved off in a Southerly direction. Jean waited about five minutes and then cautiously crept out, stretched and looked out of the opening. The column of horsemen could still be seen going Southwards. A careful search of the house, yards and barn confirmed that they had all left and that it was safe to get Mark out. He came to when Jean tried to move him and was able to assist in getting down from the pocket in the thatch. Jean changed Mark's dressings before washing and changing her own clothes. The heliograph was dug out of the hay and set up in the opening where Mark could sight it up on the sun and the depression, some two miles away and send the prearranged signal to recall Tsandra with the horses. The signal was not seen at first, but after repeated heliographing the flashing mirror acknowledgement was finally sighted. It was another hour before Tsandra appeared in the distance leading the horses, by which time Jean had prepared tiffin. The Horses were fed and watered and then the three of them sat down to eat in the loft so that they could keep a lookout from the opening. The meal made Mark feel drowsy again, but he forced himself to hold a discussion on their future plans. They could not stay at the McIntyre farm for any length of time because the ten man patrol was sure to return soon. Mark urgently needed the bullet removing from his rib cage before it festered any more or he would get blood poisoning and die. They could not go to any other homestead for fear of walking into the patrol or being betrayed by a Boer sympathizer, or anyone being threatened by the Boers for information. Pietersburg was presumably still held by the Boers and was out of question.

"Who else do you know well enough to trust and who can dig out this hardware before I go rotten in the hot sun?"

"Most of the other farmers that we have met in the Zoutpansburg area are Dutch or German and I could not be at all sure of their sympathy with the British."

"The only trustworthy person that I met at SATCO who lives up here, is Major John Ashcroft, a retired army doctor who takes out game hunters on safari along the Limpopo river. How far is the Limpopo from here?"

"I have not been, but Hamish and my father went game shooting last year. I think they said it took three days to get to the river, so that would be sixty miles or so. What good would it be going there?"

"We had quite a long chat in the store and John asked me to visit him anytime. He said that he applied his skills as an army doctor on the natives in return for help around his shamba. He has a permanent establishment and grows or shoots everything he needs. He bought enough seeds, implements and ammunition to last for a few months."

"Well if he is a bit of a bush doctor, I have got enough laudanum left to put you out while he operates. Do you want to give it a try? Can you trust him with your life?"

"It is our only chance, so let's pack up and go as soon as possible. The journey could take us more than three days with me to slow you down." That afternoon and all the next day was spent collecting essential items for the journey and packing them up so that they could be carried on the two Boer horses, which were to be used as pack horses, while Mark rode Jean's horse. There was no question of leaving Tsandra behind to wait for her people to return, if they were still alive, because on the return of the patrol she would be raped and murdered as had the other girls and women. Tsandra was very philosophical about leaving the only place that she knew and moving off into the unknown with two whites. She was very reluctant to put on one of Jean's old bush shirts to cover her breasts, which were of so much interest to Mark.

When the evening meal was finished, Jean said she wanted to spend some time at her parent's graveside and Mark said that he would accompany her. It took all the strength of the two girls to help Mark down the ladder to the ground. Mark then used an old walking stick to hobble along after Jean to the sad little mounds in the garden. Mother, Father and Hamish were buried side by side. Jean was kneeling quietly and Mark was leaning on his stick, when suddenly a doleful chant broke out behind them. It was Tsandra mourning all the dead in her tribal way. When she had finished chanting, Jean said "Couja harper Tsandra" and she came over and stood between them. Great tears started to roll down Tsandra's face and she started to sob uncontrollably. Jean stood up and gripped Tsandra's hand. Mark gripped Jean's other hand. After a few minutes the sobbing stopped and Mark felt a surge of strength flowing into his body. Tsandra said "Bwana, wanda endesha" (Boss, drive on.) and the spell was broken. Mark held both of Jean's hands and pulled her into an embrace, but so as not to exclude Tsandra, Jean pulled Tsandra into the embrace for a few minutes while the tears rolled down their cheeks. Jean asked Tsandra if she wanted to visit the shamba site before they left at first light the next day, but she shook her little head of wooly curls and said "My people are with me."

The two girls helped Mark back to the barn and then started to bed down for the night.

An ancient hand drawn map and a small compass had been found in the house, so Mark put these in the top pocket of his bush shirt ready for the journey. The tributary referred to by John Ashcroft was clearly marked and it was planned that they would aim to meet the Limpopo at the junction with the tributary to check their bearings and then follow the directions to John's shamba. Excitement and anxiety prevented Jean from sleeping and Mark heard her tossing and turning restlessly so he started up conversation. "What made your parents come out here?"

"They didn't have any choice. Daddy was at Edinburgh University and was doing his last year in engineering when he broke his arm rather badly while playing rugger and had to go to hospital. That was where he met Mummy who was a nursing sister, and they fell in love. After a while Mummy got pregnant and there was the hell of a row and the respective parents got together and decided to banish the couple to the depths of Africa and avoid any scandal. They were quickly married and shoved onto a ship with a family lawyer who had been instructed to buy them a remote farm. Fortunately the lawyer came from the country and was careful in selecting land and a farmhouse that had plenty of water and a good soil type. A contractor was engaged to build the barn and the young couple was left with enough cash to feed themselves for a year. Hamish was born while the house was still being refurbished, in fact he was born a few feet from where we are lying. And so the two proud Scottish families avoided any scandal, or so they hoped, and Mummy and Daddy were thrown into the deep end of Colonial farming with no idea of what to expect and no farming experience. There was a large number of slave families who had been released by the British a few years earlier and they slowly came trekking North back to their homelands in Kenya.

From time to time Daddy would have to take them in because they were half starved, or injured and then he got the idea of letting selected family groups build a shamba on the irrigation. This arrangement has been growing over the years and we were really starting to improve the land and look forward to better times when the war started and the raiding parties came.

"Did you and Hamish go to school?"

"Yes, sort of, Mummy taught us for four hours every day from books sent out from Scotland each year."

"Your parents must have been very remarkable people to have accomplished all this from nothing in such a short time. I haven't said it before, because we had the current crisis to worry about, but I am deeply sorry that this has happened to you, please accept my condolences."

"O Mark you don't have to put it so formally, thank you, but I am very lucky to have you here now to help me in my grief and hopefully help us get away from these terrible Boers. How can people be so beastly all because of some silly old agreement over the sale of the Cape Colony to the British that they didn't like. Greed, that is what drives them, then if there is the chance to rape and pillage innocent farmers that is all legitimate."

Jean moved across and quite unexpectedly and forcefully started to arouse Mark, first with her hands and then with her mouth, then sat astride him providing all the movement necessary to bring them both to a climax. Still panting from the exertion, Jean said. "I got to know you very well at the height of the fever and have wanted you ever since, so I just had to take advantage of you while you are still incapacitated."

Mark was in a state of shock and in too much pain to make a coherent reply. Tsandra, secretly watched the 'rape' and was amazed by the 'peculiar habits of whites'. She was awake before dawn and was already moving around when dawn broke and she looked down on the sleeping whites to see if there was to be a repeat of the 'rape', which had made her feel so excited last night, before waking them with "Sikia sana." Despite the elaborate preparations, it was some two hours before the little convoy moved off with the two girls sweeping away their tracks with branches as best they could when they had to cross soft ground. The first night's stop was most unsatisfactory because there was no water for the horses even though they kept going till about an hour before sunset. Mark was exhausted and in great pain from the motion of the horse and the previous night's 'experience', which looking back, appeared to have been almost a, 'forced performance'. Jean was stiff and ached all over, but little Tsandra took the whole thing in her stride and didn't appear distressed in any way, but kept watching to see if there was to be a 'repeat' of last night's performance. There was a lion roaring in the bush in the night so Mark sat up with his rifle while the others slept. Several times he found himself dropping off to sleep but he forced himself to Stay awake till he finally handed over to Jean in the early hours. Mark was awakened by Tsandra kneeling beside him and gently shaking his shoulder. It was fully daylight and he felt terrible.

Jean was still sleeping and he felt a real heel having to wake her, but they must get an early start and find water before the heat of the day.

It was mid afternoon before Tsandra started to get excited because she reckoned there was a water hole ahead. She had spotted the footprints of many animals radiating out from an area of thick bush. The water hole was nearly dry and a variety of species had scratched small holes to collect water to drink. Mark decided to pitch camp on some higher ground a few hundred yards North of the water hole so that their tracks would be completely obliterated by the animals coming in for a drink during the night. It took the girls ages to dig holes deep enough to collect water for the horses to drink and then to fill the water bottles with water the colour of mulligatawny soup. During the twilight, animals of all kinds came down to drink and Mark was tempted to shoot a young buck impala for the pot, but there was the risk that the shot would be heard also danger that predators coming for the carcass and then looking for something else to eat, like one of the horses. The next days march was much easier because they found good water by noon. A beautiful rocky pool at the base of a kopje. Animal tracks were everywhere. Mark decided to pitch camp on some high ground overlooking the pool and the girls soon had the camp set up and a fire going to cook the strips of salt buffalo meat. After tiffin Tsandra went off to act as herder for the horses while they grazed their fill. Jean and Mark sat under a shady tree by the fire and dozed for a while. Jean said. "Tell me about yourself."

"When Father suddenly died in Scotland, it was not till we got home that I fully realized that I had inherited the responsibility of Father's estate which had been allowed to run down due to Father's ill health. We were in the red and with the three of us at college things looked pretty grim so I left college to let the other two stay on and so that I could start to manage the estate and reorganize the place. We had to fell a mature stand of fine oaks, and use the proceeds to pay off the debts and start to improve the property. Mother, and my sister Anne seem to be coping very well since I came out here to sort out SATCO, which was in trouble. Father had sold two farms about thirteen years ago and reinvested in SATCO and had come out twice in the early stages to set it up and steer it in the crucial stages. Considering that SATCO started from scratch, it was a major achievement and an immediate success. Then about two years ago the first manager became ill and had to retire early and we got Henk van de Brecht. He was very good at first and then last year it all started to go wrong and stopped making any dividends. Father was not well enough to come out to fix up the problems and it just got worse and worse. First Henk walked out, then his assistant, Peer, walked out and we got a message from Gustav Petersen, the forwarding agent in Durban, telling us what had happened. I had to jump on the next ship available to see what had gone wrong. Soon after I arrived there were a number of mysterious attempts to burn down SATCO. We just saved it the first time and then I had the building clad with corrugated iron which saved it the second time.

It now appears that Henk was in the Boer Army all the time and was using SATCO as a base for meetings and had a large scale map in the office which was used to plan all the military operations with his friends at night. If those boxes which they had in your barn the other day contain what I think they do, and the comments about the 'job on the railway' are pieced together, then it looks as though they are planning to blow up the trains all the way to Pietersburg and perhaps to Messina on the other line.

Soon after I arrived at SATCO. we built quarters for me over the office and I was in the bath one evening when the first arson attempt occurred. Fortunately the Boers did not appear to know that there was anyone living on site and thought that they could burn down the office without any opposition. It now appears that Henk is highly embarrassed by leaving the marked map behind and that they were trying to destroy the map and do as much damage as possible. We found that the map had pin marks along the railways where they planned to blow up the trains.

I set off with the senior stable boy, Raymond, on a sales trip scheduled to last till nearly Christmas. When we were six or seven miles East of your farm, we realized that we were being followed and Raymond recognized Henk. We were hopelessly outnumbered and had to take cover on a rocky ridge and try to shoot it out. They shot our horses, then they had apparently shot Raymond. I was able to drop four or five of them and then hot foot it to your farm, in the dark, and take cover by the pool. You know the rest."

Jean said. "Henk is very annoyed that you were able to survive and beat him in his own country and then 'rise up from the dead' and continue shooting his men, but if we don't fix up your chest wound very soon it will all have been to no avail. How does it feel now?"

"It is still very sore when I move and it feels as though it is on fire."

"Here, let me check the dressings" Jean removed his shirt and then the dressings. The wound was suppurating and the two bottom ribs were blue and bloated. Jean cleaned the wound as best she could and then put on a fresh dressing but she was far more concerned than she was prepared to admit. She sniffed for that dreaded gangrene smell, but could not detect it yet.

Early the next morning, Jean took the binoculars up to the ridge to check out the landscape and see if they were being followed. "Don't forget to keep the lenses in the shadow to prevent sun flash, which can be seen for miles."

Tsandra stayed in the camp area with the horses and then returned to where Mark was lying in the sun, with the freshly filled water bottles.

Mark had passed out. Tsandra quickly pulled off the dressing and inspected the wound. She had seen similar suppurating wounds caused by spears or arrows and knew that there was only one way of getting rid of the poison. She got some clay and moulded it into a cup shape, then found some ants of a particular species and put four or five into the cup before putting it onto the wound and binding it onto Mark's body. Body warmth would dry out the clay and keep the ants where they could feast on the rotting flesh and deposit their faeces into the clay. Mark was awake by the time Jean returned 'with the all clear'. They quickly packed up and started on the next leg of their journey. On arrival at the next camp site Jean was starting to take off the dressings when she found the native remedy. "Ugh! It is ants and mud. Whatever have you put on your wound?"

"I don't know but it feels more comfortable and is not on fire."

Jean then realized that it was one of Tsandra's native remedies. Tsandra said that if Mark didn't have more 'mud packs' he would die plenty soon. Jean was horrified at the thought of horrid little ants eating away a living person, but had to admit that the ants were removing the puss and the wound looked clean. Or were they eating a living person? Hopefully the ants were only eating the rotten flesh "How much can you feel Mark?" "The whole area hurts and the fire masks whatever the ants are doing. The native remedy seems to work, so I am prepared to give it another try." Tsandra felt very important as she made up another mud pack and skilfully applied it to Mark's chest.

"Ondegi. Ondegi mingy" Little Tsanrda cried from beside Mark's horse as they plodded along the next afternoon. Jean knew that circling vultures could only mean death. But who or what had died? There had been no hunting parties out game shooting since the war started because it was too dangerous with the Boers everywhere. That number of vultures must mean many corpses. Tsandra volunteered to go forward alone to investigate and report back. Jean was becoming more worried by every additional problem or delay. An hour or so later Tsandra returned to say that there was a white man's shamba ahead and there were many dead men and animals lying around. Only the vultures were alive and slowly moving in to start feasting on the corpses.

Jean said "Sounds as though the Boers have pillaged a farm, but I didn't know that there was a farm here, there is nothing shown on the map that Father and Hamish made on their hunting trip."

The party moved up very cautiously and came up to the remains of a newly built farm house and barn. The barn had been burnt nearly to the ground but part of the house was still standing and was still smouldering. Jean wondered if there were any Boers still around and asked Tsandra to check all over the house site. She returned and said that there was no one still alive. Mark was disgusted to see the vultures ripping through the clothing of the corpses and gorging on their entrails. He could not bear to see the loathsome big birds with their skinny necks and heads reaching into the uniforms and pulling out entrails like strings of sausages. He raised his rifle and shot one large bird. The rest let out shrieks of terror and flapped away. Some could not fly because they had gorged so much and just flapped along the ground still making their dreadful screeching cries, the others went to wait in some trees. There was no human response to the rifle shot so the trio approached the house, but there was something wrong.

British soldiers had been defending the house alongside the farmer and his family, but there were British soldier's dead bodies by the barn in an attacking position. Surely it couldn't be a mutiny? Tsandra was going round the corpses looking for survivors, or was it souvenirs, when she noticed that some of the corpses down by the barn had the traditional Boer bush shirt underneath their British army tunics and she told this to Jean.

"Uitshudden, the bastards."

"What does that mean Jean?" Asked Mark.

"That is a practice that we were told about in the 'British settlers defence instructions' that was posted to all the outlying farms owned by British subjects when the war started. It means that when the Boers overrun a British position, they strip all the clothing off the troops and turn them loose stark naked in the bush with no food and no water, they soon die of thirst, hunger and exposure. The Boers then put on the British uniforms and bluff their way into British camps or British owned farms being defended by British troops, and massacre them at point blank range. It appears that this attempted massacre has not gone according to plan, because there are nearly equal numbers of corpses on both sides. We must put out the fire and check again for survivors in the ruins of the house."

The two girls started to take water from a tank to put out the last of the smouldering embers. The kitchen and wash house were nearly intact because a roof tank had ruptured with the heat and the slowly leaking water had nearly succeeded in putting out the fire in that part of the house.

"Get your bloody plates of meat off me' ands."

A distinctive cockney voice came up from the rubble where Mark was moving to get into the shade near the tank. Mark jumped back in alarm and looked down. A man's arm was buried in the rubble. "Come quickly there is someone trapped under the debris beside the tank."

The girls had difficulty in levering up the charred timbers to expose an English sergeant who was very badly injured, cut, and partly concussed.

"Cor blimey I aint 'arf glad to see you lot after those murdering, bloody, Dutchie, Boer, Bastards, they fucking nearly got me this time with their bloody dress up pantomime tricks. Me 'ead urts, me arse 'urts and I think I shit me'self when that beam fell on me."

"Just lie still while we check you over. Tsandra. Can you fetch the medicine bag from the pack horse please."

Mark sat in the shade of the kitchen while the girls administered first aid to the sergeant, Charlie Hopkins. With the superficial wounds cleaned and tied up, Charlie was then dragged out for further inspection. The main damage had been caused by the falling beam, it had ruptured some internal organs. He also needed urgent surgery or he would die very soon. Jean became more stressed with the responsibility of another wounded man desperately needing surgery.

A quick search of the remains of the house added some items of food to the dwindling supply. The night was punctuated by the howls and shrieks of the predators squabbling over the corpses and several times a hyena appeared within a few yards of where they were sleeping. When one hyena came too close in the early hours, Mark shot the ugly brute. At first light, the vultures moved in again down by the barn to start gorging on the corpses. Charlie had the plan to go to the Major's shamba for some bush surgery explained, but he chose to stay put. "Me gut's busted, I could'na make it, I've gone in the legs, you young 'uns go on and get fixed up."

Jean and Mark had a brief discussion on what to do about Charlie and decided to have a quiet day and see how he was by nightfall. They didn't have to wait very long for by mid morning Charlie was becoming delirious and called out in extreme pain. The internal injuries were proving fatal and he was passing a lot of blood. Just before noon Charlie became quiet and asked Jean to write a note to his wife and family. He got as far as "I love you all and think of you a lot when it is quiet at night"— He died peacefully with his head resting on Jean's lap while Tsandra bathed his forehead. Jean wrote a note to Charlie's family explaining the circumstances under which he had died and put it in a cloth bundle with some personal effects to send to his family when the opportunity arose. The girls found a pick and shovel and dug a shallow grave in the garden for Charlie Hopkins and then returned to where Mark was resting in the shade. The infection from the wound was worsening, because of the shattered ribs, and it was now a race against time to get Mark to surgery if he was going to survive.

Back at SATCO there was much excitement in Abdul's office because he was preparing to leave with his wife to go for a ceremony where his eldest son, Hassan, was to receive his diploma.

At eighteen, Hassan was a tall athletic boy who had done well at his studies at the college in Johanasburg. It had taken every penny that Abdul and his wife Hanna could save to pay for the fees and now they were being rewarded for their sacrifices on this hot Saturday in December.

It was late afternoon before the Suliman family returned to the SATCO office. The other staff were preparing to close and lock up for the week end. Abdul left his wife and the younger children in the office while he took Hassan on a tour of inspection.

"Now that you have turned eighteen, we must see what you want to do. I will show you how SATCO operates and you must tell me if you are wanting to start working here. You would have to start doing all the junior boys jobs till you have twenty one years old. Then we can decide where to put you and see if you can go further in the company."

Hassan had never been allowed to look over SATCO before and was very impressed, particularly by the respect given to his father by the other staff. As they returned to the office, Sasha was serving tea and Hassan was immediately attracted to her. He decided that he would like to work for SATCO and when the all important question was asked, he answered with a quick. "Yes."

It was arranged that he would start as a stable boy as soon as possible. There were several letters for Mark from his mother and Abdul was becoming more concerned about the total lack of news from the Zoutpansburg area, where Mark was last known to have visited. Finally Abdul had written a short letter to Mrs. Oakhill stating that Mark was away on a business trip when war broke out and was believed to be isolated in a remote area. More news would be sent as soon as possible.

The next day a crude farm cart rumbled into the yard and stopped under the archway. The driver jumped down and went into the office asking for Bwana Suliman.

"I have one of your sick boys in my cart." Abdul immediately thought that it was one of his own sons who had been in an accident and rushed out to find a very weak, deathly thin, Raymond lying on some sacks in the cart. The driver demanded payment for returning Raymond, so Abdul gave him a voucher for ten pounds that could be used in the store. Raymond was off loaded onto a table top and carried into the office, He had a bullet wound in his thigh and had lost the use of that leg. Abdul and Sasha went in the ambulance to the hospital with Raymond and tried to get as much information as possible about how he was wounded and what had happened to Mark.

"We was followed out Zoutpansburg hill country. I was seeing messa Van de Brecht.

We went to a ridge with rocks and waited. They came up and shot the horses and then came to get me. I got one, maybe two, then ma leg! I was down and messa van de Brecht, him plenty mad. Bwana Mark, him shooting four maybe five Boers, also one officer standing along by me. Van de Brecht, him more mad about some map, but I have no map, I jus' knows where to go. He kicks ma bad leg and I do what Bwana Mark tells me before and makes plenty dead, he kicks me some more so I jus' more dead. Nightime coming and more shooting, then all quiet but not get Bwana Mark because them Boers all keeping very low from his good shooting. When all quiet I creep away and find some good berries and hide again, then maybe after two days some xona people out hunting take me to their shamba but no fix ma leg bone. By um by me me couja harpa"

"What happened to Bwana Mark." Sasha asked anxiously.

"No more shooting, I see them Boers coming back with their horses but keeping so low them thinking the Lord was awaiting them like the others he shot." Raymond's eyes were rolling with the whites showing to illustrate his story.

"So, Bwana Mark, him must have gone like a spirit in the night cos dem Boers still a hunting like hungry jackals next day. Him must go to the farm we was a planning to go to down sunset way." The doctor was amazed that Raymond had escaped with a shattered thigh bone and travelled some two hundred miles on horseback or in a farm cart with only minor infection. The bullet had shattered the thigh bone into several splinters and then torn it's way out through the thigh muscle. "Probably a Dum-Dum, the flattened nose always does terrible damage." The doctor said.

It took two operations about three months apart to repair the bone with pins and graft the muscle and then the Doctor said that Raymond would have about 80 to 90 percent use of that leg in six months. Sasha and Mjuba took it in turns to visit Raymond in the evenings and it was good to see him gaining strength and confidence.

Tension was mounting about the disappearance of Mark and Abdul made frequent calls to the British HQ only to be told the same story that the Boers still held the Zoutpansburg area and that communications were not good in the North.

Many of the allied units still called into SATCO for supplies, and in particular to buy the sturdy Cape ponies that Gustav sent up on the train from Durban. Units of the Bush Velt Carbineers (BVC) were frequent customers for lightweight equipment, Cape ponies and use of the new blacksmith's shop on the Colonel's land across the road which Abdul had leased for a pittance.

Scraps of information could be gleaned from the BVC about how the Boer raids on farms and sabotage on the railways were carried out. This was usually followed by counter attacks by the BVC, or an ambush and the capture of Boer prisoners. It was through this source of information that Abdul found that Van de Brecht had been an officer in the Boer army for much of the time that he had been at SATCO. All at SATCO were infuriated by the deception that they had worked under for so long.

Sasha was all for going on a rescue mission with Raymond and Hassan, but Abdul would not hear of it. She knew that Mark had been invited to visit Major John Ashcroft's shamba on the Limpopo river and that was where she intended to start her search and use some of the camp followers as trackers to lead the search into the Zoutpansburg area. Increasing business kept Sasha very busy, particularly now that Abdul had given her the responsibility of a whole department which included ordering stock, much of which came from overseas through Gustav's forwarding company.

Sasha thought that there may be a way to get a message to John Ashcroft with some of the ex slaves drifting back to their home lands, but that could take years as they were so slow.

Then she got the idea of using the BVC when they next called in for supplies, only to be told that they usually only went as far as Pietersburg and not any farther North. A few days later a BVC unit called in for supplies and Sasha was able to get the officer in charge on his own in the store and explain about Mark's disappearance, and the information provided by Raymond followed by her own theory that he had gone to Major John Ashcroft's shamba for help.

The officer said. "Could I have a word with your man that got away?"

"Yes certainly, can you wait in here." She showed the young Captain into Mark's office and went to find Raymond who was taking things easy in the stables. "This is Raymond who went off with Mr. Oakhill on business and returned wounded, he can give you all the details."

Raymond repeated his version of events and added. "Bwana Mark him very good shooting, him get plenty Boers, so they keeping low so maybe him getting away to big farm that we could see towards the sunset."

Captain Clark thanked Raymond and Sasha and said that he would enquire among all BVC units in the area and get word back to SATCO.

Jean was about at the end of her endurance with the massacre at the farm, Charlie's demise and Mark's increasing weakness from infection added to the loss of her brother and parents. At first light the next day the weary little party had breakfast and had started loading up the horses when Tsandra became alarmed, and then excited.

She said. "Some of my people are near here, I can hear the bird calls that they make in the bush." "Are they friendly. Can you reply?"

"Yes, they are friendly, they are following the tribal signs that I left behind us. It is my father or my brother who comes."

Cupping her hands round her mouth, Tsandra made a series of shrill bird calls. A few minutes later a party of hunters appeared from behind some bushes at the end of an area that had been cleared as a garden. They came forward slowly with their spears at the ready. Tsandra stepped out of the shadow and called to them. The four men still came on very slowly and with caution. Finally, when they were sure that there was no ambush they ran forward and embraced Tsandra and then came to greet 'Missy Jean'. There was a lot of quickly spoken Swahili and broken English, most of which Mark did not grasp.

"Jean, please can you tell me what is going on and who are these people?"

"It appears that about half of the families in our shamba got away but some of the women and girls were raped and murdered. Tsandra had stayed to look after her ancient grandmother on the mistaken assumption that she was too young to be in danger. When the grand mother saw what was happening to the other young girls, she made an exhibition of herself so that Tsandra could slip away and hide under the bridge. The four hunters have women and children some miles further back, being guarded by the young boys. They have been following the signs left along the way by Tsandra, after they found the first one in the barn at our farm.

The Boers have half scared them to death with all their rape and murder, so the families have just been surviving in the bush and following our trail hoping to find Tsandra. They want to know if they can help so I have told them that we need urgent help to get you to the Major's shamba. They are more than willing to help and are already talking of sending out a scout to check the route to the shamba and calling up the women and boys so that we can set off right away."

Jean could see that the fever from the infection was making Mark weaker by the hour and was delighted at the thought of an escort and men to help lifting Mark onto the horse.

CHAPTER 5

ANNE

Anne Oakhill came home from the university for the Christmas holiday and was greeted with all the usual affection by her mother, but she sensed that there was grave concern just below the surface. The cattle had mostly been sold and only the best pedigree breeding stock were being looked after by two of the stable boys who had volunteered to be locked up in the buildings with them under quarantine. No one. Like no one, was allowed anywhere near the buildings. It was just a matter of rationing out the fodder till the threat of foot and mouth passed. The shouted messages across the yard indicated that the stock were in good condition and that the boys were happy to be of service, live on iron rations and receive a bonus at the end.

Anne sensed that there was a new threat tearing her mother apart. So at dinner that night she broached the subject of Mark's disappearance. "Yes dear, he is still missing and I have made enquiries through the War Office Records branch to see if he had enlisted, but they know nothing and were not at all helpful. In fact they say that the man who Mark spoke so highly of, Abdul, something or other, has been making similar enquiries at the other end. The war seems to have got to a messy stage of hit and run with the Boer army still holding the Northern part where Mark disappeared."

Agnes started to sob gently and Anne put her hand on her mother's arm.

"What is it Mummy, have you heard something else?"

The sobs continued for a while, then Agnes said. "I will get the letter for you to read."

She returned a few minutes later with a large envelope and placed it before Anne. The envelope was addressed in a very unusual hand, but was obviously a girl's writing.

Anne slid the letter out of the envelope.

South African Trading Company
Johannesburg

15th November 1902

Dear Mrs. Oakhill,

Please have forgiving for me for writing to you. I am Sasha who came from a Canal Suez Company house, then the slave camps and the mission school and now has the honour to work for SATCO.

A mother must know about her son so I have made this letter many times and this one is going to you. Please do not tell Mr. Suliman as he may be angry.

Bwana Mark is a good and clever man for everybody at SATCO and has saved us from the fires of the evil men who now hunt him because they left a map behind with plans to blow up the railways. Bwana Mark and Raymond are going for five weeks and then again on the train to Pietersburg and to the remote farms in the area.

The war is coming and we get big orders posted back and we are told he is coming back soon to SATCO. The Boers are stopping the trains so we have no more letters and Bwana Mark can not come back.

By—um—by Raymond is coming back to SATCO with a shot in his leg and we put him in hospital. He is very sick and I go many times to find what is going on. Raymond is telling me Messa Van de Brecht following them so they hide and start shooting. The horses are shot and Raymond is shot in the leg and makes plenty dead and then goes away.

Bwana Mark shooting many Boers. I am sure that Bwana Mark is getting away also and Raymond Knows where he is going. Raymond saying all Boers keeping very low because of Bwana Mark's good shooting. I am wanting to go with Hassan to find Bwana Mark but Mr. Suliman says too many Boer soldiers so no good.

So I am asking the BVC officer to help and he has promised to help me.

Please have forgiving for me writing and send help for Bwana Mark.

I remain your obedient Servant,

Sasha.

"What an extraordinary letter, written by one of the native girls working for SATCO. They must think an awful lot of Mark to actually write. What do you make of it Mummy?"

"Well dear, it gives a lot more information than the rather formal letters from Abdul Suliman. We now know that the ex manager, van de Brecht, is at the bottom of the trouble, that Mark is on his own in the bush and is on the run. How can we help him from here when there is supposed to be the British expeditionary force based in Pretoria?"

"From the reports that I have heard from the wounded boys, back from the war, at the hospital dances, the troops are just sitting on their backsides in the cities while a few Colonial Scouts do all the work. Kitchener won't move till the railway is repaired and safe to use. The Boers have control and keep blowing up the railway North of Johannesburg. A 'stalemate.'"

They talked on for a while and Agnes explained that Hugh was to spend Christmas day at home with Margaret and then the rest of the holidays at the Morgrove's house.

"Margaret and Hugh are very serious now and would dearly love to get married but they are still too young at only 18 and 19.

Ted Moregrove already treats Hugh like a son and is gradually feeding him more and more about the business so that he can take over when Ted retires. Hugh and Margaret seem very happy together, I do so hope it works out."

"Mummy, how is the market garden working out on the old swamp? Were the levels that I took any good? Did it drain properly after the ploughing?"

"Yes dear, the new man we have there, John Bellis, is very pleased with everything. He has built some sheds and has had a super crop of potatoes and now has everything growing well. We send a load into Chester market every week and the extra income is very welcome with no milk cheques coming in while the foot and mouth is about. You must not even think about going anywhere near the farm buildings for fear of infection of the stock we are keeping in isolation.

We were burning tarred rope to windward all the time but everyone else has the same idea so now you can't get tar anymore. The boys have a gun and have been told to warn off any intruders, but it is nearly impossible to keep the birds out. We have put up wire netting and so far it seems to be working. The last new outbreak was over a month ago so we must now hold out for another three months at least. We only got about half price for the cattle we had to sell off before the outbreak but that was better than having to shoot them and getting nothing. We have had to wind down our building programme on the farms and cottages while there is so little coming in and I have agreed to forgo the rent for six months on the farms that were worst affected by the foot and mouth. So you can see we are just keeping our heads above water. Without the returns from SATCO., which by the way is now showing a good monthly profit again, but I have told Abdul to plough it back for the time being."

Anne was very tired after the long day and went up to bed early but could not sleep. That letter was very disturbing, and she kept thinking of Mark out in the bush on his own being hunted down by the Boers. By breakfast time the next morning, Anne had made up her mind to go on the next available steamer to Durban to find out what had happened to Mark.

Agnes put on a front of being horrified at first, but secretly she wanted Anne to go, on the strict understanding that she went no farther than SATCO to direct operations and report on Mark's condition and the progress at SATCO. A passage was booked with the expected arrival in Durban by the end of January.

Christmas lunch was the usual huge affair with all the employees and their families being feasted in the great hall as was the Oakhill tradition. By three o'clock, the festivities were slowing down and the effect of a full, or over full, stomach and all the toasts were taking effect. People started to wish each other the season's good cheer and thanks to Agnes and go home to sleep it off.

Hugh and Margaret decided to go for a walk round the lake 'to shake down the Christmas pudding' and wrapped up well before setting off arm in arm over the crisp ground. They walked slowly along the lakeside and discussed their plans for getting married. Hugh was just into his second year at university and had two more years to go. They planned to marry as soon as he graduated and go to live in Chester close to Moregrove's office. There were plenty of houses available to rent so that was no problem. Margaret was housekeeping for her father and spending time in the office when he was away at the docks or inspecting stands of timber offered for sale.

They had reached the other side of the lake and were walking along the back of the farm buildings when there was a gun shot, and after a minute, another shot.

"Shooting is not allowed on Christmas day or Sundays, so that must be the boys in the farm buildings having trouble. Come on Margaret, we had better go and see what is wrong."

They hurried towards the end of the yards and were just in time to see Reg. Maddocks stagger round the end of the corner building before he fell into the ditch. He was blind drunk and there was blood on his legs. It took all Hugh's strength to pull Maddocks out of the ditch and roll him on to the bank. He was still firmly holding a closed, quart milk can. A little prodding finally brought Maddocks to a sitting position, Still muttering oaths and threats of. "I'll get the bastard for sacking me, I'll get his bloody cows with the infected shit in this can. Leave me alone. Bloody boys had a gun, got me' legs they did, knocked me down, I'll have the law on them I will."

"Before you start talking about the law, what you doing with that can full of manure round a registered quarantine area, there is a one thousand pound fine and five years in goal for that, you come back to the stables with me. Margaret can you run on ahead and get Mum to send for the police."

Maddocks was reluctantly frog marched to the harness room and locked in with one of the stable boys outside to keep an eye on him till the law arrived. Shouted messages revealed that Maddocks had given himself away by falling off the fence and dropping his milk can with a clatter. The boys had shouted a warning but he had kept on coming so they fired a warning shot in the air which did not deter him, but number nine shot gun pellets in the legs at fifty yards had sent him running. The police took evidence 'by shout' across the yard and then from Hugh and Margaret before washing Maddocks with carbolic and taking him off in hand cuffs.

"Just shows that you can't be too careful and that all our precautions are justified." Agnes said. "We could have lost the nucleus of our stud if we had relaxed for one moment. Christmas day, of all the gall to pick a time like that. I suppose he knew the routine, but his old drinking problem wrecked his plans. Hugh you must incinerate that filthy can right away and wash everything in carbolic including your clothes and shoes."

Anne was very excited and apprehensive at the same time as she boarded the ship at Tilbury docks and was shown to her cabin on 'C' deck. What sort of a passage would it be? What would she find at SATCO.? There had only been time to send a cable, before her departure, a letter announcing her arrival, would probably have arrived on the same ship that she was on, anyway. Would it be a good idea to look up Gustav Pedersen in Durban before going on to SATCO? The thoughts and fears tumbled round in her mind.

By the time she had unpacked in her cabin and had made a tour of the decks, the luncheon gong sounded while they ploughed down the channel. The head steward showed her to the table and the place that she had been allocated for the voyage. What a mixed bunch of people at her table, she thought, an old lady of about seventy, an American couple of about fifty, two young British officers, presumably going back to their units in South Africa, a junior ship's officer, and a middle aged woman who looked like a teacher or a governess. Conversation was very stilted at first, but the two young officers were soon trying to make conversation with Anne.

Harry Gittings was in the Royal Engineers and had spent most of his time repairing the railway tracks round Bloomfontain when they had been sabotaged by the Boers. One such section of track was being inspected by Harry when a farther explosive device in the form of a booby trap had gone off and meant that he had had to go to a London Hospital to have shrapnel removed from the corner of one eye. He was a pleasant young man but a bit inclined to be too serious and shy.

At dinner that evening Anne found out about Mike Copeland, the other young officer. He was in an infantry regiment and had seen action up the line from Bloomfontain to Johannesburg plagued by lame horses and enteric fever. When he finally got to Johannesburg, he had been shot in the back by a spent bullet or ricochet that had lodged just above his kidneys and had also been sent back to London for surgery and a return to the lines after a brief period of recovery. Neither of them had any knowledge of SATCO or the country North of Johannesburg. The journey was exhausting for Anne because of the continuous stream of would be suitors who tried to press their luck with a beautiful, single girl travelling on her own.

She was not in the mood for flirting with the worry of Mark's disappearance, and there was not anyone who caught her fancy. There was also the university studies that she was trying to keep up to date and which helped to pass the time. When at last the ship berthed at Durban, she felt a little sad at leaving the shipboard friends and more than a little apprehensive at the thought of the trip up country and what she might find at SATCO.

Anne decided to call on Gustav while in Durban. The cab stopped outside 'The Durban Forwarding Company' and on entering, she was asked to wait in the reception area while a very pleasant native girl went to find Gustav. A few minutes later the wooden floor literally shook as Gustav came hurrying down the passage. A huge hand took her hand and kissed it before he looked her over and said. "I am vary pleased that you are coming, ja. You must stay with my family tonight before taking the train. Do you have luggage?"

"Yes, it is in the cab that I have waiting outside. If you are you sure it is no trouble, I would be delighted to meet your family and stay overnight. Thank you so much."

"May I come in your cab to take you to my house?"

"Yes certainly."

"Anna is used to visitors, the hotels, they are not good, ja, plenty cockroaches, terrible food and bad plumbing."

Anne had the sights of Durban pointed out on the way to Gustav's house. It was all so strange and in some ways old fashioned. Anna did not seem at all surprised when Gustav announced that Anne Oakhill was coming to stay for a night and quickly made Anne feel at home. Gustav hurried off in the cab back to his office.

Anna instinctively knew why Anne had come to Africa and was able to give details of how the war had affected ordinary people. "You must go no farther than Johannesburg, these

Boers are worse than animals, you would not stand a chance if you got caught. I have lived in fear for my girls, they are twelve and thirteen and tall for their age so I feel that they would be an easy target for these evil men."

"They are delightful girls and so pretty, it would be a tragedy if they came to any harm."

Anna and Anne went for a sight seeing tour in an open cab after lunch. The cab driver was a trusted friend of the family who always kept a loaded revolver in his belt. The old port area with the merchant houses such as Gustav's firm, the warehouses, small factories and then the stores and hotels on the approach to the city centre. Everything was very different and most of the people were black or coffee coloured.

She was glad to be in the company of someone like Anna who knew her way round. The poverty and despair of the street children and beggars was just accepted as a way of life and nobody appeared to notice them. White people were very much in the minority but appeared to be prosperous.

The Petersens were the perfect hosts and Anne was able to relax and enjoy the company of the two girls and help them with their home work in the evening.

Departure time came all too quickly the next morning when the whole family saw Anne off on the train for Johannesburg. Anne had decided to bury herself in her books on the train trip so that she would keep up with her studies for the next exams at the university. She was hardly aware of the people who got in and got out at the various stops along the way. When she arrived at Johannesburg it was too late to go to SATCO, so she booked into a small hotel for the night and after a badly cooked dinner retired early so as to be ready for the first encounter with SATCO.

On the following morning, the cab driver turned the horses in through the SATCO. gates and stopped under the archway outside the office.

Robert Mackenzie was at his desk at the far end of the general office and looked up to see a well dressed, very attractive white girl walking briskly towards him. "Good morning, my name is Anne Oakhill and I would like to see Mr. Abdul Suliman please."

"Mr. Suliman is being very busy just now, can I help you? My name is Robert Mackenzie. I am chief clerk here."

"Thank you Mr. Mackenzie, could you please tell Mr. Suliman that Mark Oakhill's sister, Anne, is here and that I would like to see him as soon as he is free."

"Oh, Mrs, no, Missy Oakhill, it is very pleased that I am to meet you to be sure. Please be coming in here and sit down to wait. I will send for some tea while I get Mr. Suliman."

Anne was ushered into Mark's office and sat in a comfortable chair by the side table while she looked round and tried to take in as much as possible of her surroundings. A chink of china cups made Anne look up and see a tall, very beautiful girl coming down the stairs from Mark's quarters with the best tea service on a tray. Anne was amazed by the elegant and very sophisticated girl who came into the room and put down the tray and said. "May I pour some tea for you Miss. Oakhill?"

The letter was still in Anne's hand bag, and she could still remember some of the passages in it and also some of the comments in Mark's letters. "Yes please, would you be Sasha?"

Sasha blushed. "Yes"

"Please sit down Sasha, I would like to talk to you about my brother Mark's disappearance."

Anne got the letter out of her bag and said. "It was extremely kind of you to go to the trouble to write to my mother. Thank you very much, it means so much to just get some news."

Sasha sat down and said. "I hope that you were not angry with me because I wrote asking for help. Since Raymond has come back with a shot in his leg I have known that Mark, Bwana Mark, is in trouble. He is not dead, I am sure that he was getting away but he may be wounded also and he is being hunted by the Boers because of the map left behind by Messa van de Brecht."

"What do you know about the map Sasha, why was it so important?"

"That is where the map was." Said Sasha pointing to a lighter patch on the wall below a large hook. "All our customers were marked with pins but there were other marks put on the map by van de Brecht along the railways. Bwana Mark showed me the marks along the railways so we are hiding the map for the Boer occupation. Would you like me to get the map?"

"Yes please."

Sasha went to the cellar and Robert Mackenzie appeared again to say that. "Mr. Suliman sends his apologies but he is having trouble with unloading the dynamite for the mines, he will be back by noon."

"Thank you Robert."

Sasha returned with the map and laid it on the table. "After all the trouble, I am not hanging it up again because the Boers have their spies everywhere and may burn the office again."

"Very wise. Can you show me the marks when you have had your tea?" Sasha blushed again and nervously sat down while she drank her tea. Anne could not help noticing that Sasha picked up the cup with familiarity and wondered how many times she had used it before with Mark. Sasha explained all the normal pins on the map and then the new pin marks along the railways.

"You know that the BVC officers are telling us that Messa van de Brecht was in the Boer army all the time that he was working here. We are sure that he was making secret plans when he had meetings at night with his Boer friends. You are the only other person to see the map since we took it down."

Anne followed Sasha into the cellar as she put the map back into it's hiding place and took notice of all the firearms, ammunition and goods of high value stored there.

"Do you have much trade in these firearms?"

"Oh yes, we supply the farmers and hunters and now the new army units come in with large indent orders because their own supplies do not come in time. We never let anyone come in here. There is only a small stock in the store for the customers to see."

As they walked back to the office, Anne asked if she could have a look round SATCO.

"Please may I arrange for Mjuba to look after the store while we are away."

Mjuba was introduced to Anne and then took over minding the household section. Anne was pleasantly surprised with the 'Quarters' and could see that the furnishings and ornaments showed signs of the female touch.

"You have made the 'Quarters' very comfortable for my brother, I hope that he appreciates it." Sasha blushed again and led the way to the room used by Mjuba. They then went through the office, household, general merchandise, stables, warehouses and machinery sheds. "Since Mark, Bwana Mark, has gone, Abdul has leased some of the colonels land across the road and we have put up a new blacksmith's shop, fodder sheds and stables for the army horses. That is big business now."

All the buildings were very new and were bustling with activity. The smith had a long line of horses waiting to be shod and the ring of his hammer on the anvil was a familiar sound from the many times that Anne had taken a horse to be shod back home. Sasha quickly went through the mail which Mjuba had brought in and singled out those items for the household section. The two girls went into Mark's office and Sasha read a letter which had been pinned to a bundle of invoices. "Gustav says that he has a very interesting man coming on a ship, he is a miner from Cornwall and he suggests that he could be of interest to SATCO. to service the mines. Where is Cornwall please?"

"It is in the South West of England and that is where they mine tin, copper and sometimes silver." "Do you do much business with the mines round here?"

"Oh yes, we do a lot of business with the mines, we supply dynamite for blasting, rock drills, hand tools, miners lamps, rubber hose and lots of new machinery; it is a very complicated business."

"Is there a mining expert on the staff here?"

"Well, not now, we had Henk and Peer who were both trained in explosives and mining machines but now that they have gone we have nobody. Abdul does as best he can, but he can only arrange the supplies that are ordered."

"Perhaps it is worth sending for this experienced Cornish miner to see if he is suitable to look after the mines. What do you think?"

"Please, you are asking me very big questions and I am only just made the supervisor in the household section."

"But you are very much a part of SATCO, now, aren't you? I would value your opinion."

Sasha was all embarrassed for a moment, and then smiled at Anne and said.

"You are very like your brother. He would talk to me about SATCO as though it belongs to all of us here. These questions are for Mr. Suliman and Bwana Mark, but if this man knows about mines perhaps he can help the mines to make good business."

"I will talk to Abdul and ask him to send for this man for an interview as soon as possible."

Sasha said that she had to get back to her section and excused herself.

Anne talked to Robert Mackenzie for a while about the bad debts that had been allowed to accumulate by Henk and was pleased to learn that all the accounts in the Southern region had now been paid, probably because the British administration was now in control and the fear of a forceful collection was a motive for settlement. Even some of the large overdue accounts farther North were starting to come in. This was having a dramatic effect on the current month's results and the account was already over 50,000 Pounds in credit at the bank.

"What are the terms of the lease on the Colonel's land?"

"We are having five years with the option to buy anytime at the original valuation. They did not want to lease at first but desperately needed the money to start paying off the Colonel's son's gambling debts."

Footsteps sounded in the doorway and Anne turned round to see someone she assumed to be Abdul walking up the office.

"I am sorry that I could not come sooner Miss Oakhill. I am Abdul Suliman and I am very pleased to meet you."

"I am pleased to meet you Abdul and please just call me Anne. Anyway, what was the problem with the dynamite?"

"Well, it is all because of the Boer spies and the commando raids. Gustav sends it up with a British army guard and I have to count it, sign for it and personally supervise the delivery direct to the mines still under guard. It just takes time, but it is very good business."

"I am pleased that you are so careful, we don't want the Boers going round armed with explosives and blowing things up."

"They have stolen some dynamite from another company, who did not have a guard, and they are blowing up trains all the time. We lost some of our supplies in one of the trains that was derailed. Have you looked over SATCO. yet?"

"Yes thank you, Sasha took me on a quick tour, but perhaps you could show me the Colonel's land in more detail sometime."

"I would be pleased to whenever you wish. It is nearly one o'clock, what would you like to do for lunch? Mark usually had it sent to his office from the quarters."

"That sounds fine."

While Anne was using the bathroom, Sasha and Mjuba laid out a cold lunch in Mark's office and they all sat down for lunch. Anne showed Gustav's letter to Abdul and said.

"Do you think that we could use a mining expert to service the mines? Should we send for this man, who has been recommended by Gustav, for interview. I have heard that the Cornish miners are in great demand in other parts of the world."

"Now that we have lost Peer and Hank I have to do most of the mine work myself, but I am having no knowledge of mines. So we could employ this man if he is good. I can send for him right away."

"Yes please do that Abdul, I am sure that we can rely on Gustav's judgment.

Sasha has told me all that she knows about Mark's disappearance, but you may be able to add something."

Abdul thought for a moment before answering, but could not add anything to what Anne had already gleaned from Sasha. Anne moved into the quarters and spent her time between following up all the information about Mark's disappearance, getting to know more about SATCO and working at her studies. At the end of the first week she asked Abdul to show her over the Colonel's land.

Abdul had two horses sent round so that they could ride over the property starting with the lower road frontage and then up through the scrub onto the small hill at the far end. There was about 200 acres in all. The Boer army, followed by the British army had camped along the two road frontages and most of the trees had been cut down for their cooking fires, so it looked a lot different from the start of the war.

"How much does the Colonel's son want for the whole lot Abdul?"

"The valuation was 50 pounds per acre which is 10,000 pounds for the 200 acres but what would we do with it? We are only leasing ten acres for the holding paddocks and sheds. Do you have something in mind?"

"Yes, an idea is forming in my mind that we can discuss later."

They rode back with Anne deep in thought. On each of the next few days Anne went to British HQ and after three visits actually got to see one of Kitchener's staff advisors, Major General Broughton, who promised to send an immediate order to all the patrols going North to enquire about Mark.

"You must keep calling my dear, we could have some news any day now."

He was becoming obsessed with the idea of a beautiful young English girl in distress visiting him in his private office and Anne was not surprised when he suggested joining him for dinner sometime, but Anne decided to keep the enquiries on a strictly formal basis.

Abdul had talked about the young couple that Mark had met on the train, George and Heather Bridgeman, so Anne decided to look them up.

CHAPTER 6

SHEEBA

After two days of travel at a frantic pace, Jean's party, guided and assisted by the natives from the shamba, were within a few hundred yards of their destination. Smoke curled up from a small clearing just ahead and they could see the tops of some thatched huts.

A deep, throaty, blood curdling roar came from a thicket by a bend in the track.

Everyone froze. "Lion." said Jean.

Mark was just sufficiently conscious to pick up what was happening and said. "Get me my rifle." While Jean was deciding whether to give Mark his rifle or use it herself, the most amazing sight came into view in a patch of sunlight some fifty yards along the track. Two teenage girls were coming down the track with a fully grown, rather plump, lioness on a lead.

The lioness stopped and sniffed the air and all the natives in Jean's party just melted into the bush. Jean quickly realised that the lion was tame and called out. "We are coming to see Major Ashcroft, please may we pass." She then repeated the request in Swahili. The two girls giggled sheepishly and signalled them to come forward. When they were a bit closer, the older of the two girls said.

"Sheeba will not hurt you if you are kind to her, you must stand very still and let her smell you all over so she is knowing you, then we can go on together."

Jean was amazed that the girls spoke English so well, not to mention the tame lion smelling her trousers and nuzzling her hand. When the lion had 'accepted' the party, they moved forward again. "Do you live at Major Ashcroft's shamba?"

"Yes, we are his daughters. Sheeba was rescued by Papa as a cub and she lives with us now and we take her for walks while she is pregnant."

Word of their approach had obviously preceded their arrival, for John Ashcroft was standing on the veranda of his hut complete with a welcoming party as they approached.

"You must be Alistair Macintyre's girl with your wounded friend, please let me show you to our first aid hut."

He led the way to a small hut comprising two rooms with wide verandas and large windows. They very carefully lifted Mark off Jean's horse and carried him into the hut and placed him on the high table in the middle of the room. There was a bed close to one wall and a rack of bottles and instruments on the other wall. John Ashcroft asked Jean to remove the clothing and dressings from the wound areas and tell him the extent of the damage as she worked. A tall, good looking native woman of about thirty went into the second room and started to light a fire in a small mud brick stove and sterilize a basic set of surgical instruments. John took Jean into the other room and said. "The chap is in a pretty bad way, you must realise the danger of operating, also you must realise the predictability of events if we don't operate."

"Yes, I am fully aware of the position, but please will you operate and try to save his life, you see, I have become rather fond of him, though I hardly know him yet."

"Yes, I will operate but I must start right now because the good light will only last for another four hours or so. Do you have any experience in these matters?"

"Yes, I have helped my mother operate many times, do you want me to scrub up and assist you?" "Yes please."

They went over to where the instruments were just coming to the boil. "This is my wife, May. This is Miss. McIntyre"

"How do you do. Please call me Jean, thank you for getting started so quickly."

"Hello Miss Jean, we heard that you were coming, so we made ready. Please wash very carefully and put on this shirt."

After scrubbing up, all three put on old long sleeve shirts. John then looked Mark over and put him out with chloroform. Jean said a prayer to herself as she laid out the instruments and watched John probing into the festering ribs.

"I shall probably have to remove at least two of the shattered ribs and hopefully I will find the spent bullet within reach underneath."

Once John had made a long incision and pegged back the skin, he skilfully used a sort of butcher's boning technique to completely remove the two lower ribs, both of which were shattered into many splinters and infected. Then using a spoon like instrument he searched for the bullet and found it buried under the third rib and dropped it into an enamel dish with a clatter.

"That is the bastard that we have been looking for, now we can scrape away some of this damaged flesh and sew him up. Are you coping alright Jean?"

"Yes thank you."

The operation had taken over an hour and Jean felt physically and mentally exhausted by the time Mark was cleaned up, sewn up, with new dressings and with May sitting by his side to monitor his recovery.

"You look about done in girl, come over to the house and have a stiff brandy, it'll do you good, May is used to looking after patients after operations."

John led the way into his hut which was furnished with furniture made out of timber from the bush and covered with animal skins of many kinds. They sat down on easy chairs and John's daughters came in with Sheeba. Jean was smelt all over again and then Sheeba flopped down and rolled onto her back and demanded that her chin was rubbed, just like a fireside cat. Sally and Sarah brought in the drinks and then sat down with their fruit juice. As he sipped his brandy, John said. "Did you sew up that wound on his leg?"

"Yes I had to do what I could, because when I found Mark my parents and my brother had already been murdered by the Boers and I was on my own."

"That must have been a terrible ordeal for you. You have been a very brave girl to achieve so much without any help. Oh by the way, I have arranged for your natives to bunk down in my shamba,

I think that they all came from the same area and then the same slave camps and seem to get on well together. Little Tsandra has palled up with my girls and will be sharing their room in the new wing down that way." Said John, pointing down a passage leading off the main room.

The hut was built in typical African style with a huge central room, with a high ceiling, in which they were sitting, then there were radial suits of rooms leading off in various directions.

John and May's rooms, the new wing for the girls, the kitchen and bathroom wing where a large mud brick stove burnt 24 hours a day, and the original two rooms which were now the visitor's suit.

"Where would you like to sleep. Here or in the first aid hut? On second thoughts perhaps it would be better if you slept here for tonight and get a good rest, then see if you feel up to playing nursemaid tomorrow. They can be very demanding when they first come round you know."

"Thank you, perhaps I will take your advice and sleep here, you are right I am dead beat, particularly after that stiff brandy. Can I relieve May while she comes up for dinner tonight."

"Yes that would be fine."

Jean had a hot bath and felt a lot better by sundown when they sat down to dinner which comprised roasted leg of reed buck, yams, sweet corn and fresh fruit. As soon as Jean had finished the meal, she hurried down to relieve May.

"How is he, is he awake yet?"

"Yes he has been awake for a while and he thought it was you looking after him, he is still very feverish and is in pain when he is awake. He will only be awake for a few minutes at a time for the next few days, just give him plenty to drink when he is awake. If you are alright, I'll go and have dinner now."

When May had gone, Jean brought the lamp closer and checked Mark carefully. He was sleeping deeply with regular breathing but he was still very hot and feverish. Just before May returned, Mark woke up and was obviously in great pain. He drank some fruit juice and asked Jean where he was. "We arrived safely at John Ashcroft's shamba and he has taken out the bullet so now you can just rest and get well again. John's wife, May, will look after you during the night. She is very competent and I will not be far away."

She was kissing Mark good night when May returned. "Good night, you be good for May."

May came in and started to make up the bed in the other room and Jean left.

John was sitting on the end of the settee with Sheeba's head in his lap fondling her ears when Jean walked in.

"Don't be surprised if Sheeba comes to visit you in the night, she has the run of the house and likes to check up on everyone as though we are her cubs."

"I think I will turn in now, good night" Sally and Sarah came over and kissed Jean good night and then took a lamp to her room. Jean was asleep as soon as her head hit the pillow.

Mark woke in the early hours and May was quickly at his bedside checking his pulse. In his half drugged state, Mark thought it was Sasha holding his hand, then when she asked him how he felt, he realised that the voice was different and started to get his bearings.

"I have a terrible headache, I feel sick and my chest hurts, but the fire in my ribs has stopped. After a drink Mark dropped off into a deep sleep which lasted till long after sunrise. Sa—nne-na—nussu (10. 30) as May called it.

Jean had been awakened by Sheeba licking her arm just after sunrise so she got out of bed and stroked Sheeba's head and talked to her. The girls heard Jean talking and came in with Tsandra and all three took Sheeba for her before breakfast walk. Jean dressed and went to see Mark who was still sleeping so she returned to the kitchen to find the two house girls from the native quarters already preparing breakfast.

Breakfast was a leisurely affair eaten in the shade on the veranda, mealy porridge, melons, and fruit juice. Sheeba lay snoring in the doorway twitching her tail in her dreams close to John's feet. May joined them for breakfast while one of the house girls kept an eye on Mark.

"You seem to have quite a routine drill for operating and looking after patients."

"Yes we have worked out a system, we get quite a few from the war, mostly wounded natives, then there are the spear wounds from fights among the natives, usually over a wife. Never any money changes hands, but they usually pay in kind by sending their family to work in my fields for a while or with gifts of animal skins or meat. I go to Johannesburg every few months for supplies."

After a long pause, John said. "My first wife died from cholera in India many years ago then I retired from the army and came out here and set up my shamba to take out hunting parties which paid very well for a few years, but then I became sickened by the rich city folk who came and professed to be hunters, just wounded anything in sight and then wanted their photo taken 'to show the folks back home'. We often had to go and make a clean kill which was always very dangerous. Now I only take out a few of our native gun bearers, who are all excellent shots, or friends when we want some meat, a bit like farming really. May came to me as a house girl and we have made marriage vows to each other, so as far as we are concerned, we are man and wife."

John took May's hand and they looked endearingly into each other's eyes. "May has produced two wonderful daughters and we are very happy together. I run a school class, for those who want to attend, about four mornings a week. We have a mixed bunch of children and a few adults attending. This means that some of them can go and get better jobs or more education in the towns. We have a very simple, happy lifestyle and I still have a small pension from the Army Medical Corps and a few investments to pay for the things that we have to buy in Johannesburg."

"What was that! Sounded like a gunshot." said May. Then as everyone was listening attentively there were two more louder, more clearly defined, rifle shots, then silence, then a few well spaced shots. Sometime later, a small, breathless native boy came up to John and started pouring out a report in Swahili. Jean gathered that there were several small boys watching a group of Boer soldiers about a mile away.

"They were starting to cook a meal when the cooking pot and the fire blew up. The Boers then started to shoot at any likely hiding place, but there was nobody there. The boy's eyes were rolling and his arms were gesticulating violently to illustrate his story.

"Kwenda fuata" said John., and the boy ran off.

Tsandra, Sally and Sarah had finished their breakfast and were sitting on the edge of the veranda hanging onto Sheeba as she was becoming alarmed by the sound of gunshots. Tsandra said something to the other girls who then started to giggle.

John could not see the joke and asked gruffly. "What is your private joke?"

After a while Sally said. "Tsandra thinks Bwana Mark was blowing up the cooking pots, ha ha." "And how does a sick man, flat on his back, blow up a cooking pot a mile away?"

Tsandra, with Jean's help, explained that Mark had taken some 7mm Mauser ammunition from the dead 'advance party' at the farm and had got Tsandra to put two or three rounds into each of some hollow logs left at each campsite so that any one following them was likely to give themselves away by using 'a convenient piece of firewood'.

"John said. "There are about ten Boers in that party and they have been seen going to each homestead in the district according to my scout boys. I think that it is time that we went to ground, particularly with Mark in his present condition."

"I will make ready" said May as she left the veranda and went into the hut to start moving furniture.

A large steel plate was exposed from underneath some mats in the main room which exposed steps leading into the cellar. The girls then went quickly to work fetching fresh water, food, bedding, lamps, rifles, ammunition, and a stretcher. May said. "Can you help to move Mark, please."

"Yes of course" Jean followed May to the first aid hut and they gently rolled the sleeping Mark onto the stretcher. May took the front and led the way into the cellar where they gently rolled Mark onto a bed in the centre of the room which was now lit by several lamps. Jean was surprised at the planning that had obviously gone into the design and construction of the whole complex. Though not outwardly apparent, the whole house was built on a slight mound made from the earth that had been excavated from the cellar. Numerous giant bamboo tubes let into the top of the cellar walls gave both ventilation and minute glimpses of the outside world. Jean, Sheeba and the girls went into the cellar and John dropped the hatch and replaced the rugs. John then did a patrol of the area removing any trace of evidence that he had visitors. One of the house girls was sent to summon the village head man from the native quarters and when he arrived there was a quick discussion which sent him running back to batten down and send all the women and children to the emergency camp hidden in the bush. John then spent some time in the first aid hut and there was the chinking of glasses and bottles. An hour or so later the head man came into view leading a party of Boers surrounded by spear brandishing warriors. They came straight up to John's house with rifles at the ready. An animated discussion in Africaans, broken English and Swahili took place and finally John agreed to let two soldiers search his hut.

While this was taking place, John suggested to the man in charge that they might like a cool drink of native beer. Greedy smiles broke out on the Boer's faces and they followed John into the first aid hut where he had set up an evaporative cooler made from wetted reeds surrounding the bottles of native beer. The Boers drank thirstily and then started to sit around in the shade of the veranda. The man in charge then went up to the house and insisted on personally searching again and visited each room with his revolver drawn and pocked into every cupboard and under each bed with a stick.

Another group of men returned from a fruitless search of the native quarters and then after some more beer they started to relax. John then gave them all some more beer and some meat before they departed at high speed. Jean had been watching the socializing through a bamboo tube and wondered what John was up to.

Some time later, a scout boy came running back to report that the Boers had gone 'plumb loco' then ridden off at great speed and that the followers were having trouble keeping up with them. John moved back the settee and rolled back the mats before lifting the trap door so that Jean, the girls and Sheeba could come out.

"Why waste all that beer on the Boers?" Asked Jean.

"Just you wait and see." Said John with a whimsical smile.

It was decided to keep Mark in the cellar while there were Boer patrols in the area. May helped Jean move her bed into the cellar and set up everything that she might need for herself and Mark. The sun was getting low in the sky when a scout boy came running up to the veranda with his eyes popping and his arms waving to support his report.

"Askari, they have gone 'plumb loco', they all ride in different directions, they drop their banduki (Rifles) and equipment, shout and even take off their clothes, some are running around on foot, some are on horses, they go to the river and will drink it dry they have such a terrible thirst, what can we do Bwana?"

Suppressing a smile, John said. "Kwenda, keep a good watch on the askari, even in the night and report what you see in the morning."

Jean's curiosity was getting too much for her, so she said. "Please tell me what you laced that beer with, it must have been very potent."

"Shouldn't give away trade secrets you know, but let us say that the second round of drinks was not the same as the first. We collect and distil the juice from a certain type of fungus which grows around here. The natives use it to catch animals. It has a slow acting effect and makes them hallucinate and go into a sort of trance for a long time. I think that they get a sense of searing heat and that is why humans strip off their clothes and drink like there is no tomorrow. They loose all sense of time and direction and each time they have a drink, it reactivates the toxins in their bodies. I have not seen it reacting on a whole group of men before, but we know it effects people differently. Usually they don't even know their own family for a while."

"What do you think will happen now John?"

"Hard to say, they will probably stumble round in the bush for a few days, but will keep to the river because of their terrible thirst. Eventually they will reform their group, probably in about a week and feel very embarrassed because they have lost all their clothes and equipment, not to mention their memories, and be late returning to base. I don't think that they will bother us any more for a while.

Just visualize them reporting to their superior, 'first the cooking pot was shot at but there was no body there, then we lost our memories, our sense of direction and all our equipment and took twice the usual time to get back to base."

John rolled round in his chair in convulsive laughter while everybody shared in his mirth.

Mark had been half awake and became curious about the cause of the mirth and called out. "What is so funny?"

The two girls told Mark about the success of his booby trap and John's beer and he had to hold his chest because laughing made it feel as though it would burst.

"Jean, I must get word back to SATCO, can you please ask John if he has any means of getting a message through?"

"I will ask him now." Jean went up to the veranda and asked John.

"Yes, we have a family of Bushmen, Ruga Ruga that we helped, you know how they can cover the ground. They can do at least fifty miles a day. They go to Joburg' for me if there is anything very urgent and are back in about ten to twelve days. We usually send two so they can take it in turns to lead and set the pace. Amazing people, just happy to be of service because we saved the lives of their parents when they were shot by a party of drunken Germans, said that they had shot a couple of monkeys. The professional hunter running their safari brought them in here for surgery. I was able to fix them up, good as new now. It is their two sons who run errands for me. We can get them here in a few days while you write the message for Mark."

"What if they get caught by the Boers, surely they are in danger of being captured."

"Yes they are, but the little buggers have their own tracks and they have a way of keeping out of trouble, just run through the bush like a puff of wind and they are gone."

Jean set up two lamps and started to write to Abdul as Mark dictated.

The middle of nowhere

Dear Abdul,

This letter is being written for me by a friend who is looking after me at present. We can't provide much information as this letter may fall into the wrong hands, so please be very circumspect with your answer. The messengers will rest for two days with you before returning with your reply. Raymond was shot and apparently killed, but we later found out that he was wounded and got away. Later I was seriously wounded. The person from the mission would know where I would go for first aid. The bullet has been removed—(Mark had gone into a feverish sleep at that point) John was summoned. "Keep a cold compress on his wounds and his forehead to reduce his temperature and let me know if there is any change in his condition."

May took over nursing Mark so that Jean could continue writing in the sunshine on the veranda.

The patient is sleeping now so I will continue writing this letter. Our friend has done an excellent job of removing two shattered ribs and the Dum Dum bullet beneath them. The patient is recovering well and sleeps a lot of the time at present. The facilities here are good and we have every confidence that the patient will make a full recovery in time. We will keep you informed of his progress. Please do not attempt to find out where the messengers come from as this may put all our lives at risk. There are patrols from both sides in the area. Our patient would like you to write to his mother with this news, he sends his kindest regards to all at 'The Company' and asks that you take good care of the messengers.

With kindest regards
Jean.

CHAPTER 7

A BIT O' WRECKING

Anne arrived at George Bridgeman's office to be greeted by a junior draughtsman who brought George to the front counter a few minutes later.

"Mr. George Bridgeman?. I am Mark Oakhill's sister, Anne. How do you do."

"I am very pleased to meet you Anne. Have you had a good journey?" "Yes thank you, and I have been informed of the news about Mark's disappearance and felt that I must meet you and your wife after all the glowing reports in Mark's letters."

George went grey and tears were welling up in his eyes.

Then with difficulty, he said. "I have lost Heather, the Boers followed us from our house to our supposedly 'safe lodgings' and murdered her when I was out the next day."

"I am most terribly sorry to be so tactless, you poor man, please let me arrange for you to have a cup of tea while you compose yourself."

Anne went back to the front counter and asked the draughtsman to get some tea. They drank their tea in silence and then Anne said. "Would you like to tell me about it?"

"We were terribly busy with extra work from the mines after war broke out and it was just by chance that I got word that I was a Boer target because I had done work for British companies. I hurried back home and picked up Heather and we went to an old boarding house that we knew of. The next day I came back to the office to pick up some instruments and work in progress and quickly returned to our 'Secret lodgings.'

It was horrible what they had done to her, and she was pregnant too. The Army reckon it was a reprisal murder to warn me off working for British firms."

There was a long silence, then Anne said. "You will probably be aware that Mark is missing somewhere up in the Zoutpansburg hill country, his boy was wounded, but was able to escape and was helped to get back to SATCO. That is all we know."

"The British do nothing but sit in Pretoria while a few Colonial Scouts hunt the Boers in the North. Kitchener seems to have run out of steam and is paralysed by the loss of the railways, due to the commando raids to blow them up all the time. I wish we had someone with the guts to show them who is boss round here."

They chatted on for a while and Anne realized that she was becoming very much attracted to this fit young Englishman who had carved a pioneer business for himself out of this strange, dark continent. His services seemed to be in constant demand by the mines, the new industries and the local government.

"Would you care to join me for dinner one night soon?"

George paused, then said. "Yes that would be most enjoyable, but you see, since loosing Heather I have not been able to go out and face people 'en masse'. I'm sure that you understand."

"We don't have to go to a restaurant and be on show you know. We have very comfortable quarters at SATCO and I enjoy cooking, so how about Saturday at eight?"

"Thank you, that sounds good, you are most kind and I will be very glad to accept." Anne went back to SATCO. not quite sure if she had invited George on passionate or compassionate grounds. May be it was a bit of both.

Sasha was very excited and rushed to meet Anne as she rode into the yard.

"There are two messengers and a letter from Mark. I will bring the letter to Mark's office."

Anne had just sat down at the desk, when Sasha came in with two strange looking, very small natives who greeted her by placing their hands on their own chests and then on hers. They grinned happily and spoke in a language of hisses and tongue clicking sounds. Sasha did not fully understand their spoken language but was able to 'communicate' by mime and signs.

The letter was addressed to Abdul, but that was understandable because how was Mark to know that she was now at SATCO. When Anne and Sasha had read the letter, Sasha said. "Bwana Mark has been taken to Major John Ashcroft's shamba. He was an Army doctor and saved the lives of the parents of the messengers, so they are happy to run errands for him. I do not know this Jean who is writing the letter. Is there anything that you would like to ask the messengers?"

"Just how is Mark, how sick is he?"

There was much miming, and one of the bushmen lay on the floor while the other bathed his forehead with an imaginary sponge. Sasha said. "I think he is having a fever after an operation. He looks very weak."

"Please thank the men, and ask when do they return."

"They have been here before many times so we know that they will return the day after tomorrow when they have rested and fed enough to make up for the journey. They have run about 200 miles through the bush in about three and a half days. That is what these Bushmen can do. They have overcome the big distances by learning to travel with little effort and at great speed and then rest and take on food. You can see their buttocks are small now but when they are ready to go again they will have fat little bottoms to use on the return journey."

Anne gave the sign of friendship and the two little men went off to rest, grinning happily and talking in their own language.

"There was a separate letter for me, also a letter which has to be forwarded onto Jean Macintyre's grand parents in Scotland and a letter for Mark's mother."

Anne read Sasha's letter which was very personal and tears came to her eyes when she read about how Jean had lost her parents and brother and then had to endure all the hardship of taking Mark to a doctor out in the middle of nowhere. It was a miracle that they could find a surgeon and save Mark's life. Perhaps there would be some medicine that the men could take back to help with Mark's recovery.

"Sasha, do you know of a good doctor who we could ask if there is some special medicine that we can send?"

That evening Anne sat in Mark's sitting room and wrote a long letter to Mark with all the news from home and a brief report on 'the business.' There were also letters for Jean and John Ashcroft thanking them for looking after Mark so well.

Sasha wrote a long, very personal letter to Mark.

As Anne was addressing the envelopes there was a noise of voices in the yard below. Stopping to listen she heard the unmistakable Cornish accent and realized that the miner had arrived off the train with a cart load of stores sent up from Durban. Having decided to put off writing to her mother till later, Anne went down to the office to find Sasha talking to a wiry little man with a craggy face and huge hands.

"This is Miss Oakhill, this is Tad Trevenick who is coming from Gustav Petersen. Tad put out a gnarled paw and shook her hand, surprisingly gently.

"Being greatly pleased to met you, ma-am."

"How do you do Tad, I hope that you have had a good journey. Would you like to come in here and tell me about yourself?"

Anne didn't need to ask many questions once Tad got over his initial shyness, he just poured out his life story of being a powder monkey as a boy, a shift captain, a mine captain, and latterly a mine manager when the mine fell into poor finances. Sasha brought numerous snacks and cups of coffee which Tad devoured as though he hadn't eaten for days. It was arranged that he would stay in lodgings nearby and return to meet Abdul in the morning.

"Amazing people in Cornwall, Sasha, they are natural miners and still have the cunning of their ancestors as smugglers and wreckers"

"What are wreckers please?"

"Wrecking was what they used to do off the rugged coast of Cornwall. They put up false lights in place of the lighthouses so that the ships would run aground on the rocks so that they could salvage the cargoes on the shore. They made a good living from smuggling wines, spirits and tobacco from France and Spain and with a few wrecked ships cargoes now and then as a bonus."

Abdul could see that Anne's mind was already made up when Tad's interview started in the morning. So Tad was engaged as a 'mining expert', not that he knew much about the very deep mines in the area, but the principals were the same as those used in Cornwall and he would pick up the detail soon enough. Having taken the lead in engaging Tad, Anne now felt more confident and suggested to Abdul that SATCO should buy the Colonel's land right away. There was enough in the bank and they could make an offer of up to 8,000 pounds cash. A meeting was held in Mr. Foster's office at the bank, and a tentative offer of 6,000 was made and then negotiated slowly up to the expected valuation of 7,500. Anne also proposed that some houses should be built for employees on the land. Abdul was horrified at all the proposed expenditure and was very reticent with his comments. Anne did not elaborate at the time but decided to talk it over with George over dinner that evening. The Colonel's son accepted the final offer and the transfers were drawn up. Abdul arranged for Tad to start visiting the mines with Hassan during the next week and become familiar with their workings.

The local economy was now largely based on the gold mines in the area. The war and instability in Europe had caused a loss of confidence in the stock markets of the world so people were parking their money in gold bullion, thus driving up the price of gold so that the mines were now getting much higher gold prices and were increasing production as fast as possible.

Anne was glad of the moral support and local knowledge from Sasha as she prepared and cooked a special dinner for George that evening. They were to have savoury rack of lamb followed by apricot flan in a special French chocolate sauce. Sasha sensed that there was more afoot than just a business meeting over dinner and entered into the spirit of the game of 'trapping your man'. Sasha suggested that she should wait at table for the first course and then leave Anne to serve the suit and coffee. Anne was in agreement on the understanding that they cooked enough for Sasha and Mjuba as well. The formal part of the dinner went as planned and when George and Anne were alone they pooled all the knowledge that they had about Mark's disappearance, wounding, operation and current recovery and possible ways to get him back to SATCO. and hospital for more treatment. They talked into the early hours of the next morning over brandy and coffee till their eyes would not stay open any longer. Finally George got up to leave and Anne went down to see him off and kissed him firmly on the lips as they parted. She may have to live with that memory for a long time, as George was still grieving for Heather.

Anne awoke early the next morning with her plans for the land and houses on the ridge flooding out onto paper. She traced the drawings of the Colonel's land and then superimposed her ideas for a village onto the tracing. Later in the day more ideas came flooding out and more tracings and more plans were sketched and improved. At the end of two days with her pencil, Anne decided to ask George to make a set of professional drawings so that estimates could be obtained for the cost of the buildings. This provided an excuse for George to come over for dinner on two nights later in the week. He then took the sketches back to his office to start work in earnest.

Tad was not sure how to treat Hassan at first, but soon found that he was much better educated than himself and had a quick and retentive mind. He even started to enjoy passing on his practical knowledge of underground mining and in particular the use and handling of explosives. Hassan was a willing and enthusiastic student. At the end of the week Abdul called Hassan and Tad into the office to check on their progress.

"How do the mines here compare with the mines that you worked in before?"

"They be much deeper, but when ees' under ground, they be much the same, blasting be different 'cos the rock's different, you'n be more mechanical like. I can see there be better ways 'o winning the lode, plenty 'o work for me' family when they be 'ere."

They then went on to discuss the equipment that SATCO supplied and what additional items were needed. Hassan had told Tad about the Boer occupation and how they had just commandeered all the supplies that they needed without any payment. Tad was deeply worried.

"Th' an be ways 'o getting paid in kind by they Dutchies, I'll show 'ee one day."

A letter arrived from Gustav the next morning giving details of a special trading ship on a good will trip to try and restore the Dutch reputation as 'honest traders'. She was due to berth in Durban in a few days time and was fitted out as a floating showroom for exotic foods, wines, French silks and clothes, German tools, mining equipment, explosives and firearms. Abdul could not spare the time to go himself, so he sent Hassan and Tad so that they could combine the trip with bringing up another consignment of explosives. "You can spend a few days looking over the ship and the other Durban merchants."

That evening Tad had a wicked twinkle in his eye as he sat in the Petersen's dining room enjoying some French brandy that had been sent from the ship as a sample. "We still have to square off they Dutchie's debt from when they robbed the master's store, getting timely for a bit 'o wrecking, I'm thinking."

Anna was horrified, but Gustav just smoked his pipe and nodded. They sat up till the early hours and slowly a plan was worked out with the aid of more brandy and black coffee.

There was to be a formal reception for the ship's officers and the local merchants at the Dutch commercial Attache`'s house the very next evening. Gustav knew it would be a very heavy drinking affair by the amount of alcohol sent ashore, presumably to soften up the merchant's purses. Many of whom still had very strong anti-Dutch sentiments after the crimes committed by the Boers.

Tad was dressed as a telegraph boy and went on board the Ambrosia with a formal invitation for the crew to join a quayside party being held outside a bordello. The madam had been paid a large sum of money to reduce her rates for the night and serve free wine to patrons. Having delivered the invitation, Tad went into an empty cabin and slipped off his uniform and put on workman's clothes that he had carried in a haversack, suitably marked with the post office emblem, and waited for his chance to climb up onto the bridge. When there no one around, he quickly climbed onto the bridge and removed the brass plate covering the compensating magnets on the binnacle compass, (normally only used to 'swing' the compass on a new ship), and moved the magnets some 15 degrees, and replaced the cover. After the crew had gone ashore for the party and the 'Watch' had retired to the mess deck for some serious drinking, he slipped ashore. By eight o'clock the Ambrosia's crew was either in the bordello, drunk, or both.

A battered old tug was used by Gustav's timber wharf for pulling the ships up the river and moving the lighters and barges. Gustav had fired up her boilers with carefully selected seasoned timber so that she would not emit any smoke from her rusty funnel.

On a signal from Tad and Hassan, Gustav knew that it was time to move the tug up to the Ambrosia's seaward side and go aboard with five of his best men from the timber yard. They were all masked and armed with batons and some extra bottles of brandy. The four men on watch were overpowered and force fed a bottle of brandy each, and then locked in the forecastle store room.

With just a rhythmic hissing, the powerful little tug moved the ship ever so slowly up river above the old slavers camp to a disused wharf. Gustav slipped away for two hours to put in an appearance at the formal function. More men were waiting at the wharf and soon a frenzy of activity started as cranes were used to swing selected items into the lighters waiting alongside. French brandy and wines, silks, tools, canned food, explosives and anything else of high value that they could find.

At midnight everyone except Tad, Hassan and the original boarding party left the ship. The tug swapped sides and slowly pushed the Ambrosia out to sea while the boarding party lit her boilers and started to raise a head of steam. When they were some five miles out to sea the watchmen were force fed another half bottle of brandy and released, not that they were capable of going anywhere, and their tormenters slipped over the side into the tug which then hurried back to the timber loading wharf. A string of loaded lighters was ready to be towed farther up river to be hidden in some overgrown backwaters.

By the usual starting time, a gang of men was seen going into the timber yard for a day's work. The Ambrosia's officers had arrived back at the wharf between five and six o'clock to find their ship just a dot on the horizon with a wisp of smoke curling from her funnel. There were a few very drunk crewmen hanging round on the wharf, all swearing that they knew nothing of the ship's departure.

A pair of binoculars was produced and the Ambrosia's captain went up to the customs house steps to get a better view of his mutinous ship. He mouthed every oath he could think of and then rounded on his men like a bear with sore balls. Not knowing what to say to appease their captain, the crewmen ashore adopted a 'conspiracy of silence'. Meanwhile the Ambrosia's funnel was emitting more smoke indicating that her boilers were being coaled afresh. Finally, the Ambrosia's bow swung round and she started to come back to harbour, but not along the marked channel.

It was not long before the Ambrosia ran aground on a sand bank on the far side of the river mouth and put down a lifeboat which was rowed up to the quay. By this time the captain was beyond reason and he charged aboard the lifeboat and bellowed for the oarsmen to row him out to the ship with the utmost speed. Before the captain was aboard his ship, he was shouting for full steam ahead and threatening his crew with 'mutiny'. Once aboard, on finding that part of his cargo was missing the threats were changed to 'piracy on the high seas'.

Eventually, a change of tide and full steam astern floated the Ambrosia off the sand bank and she was able to return to her berth on the quay. An immediate inquiry was started and all the port officials were brought in for questioning, but as they all had been at the reception there was no body who could give evidence of any clandestine activities ashore or aboard the Ambrosia. It was therefore decided that the captain's theory of a secret rendezvous at sea with another ship was the most likely answer. The watch keepers excuses of being locked in the forecastle store and being so drunk that they did not know what was happening were ignored and went against them.

Not wanting to become embroiled with a foreign ship's disciplinary problems, the port officials suggested an early departure so that the matter could be sorted out at the Ambrosia's home port. Tad and Hassan had already left with an official consignment of stores and explosives and said nothing of their escapade on their return to SATCO. The Ambrosia ran aground again on entering Cape Town harbour and had to go into dry dock for repairs. This, combined with the disappearance of about half the cargo invoked the fury of the Ship's owners and the companies that had sponsored the 'good will voyage' The Durban Forwarding Company had purchased large quantities of the cargo as soon as the ship had docked at Durban, so it was quite normal for the goods to be sent up to SATCO and invoiced as usual. But what was not normal was the high number of credits for 'goods damaged in transit'. Gustav had to do a lot of fast talking to get Abdul to accept the 'compensation' for the stock that the Boer army had 'commandeered'.

Anne was pleased to see Gustav again during his brief visit to SATCO., and listened intently when the 'compensation scheme' was explained to her. "Cunning little man, Tad, he can't help himself when there is a bit o 'wrecking' in the wind. Fortunately no body got hurt, just a few sore heads the next day. Did you find out how long the Ambrosia will be in dry dock?"

"Captain of the next ship up from Cape Town told me that she hit some plenty big rocks and has some plenty big leaks, so she may be there a few months, ja. We are having our own very secret commando raid, ja."

Gustav was interested in Anne's latest project and made some useful suggestions as they rode round the two hundred acres. "It needs a new road along the ridge and some new trees planting. One of those new windmills would pump water up to the top to supply the houses that you plan to build. Mark's idea of building a blacksmith's shop, a bakery and some small shops along the main road makes good sense to me also, ja."

Gustav went back to Durban on the next train but Anne's plans were already including the ideas put forward by Gustav.

A long session was held with Mr. Foster at the bank, and he was only too pleased to have the opportunity to issue a mortgage to cover the cost of the buildings, with SATCO as security. His eagerness to issue a mortgage alarmed Anne, so she visited the company solicitor for advice.

"Got to isolate your self from the parent company when entering a new risk venture, so that if anything goes wrong the bank can't draw on SATCO. my Dear.

We can form a new company that is independent, but it must then provide it's own security for the mortgage. That may mean that you have to put in more cash to start with. These bankers will only take on a very safe bet. Let me know when you are ready to make a move and I will draw up the deeds immediately and get the new company registered."

CHAPTER 8

COMMANDO HILL

During the rest of February and March, Anne saw George regularly as the plans were firmed up for the new company and the buildings.

Another exchange of letters with Mark took place so they all now had a good idea of each other's situation.

Six small leased shops, a company owned bakery, blacksmith's shop and wheelwright were to be built along the side road opposite the stable gate. A bore was to be sunk, as directed by a dowser, and windmills were to be used to pump water, in stages, up to a huge tank at the top of the hill. The road suggested by Gustav was surveyed by George's surveyor and estimates obtained for it's construction, but the quotations were outlandish.

Tad heard of the plans to build the road and volunteered to blast a road up to and along the ridge. "Same way as wee'n put roads to new mines in Cornwall."

So Tad was put in charge of a team of well built young Africans to build the road over the next month or so. Large quantities of dynamite would be used to remove rocky outcrops and break up the boulders. Anne realized that the project had started in a low key fashion but that as yet there was no name for it.

Finance came from 7,500 pounds of recouped bad debts used to buy the land, 20,000 pounds from 'compensation' resulting from SATCO's own 'Commando raid' and a 30,000 pound mortgage from the bank to be used to build the first of the houses and shops that were planned, still leaving a healthy balance in the bank which could be sent to England to help restore the damage done by the foot and mouth disease.

Ideas for a name were mulled over in Anne's mind and discussed with George at length but nothing came up that appeared to be suitable. Then suddenly she had it in the wakeful early hours, "COMMANDO HILL." There was now only the need to obtain approval from Mark and Mother before the project could start. What would Mother think of such a large project?

"You being so young and fit has made it possible to withstand the wounding, infection, and the shock of the operation. Your recovery is very pleasing and we can expect you to be able to ride a little for a few hours at a time by next week.

"I can only thank you for your skill as a surgeon and all the help that I have had from your family and Jean. How can I ever repay you?"

"Don't try, just keep on as you are and give me the satisfaction of seeing you take up a normal life again."

John put down his stethoscope as Mark got off the 'op' table in the first aid hut, now that the check up was over.

"What are Jean's plans now that she has lost all her family in Africa, will she return to her grand parents in Scotland?"

"She has no immediate plans to go to Scotland for obvious reasons, and you see she has never met any of her family over there. For the immediate future, she plans to go to Johannesburg and then review the situation. She will inherit the McIntyre farm, once all the bumph is sorted out, but that would not be a suitable future for a single girl on her own in the bush."

Another series of letters had just arrived by Ruga Ruga when Mark reached the hut, so Jean came over and sat next to Mark as he opened the one addressed to him.

Johannesburg

My Dear Brother,

As you can see I have come out to help find you and assist in any way possible with your recovery, now that we know that you are recovering from wounds. There is also a letter from your friend and a small parcel of medicine for your doctor that we got from the doctor in the hospital that fixed your boy's leg. We are so restricted in what we can say or send to you. I do so hope that you are feeling better and getting stronger and will soon be able to return to us here. Mother was worried sick by the first report that you were missing. Then there was a letter from the person from the mission giving details of your boy's return and your apparent escape, so I decided to come out and see for myself.

The business here is booming and we have great opportunities at present.

We have purchased the land across the road, at less than the original valuation because the colonel's son was desperate to pay off his gambling debts before the loan sharks move in, so we can now form a separate company to develop the whole area, as I think you had intended, from what the staff here tell me. Plans have been drawn up and we are getting estimates for construction.

The solicitor has drawn up documents for your approval which are enclosed for your signature. Please say yes. I'm so excited to be associated with something new.

We have sent the same detail to Mother and asked for her approval as well. George has been a wonderful help in drawing up all the plans, giving advice and getting estimates, he is so businesslike and knows where to go for everything that we need.

How do you like the name COMMANDO HILL for the new project?

Did you know that Heather was murdered just after war started? George had become a target because of his work and they went into hiding but were followed and it was too late. Terrible for poor George, he is such a dear.

How soon will you be well enough to ride again and think of getting out? Mother's last letter says that the foot and mouth disease outbreaks have stopped and that they only have a few weeks before the quarantine period is over. Our stock has survived so far, and we have even had one calf in the time that they have been locked up. It will be years before we have a working herd again. Your staff have been so kind and helpful that I feel almost at home in your quarters, even though it is in the middle of Africa.

You are so lucky to have the girl from the mission, she is so capable and thinks like one of the family already. We have a new mining expert from Cornwall on the staff, and he has already lived up to the reputation of people from that part of the world. He is a valuable asset and I will tell you more in person. Hassan and the Cornishman are working together servicing the mines and the manager is very pleased to see his son bringing in good results already. The BVC call in regularly for supplies and we have asked for their help to get you out when the time comes. We get the only true updates on the situation from them regarding the area to the North.

Hugh and Margaret are to be married as soon as he graduates and they will live in Chester with Hugh working in Morgroves. Ted is already schooling him up into the business and Mother is very pleased with the idea.

I have more exams at the university later in the year so I am keeping up with my studies and have even been to lectures here in Johannesburg to try to keep up with the work and not miss a year. It would be such a bore to have to do it all again. George and I are becoming very fond of each other, but it is much too soon for George to think of anyone else yet.

You are very fortunate to have such good friends to look after you and nurse you back to health out there in the middle of nowhere. I am keeping Mother informed of all that is happening here and her last letter was much happier now that she knows that you are in safe hands and recovering.

Write soon.
Love Anne.

Mark had placed the letter between them so that they could read it together.

"It hasn't taken sister Anne long to get into the swing of things. What she has proposed is more or less what I had planned anyway, but this new housing venture is mostly her idea. I like the name that she has chosen and the money side seems simple enough. I only have one reservation and that is 'should we be sending dividends back to Mother to help overcome the foot and mouth crisis?. There is no mention of how the estate finance is going. I suspect that Mother has just tightened her belt and is riding it out. Country people are much more resilient than city folk in a crisis. Thank goodness we got rid of all the debts before I left. How is your family in Scotland surviving with the foot and mouth?"

"I have no idea, you see they make a point of not writing as punishment for my parents, so childish really, they just arrange for books to be sent for our education. I am considering joining John's classes, but I'm not sure if I'll be a student or a teacher, perhaps a bit of each. How are you feeling now that you can exercise and walk around?"

"I can feel myself getting stronger every day and I am fine till I have to use my chest muscles to cough or laugh, or when I have Sheeba on her lead, she is so strong, I just have to let her go. But she is very good, she just goes to socialize with her friends for a while and then comes back to her compound for the next meal. When are her cubs due?"

"John says that it could be any day now. The first signs will be restlessness and a change in her behaviour pattern."

"We must write to Anne and also all at SATCO and this time I will write another separate letter for Mother to put her mind at rest. It is so ridiculous having the railway line all the way up to Pietersburg, and still no trains, just because a few Boer saboteurs, with a few sticks of dynamite, keep blowing up the trains, while Kitchener 'rests' his men in Pretoria. He has an army at his disposal that could round up the Boers in no time, if he put his mind to it. I am just itching to get my hands on that van de Brecht bastard for what he did to SATCO, your family, thousands of poor farmers and now the railway. Just give me another few weeks and I'll show them. Sounds as though that Cornishman, is a very useful man to have around."

Mark sat on the veranda with Sheeba in her favourite place in the shade, alongside the camp settee, which was made from poles lashed together and covered with animal skins, and started to write some letters. There were letters to Anne, Abdul and his mother. There was also a very private letter for Sasha. In the letter to Anne he suggested that the Cornishman might be spared to come up with Raymond with 'plenty of his tools of trade', but only if they were willing to risk the Boer patrols. He added that it may be possible for them to travel part of the way with a BVC patrol. Mark returned the solicitor's documents with his signed approval to proceed with the COMMANDO HILL housing venture. Jean read through the letter to Anne without comment till she got to the bit about Tad and Raymond coming.

"And just what has our wounded hero got in mind? You are in no fit state to go chasing Henk along the railway."

"Just thought I might liven up the stalemate and help to get some trains running again."

At supper time Sheeba was becoming very distressed and padded in and out of the house and her compound and then started scratching at the trap door into the cellar. John got the idea and rearranged the furniture so that Sheeba had a way into the cellar from behind a repositioned bookcase. By midnight Sheeba was in labour and the birth of her first cubs was imminent. It was decided to leave her to have her cubs in the place of her choice and keep an eye on her from a distance.

John and May sat up all night while the rest of the household went to bed.

Jean was awakened in the early hours by a plaintive mewing like that of hungry kittens. As she slowly gained awareness she realized that the cubs had arrived and went out into the sitting room where John and May were sitting holding hands, in the lamplight, in a state of excitement. "How many has she had?"

"We think it is three. It is too dark to see but we were aware of each birth and then the cleaning of each cub. They seem to be very hungry, so we expect Sheeba to stay with them and feed them for the first day or so till she has recovered and the cubs have had enough milk to sleep quietly, so that she can go off to feed, as she would in the wild."

Just before lunch Sheeba emerged from the cellar, sooner than expected, and took up a protective lioness stance, growling from the depths of her throat. Everybody froze and Sheeba ignored them and then padded off to her compound to find some food. The cubs were sleeping. John said that no body should go near Sheeba till she had overcome the instinctive protectiveness for her cubs. Sally and Sarah were longing to see the cubs and play with them. It was so frustrating to be able to hear them but not see them.

A 'PS' was added to all the letters advising that Sheeba's cubs had arrived and that all appeared to be going well. The Bushmen Ruga Ruga arrived and after a lot of mime and signs to check on Mark's condition first hand, they took off into the bush with their happy grins and bundle of letters.

Sasha saw the Bushmen come into the yard and quickly ushered them into Mark's office where they gave their greeting and sat down on the floor to wait and eat the food that Mjuba brought for them.

Anne was out with George on Commando Hill checking on the final stage of Tad's new road, blasted out of the solid rock in places. To her delight, Sasha was handed a letter addressed to her personally and she opened it while only the Bushmen were around

The Middle of Nowhere.

Dearest Sasha,

I hope the Ruga Ruga remember to give you this letter personally, as arranged. Thank you Darling Sasha for all that you have done and are doing in my absence for the good of the company and also helping my sister Anne. You must have talked freely about our plans for the vacant land and now Anne has taken it a step farther with an even more ambitious scheme to build some houses as well. I am very pleased that you two get on so well together. It is a great relief to have the bullet removed, along with the two shattered and infected ribs, and I am feeling stronger every day.

John has a very simple and happy lifestyle and I find it a perfect place to recover. All I need is you, my Darling Sasha, to make my life perfect. Please can you take tracings off the wall map in the sections with the additional pin holes between Johannesburg, Pretoria and Pietersburg and send them back with the Ruga Ruga.

I am always thinking of you and want you to be with me all the time, you are everything to me. Please take care of your beautiful self.

With all my love.
Mark

George and Anne returned for lunch and were given their letters. The Bushmen did their miming act depicting Mark walking around and moving fairly freely but there was a limp from the leg wound. They then went off to rest and get ready for the return trip. Tad then came into the office to discuss the next stage of making the road now that it was roughed out. He said that it was ready for grading with horse scoops and the addition of some gravel.

Anne agreed and then asked Tad what he thought about going North to find Mark with the next BVC patrol. Tad volunteered after only a moment's thought.

"Letters have gone to me' wife and brothers telling them to sell up and come out, so I'd need to be sure that they would have a house and work while I'm gone, can ee' tell me that?"

"How many brothers Tad?"

"There be two brothers and me' wife and four children."

"We can arrange a house and offer work for a while and there is plenty of work in the mines for good men all the time. Tell them to come to see me as soon as they arrive and I promise that I will look after them. You may even be back before they arrive."

Raymond was keen to get back into the bush and join in the hunt for the Boers who had shot up his leg. It was now just a matter of waiting for a suitable BVC patrol going North.

Sasha took the map up to her room and spent hours tracing the detail required onto some of the tracing paper that George had given to Anne for the proposed layout of Commando Hill. The finished tracings could not be folded so they were rolled up and put into a native arrow quiver made out of a hollow stem and bound with leather.

As usual, George produced very elaborate drawings for the Commando Hill project. The shops and buildings along the road were all in keeping with the period and each had an individual character to suit the proposed use. Dwellings were incorporated into the designs over each shop so that the whole complex was self sufficient with gardens at the rear. A long, wide veranda ran the entire length of the shops so that patrons could keep out of the hot summer sun or the winter rains. When the plans for Commando Hill were shown to Anne there was a large British Colonial, two story house drawn in the picked position at the top of the ridge. There was then a series of medium sized houses and lower down, a street of cottages. Anne tackled George about the big house.

"Who is that for?"

"I thought that if you married me a bit later on, you might like to live there."

"Do I take that as a proposal of marriage?" "Well, er, yes that was what I had in mind, but didn't know how to put it."

"You dear shy man, I'm very flattered and the answer is yes, oh yes." She kissed him and stood holding him at arm's length with a broad grin on her face.

"It doesn't have to be built right away, but it is important that provision is made for a house right away, so if you would like to live there later, the area will be properly planned to include the house and grounds."

She kissed George again and told him that she liked his idea but there was a lot to do first, including her next exams. George was delighted and hugged and kissed her passionately.

Then Anne said "I would like to get Abdul and his family into one of the houses on the ridge, it is important that he has first choice. I was thinking that we could make occupancy conditional on employment at SATCO and only charge a nominal rental for the senior men. What do you think?" "There are ways of having 'tied houses' that the solicitors can work out.

It is also a way of rewarding the senior staff and keeping them faithful to the company. A two way benefit."

Abdul was very pleased with the idea of having a new house on the hill, if the project went ahead. There was only the reply from Mark's mother awaited and this was due any day now. Sasha collected up the letters for Mark and gave them to the Ruga Ruga with the roll of drawings and the personal note for Mark and off they went again, still happy to be of service in their special way.

Several recent attempts had been made to get an army train through to Pietersburg, but each time the track was blown up or the train derailed by sabotage. By May, the troops had become reluctant to go up the line, only to be sabotaged and shot at by the Boer snipers while they tried to repair the track. They said it was 'like shooting fish in a barrel.' More British patrols were sent up the line but they did not know where to look for the explosive charges that had been laid under the track and seldom found any signs of sabotage before it was too late.

Some two weeks later a BVC patrol came into SATCO for supplies and fresh Cape ponies and Anne found that they were to go straight to Pietersburg to join up with another unit. This was the chance that she had been waiting for. The young Captain in charge agreed to take Raymond and Tad with their pack horses as far as Pietersburg, but they must be ready to leave at first light the very next morning. Raymond knew the drill for packing the essentials for bush travel and Tad knew what he needed in the way of dynamite, primers, slow fuse and instant fuse. Sasha came down to the stables where they were loading up the saddle bags ready for the next morning and added two boxes of the special ammunition for Mark's high power rifle. Provided he was strong enough, he could always defend himself if he had his rifle and ammunition. She also sent two spare rifles and two revolvers with ammunition.

The patrol set off just after six as the dawn was breaking over Commando Hill and headed North up the road towards Pretoria and Pietersburg. It was expected to take about six to seven days to do the trip, if they had clear passage without any encounters with Boer patrols. On the fourth day out, Tad and Raymond, who were travelling nearly at the rear of the column, heard orders being shouted ahead and then were told to dismount and take cover in some scrub at the side of the road. A party of twelve men was sent off ahead to check out the tracks of some Boer wagons that had been seen up ahead when they had been crossing a steep gully. The scout party returned at dusk to report that the wagons definitely contained Boer soldiers and had taken the road for some miles and then veered off to the North West and had formed a laager, or camp, for the night. Captain Fisher decided to move the main party up the road for about two miles in the twilight and then make a short stop while two attack groups were sent off to creep up to the Boer position in the darkness and keep them under observation till just before dawn. The main party would have time to have a meal and rest and then be able to follow the wheel tracks with a shielded lantern and arrive at the laager by dawn.

A simple plan that had a good chance of succeeding. Tad and Raymond seemed to have only just gone to sleep when they were roughly awakened, given some stale bread and jam and a swig of tea before they headed off into the darkness. Progress was slow and cautious, so it took over three hours to cover the last few miles to the Boer's laager. All was in readiness for the attack by the main party well before dawn, and it was assumed that the other two groups were already in position. The pre-dawn glow started to appear in the sky and the outline of objects at ground level became more defined.

Suddenly there was the outline of three covered wagons only about one hundred and fifty yards down the hill. Horses started to neigh and jerk at their tethers, then a shot rang out, then a volley of shots followed by shouts and screams. The Boers had nearly been taken by surprise. It was the horses that had woken up some of the Boers who were now trying to get out of their small tents as the attack started. More shots and more shouting as hand to hand fighting broke out in the laager. Prisoners were rounded up and their hands and feet securely tied while the laager was systematically searched for weapons, wounded and stragglers. This was nearly complete and Captain Fisher was standing close to one of the wagons supervising his men when a single revolver shot rang out. Captain Fisher fell with a groan and a blood stain spread across his shoulder. Two burley troopers sprang into the wagon and dragged out the Boer officer who had been hiding there under a tarpaulin. The Boer officer was tied up, none too gently, and put with the other prisoners. A medical orderly attended Captain Fisher and found that he had been shot in the upper arm and would survive with prompt hospital treatment. He was then carefully put into the wagon recently vacated by his assassin. He told his sergeant to take charge and get to base as soon as possible and then passed out with the pain. Sergeant Danny Morgan soon had the prisoners digging shallow graves for their fallen comrades and two of his own men. Two of the wounded men were put into the wagon with Captain Fisher. The other two wagons were burnt along with the prisoner's equipment. At the end of the next day's travel it was decided that travel with the wagon was too slow so the wounded were put on horseback, the wagon abandoned, and travel resumed at the normal pace. They arrived in Pietersburg on the seventh day and Tad and Raymond stocked up before heading North West on their own. Raymond had memorized Mark's description of how to find the shamba and had no trouble in finding the land marks while travelling as fast as they could.

The warning calls of the scout boys alerted Raymond that they were approaching habitation and he soon saw the smoke from the cooking fires and the roofs of the thatched huts. A party of warriors challenged Raymond and Tad, and after an exchange of bird calls and a brief discussion they were escorted to John Aschcroft's hut to meet 'Bwana Doctarti.' Mark had been alerted that two 'friendly' men were coming and was in the first aid hut with his rifle at the ready till he was satisfied that the visitors were bona fide and that the scouts had not been tricked.

Raymond was delighted to see Bwana Mark and kept on touching the scars on his leg and rib cage in wonder at the fast recovery. After all that they had been through together, there was a strong bond between Mark and Raymond. As soon as Mark and Raymond had greeted each other, there were formal introductions all round. Then just as everyone was sitting down to a drink on the veranda, Sally and Sarah arrived with Sheeba on her lead from her walk. Sheeba was very unsure of so many strangers and checked them all very carefully before going to feed her cubs in the cellar. The cubs mewed like hungry kittens and then it was possible to hear them suckling greedily. Raymond and Tad were allocated the first aid hut as their quarters on the understanding that they moved out if there was an emergency. Mark started to study the tracings of the map that Sasha had sent up with the Ruga Ruga and then began to work out the Boer's 'modus operandi' for blowing up the trains and attacking the crew from a vantage point along the track. Sasha had sent up two revolvers, two rifles and plenty of ammunition.

Tad had his own plentiful supply of dynamite, primers and fuse. Now that Mark's wounds were healed and he was gaining strength and self confidence every day, he was anxious to be involved with the final defeat of the Boers. Jean was horrified at the thought of Mark getting involved, particularly after the loss of her own family and the pain and suffering that she had experienced first hand. This was further accentuated by her 'little secret'. But the presence of Tad and Raymond only gave Mark more confidence to go and finish off the Boers, so he started exercising and going on hunting trips and also joining Sally and Sarah when they took Sheeba for walks which sometimes included shooting game which Sheeba was allowed to 'kill' and then drag back to the party knowing that she would be given the remains of the carcass once a few steaks and joints had been cut off for the humans to eat. Jean kept herself busy helping John with his daily surgery and school classes and was pleasantly surprised to find that some of the natives were up to high school standard and still seeking more knowledge. There was a terrible shortage of books, but this did not deter John in his endeavours to bridge the gap between a tribal people and the present day.

May spent a lot of time working with Jean in helping John and with her 'woman's perception' soon realized that Jean was already some months pregnant.

After another few days Mark was full of confidence, and in spite of considerable pain after exertion, considered that he was nearly ready to take a patrol along the railway.

On the return from a hunting trip, Mark was getting some clean clothes out of the laundry area when he overheard John and May talking.

"I am sure that Jean is with mtoto, she has not had the curse of the moon for a longtime and she is making the big titties."

"How stupid of me not to notice, been too busy, but now that you mention it, she has been very fussy with food and has avoided anything fatty. Just thought that she was trying to control her weight."

Mark was shocked, and went off for a long walk to asses the situation. If Jean was pregnant, and he was the father, was he 'honour bound' to marry her?, but he was hopelessly in love with Sasha, who was of mixed race, with some of the social stigma problems that society placed on people of mixed race married to whites. What were the options, marry Jean and still keep Sasha, but that was not fair on Sasha or Jean. Abandon Jean, because she took advantage of him while he was incapacitated, and marry Sasha. He must confront Jean and confirm that she is pregnant and then decide how to take the next step. That night as they lay in bed, Mark remarked about her enlarged breasts and her frequent visits to the bathroom. Jean became very tearful and finally admitted that she was pregnant.

Mark pretended to be shocked and asked if it was possible to become pregnant after just one very brief penetration.

"Oh yes it is with two young healthy people. I should not have given in to my desires and realised that you would 'perform' even when you were recovering from serious wounding."

"If you are pregnant, and think that I am the father, do you expect me to do the honourable thing and marry you?"

"That is very noble of you, do not rush into anything, we will just have to wait and see how things work out."

CHAPTER 9

THE RAILWAY

The patrol comprised Mark, Raymond, Tad and three of the warriors from the McIntyre irrigation shamba. They made good time to the rail head at Pietersburg but did not contact the BVC out post there and after buying some more supplies headed off for an area that was marked on the map where the track went through a cutting about 50 miles to the South. The three warriors went on ahead to read the signs and returned to report that there had been a battle between white men and that a 'garry' lay wounded round the next bend. Mark decided to skirt round the cutting and get a general view from the Eastern rim of the cutting before going down to the trouble spot marked on the map.

Sure enough there was a 'garry', or train, just as it had been abandoned when the crew had been ambushed and killed. An open flat car had been pushed in front of the locomotive and this had been blown right off the track by an explosive charge under the sleepers. The locomotive's front bogey had stopped just short of the damaged section of track thus leaving the locomotive tipped forward. All the goods wagons had been pillaged and there was evidence of many corpses having been devoured by the scavengers. Fighting must have been very intense by the number of empty cartridge cases on both sides.

As there was no sign of life, Mark posted the warriors as scouts and then went to asses the damage at close quarters with Tad.

Tad was a genius at fixing things and when faced with wreckage that was in the way he just blew it out of the way with a small charge of dynamite.

At the end of four days of back breaking work, the wreckage was cleared, the rails roughly repaired, even if they did have a terrible kink in them, and it was time to see if the train could be moved up the line to Pietersburg. Another day was spent cutting fire wood for the boiler and checking for any other damage to the train or the track.

Soon after first light on the next day the pressure gauge was slowly creeping up to the working pressure of 150 pounds per square inch. Tad was quite at home with boilers and railways after his experience in the mines so he assumed the role of engine driver as a matter of course.

Mark positioned the scouts at the rear of the train, so that they could not be surprised from behind, with himself and Raymond on the foot plate with Tad. The horses were put in one of the empty cattle trucks. There was much shrieking of tortured metal as the wheels were eased slowly over the damaged section of track before they could gain speed and go North to the next trouble spot marked on the map. The train took some four hours to travel the thirty or so miles to the next trouble spot marked on the map, but Mark asked Tad to stop about one mile short of the marked position, on a bend. The fire was reduced to a glow, and the party set off on horseback for a 'recce'.

With extreme caution, the party rode along the track towards the next marked position and looked out for any signs of sabotage or Boers. Mark found the exact location marked on the map for sabotaging trains. This was an open area with a rocky outcrop on one side, the perfect place to set off a charge and then shoot up the crew from cover among the rocks. The Boers had been very well trained in the art of sabotaging trains, probably by Henk van Brecht.

Tad found the charges under the track and carefully removed them, then put back just a small slice off the end of a stick of dynamite with the remark. "Mustn't let the bastards think that the charge 'as been took away."

A scout came running up very out of breath and told Mark that the Boers were camped only half a mile or so round the next bend by a stream and were lying round lazing in the sun. The horses were led quietly away while Tad buried the majority of the original charge in the most likely place that would be used by the Boers to shoot up the train from, and then the wires were relayed and hidden.

It took about half an hour to raise a head of steam before the train could move off again. The plan was for the train to move forward with as much noise as possible, to alert the Boers, while Mark and a scout slipped off the train and hurried through the bush towards the Boer camp to cut off their line of retreat. Tad accelerated and slowed to make the trucks 'take umbridge' and during a period of low speed Mark and the scout slipped off the train and ran off into the bush towards the Boer camp.

The sudden arrival of a train on a line that was supposed to be still blocked farther back, took the Boers completely by surprise. There was a panic to get to their strategic positions before the train came into sight round the corner. The plunger was quickly connected to the ends of the wires, positioned in the same place by Tad, and the Boers then took cover behind the rocks and got ready to shoot up the train crew. Smoke belched from the funnel as Tad threw green sticks on to the fire to ensure that they were seen. A very tall man with a blond beard crouched over the plunger waiting for the moment when the locomotive was over the charge.

But something was wrong. There was not the usual sacrificial flat car out in front. What did this mean? While considering this new turn of events, he missed the ideal moment when the locomotive was over the charge and thrust down the plunger as the first truck was over the charge. There was a loud bang and an impressive cloud of fine dust and smoke, but no damage to the train which was immediately braked to a halt by tad. Simultaneously there was a large explosion in the rocky outcrop where the Boer riflemen were hiding and several were killed or mortally wounded by flying rock fragments.

Mark and the scout were still hurrying through the bush when the explosions went off.

The remaining Boers fired a few shots at the locomotive and then panicked, thinking that they were under attack by a superior force, and fled to their camp to pick up a few essentials before mounting their horses and charging off in a Southerly direction. Mark and the scout were able to account for two more Boers before they were out of range. Even so, Mark sent the scout after them with the instruction to fire the odd shot to prevent them regrouping and coming back to attack again. In the meantime, Tad had moved the locomotive up the line to where the line crossed a creek and was supervising a bucket chain to refill the water tanks on the locomotive.

There was one more ambush site marked on Sasha's map a few miles up the track towards Pietersburg, so after loading up some tents and stores left behind by the Boers, they moved off to the North for the next three hours at a very slow pace constantly looking out for any signs of trouble and then stopped a few miles short of the next trouble spot marked on the map.

The horses were being off loaded and Tad was raking out the furnace on the engine when a burst of rifle fire came from behind an earth mound close to the track. Two of the horses were killed and one of the scouts was wounded before Mark could grab his rifle and get into position to return fire and stop the Boers from shooting unopposed. Was the map wrong or had the Boers found that this was a better position than that marked on the map or were they informed that a train had got through? Was there a charge under the track? Tad checked as best as he could but found nothing. From the elevated position on the tender, Mark could see the fold in the ground being used by the Boers and was able to shoot two of them before they could move to a safer place. After a while, a stalemate situation developed with each side behind adequate cover and able to place well aimed shots as soon as a target was presented by an enemy. Tad tied a slice off a stick of dynamite and a carefully measured length of fuse between two pieces of wood to make a crude form of hand grenade, and then suggested moving the train forward, closer to the Boer position, so that he could lob his home made grenade over the bank that was protecting the Boers and flush them out and give Mark some running targets as they fled for the trees.

The plan worked reasonably well, but the footplate became aligned with the Boer's line of fire which made it impossible for Tad to have a view of his target when he lobbed his grenade from behind the steel wall of the tender resulting in it landing some distance to the right of the of the group of riflemen. However, the flying rock fragments, the explosion and the threat of more grenades to follow made the Boers vacate their position and run for the trees. Mark was able to drop two more of them and keep the others running headlong through the bush to where they had left their horses.

A few minutes later, while they were attending to the wounded scouts arm, a volley of shots rang out in the direction of the fleeing Boers, then nothing, then another few shots, then total silence. Could the Boers have run into a British patrol? Or was there some other reason?

After another few minutes the suspense was too much, so Mark asked Tad to blow the whistle on the train to alert any possible British patrol of their presence. The signal was obviously understood because after another few minutes a BVC patrol emerged out of the bush with a group of prisoners, roped together, walking in front of them. The young Captain in charge of the BVC patrol was amazed to see a group of 'irregulars' in charge of the train this far North, because all previous attempts to get through had failed. After a brief discussion, one wagon was cleared out of debris and the Boer prisoners were tied up securely and locked inside. It was decided that the patrol would ride on the train and provide an escort to Pietersburg. While they were travelling, Mark questioned the Captain about the state of the war, the patrol activity and the latest news from Johannesburg.

Captain Clark found that Mark was the person whom Sasha had asked about back at SATCO and then became very cooperative. As they rolled into the outskirts of the city, Tad blew the whistle and people came out along the track and waved and shouted excitedly. News of their arrival must have preceded them, for the garrison commander came to the station to give them an official welcome and wanted to know how some 'irregulars' had salvaged the train and got through. He then offered every assistance and accommodation for all. It was wonderful to have a hot bath and a change of clothes after sleeping in a wagon or on the ground. At dinner that night Mark was questioned by the BVC officers about his adventure and wounding. The next day, the garrison Commander arranged for a special train to be made up in the shunting yards. It had two flat cars at each end with the engine and three wagons in the middle. The goods wagons were shored up with timber sleepers on the inside and slits were cut for use by riflemen. While the train was being got ready, Mark visited the Army doctor for a check up, to be given a clean bill of health but was told that he was doing too much, too soon. The wounded scout had his arm attended to by a doctor and it was then put in a sling.

It was arranged that a BVC escort patrol would go back to the Major's shamba with the three scouts and some extra stores while Mark, Raymond and Tad would join the train and it's escort and go back to Pretoria and Johannesburg. That night Mark wrote a long letter to Jean and the Major explaining that he was going back to SATCO for a quick visit and would come back on the next available train.

A crew of eight plate layers, some spare rails and tools were loaded onto the second flat car so that the damaged rails could be repaired en-route. Just before they set off there was a heated argument between the BVC officers about the prisoners. It was decided to move the plate layers to one of the goods wagons and tie the four Boer prisoners to some spare sleepers on the leading flat car so that any Boer saboteurs along the way would see who they would blow up first.

The journey South was uneventful till they got to the damaged section of track which Tad had marked with a piece of white cloth tied to a pole. Everyone was at full alert while the plate layers toiled away to replace the twisted rails.

It took six hours to complete the job and when the train moved forward again a meal was eaten on the move. The delay for the repairs and the constant look out for sabotage made a nerve wracking trip but there was one major advantage, in that they had Sasha's map with the danger spots marked so that a foot patrol could walk in front of the train looking for any signs of trouble in these sections. No signs of trouble were found in any of the Southern marked sections.

As it got dark a lantern was set up on the leading flat car close to the prisoners to make sure that they were clearly visible to any would be Saboteurs. It was in the early hours of the morning when they finally rolled into Pretoria. Several sentries posted along the station became alarmed and looked as though they were going to open fire on the train and it's crew. But the familiar sight of the BVC uniforms and much waving and shouting finally convinced them that it was not another Boer trick and they were escorted into the station master's office. The British officer in charge of transport finally appeared, still half asleep, having been summoned from a comfortable bed with his mistress in the station hotel across the street. There was obviously some professional rivalry between the BVC and the British forces.

"You bloody 'irregulars' think that you can go charging about on a military train in the middle of the night without any movement orders or signalling system. You could have run the boiler out of water and blown yourselves up and wrecked the engine. Not to mention the risk of running into another Boer booby trap." "Yes sir, but you see we have a very competent civilian engine driver and a Boer map showing where all the booby traps are to be placed, so we were able to slow down and walk along the trouble spots looking for any sabotage."

"You say that you have a Boer map, where did you get that from?"

"I understand it was copied from a large wall map used by a Boer Major van de Brecht when he planned the whole thing before the war broke out, he was an explosives expert I understand."

It took till late morning to clear the red tape and get going again and they finally rolled into Johannesburg late in the afternoon. Mark quickly collected his party and headed for SATCO.

Anne was up at the building site with George Bridgman, but Sasha was in the office finishing off for the day and counting the day's takings and looked up to see Mark and his party enter the main gate. She was tempted to rush out and embrace Mark, but decided to wait and went up to her room to change and do her hair.

Having given instructions for his men to be fed and given accommodation, Mark walked into the office and went up stairs with his rifle still slung on his shoulder. Sasha watched through a window and noticed that Mark walked with a slight limp and was a little stiff in his movements. Mark was cleaning his rifle when Sasha appeared in the doorway looking thinner and more mature than when he had last seen her, but even more desirable. They both rushed forward and met in a passionate embrace and a lingering kiss. The feel of her taut and shapely body was so exciting that desire just welled up and all the old feelings returned, they both knew exactly what they wanted at that moment.

Horses hooves clattered on the cobbles in the main entrance as Anne and George rode into the yard and handed their mounts over to the stable boys. Sasha returned to the store. Mark was surveying all the female clothes and belongings scattered round his room as Anne came into the room and embraced him. She then stood back and looked him over and said. "I suppose that I shouldn't hug you as it would hurt your wounds, anyway, how are you dear brother, other than looking thinner and much more suntanned?"

"Now that the bullet has been removed and I am all stitched up, I am practically as good as new, thanks to John Ashcroft and expert nursing by Jean and John's wife May."

At this point George Bridgman came into the room, shook hands and they exchanged condolences about the loss of Heather and Mark's capture and wounding. George then insisted that they all go out to dinner together and said that he would be back at eight to pick them up and hurried off to change. Brother and sister then sat down in Mark's sitting room and filled each other in on what had happened in their respective lives over the last few months.

It was 7. O'clock when Mark realized that he had to bath and change for dinner. While Mark was in the bath Anne and Sasha set up a camp bed for Anne in the living room. Putting on formal clothes was so strange after roughing it in the bush for so long that Mark felt as though his tie would strangle him. Over dinner, George told Mark that he and Anne were engaged to be married in about 12 month's time. In the meantime Anne had to go back to Oxford and cram for her finals exam. There was a ship leaving for Southampton in two days time and it was essential that she took up her booking if she was to have any time at all to prepare for the exams. George became very melancholy at the thought of Anne going so soon, but as Mark pointed out, he had the trip over, the wedding and the trip back as a honeymoon to look forward to in a year's time.

"You lucky son of a gun, you have got the pick of the litter."

Even though Mark was dog tired he sat up half the night going through Abdul's accounts and writing to his mother while Sasha kept him supplied with cups of coffee.

In spite of all the extra expenditure in recent months on the Commando Hill project, there was still a healthy credit at the bank, so Mark decided to send a large dividend to his account in England for his mother to draw on. Extra investment was badly needed on the property to compensate for the effects of the foot and mouth plague that had ravaged the farms in England, and on the Continent of Europe where the disease had come from. Foot and mouth was so easily spread by birds, travelling animals and humans and all cloven hoof animals are effected.

Mark said to Anne and Sasha at breakfast the following morning. "There is no question of me going back to England yet, I have to finish off doing my bit in getting the railways running again and I also have to get Jean safely out of the bush so that she can sort out her affairs in Johannesburg. I have written to Mother and given her a 'sitrep' and a dividend based on the excellent status of SATCO. which is thanks to Abdul, you Sasha, all the employees, as well as Gustav and of coarse George.

Oh yes, I must not forget Tad and his 'little bit of Wrecking' which paid for the thefts by the Boers about three times over. A very handy chap to have around when there is a bit of trouble that needs fixing.

I have complete faith in all the staff and all the men in the store and warehouses. There is plenty of demand for all our goods and services after the wartime shortages and we can only expect it to continue for some time to come. As for the building, we have George to keep an overall eye on things and we can engage an architectural supervisor to work for George, if he is agreeable, so that he is free to spend most of his time in his own business."

Anne said. "Yes that sounds fine, to have a pair of eyes and ears on site at all times so that George will hardly ever have to leave his office. How many houses do you want built?"

"I was thinking of doing it in stages, say houses for Abdul, Mackenzie and Tad with cottages for each of the most senior men in the warehouse to start with. But the new shops, blacksmith, wheelwright and fodder store must take priority to ensure that we get the immediate revenue available from the land on the other side of the road while the post war boom is still with us."

"When do you plan on going back to the Major's shamba?" Asked Sasha.

"I have to go to Army HQ in the morning to get clearance to travel on a train going North, but there is some flap on about some war correspondents having priority. Let's get the trains running and business back to normal before we get bogged down with the bumph and propaganda merchants, but you know how the Army staff like to play up for the newspapers. I am hoping to get away the day after tomorrow, may even have official movement orders next time.

Anne, you must hurry now to catch the train to Durban, safe trip, love to everyone, take care and write soon." Anne kissed Mark and Sasha and got into the waiting cab.

Mark was welcomed at BHQ as a hero and much to his surprise was given immediate authority to travel back to Pietersburg on a special train that was being made up with an official crew and an escort which included a Vickers Maxim machine gun capable of firing 550 rounds per minute.

On returning to SATCO, Mark called in Tad and Raymond to explain that they would need all their stores and equipment made ready and be down at the station by 0530 Hrs. in two days time.

Mark spent the rest of the day picking up medical supplies, books, implements, food and equipment for John Ashcroft. As Sasha moved around the quarters preparing the evening meal, Mark could not take his eyes off her, she was thinner, more mature looking, and had a more confident air about her which aroused Mark greatly.

"Thank you for all that you have done for SATCO and me while I was away, it was very comforting to know that you were safe here and looking after things for me. You are more beautiful than ever and your movements are poetry in motion."

"I love working at SATCO. And I have a good life now thanks to you and all the people here, but now you have missy

Jean and Raymond tells me that she is pregnant and wants you to marry her, and she is white."

'That is not important and does not stop me loving you and wanting us to be together all the time."

Sasha looked as though she was about to start crying, so Mark held her and said. "I do not want to marry Jean, but as you say, she has ideas that I should marry her. It is very difficult to believe that she got herself pregnant from the one time that she forced herself onto me when I was still very weak after the wounding. I love you Darling Sasha and I want to marry you as soon as I can find a way out of the problems. As I have said before, the colour of your skin only makes me love you more, you just have a healthy sun tan my Darling. I do not worry what other people think, and I think that many people are becoming more broad minded." Sasha went very quiet and served up the meal without speaking. They eat in silence, each wrestling with inner thoughts and desires. Clearing away the meal was also done in silence, then as Sasha was drying her hands Mark heard her sobbing and went over to comfort her. Sasha buried her face against Mark's shoulder as great wracking sobs shook her whole body and he held her tightly. Mark gently wiped her eyes and kissed her forehead and said. "Surely we can still make love and enjoy each other when I am here, for we both have had the most wonderful experience together and nothing can ever change that."

Sasha relaxed a little and Mark kissed her passionately and she started to respond by pressing her taut body against him and moaning gently.

After a long time, the embrace was released and they walked hand in hand over to Mark's bed. Sasha undid some buttons and let her clothes fall to the floor and started to very confidently undress Mark and pull him down onto her. It was so wonderful for both of them to feel him sliding inside again. Mark found that Sasha was more demanding and totally uninhibited in the way that she fondled and kissed him and then wanted a forceful penetration again and again and they climaxed together. Dawn broke and the first rays of sunlight came into the room and Mark gently kissed her shoulder as Sasha started to stir sleepily. She felt him hard against her and turned to face him so that she could guide him into her again.

Mark was in the yard at 7 0'clock when the employees started to arrive for the day and greeted each with a cheery. "Jambo, Habari" ("Hello, how are you") for he was feeling on top of the world.

Hassan was loading up two carts with tools and machinery parts for one of the mines and said that he had good orders for dynamite for all the mines and would have to make another guarded trip to Durban very soon for more supplies. Mark said. "Kwenda, pacy pacy sana" (Go, very quickly) This was because explosives sales were one of the most profitable parts of the business and it was vital that competitors were not allowed to muscle in on SATCO's key customers.

A young architect had been selected by George Bridgman to be vetted by Mark as a building supervisor, so Mark and Sasha spent the rest of the day going over the drawings and estimates with him, to asses his ability. Mike Copeland had gained some experience in Cape Town and quickly grasped the outline of what was required for Commando Hill, so Mark confirmed his appointment with the instruction that he was to submit progress reports, accounts and drawings each quarter through George.

Mjuba had the evening meal ready when Sasha and Mark returned, exhausted after a long day ensuring that Commando Hill would proceed as planned.

During the meal Sasha became worried about Mark going off into the Boer danger area again and gripped his arm with her strong fingers and looked into his eyes with tears welling up at the thought of loosing him. "You have Abdul and the staff here to look after you while I am away and Abdul treats you almost like a daughter now that he has come to know you better."

"Yes they all look after me very well, but I want us to be together all the time. You are so exciting and I want to come with you so that I can help you."

"Oh my Darling Sasha, how I wish that you could come, but it is much too dangerous and we have to 'rough it' a lot of the time. I am very honoured that you want to be with me, but not on this trip my Darling. You stay here where it is safe and give me the comfort of knowing that you are being well looked after and among friends. We always have the happy thought of my return to look forward to."

The early start came all too soon the next morning and Mark felt both sad at leaving Sasha and excited at the thought of seeing everyone at the shamba with the opportunity to help finishing off the Boer resistance. Tad rode on the foot plate with the regular engine driver, with the map, to point out the marked trouble spots while Mark rode in the first 'armoured' truck. There was no problem at any of the marked trouble spots, but when they were only about 20 miles South of Pietersburg, there was a tree across the line which caused Tad to reach across to the controls, past the regular driver, and jam on the brakes and bring the train to a screeching halt just a few feet from the obstruction. The sergeant manning the machine gun on the flat car, just in front of the locomotive, started to traverse his weapon in a menacing manner but there was nobody in sight. A party of men, armed with crow bars, was detailed to move the tree off the line while everyone else was at the ready. The tree was half off the track and the party of correspondents was milling around getting in every ones way when a volley of shots rang out and several men and two journalists fell. Mark spotted the muzzle flashes in the trees about 100 yards away, and with the aid of his field glasses, was able to pinpoint where the Boers were concealed and opened fire. "Tad, can you go to the machine gunner and show him where the Boers are and get him shooting in the right direction."

"Yer' I do that for ee."

The sergeant manning the machine gun was an expert marksman and now he was pointed in the right direction, placed well aimed, short bursts of three to five rounds each, into the Boer position which sent the few survivors running further back into the trees. The Vickers Maxim was at its best in this type of warfare and the fleeing men were cut down by the new cordite propelled bullets travelling at 2,440 feet per second as though by an invisible scythe.

A 'number two gunner' knelt beside the Maxim to feed in the ammunition belts and keep the cooling water topped up. Only the Maxim barrel and the top of the gunner's heads protruded above the top of the double wall of sand bags built around the rim of the flat car. A few extra bursts were sprayed along the edge of the trees in case there were any Boers lurking there who might return fire later.

All was quiet for a while so the crow bar party ventured out again and started to roll the tree off the rails and had nearly finished when another volley of rifle shots rang out and some of the crow bar party were hit. The machine gunner soon had the Boer position on the other side of the track in his sights and raked their position with deadly effect.

Mark said. "They must have been there all the time just waiting for the next appearance of the crow bar men, and held their fire till now, the bastards. None of them are still alive thanks to the Vickers Maxim. We would have been in big trouble without our expert gunner with that number of Boer riflemen hidden on two sides of us."

"Yer' be like a scythe, just cuts 'em down like cutting corn." Said Tad.

Mark climbed up to an elevated position on the tender and could see some more Boers half hidden in another fold in the ground and started picking them off one at a time.

The crow bar party was now reduced to three out of the original eight, so three troopers went round cautiously looking for any more enemy snipers or wounded but could not find any.

The Major sent out more men to finish removing the tree and to bring back their dead colleagues, and then went round himself with his revolver drawn to make sure that all was secure from any heroics from the wounded. The Boers had had tufts of local grass and bushes tucked into their hats and clothing which was why they had been so hard to distinguish from the scenery at 100 yards. Somehow, at the start of the skirmish, one of the journalists had got detached from the rest of the men while he was taking photographs, and got taken prisoner and dragged away and tied onto a horse by a very determined separate group of Boers from farther down the track. A search party found the tracks of the horses where they had caught the journalist and then ridden off at high speed. It was too late to try to follow them as they would be miles away by now. There were two badly wounded Boers who were carried in, searched for weapons, patched up and then questioned. The only coherent response was fear and amazement at the effectiveness of the Vickers Maxim machine gun. One of the prisoners had an uncle who fought in the Zulu wars and saw the Gatling gun in action and came back with stories of thousands of Zulu Impi being mown down by a few well trained British gunners and said that he now believed the amazing stories told by his uncle.

Obviously the Boers had only expected to encounter the usual rifle fire from a few inexperienced and inaccurate riflemen and then be able the take the train and loot its contents.

As the train moved forward again the gunner fired a few bursts into the tree line just in case there were any Boers still in hiding there. Mark was itching to have a chance to fire the Vickers gun and when the train stopped to take on water the sergeant said. "Would you like a shot sir?"

Mark's face lit up with delight as he said. "Yes please Sergeant."

A simple target was set up while the bucket chain was filling the tender with water from a small creek. Sergeant Howe gave a brief instruction and warned Mark that. "The aim climbs to the right. Start low left and let the gun follow through to high right for each burst. Best to fire only about five rounds to each burst to conserve ammo' and see where your shots strike before the next burst."

Tad volunteered to be Mark's number two and feed the belts into the breech. The first burst took Mark by surprise because of the light trigger pressure and the violent vibration of the gun's high speed reciprocating action. Holding the gun firmly, Mark fired several bursts into the log set up at 100 yards and the hits were clearly audible as the bullets smashed into the dry timber causing splinters to fly off the centre. A cheer went up from the men standing alongside the engine. Sergeant Howe said. "You are not only a crack shot with a rifle but you are a 'natural' with the Vickers too. I'm very glad that you are on our side sir."

Mark blushed and thanked the sergeant. Mark asked. "Do the Boers have any machine guns or field pieces?" "Yes, they had some very old Gatling guns that had been salvaged from the Zulu wars and some German field guns down South but they never got them this far North due to the poor transport and lack of ammunition. Most of the Boers are very good, bush trained, rifle shots. Some of our raw recruits straight out from the old country could not hit a barn if they were inside it. It is mostly very small groups of Boer riflemen working independently now. Just bloody bandits claiming to be soldiers and they rape, murder and pillage wherever they go. We hear that some of the captured Boers are becoming smart-arses and 'crying foul' and the stupid pen pushers in Pretoria actually believe the lying bastards. Take no prisoners, that is the safest way, particularly after what they have done to the women and young girls, if my wife had been raped and murdered, I'm sure that I would go 'blood mad' and shoot every Boer in sight and ask no questions, just as most of the few remaining farmers are doing. We have been ordered not to take prisoners, if possible.

There is the hell of a row over some silly old German Missionary who disobeyed Army orders and took off on his own with two mules pulling his cape cart through Boer territory and finished up with a 7mm Mauser bullet for his breakfast. The armchair officers actually believed some lying, Boer infiltrator, who was mistakenly allowed to join the BVC. He is now the star witness in the court martial of some unfortunate Australian officers, Morant, Handcock and Whitton, who had served with great distinction and nearly finished mopping up the last of these Boer bandits.(The Dutch infiltrator had been caught and admitted selling British uniforms to the Boers, but because of the political pressure, this was conveniently overlooked.)

The Australians are calling it a 'kangaroo court' 'cos the poor bastards are 'guilty' no matter what. The prosecution has bribed some dodgy witnesses to ensure that they win. We have been told.

Kitchener issued an order, through Colonel Hamilton, 'take no prisoners.' The false accusation of the Australian officers started because some men who had been disciplined by the

Australian officers put in a complaint and also that the German government was given false information, by the Boers, about their precious missionary being supposedly killed by the BVC. The prosecution has apparently bribed their witnesses to make a case against the Australians to ensure that they get a conviction.

The two faced old missionary was acting as an informant for the Boers and the Australians had seen him talking with the Boers and so made sure that he saw nothing of interest and just fed him bullshit stories that he could pass on to his Boer mates. Our theory is that one of these bullshit stories was relayed to the Boers and it backfired on the missionary, so the Boers followed him out of town and shot him with one of their 7 mm Mauser rifles and then put out the story that the Australian BVC. officers were involved in his murder. The stupid Pretoria mob didn't even bother to check on the type of bullet still in the missionary's guts. Bloody armchair amateurs. The BVC. were all issued with British 303's, so it could not have involved the BVC.

SNAFU! (Situation normal, all fucked up) The only good Boer is one who has had scrambled 303 for breakfast."

"Thank you for the background information, that was most interesting, it is terrible about the false accusations against the Australian officers, what can be done to put things right?"

"Sack the silly old duffers in Pretoria and put in men like you sir, who understand the type of terrorist war we have here. How can you fight 'by the rules' against lawless bandits?"

"You have a wonderful new weapon there that can change the history of the world."

"Yes sir, that is right, but let us hope that the enemy does not get them as well."

The rest of the journey Northwards was uneventful and it was late evening when the train pulled into Pietersburg. Mark and his party were asked to join the troops for an evening meal before booking into a small hotel for the night.

CHAPTER 10

MOPPING UP

First light saw Mark and his party saddling up and heading off for the Ashcroft shamba.

The war correspondents had had a very heavy drinking session the night before and were nowhere to be seen even though they had pestered Mark for a 'story' on his exploits as an 'irregular'. Mark was glad to be able to slip away quietly without any publicity before they got over their hangovers.

Ghillie's training came back to Mark. One day when trudging through the heather Ghillie had said. "Always keep a low profile, never let the enemy know anything about you, keep him guessing, and you can then often use bluff and get away with amazing successes. When the time is right, strike quickly before the buggers 'ken what is going on. Good planning and surprise will win the day even when ye are outnumbered four to one."

Ghillie was an excellent teacher and a strategist as well.

It was amazing how all of Ghillie's training was just falling into place. Without it, Mark would have died a dozen times already, and so would scores of other innocent people.

Six heavily laden pack horses slowed down Mark's progress as they trekked towards the river junction and the Ashcroft shamba. On the third day they found the tracks of about ten men on horseback. Raymond was sure that they were Boers because of the small hoof prints, rough shoes, and even some unshod horses. Proceeding with extreme caution, they came up on the Boer camp just after dark that night. Raymond went ahead for a closer look and returned after half an hour to report. "Bwana Mark, plenty Boers, saw six, probably ten there, horses look sick, no sentry, just the fire going, they have chicoola now."

Mark said. "We will draw back a little, have our meal without a fire, and attack them when they are in their deepest sleep in say about two to three hours time."

"I was thinking maybe you could use a few of 'me grenades to soften them up like" Said Tad.

"Yes that is an excellent idea Tad. Have you got what you need to make them up?"

"O yer, there be plenty of Dynamite and fuse to tickle 'em up with."

Cold bully beef, beans, stale bread and luke warm tea made up the pre-attack supper, but in the excitement of the moment, the drabness of the menu went unnoticed. The horses were left back at camp while the attackers moved forward cautiously through the bush. Glowing embers of the Boers' fire were spotted through some trees and the party halted to finalise the plan of attack. "How many grenades have you made up Tad?"

"There be four ready for lighting."

"That is fine, can you and Raymond take two each and lob them into the Boer camp and then draw back to the cover of the trees while I cover you from the left hand side. Give me about five minutes to get into position and then get your grenades in as fast as you can. We should be able to take them completely by surprise."

The first grenade landed between two bivouacs and the second landed beside the fire and exploded almost immediately showering the camp with burning embers. Very angry, half asleep Boers stumbled into view just as another grenade went off between two bivouacs. The last grenade added to the carnage and confusion. At least two Boers were very fast to respond and started shooting in the direction that Tad and Raymond had taken. Mark's chance came and he was able to shoot the remaining Boers lying beside their tents. Then all was quiet for a while.

A dirty, off white garment was waved from the farthest tent in the group and a youthful voice started to call for mercy. There was no way of telling how many men were still hidden in the tents while one boy of about sixteen stood waving his 'white flag'.

Finally Mark shouted. "Take down all your tents and put all your weapons where I can see them and show us how many men you are still hiding." The boy quickly unhooked the guy ropes and rolled the tents up to reveal two wounded and six dead men.

"Move the weapons to by the fire and stand back." The boy complied.

"Stay where you are with your hands up. One move and we will shoot you."

The boy looked terrified and kept looking down to where the wounded men lay. Mark kept them covered while Tad and Raymond moved slowly forward. A quick nervous glance by the boy made Mark check the wounded men again. He was just in time to see an apparently bandaged arm swinging in line with Raymond. A well placed shot blew away the man's arm and the revolver wrapped in strips of cloth, thus saving Raymond's life. Mark reloaded and moved in closer from the left flank. The man who had tried to shoot Raymond was dieing anyway because he had a stomach wound that was proving fatal and he died a few minutes later. The other wounded Boer was shot in the shoulder and would survive with medical treatment. He was the only survivor other than the boy who they found out later had been press ganged into service from one of the farms that the Boers had pillaged along the way.

"Bloody kid is so scared 'e 'as shit 'is breeches, poor little bugger stinks, we must throw 'im in the next river." Said Tad.

"I was not reckoning on attracting a prisoner and a boy. Any ideas?" Said Mark.

"Y'oum ally's shoot the buggers—kind' a defensive like." Said Tad.

"The thought did cross my mind, but we should not descend to their level of cruelty, however we do not want to reveal the position of the shamba to any Boers."

The scouts brought over the two prisoners and Mark gave them the option of taking a horse and some food into the bush to find their way home, or remaining tied hand and foot strapped on a pack horse. The wounded Boer opted to take his chances in the bush. The boy seemed to be overjoyed to be free of his tormenters and gladly agreed to go along with Mark's party. One horse was a bit lame on the hoof that was missing a shoe, so it was loaded up with a portion of food and water and after his wound had been patched up from the first aid kit he was sent on his way. One of the scouts was detailed to follow at a discreet distance for an hour or so to ensure that the Boer did not pull any tricks. Raymond seemed over confident that the departing Boer would not give any trouble. Finally he admitted to having laced the water bottle with the juice of a plant that acted like senna pods.

Tad said. "Both the buggers have the shits now. That stuff be mighty powerful and makes you able to shit through the eye of a needle at 100 yards. You'm be a crafty black devil Raymond."

Raymond just grinned. While the scout was away, the camp site was searched and all surplus equipment was burnt. Anything of value was salvaged and put onto the pack horses and all evidence of the attack was removed. Mark's party now had eight extra saddle horses and four extra pack horses to add to the entourage, so it took an age to get ready to move off. It was therefore decided that as they were only about one and a half days ride to the shamba, they would keep saddled up and keep moving to save the effort of 'out spanning and in spanning' for a major halt.

As they plodded along, Mark positioned himself alongside the boy and started to question him about his background and just how he had been 'press ganged' into joining the Boer patrol.

"Ya, I am only part Dutch, my mother was Belgian and my father was part Dutch and part English. When the Boers raided our farm my poor mother was raped again and again and I was made to watch, then they took all our food and horses. My father, he tried to stop them raping poor Mama, so they shot them both in the kitchen." Great floods of tears rolled down the boy's face and he sobbed uncontrollably for a while.

"How did you avoid being shot?"

"They had heard that I am reading many books and have learnt to be a vet for horses so they forced me to go vith them to look after their sick horses, but they have no medicine and no horse shoes so I do not make the horses much better and they are very angry. I am threatened for my life every day if a horse dies or goes lame."

"Do you want to go back and join the Boers?"

"No, I vill kill them for what they are doing to my mother and father, I have no home now, they have burnt our farm and taken all our horses and cattle. I vill work anywhere with animals and I want to make more learning with animals and become a vet."

"How would you like to go to school for a few hours a day in return for working with sick people and sick animals?"

"Dat would be velly fine for me. Where is such a place?"

"I may be able to arrange this for you, but if you have any reservations, tell me now so that we do not waste other people's time."

"I am not having any, how do you say, reservations, but tell me, where is such a place, in Joburg. Maybe?"

"Just behave yourself and help the askari and I will see what I can do for you, but I am not making any firm promises on behalf of other people."

When the enlarged 'patrol' approached the shamba, Raymond went on ahead to warn the Major's scouts of their arrival in case the number of horses caused alarm. John, May, Jean and the girls were waiting on the veranda as the long line of horses came up the gentle slope to the shamba.

Despite being dog tired Mark was excited to be with friends in a familiar place again. Jean ran forward, and in spite of her enlarged profile hugged Mark as he jumped down from the saddle. May and the girls then came and gave him a kiss. John beamed with pleasure and shook everyone's hand, pleased that they had all returned safely. Finally it was the boy's turn to be greeted.

"Who have we got here?"

"Je m'appel Marcel, Mousieur."

Mark stepped forward and explained Marcel's presence and then asked John if he could take on an assistant—cum student. "Happy to have him in the unit provided he plays by the rules, but if there is any trouble he will be frog marched out of camp by my askari. Do you understand Marcel?"

"Ja, I am understanding, I vill make no trouble, and thank you. Please may I wash for I am velly sore."

"And smelly." Added Tad.

Mark explained what the problem was and John laughed and suggested that the girls might like to take him to the bath room to wash him and then dress his sores in the first aid hut.

"Good experience for them" He said with a twinkle in his eye.

A very sheepish Marcel was led away by Sally and Sarah.

"Dinner is at sundown so I suggest that you have a bath and rest till dinner when we can hear your news over the meal." Said May.

The first aid hut had grown in the form of a ward or dormitory with six beds since Mark had last seen it so there was plenty of room for Tad, Raymond and Marcel. While Mark was in the bath, Jean brought him up to date with the news from the shamba.

"Sheeba has taken her cubs to a cave in the rocky area up on the other side of the river, but she still comes for food and a rest about twice a day. It was a marvellous sight when she took the cubs out of the cellar, they just followed her like playful kittens gambling along behind her, but Sheeba growled so we did not make any move towards them. I do wish she would bring the cubs up to the house one day. May is confident that Sheeba will bring them all trooping up to the house when she feels that that they are old enough to leave the cave. As you have seen, John got the men and women from the village to extend the first aid hut. They had the hut finished in two days then they put down a clay floor and stamped it in for two days before we got the beds made. We have plenty of capacity for any emergency now. There have been no more reports of Boer patrols in the area, but we have had reports of columns of smoke being seen a long way South, presumably from pillaged and burnt farms. Those poor people, they are so vulnerable to attack by the Boers.

"Tell me what you have been up to lately." Said Jean, as Mark lay in the bath.

Mark drowsily summarized events and it was only Jean's prompting that kept him awake.

"Come on get out of the bath and have a sleep or you will fall asleep at the dinner table."

Jean had to wake Mark in time for dinner and he was still half asleep as he struggled into his clothes.

May had excelled herself for the 'welcome home dinner', the spread on the table included, an assortment of roasted meat, liver, kidney, fish, and a whole assortment of new vegetables grown in the new wire mesh enclosures down by the river and fruit of many kinds. John produced a bottle of white wine and some brandy which had a very soporific effect on the weary travellers.

With much effort to keep alert, Mark summarized events as he knew them and then Tad gave a colourful account of the 'wrecking escapade' in Durban.

Marcel was fascinated at the thought of a fully grown lioness coming up to the house for an evening meal and could not wait to see her, but all the extra activity and strangers present caused Sheeba to stay away from the house, so Sally, Sarah and Marcel took her food down to the river bank and called for over an hour before Sheeba warily swam across and slowly came up to them. At first Sheeba would not go near Marcel, then slowly gained confidence and came up to him and smelled him all over and licked his hand with her rasping tongue. Marcel was dieing to stroke and cuddle her but had been told that strangers must stand perfectly still till they are fully accepted. Sheeba took her meat and swam back to the cubs without the usual show of affection for the girls.

Breakfast was the usual leisurely affair on the veranda and plans for the day were discussed. The extra supplies of books, food, tents, ammunition and equipment were very welcome, but the extra horses would pose a huge burden on the limited fodder supplies grown for the few horses and cattle that John kept for his private use. A foraging party would have to be established each day to herd the grazing horses along the river banks where there was plenty of feed. They now had spare horses to trade with any passing travellers (if there were any).

"From what you have told us, it sounds as though the Boers are about done for, particularly now that Kitchener is able to run regular train loads of men and supplies up to Pietersburg. You did a wonderful job in opening up the railway for him, I only hope he appreciates your efforts. However there are still the odd Boer patrols on the loose and it may take months to round them all up. What has happened to that Boer who used to work for your father, Henk van de Brecht.?"

"We have not heard of him for some time, but from what we have been able to prize out of prisoners, we believe that he is still on the loose with about 20 men from his original company of about 50 men and is probably hanging about the railway with his pack horses still loaded with dynamite waiting for a weakness to show and his chance to blow up another train. Captain Fisher of the BVC is out of hospital now and is in charge of counter terrorist activity along the railways, so Henk had better look out."

The wound area on Mark's chest had been giving him pain for some time and Jean recognized the signs of infection working it's way out of the wound and insisted that John be informed and it was arranged that Mark would be checked over the next morning as soon as the light was good enough. "You wouldn't take my advice and did far too much too soon, so now you have a suppurating wound where the lesions have partly torn and allowed infection to set in because of all the exertion you have been doing, we will have to operate and put in drain tubes again. The sooner the better, like right now, Jean please get May and we will start immediately."

John operated on Mark for over an hour with Jean and May assisting. Marcel was allowed to be an observer. The drain tubes were inserted into the wound so that the puss could be drawn out and the wound area kept flushed clean till it fully healed.

May was at his bedside when Mark came round. He felt terrible and wanted to vomit but could not. May gave him a small drink and bathed his sweating body to replace the moisture that he was loosing. It was nearly a month before Mark was free of the drain tubes and recovered from the effects of the operation.

CHAPTER 11

SHEEBA'S REVENGE

Sheeba had started to bring the cubs down to the river most evenings while she swam across for her food. The cubs would swim after their mother a short distance and then turn back and wait for their supper on a sand bank. Gradually one of the cubs came further each evening till he actually came ashore and shook himself dry and padded along after Sheeba to where Sally was holding his meat. The cub sniffed the meat then Sally, then put out a paw and patted Sally on the leg. Sally did not move. Sheeba came up and rubbed the length of her body against Sally who stroked her head and ran her hand along the length of Sheeba's back. The cub came up again and playfully patted Sally's leg and gave a mock snarl. Sheeba took the meat and put it on the ground and then stood between the cub and Sally while the cub used his milk teeth to tear off small strips of meat. It was another week before all three cubs came across for their food.

"Sarah, look at their dear little faces and their spotted jackets, I'm so glad that they have finally accepted us and come to feed each day."

The evening feeding ritual progressed slowly with the cubs gaining confidence but never showing the depth of affection that Sheeba had for the whole family. The cubs were tolerant of humans approved of by their mother but were wild lions in every other way.

During lunch the next day, one of the scouts ran up to the hut to say that a party of Boers was in the area and had murdered two of the young scouts by torture while trying to extract information about the shamba. Contact had now been lost with the Boers.

Extra senior scouts were taken from the fields and defence preparations were put into high alert.

Marcel and the girls were waiting for Sheeba and the cubs to come for their supper that evening, but they did not come. Suddenly there was a terrible commotion and a rifle shot rang out from the area of the cave, more sounds of snarling and crashing in the undergrowth. Mark was soon on the alert with his field glasses and rifle and quickly ran down to the river with Raymond and Tad, both of whom had had the foresight to bring their rifles. Having crossed the river, it became apparent from the tracks, in the dust that the Boers had been using the rocky high bank above the river, close to the cave, to spy on the shamba, when Sheeba had taken the matter in hand. It was some minutes before Mark's field glasses picked out Sheeba standing on a rock with her tail lashing from side to side. In front of her was the prostrate body of a man. Creeping closer, Mark was able to identify the prostrate body as that of Henk van de Brecht. He was not dead, but was rapidly bleeding to death from the huge gashes inflicted by Sheeba's claws on his arms and chest. His stomach was ripped open and there was a large cluster of dust covered entrails visible at his side. His rifle was close by but he was either too weak to use it or afraid that any movement would invoke another mauling from Sheeba. Two of the cubs stood at the entrance to the cave snarling and hissing, but there was no sign of the other cub.

There was no point in trying to intervene unless Henk tried to get hold of his rifle, so Mark handed the field glasses to Tad and Raymond and asked them to go down river to follow the Boers at a distance while he kept a 'bead' on Henk in case he made a grab for the rifle. Tad and Raymond crept away and headed downstream. Mark lay covering Henk for about half an hour, then he saw his body slowly go limp and slump face down in the dust, apparently dead from loss of blood and shock of the mauling. Sheeba came forward and hooked at the body with her claws extended. There was no response so she pawed at it again and turned it over. Still no response, so she pawed it more vigorously and stalked away to where the cubs were standing, licked them affectionately and went into the cave. On getting closer to the cave, Mark started to call Sheeba and she came out and greeted him cautiously. Then Mark saw blood spots on the ground leading to the cave and saw fresh blood on Sheeba's jaw, presumably from licking her wounded cub.

Mark hurried back to the shamba to get a lamp and help to distract Sheeba while he went into the cave to check the wounded cub. John decided that the only way to get into the cave was to drug Sheeba, so she was fed some inoculated meat and she slowly became drowsy and finally lay down totally relaxed with John standing by with a loaded syringe in case she came round too soon.

Mark and Marcel went into the cave while Sally and Sarah kept the other two cubs distracted with morsels of meat tied on lengths of string. Inside the cave, they found the brave little boy cub with a clean gunshot wound to his hind leg. The bone was broken and he had lost a lot of blood.

Marcel fetched the syringe and quarter of the dose was injected into the weak and protesting cub's good leg. He soon became drowsy and relaxed and Mark and Marcel were able to carry him out into the fading light. Four men from the shamba carried the cub back to the first aid hut so that John could set the bone and sew up the wound. The cub would have to be kept in captivity till the bone was fully knitted together again, probably about six weeks.

During the rescue of the wounded cub John had monitored Sheeba's recovery but Henk's body was forgotten, so when a burial party did finally arrive the hyenas had already started the grizley process of dismembering the body with their incredibly strong teeth and jaws. As Sheeba was still very groggy, John slowly led her back to the cave, he then got May and Marcel to help him to operate on the cub for the next hour or so and then made up a harness that fitted in a kind of hammock. When the cub came to he was suspended some three feet off the ground with his leg securely held in a plaster.

I t would be necessary for relays of people to play with the cub and feed him to ensure that his limbs stayed healthy while not being used. Mark was assembling a party of warriors to join in the hunt for the Boers when there was a very loud series of explosions some distance down river causing echoes off the rocks and sending flocks of shrieking birds into the air above the mopani trees along the river bank.

"I bet Tad had something to do with that, did he take any dynamite?"

"No, I do not think so, they just took their rifles and hurried off." Said May.

"Then that must have been Henk's supply of dynamite that he has been carting round on his pack horses while waiting for the opportunity to blow up more trains. I hope our chaps are alright.

I must hurry now to see if they need any help." Mark and his party went off down river for about half a mile and were rounding a bend when Tad, Raymond and the warriors came into view with four prisoners and their horses.

"What happened Tad?"

"W'em saw them dynamite boxes was off loaded while the 'orses was allowed to feed, so w'eem made a bit of a diversion with a blindfolded wart hog piglet wot 'ad a prickly leaf stuck up 'is arse to give me time to set a fuse for the boxes of dynamite.

Must 'av bin over 200 pounds, hell of a bang, blew 'em to smitherines, wot was close, and them others is deaf as posts and 'powder daft' with being too near. Wot do we do with these Dutchie bastards?"

"We do not want them hanging round here, so how about we give them a lame horse and some food and send them South with some scouts following." The prisoners did not look very happy at the thought of going South towards British lines, unarmed and being followed by some scouts to make sure that they did not try any tricks and kept moving in the right direction. The prisoners were not to know that the scouts would turn back after a few days.

Jean was pleased to see Mark return unharmed and tried to persuade him to stay for another week before going back to Joburg and SATCO, but Mark was keen to see Sasha and wanted to leave very soon.

Marcel took it upon himself to look after the wounded cub and a depth of understanding developed between them. Sally and Sarah also took it in turns to feed and exercise the cub.

There were a few very tense moments when Sheeba came in and tried to take the cub by pulling him out of the hammock. Finally after much coaxing she conceded defeat and became resigned to visits with lots of licking round the plaster encased leg. The two girl cubs were now coming across the river each evening and spending time with Sally, Sarah and Marcel.

Later that evening when all was quiet and everyone was gathered on the veranda, Mark said.

"Tad you never did tell us how you created a diversion with the ngulube, or wart hog piglet, they are fearsome creatures and as tough as old boots."

"W'al 'eem be the blacks wot got 'eem, them found an ardvark 'ole wot them pigs was living in and stomped back a bit. Them angry pigs shot out like, all fired up to get at anything, the blacks threw sticks for 'em to chase, then the piglet came out and quick as a flash Raymond had a shirt tied over 'is 'ead and a thorn branch up 'is arse. Did 'em go. Squeeling like all the she devils in hell was after 'im, the boar and sow then came to the rescue of their run amock piglet. The more th'em tried to 'elp the more the piglet ran towards the Boers who then attacked the pigs with sticks an all hell went up. That was when I was able to set a fuse. We was just creeping away when the crazed piglet came back towards the boxes with the boar, sow and the Boars all following. That was when she blew. Them bloody Boars won't want fire crackers for Christmas. They be powder daft from being so close, most go silly as a wheel, and 'arf daft and deaf they be. Just you wait till I tells me brothers about the piglet trick, th'em piss 'em selves laughing."

Tad had everyone rolling round laughing and Mark had to hold his chest to over come the pain from laughing so much.

Leaving the shamba was an emotional wrench for all concerned. It was considered that they might stay at the McIntyre shamba for a while to give the natives time to rebuild their huts on the irrigation and get some crops planted. If necessary, some warriors could follow Mark into Johannesburg and then take back any essentials to replace what the Boers had pillaged or destroyed.

John Ashcroft was glad to get rid of the extra horses as they had been a real burden on the limited fodder supplies. Marcel was undecided at first about going to Johannesburg, but finally decided to stay on for a while and attend John's classes and look after the cub. There were many fond farewells with promises to return whenever possible. The long convoy of pack horses and riders slowly wound its way down the hill and out of sight. John and May stood on the veranda with the girls and Marcel. The house suddenly seemed very empty and they felt alone once more.

The cub's leg was due to come out of plaster in another two weeks time so Marcel and the girls had their hands fully occupied gradually letting him do a little more each day, and there was still the problem of how Sheeba would react to her cub being held in captivity and then returned to rejoin his family.

Raymond and the senior warriors headed the convoy and kept up a brisk pace so that they could secure the water holes and set up camp while the slower pack horses and natives on foot came along at their own pace. Mark, Jean, Tsandra and the junior warriors brought up the rear with Tad scouting along the length of the column. It was with mixed feelings on the fourth day that Mark and Jean rode into the McIntyre barn and jumped down from their saddles. Nothing much had changed, a few more items of harness and equipment had been looted, the irrigation fields had been stripped of anything that was ripe enough to eat but fortunately the buildings had not been damaged any more. Returning to the place where her family had so recently been murdered proved to be too distressing for Jean so she begged Mark to leave after two days. Raymond volunteered to stay on for another week and help the natives re-establish their shamba before returning to Joburg. So on the third day a small party of warriors accompanied Mark,

Jean and Tad to Pietersburg to return to the farm with seeds and equipment, purchased by Mark, for the shamba and the McIntyre Property.

Sale of the surplus horses yielded more than enough to pay for the supplies to be sent back to the McIntyre Farm and the warriors set off leading just two pack horses and headed North. Jean, Mark and Tad walked back to the station to pick up the next train to Joburg.

An officious sergeant tried to make an issue out of Mark carrying a rifle on to the train, so Mark told him to fetch over the officer in charge. When the officer eventually arrived, Mark explained that it was largely the result of having that particular rifle and his marksmanship that the trains were now running at all.

Tad couldn't contain himself.

"See 'ere jist you get through your thick skull that the marksmanship of me' boss 'as shot more Boers than you've' 'ad 'hot dinners. We was the 'Irregulars' wot got the first train through to 'ere, Can't you show a little respek' and thanks fer wot we done?" After an embarrassing back down, the young captain apologized and gave a note to Mark to be taken to British GHQ suggesting that he be issued with a travel warrant permitting him to carry fire arms and ammunition on the trains at any time. The train was over an hour late leaving and then its progress was painfully slow so that the lookouts in the flatcar in front could have a chance of spotting any signs of sabotage.

It was after midnight when Mark's weary party eventually arrived at SATCO. The askari answered when Mark pulled the bell cord and then let them in through the main gate. Jean was amazed at the size and complexity of SATCO during a quick tour of the offices and stores area and then became more practical while she helped Sasha prepare a meal which was served in the general office for the hungry travellers. There was a letter for Tad advising that there had been a delay in selling the house because most of the mines in the area were closing down, but his wife and brothers, their wives and all their children were hoping to be on a ship in a few months time. Agnes Oakhill's letter contained the best news of all. The foot and mouth plague was over and the stock were out in the fields again enjoying their freedom and more calves were expected soon.

Jean was not sure how to take the letter from her Grandmother. The guilt for banishing the young couple all those years ago was very apparent now that three out of the family of four were dead at the hands of the Boers. There was a very strong plea for Jean to return to Scotland and be taken care of by her maternal grand parents.

The idea of social life in a city did not appeal to Jean at all. A short visit was all that was necessary, and then what?

She had been hoping that Mark would propose, but it was now confirmed that Mark was very much in love with Sasha which was demonstrated by their joyous reunion and resumption of living together again in the quarters while Jean had to sleep on a camp bed in the living room.

CHAPTER 12

JEAN

Mark had offered to buy the McIntyre farm and put in a working Manager on a profit share scheme. That sounded like a good idea, but who would want to live on an isolated farm in the African bush? Jean was glad to accept the offer at a very low valuation. There was also another letter from Agnes with more news, Anne had passed her exams and the home farm was steadily improving. The news from Scotland was not so good, Gillie's wife, Alice, was diagnosed as having TB. The doctors were recommending a change of climate as the only way of preventing the disease taking hold completely.

"How soon do you want to go back to Scotland?" Mark asked Jean at breakfast. "Oh, whenever there is a boat leaving Durban, but I will have to wait till the farm is settled, so I will have to get a job and save up for my ticket." "Don't worry about the ticket, I will arrange for SATCO to pay for your ticket and whatever you need for the journey, after all you have done for me. I can arrange for Gustav to book you a passage as soon as you are ready, I expect that you will want to do some shopping for clothes and all the personal things that you have lost before you go to the ship."

"We did not have much, we lived a pretty Spartan existence, but I would like to get some clothes to wear on the ship, these are pretty tatty and not quite the thing to wear for shipboard life. When do you plan to return to England?"

"I would like to get everything at SATCO running smoothly and feel comfortable about leaving it for, say, two years before returning to see that all is well and on the rails. There is also the work going on at Commando Hill that Anne started. George is very reliable and his young assistant is doing a good job, but I would like to at least see some of the houses finished. The shops are already finished and are in full swing and already trading very well, which is entirely due to George and Abdul pushing the project along and keeping pressure on the contractors. Perhaps you could visit my aunt and uncle in Scotland and exchange news with all at Glencairn and in particular, send me a report on the health of Gillie's wife, Alice. The poor dear has TB and I am so lucky to have had the benefit of their friendship and training before leaving England and would like to help any way I can. It would be a tragedy if Alice gets any worse. Another few months should give me enough time to do all that needs to be done here, unless there is a crisis back home. How about you go and buy some clothes this morning, then go to the site for the proposed new branch store and I will meet you there as soon as I am clear of the meeting with the bank manager and we can all go out for a slap up dinner with George and Anne."

"Yes, that sounds perfect. Now that I have spent a few days exploring the city for the proposed new branch store, I feel more confident and can find my way there without the need of a stable boy to navigate for me. I will see you there about two o'clock."

While the 'proposed branch store survey party', comprising Jean, Raymond and sometimes Abdul, had been off each day, Mark and Sasha had systematically gone through every part of SATCO and all the new ventures and were pleased with what they found. Sasha was obviously enjoying working together with Mark in the business and was also working long hours in the store.

CHAPTER 13

VENDETA

Mark was becoming worried about Jean's advanced pregnancy and the reaction of the grandparents to a single girl either pregnant or 'with child at foot'. However, the progress at SATCO. took his mind off the problem most of the time and he relaxed a little. The meeting at the bank took longer than expected because the title deed for the colonel's land had been mislaid and Mark was becoming worried about meeting Jean to check out the site for the proposed branch store, owned by an old Indian trader, on the other side of town. They had arranged to wear all their oldest bush clothing and ride just average hacks from the stable so as not to alert the trader to their real worth. Finally the title was found and the meeting was concluded and Mark could hurry to the Indian's store.

It was nearly three o'clock when Mark arrived and hurried round the corner onto the veranda expecting to find an impatient Jean, but there was only the old Indian sitting on a chair, made out of a cut away barrel, grinning through his rotten and stained teeth with his 'come in and buy look'. The Indian got up with surprising alacrity and tried to usher Mark into his rat infested shop. "Velly welcome please, kind sir, I haf' many good things inside, please." Mark rechecked the street number and location again and all seemed correct. He then approached the Indian again. "Have you seen a tall English girl waiting here please?"

"I am not seeing any Engleesh girls here today. I am having velly much pleasure for Engleesh to buy in my shop. Maybe you want to buy something for the Engleesh girl from my shop?"

Mark strode into the shop and looked around in the dimly lit interior. Foul smells of stale curry and excreta greeted him as he pushed through a curtained doorway at the rear which led into a living area, or if the smell was any indication, a dieing area. "Jean, Jean." He called, but there was no answer.

He then pushed through a wooden door, which was sagging on it's hinges, and into a yard at the rear of the shop. The yard led to a lane and still there was no sign of Jean or her horse and Mark was just returning to the shop when he noticed the hoof prints of a freshly shod riding horse in the dust. Mark was on his knees carefully checking the hoof prints when the Indian appeared in the doorway. "Engleesh girl not coming here please. I am not selling anything that was dropped here." Mark was sure that the hack had just been re-shod and that Jean had been in the yard. Farther up the yard the hoof prints were partly obliterated by the wheel tracks of a light cart that had stood in the yard and then moved off into the lane towards a busy street. The signs looked ominous. Mark grabbed the scrawny bundle of rags and shoved it into the back room.

"Those tracks tell me that you are lying through your rotten teeth and that my friend was here with her horse and that she was possibly taken away in a small cart."

Mark was so angry that he did not notice the Indian's hands move under his filthy clothes.

The shining curved blade of a razor sharp kukri flashed in a shaft of sunlight coming through a crack in the wall, just in time to allow Mark to draw back and avoid an amputated arm. Grabbing the nearest weapon, which happened to be a large wooden stirrer sticking out of a cooking pot, Mark started to parry the deadly blows made by the kukri. The Indian was shouting abuse and dancing around a packing case, which served as a table, while he hacked and slashed at Mark.

Mark was very aware of the limitations of a wooden stirrer versus a kukri and was looking round for a better weapon when the Indian tripped on his ragged clothes and Mark was able to dart forward and inflict a heavy blow on the man's shoulder.

Judging by the 'crack' he had probably broken the man's collar bone. The Indian's arm went limp and the kukri fell out of his hand and went spinning across the dirt floor by the stove.

Mark grabbed the kukri and held it to the Indian's throat. "I will tell you about the Engleesh girl but first I am needing velly many pounds kind sir." Mark drew the razor sharp blade across the scrawny neck and wildly bobbing Adam's apple.

"You are keeling me so I will not be telling you about the Engleesh girl."

"You tell me everything very fast or I will start cutting deeper into your throat, now start from the beginning."

The Indian's eyes strained to see the blood dripping from the blade and a wave of terror racked his body. "For just five pounds I am telling you velly fast."

Another incision was more effective than words.

"Very pukah sahib coming to my shop and telling me he must hide to watch a mem—sahib on a horse. He paid me just a few shillings and left his cart and driver in the yard. The mem-sahib coming and the driver used his pistol to make her come into the shop so he can make her tied up in the cart. The puckah sahib taking some of my sacks, may he be made destitute and may his sons and daughters be with the plague, to cover the mem-sahib and they go away velly fast. The driver was riding the mem-sahib's horse."

"Who was this puckah sahib, has he been here before?"

"I am not seeing this sahib before, just a few shillings, that is all he paid me for so much trouble.

"What did the sahib look like, was he English or Boer?"

"Young sahib Boer, and also driver, Boer who was riding the horse that way."

Scrawny fingers pointed in the direction of the lane and the busy street, thus corroborating the signs in the dust. At least that part of the story was the truth.

"How long ago did they go that way?"

"For just five pounds I will tell you everything."

Another slice into the Adam's apple and a promise to pay five pounds had the Indian pouring out his more embellished version of events, but there was still nothing new other than the fact that the sahib seemed to be very fussy about his appearance. A bell was ringing at the back of Mark's head. Some body had been described as a very natty dresser, but who was it? Suddenly it came to him. Abdul had been showing Mark a formal photograph of the SATCO staff taken a few years earlier and had commented on Peer's appearance in the photograph. Mark could remember the wavy blond hair, the boyish face and the very latest collar and coat style.

"Describe the man's hair, how old was he and did he have a collar and tie?"

"Oh my, sahib had the yellow hair with the waves, a collar and tie and a velly good coat, now I am needing another five pounds to make my arm good." Mark reluctantly gave the Indian another five pounds and said that he would be back later. "Sahib, the man was very young to have such a good coat and a new spring cart, they went away about one hour ago, now I must make my arm unbroken at the medicine man."

Mark rode straight to the British Army HQ and asked to see his acquaintance from the railway episode. After a long wait, he was ushered into Colonel Wilkinson's office and asked to sit down. "You say that your friend, Miss McIntyre, was abducted this afternoon, but isn't that a police matter?"

"No, I do not think so, because it appears that this is part of a vendetta by the Boers because of my involvement in intercepting plans by Henk van de Brecht and his followers to blow up the railway and then getting the first train through, followed by Henk's demise by courtesy of a friendly lioness. There is evidence that the abduction was carried out by van de Brecht's assistant, Peer. Do you know if these people still have an operational unit commanded by Peer Spellman, and hiding somewhere in the bush close to the city?"

The colonel sent for his intelligence officer who came in with a number of files under his arm and was given an outline of the situation.

"Got a file on van de Brecht sir, you say we can close the file when we add that he was mauled to death by a tame lioness. Should have more of them on our side, what? Now this Peer Spellman fellah, as you say, worked for van de Brecht as an explosives expert at SATCO, your company I believe?"

"Yes, that is correct."

"Now we have a gap in our file, but there is an unconfirmed report that as an explosives expert he was training young Boers in laying charges and the sabotage of trains when he lost one of his recruits in a nasty 'accident', he was very cut up about it. Our man says it was an engineered 'accident', because of a jealousy triangle, all 'homos' you know. The last unconfirmed report we have is that 'pretty boy' Peer has his own commando unit on a roving commission that operates both in the city and elsewhere to raid farms for food and horses. They appear to be able to go to ground in the city somewhere. That is all I have sir."

"Thank you major, can you fill in Mr. Oakhill with any more details that may be of assistance in finding Miss. McIntyre."

Mark followed major Scanlon into his own office, and during the next hour or so, became amazed at how well informed the major was on past and present Boer activity. Peer was definitely still at large and was still operating his own unit which was not fully defined or located. They seemed to target a number of vendetta type operations on civilians who had contributed to the downfall of the Boer army.

"Spellman and his gang seem to have assumed dual identity so that they can just melt back into the community at any time. We believe that Spellman was responsible for the murder of the retired colonel who had land opposite SATCO., George Bridgeman's wife and numerous other people in the city including the banker who cooperated with the army in trying to capture Spellman when he came in to draw money for supplies. There was a spy in the bank who tipped off Spellman and he never came to draw the large sum of cash that he had arranged to collect. We still have a watch on his account in case he comes back again.

Now, I will arrange for one of my undercover men to make contact with you at SATCO. and hopefully he will be able to help you to find your friend and Spellman as well."

Mark thanked major Scanlon and hurried back to SATCO.

Just a few hours of a more relaxed lifestyle had resulted in a disaster. The Boers were still very much in operation in a terrorist style that was much more difficult to deal with as you didn't know who was a friend and who was an enemy.

How did that bastard Spellman know that he was negotiating to buy a property on the other side of town and had arranged to meet Jean to check out the suitability of the location before putting in a bid through an agent. There must still be a spy in the bank or even at SATCO.?

The spy could be Maria's sister in law who worked in the Bank. I must ask the bank to check her out and advise major Scanlon if they find that she is a suspect.

It was after eight when Mark and Sasha had just finished dinner that major Scanlon's undercover agent called. Frank was older than Mark had expected and he was very unsure of Sasha being present at first but soon came to accept her as she joined in the discussion and provided a lot more local details.

Frank was about fifty but was still very fit and alert, a real professional in his field. Frank suggested that they could use Spellman's weakness for small boys to draw him into a trap, namely a sleezy bar at the other side of the city where deviants met pimps who procured small boys for a price. The following evening Frank and Mark were inside a delivery van parked opposite the 'Reef Bar', and with the aid of binoculars, scrutinized every patron entering and leaving the bar.

At the end of a week, relays of observers had not seen any signs of Spellman or his known associates. Mark was becoming more and more despondent and despite Frank following up many leads, still there was no sign of Spellman or Jean.

In her usual lateral thinking way, Sasha came up with the only lead that produced results. There was a village some miles North of the city where a wicked old Arab slave trader had set up business selling human flesh, including many half cast small boys, and the usual assortment of young girls.

Heavily disguised, Frank and Mark drove out to the village the following evening in a light spring cart.

It was necessary to make several discreet enquiries and pay several bribes in order to be accepted as bona-fide and get access to the sale. The Arab trader had his own thugs stationed all round the ancient grain store that was used as a sale ring. The sale was due to start at eight that evening so Frank and Mark arrived a few minutes early but the whole building was already packed with a mixed collection of buyers and spectators.

After a lot of showmanship and typical 'eastern picture talk' the Arab slave trader signaled for the first of the merchandize to be displayed. The half cast girl was probably only about eighteen and was terrified. At the height of his sales speel the Arab gave a nod to his assistant who tore off the only garment the girl was wearing and pulled her down onto a contraption that was a cross between a gym horse and a camel saddle, thus revealing her most intimate parts for all the crowd to see. The Arab's speel was reaching a crescendo as he assured the audience that she was a virgin and invited anyone placing a bid to step forward and check. "As Allah is my witness it is the truth."

The girl screamed when a bidder touched her most sensitive place, causing her bladder to discharge forcefully. Frank spoke Arabic, so was able to give Mark a running translation. More men stepped forward to where the poor girl was spread eagled on the 'horse' and verified the Arab's claim by pulling the lips of her vagina apart, the bidding quickened and she was very soon sold.

Having aroused the audience with a 'top shelf item', the Arab fielded a variety of girls of many mixed races for the next hour or so and then started with the small boys who were brought in stark naked. Some of the audience started to drift away leaving only about twenty men and a few women who moved forward under the powerful paraffin pressure lamps used to show off the merchandize.

Frank and Mark had to move forward but kept just out of the brightly lit area under the stage.

As the third boy of about eighteen was being spread eagled on the 'horse', two men stepped forward and started to fondle the boy's genitals.

"Frank, see that 'Arab' on the left, he has very effeminate white hands."

Frank could see the white hands as they fondled the now fully erect small penis. "Yes, I see what you mean, his lust has made him careless with his disguise. That could be our man."

"Or the dapper little man next to him could be Spellman, they are both phoney and in disguise and need following."

The Arab slaver became annoyed and said. "You do not buy the boy, so you no make play with him. Now how many pounds for a beautiful boy? Better than having just one woman, always make pleasure for you."

The boy was sold to a 'Madam' who was standing at the back, presumably for some sort of 'house of pleasure.'

"Frank keep your eyes on those two while I go and get the cart."

The next three boys were quickly sold to another 'Madam' and the sale was drawing to a close as Mark started to edge towards the door. As Mark returned with the cart, he saw Frank come outside and start following the two phoney 'Arabs'. When the spring cart drew alongside, Frank jumped in and Mark let the horse amble along at a discreet distance from where the 'Arabs' were walking towards their cart on the other side of the small village. Their cart was standing under a clump of trees with the horse tended by a small boy. Some form of payment was given to the boy and the 'Arabs' drove off slowly towards the city.

Mark waited in the shadows behind some ramshackle buildings till the other cart was just visible on the road in the pale moonlight and then followed along the road to Johannesburg. On the outskirts of the city Frank said.

"It will be too obvious following in another cart, so please drop me off and I will follow on foot while you can try to keep pace with them and follow in a parallel street one block to the East of this one. Anyway, I will see you back at SATCO. in the morning if we get totally separated."

It was necessary for Frank to jog trot for the first block to catch up with the two men in the cart. He then walked at a steady pace keeping to the shadows when possible. The shadows were interrupted by the occasional shaft of bright light coming from hissing Tilley pressure lamps in shops or houses. While passing close to the pools of light Frank adopted the old army method of maintaining your night vision, by firmly closing one eye in the brightly lit areas. The cart was now entering a fashionable residential area where many of the wealthy coloured merchants lived. Suddenly the cart turned into a narrow alleyway and went in through heavy iron studded doors, which appeared to be the rear entrance to a large mansion fronting on another street.

Mark was travelling slightly faster than the other cart and waited at each intersection to check that the other cart was still in sight one block away and then hurried to the next intersection to check again. This technique was successful for four intersections and then the other cart failed to appear.

How was Frank keeping up? Had he lost them? Had he been sighted and taken prisoner? Mark could not resist turning the corner, travelling the length of the intervening block and then turning back along the street where the other cart was last seen. There was nothing moving in the street, just a few large houses with light coming out of the odd window. Most of the houses were set back from the road and had a high wall in front with elaborate wrought iron gates. The service lanes were placed at the rear of each row of houses for access to the stables and for the night soil carts to do their pick ups. A sudden movement caught Mark's eye as a dusky figure separated it's self from the shadows and hurried over to jump into the cart.

"Did you see where they went?"

"Yes, the second service lane from that corner and the third house along. Can you drive slowly round the block so we can check out the front of the house for the record before returning to base.

The front of the house was the very opulent, as Frank put it, with huge wrought iron gates, and ornate wrought iron panels let into the wall at intervals, but thick shrubs prevented a close look at the house. Lights were burning in one room and the roof of a stable or out house was visible to one side and to the rear. It was now one o'clock in the morning, so Frank returned to SATCO with Mark and spent the night on a spare bed in the sitting room.

Frank was off to British HQ early the next morning to submit his report on finding Spellman's hide out and to try to get some action in rounding him up. But as Colonel Wilkinson pointed out, there was not much to be gained in capture of the leader, he wanted the whole commando unit eliminated at one time, if this was possible.

A messenger brought a note for Mark from Frank explaining that the best he could do was to get authority to put a 24 hour watch on the house. The owner of the house was found to be a well known priest who was considered an eccentric and belonged to the local catholic Church and disappeared for months at a time 'doing missionary work among the natives.'

A perfect cover for Spellman's Jeckel and Hyde lifestyle.

Jean rounded the corner and there was the shabby shop front of 'Mahindar Singe—General Merchants' with vacant land at one side and to the rear. It was hot and airless and Jean was glad to jump down and stand in the shadow of a building diagonally opposite and wait for Mark.

Her advancing Pregnancy was now becoming a burden and she hoped that Mark would not be held up at the bank. Now that she had failed to seduce Mark, her life seemed to be in a mess and her mind was busy planning on how to handle the grandparents on the return to Scotland. What would her grandmother and grandfather be like, would she want to stay in Scotland, would there still be all that ill feeling that had driven her parents away?

All these thoughts were churning round in Jean's mind and she did not take particular notice of a heavily built man in a bush shirt and a felt hat come out of the shop and amble across the road. "Do not do anything stupid, I am having a pistol in your back. Now move slowly to where that Indian is sitting outside the shop."

"No I will not, who are you, anyway? Now go away at once."

Jean was furious and had no intention of complying with the man's demands.

Rough hands grabbed Jean's arm and forced it up her back till she was sobbing with the pain and she feared for her unborn child if there was any more violence. As they crossed the road, Jean saw that the man had a pistol in a brown paper bag. The Indian leaped to his feet as they approached and disappeared into his evil smelling shop.

Inside the shop, Jean was also grabbed by another man who forced her into a back room where she was put on a packing case and securely tied up. The Indian tied a large knot in the centre of a strip of cloth and this was forced into her mouth as a gag and the ends were tied behind her head. A coarse weave sack was pulled over her head and shoulders and another sack was pulled over her legs, a cord was tied round her neck and the other end was tied to her ankles so that if she tried to straighten her body she was strangled. The second man fetched a small cart and started giving orders for her to be loaded into the cart.

More empty sacks were then thrown over her. The man who appeared to be in charge then jumped into the cart and drove out of the yard, along a gravel lane and onto a paved street. Sweat was rolling off Jean's face and body and she felt as though she would asphyxiate in the heat.

Will power made Jean try to concentrate on the direction taken by the cart, but after several turns it appeared that they were weaving in and out of back streets. The smell of Asian cooking wafted into the sack, but the location was completely strange. Suddenly the cart stopped, there was a signal tapped onto a wooden door, the creaking of hinges and they moved forward again into an area smelling of stabled horses.

A few commands were given and Jean was manhandled up some wooden steps and into an upper room of some sort. As the sacks were removed, a crude blindfold was put over Jean's eyes. She was then tied into a chair and the gag was removed. Her mouth was so dry that it was some minutes before she could even croak out a request for water. A small child was sent for the water which was brought in a battered enamel mug and held to her mouth. The cool water revived Jean a little and she realized that she could see under the blindfold. The half naked child was a coffee coloured boy with big blue eyes. The men and the boy then left. After what seemed like an eternity, the boy returned with a bowl of mealy corn porridge which he proceeded to feed into Jean's mouth with a battered spoon.

Between mouthfuls, Jean started to talk to the boy in Swahili. His name was Hassan and he had been sold along with his Kikuyu mother at a slave auction by his Arab father. Since he had been taken from his mother and brought here he was being used as a sex slave by the white priests and was very unhappy.

Approaching footsteps made Jean caution the boy to silence. The booted feet came into the room and stood in front of Jean. A sack of heavy metal items was dumped on the floor and to Jean's absolute horror the man proceeded to put steel slave manacles and chains on her wrists. The ring at the other end of the chain was then secured to a ring in the wall with a sturdy padlock. A bucket was put in reach of the chain and the boy was roughly told to remove the blindfold and cords, collect the plate and spoon and the two departed down the steps. Now that the blindfold had been removed, Jean could see that she was in a loft over some stables with horses moving about underneath. Everything was very solid and well built. There were rows of bunks just visible along a wall near the back of the room and a long table and benches were in another corner. A stack of chaff bags was placed close to the top of the steps, presumably ready to be moved across the room when necessary to conceal the occupants. While all was quiet, Jean was glad of the opportunity to use the bucket and exercise her cramped limbs. The manacles bit into her soft skin, but by holding the weight of the chains it was less painful to move around. Hassan brought food and water twice a day but the man was never far away so it was only possible to exchange a few words at a time with him.

Hassan reckoned he could climb out of the yard below, crawl along the top of the wall, and onto a tree in the front garden, but he did not know where to go because he had never lived in Johannesburg.

By the end of a week, Jean had been able to convince Hassan that if he could get out of the front garden he only had to ask for directions to 'SATCO' and he would be safe and looked after but must tell all he knew about the house, stables and her imprisonment to Abdul Suliman and Sasha.

There was no moon at present so it was now or never. Hassan was becoming weak, from constant abuse by the priests, but this further convinced him to try for freedom. Scaling the stable yard wall at midnight was harder than he expected and his fingers were raw and bleeding when he reached the top. He lay on the top of the wall for a few minutes to get his breath and then ran along and jumped into the overhanging branches of a big ornamental tree in the front garden. Only the thin ends of the branch were close enough and they snapped under his weight. Hassan lost his grip and fell down through the lower branches which partly broke his fall to the ground. Terrible pain shot up his arm as he slowly got to his feet.

His arm was bent the wrong way. Something must be broken, but he must get out pacey pacey sana (Quickly—very.)

Designers of the wrought iron panels in the front wall had not considered how a desperate small boy could fold his body to fit into the pattern of an ornate scroll and squeeze through.

Hassan was not able to use his damaged arm and fell heavily onto the footpath causing him to cry out with pain. Freedom at last gave Hassan the energy to pick himself up and run as fast as he could for about quarter of a mile. Sobbing with pain and exhaustion, Hassan hid in some shadows near an old warehouse. Fear of white men and their stinking cities crowded into Hassan's mind as he lay in a state of terror till dawn started to break. Workmen were starting to shuffle along the street. Two men approached and they were speaking in his tongue.

"I see you my father, help me."

The two men took little notice of another beggar child till one man noticed the boy's dislocated arm and fresh blood on his clothes.

"You are hurt, how did it happen?"

"I fell when running away from the devil priests. Please help me find good people at a place called SATCO."

"We do not know a place called SATCO but our boss is a good man and can make your arm straight."

Somewhat reluctantly, Hassan followed the two men to the tannery where they worked. The boss was at the gate checking the men in for work and he told Hassan to wait out side his office till all the men had arrived. He then walked quickly along the stinking pits of tanning solution and frames of stretched hides. Hassan was still terrified when the boss man returned.

"Couja harpa mtoto."

Hassan followed him into the office. "What you bin doing boy?"

"I fell when running away from them dog devil white priests, Bwana."

"I knows your body from when I was a butchering, sit here an I make your arm straight."

The strong African foreman gripped Hassan's wrist and pressed against his shoulder and with a twisting motion which clicked the dislocated shoulder back into place. Tears rolled down Hassan's face and through his blurred vision he could see that his arm was now back where it should be, but it still hurt even when put in a sling. Taking a rough sandwich from his lunch bag and giving it to Hassan the foreman said.

"Where are you going boy?"

"I must find a place called SATCO where there are good people who will help me. They speak our tongue and will understand me."

"I know SATCO, we get tools from there. I will send one of my boys to show you the way."

Sasha was making up an order to send to Gustav when a stable boy came in with two frightened looking small boys. Having got the gist of what had happened, Sasha gave the older boy a tip and sent him back to his boss and then started questioning the younger boy, who still had his arm in a sling.

"Yes, white girl in slave chains send me to SATCO to find you and to get help because you speak our tongue and will give me a reward."

"Can you find where the white girl is?"

"Maybe, very big houses, big walls, iron flowers in the walls where I was climbing out, dog devil priests living there. Near tannery where the boss man made my arm straight." Sasha knew the tannery where the messenger boy came from, so that gave the general direction.

Mark and Frank had found where they thought Spellman was hiding and that was not far away so it was all starting to fall into place, piece by piece. Mark went with Frank to British HQ. to have another attempt to get the army to raid the Spellman house and rescue Jean, but Colonel Wilkinson was adamant that he wanted to catch the whole unit at once.

It was so frustrating trying to get any action from the army and Mark felt guilty because of Jean's pregnancy and the need to do the honourable thing and rescue her as soon as possible.

He returned to SATCO feeling depressed and angry. Hassan had nowhere to go so Abdul arranged for him to become a trainee stable boy for the time being.

Jean had got to know the sounds of the establishment during the week. Soon after dawn each day the horses were fed and watered, the stables were cleaned out, and sometimes horses were put into a cart or carriage during the morning, various delivery carts went along a rough track nearby, but always she could hear the heavy doors into the yard being closed and barred after anything went in or out.

In the early hours of each morning she was awakened by the stinking night soil cart with its clanking buckets and the drivers shouting abuse at the poor horses.

Hassan's escape was noticed at dawn the next morning when he was not there to help feed the horses. Shouts and the banging of doors could be heard for about an hour while the search was in progress. At first they were convinced that the boy was hiding somewhere in a building and searched behind every sack of fodder or pile of hay, but later concluded that Jean had arranged his escape. The burley Boer questioned Jean and accused her of organizing the escape.

"How can I help a boy to escape when you have me chained up in here where I cannot even see what it is like outside. Where am I, Who are You, Why have you taken me prisoner?"

"Quiet girl, I ask the questions round here. You will pay for helping Oakhills and the boy. The boss has some 'pleasure' arranged for you when the men come back tomorrow."

The next night Jean was awakened by the night soil cart as usual but amongst the clanking of buckets, she could hear the footsteps of many men and muffled voices. She estimated ten or twelve men came up into the loft and started to stack their rifles against the wall behind a freshly built screen of chaff bags. The smell of hot food wafted into the loft and Jean could hear the men serving out the food and sitting down at the table, eating noisily and demanding beer. More food and some beer was brought from across the yard by a native girl under the supervision of the burley Boer, who appeared to be in charge. "No noise, or I will personally cut your tongues out, now sleep and be ready for the next night soil cart."

The men were exhausted and were soon snoring and Jean could hear the bunks creaking as they turned in their sleep behind the screen of chaff bags. The only sound now was creaking bunks and snoring. The men slept for most of the next day, only moving when food was brought in from the house.

Just before the night soil cart was due, the Burley Boer came into the loft and roughly woke up the men and got them ready to move. By listening very carefully, Jean could just distinguish the sounds of two night soil carts pull up outside the doors into the lane. On a command, the men filed quietly down the steps across the yard and into a phantom night soil cart. Then with much clanking of buckets, the two carts moved off with the usual shouts at the horses. At least Jean now knew how the Boers got in and out of the city when they had a raid in the city area. Jean had heard that the council had a depot some miles out of the city where the night soil carts were emptied and then stored during the daytime. A sense of purpose now gripped Jean, she must let Mark and the police know how the Boers get in and out of the city at almost any time. The new boy who replaced Hassan was younger and was in a permanent state of terror and did not notice that Jean kept a fork after one of her frugal meals. The next day was spent scratching a message at the base of the heavy wooden wall at the extremity of the reach of her chains.

CAPTURED BY BOERS AT INDIANS STORE—COMMANDOS TRAVEL IN AND OUT OF CITY IN NIGHT SOIL CART—ABOUT TWELVE MEN SLEPT HERE AFTER A RAID LAST NIGHT—JEAN.

The night that Hassan had escaped there was no commotion till the morning when the horses were fed, so it appeared that he had got away alright, but had he been able to get to SATCO and get help. The next 48 hours were going to indicate his success or otherwise. At the time when the night soil cart was due the next night, the burley Boer came and roughly blindfolded Jean, tied her up and removed the slave manacles. As before, the blindfold gave her some vision in the lamplight down at floor level.

When the carts arrived with all the usual clanking of buckets, Jean was carried down the steps, shoved into the cart and seated on a bench. A few minutes later two men got in and sat opposite her, the doors closed and the cart moved off Now that the manacles and chains had been removed Jean felt that she had some chance of escape, but how? The two men opposite started making lewd suggestions about her pregnancy and how she was going to 'loose her virginity' again when she was allowed to give pleasure to all the men in the commando unit.

Light was now coming through the crack round the door and she could see two pairs of shiny black boots and their owners were well spoken and appeared to have some authority. Jean became sick with fear at first, but then the fear made her more determined to escape. After about half an hour of fairly brisk travel Jean became aware of the ultimate stench of sewage as they approached what probably was the council depot. Dawn was not far away and more light was filtering into the cart now. The two pairs of shiny black boots were clearly visible and the men were well dressed in black suits, up to the waist anyway. The cart must have now entered a building of some sort because it was darker and there were the sounds and smells of stabled horses. Both black boots got out, some orders were given, and Jean was bundled out and up into a loft and left tied up. It was not very long before she was taken down into a stable and tied onto a horse. Her horse was then tied to another horse ridden by the burly Boer and they joined a group of riders and headed off. It was now starting to get lighter and it was wonderful to be out in the open away from that terrible smell coming from the long trenches where the sewerage was tipped and then buried.

Jean felt at home in the saddle and was attuned to every chance of escape. They were heading North East or North East by East according to Jean's reckoning from the sun. There was no sign of the black boots, so they had presumably left the depot earlier.

Mark returned to SATCO. in a state of excitement after a long session with Colonel Wilkinson at BHQ. It had been finally decided to make a dawn raid on the Spellman house because there had been another raid in the city. Forty carefully trained men were to move in at 0500 hours and assault the house from all sides. Mark was to be allowed to be an observer from a safe distance and hopefully be able to rescue Jean when the troops had the building secure. As there was a lot of political tension, the attack was to be 'on the QT.' with no shots fired, if possible, and no disturbance in the area. The horse drawn troop carriers were to drop off the men about quarter of a mile away and the men were then to move towards the target on foot, in small groups to take up position ready to attack at 0500 hours.

On the stroke of five 0'clock, Mark saw the men start scaling the walls and dropping down into the front garden and forming up in front of the house. Two men moved up to the door and there was then the splintering of wood and the front door burst open. Men poured into the house and started a room by room search.

After some ten minutes the officer in charge came out and told mark. "The birds have flown, the house is secure so you can go in now." The front gate had now also been forced so Mark was able to just walk into the house. A group of wide eyed, half dressed native servants was in the hall. "What have they told you?" Mark asked the officer in charge.

"Only that they were kept here by blackmail and paid a pittance by two 'priests' who came and went at various times and that the 'priests' were very partial to small boys."

"The boy that escaped said that Jean was kept in chains in a loft over a stable, so I must go and see if there are any clues."

"Sergeant, please go with Mr. Oakhill to the stable."

"Yes Sir." Mark followed the sergeant across the yard to the stable and up wooden steps into the loft. There were steel rings, chains and slave manacles against one wall. Mark knelt down to examine the chains with the aid of a lantern, and finally saw the scratched message on the wall. Mark asked the sergeant to bring over the officer in charge to let him see the message first hand. A quick council of war was then held in the front hall and it was decided to move the troops to the council depot as quickly as possible and capture the Boers before they moved again.

Mark's frustration mounted when they found that the Boers had left the depot about an hour ago. They found the night soil cart with a simulated body and the cramped space inside for about twelve men. They also found that some of the convicts who worked on the sewerage farm were able to give a lot of detail on how the Boers operated. The council overseers at the depot said that they knew nothing and appeared to be 'manipulated' Boer sympathizers, but this could not be proved.

By this time Frank and a team of his 'I' Corps men had arrived and were starting to question everyone and make copious notes. The military machine seemed to be quite pleased with it's self now that two nests of Boers had been flushed out of the city. The fact that none had been shot or caught did not seem to worry them too much provided that they were out of the city area.

There was no way that Mark could get the Colonel to send a patrol off immediately to round up the Boers and hopefully find Jean.

"This type of operation must be carefully planned and it will be two or three days before we can put together enough information to send out a patrol." Was all he could get out of the colonel.

Mark's frustration was at breaking point. He realized that the only way to give chase was to return to SATCO and form his own Patrol with SATCO. personnel. He made out that he must return to SATCO for a meeting and hurried back to his office.

Raymond, Tad, Hassan and Mark equipped themselves for bush travel and armed themselves with rifles and revolvers. He had time to give Sasha a hug and a kiss before setting off across the wasteland at the rear of the depot where the Boers were thought to have gone bush.

Slowly crossing the area at the rear of the depot enabled Raymond to pick up the tracks left by the Boers. The patrol then followed the tracks in a North East direction. The Boers had about a five hour start on Mark's patrol, so they must hurry if there was to be any chance of finding Jean alive.

Jean's body ached in every muscle after the long day tied to the horse and having to ride in a cramped position while the Boers headed North East in a confident manner. Even though the sun had set and it was quite dark, they kept on for another two or three hours. At what Jean reckoned was about eleven o'clock, they went into single file and entered a heavily wooded area with numerous rocky outcrops. They were now climbing steadily. Suddenly the track ended in a clearing with a camp fire and tents. The horses were tethered in the clearing to graze and Jean was led away to a tent on it's own and chained to a nearby tree. The Boers cooked a meal and eventually food and water were brought over for Jean.

There was absolutely no chance of escape, so Jean decided to let exhaustion take over and slept soundly till first light the following morning. The aches and pains that had built up the previous day were mostly gone and she felt ready for an escape attempt, but that infernal chain securely padlocked to her ankle only left one option. Cut off her foot, but there was not even a bully beef tin, with a jagged edge that could be used to sever her foot. As the day wore on, the Boers started to emerge from their tents and were busy with camp chores till mid day. The horses were taken to a small pool below the camp and allowed to drink and the Boers were shouting lewd suggestions in her direction which made her sense that the earlier suggestions of 'pleasure' were not an idle threat. The fact that she was eight months pregnant did not seem to worry them at all.

Two horsemen rode confidently into camp and were greeted with some deference by the men. There was something familiar about the smaller man and when he took his hat off Jean recognized the curly blond hair of Spellman from the staff photograph at SATCO. The two new arrivals were the two black booted men who had travelled in the night soil cart and had presumably changed their clothes and taken another route to the camp. After some discussion with the men, the older of the two black boots gave some instruction and the men let out a series of excited shouts and came running over to Jean's tent. The chains were hastily removed and she was dragged to a rough table under a tree. The men started yelling at her to remove her clothes and when she refused they tore her clothes off and she was held down on the table stark naked with her very prominent abdomen feeling as though it would burst. Some of the men started to fondle her and arouse themselves.

"Who is first, looks like she is a virgin, ha, ha, we have waited a long time for this, we will teach that bloody Oakhills a lesson for what he has done."

Spellman singled out a youth of about 18 and said "Let him be first, I think he is a virgin also." There were loud laughs as the nervous youth tried to arouse himself without success.

"He is no bloody good, let me be first, I am ready." A tall man of about 30 stepped forward amidst a lot of shouting and jeering.

"He will open her flower, he is as big as a horse."

Jean could not see all that was happening, but she felt the forceful penetration and was sickened with the pain and the humility.

Spellman exposed himself and tried to get Jean to give him oral stimulation. As soon as the opportunity arose, she bit his member so hard that blood spurted from the end.

"You bitch, you will pay for that, just you wait." He retreated and bound up his member in a dirty looking handkerchief and was still crying with the pain.

After the first man, Jean was in a state of shock and felt sick and just prayed that it would soon be over. When the sixth, or was it the seventh, man was on her, a volley of shots rang out and the man on her gave a groan and fell to the ground. The men holding her were either dead or wounded leaving her to struggle off the table and collapse on to the ground.

She hid under the table in the first of a series of contractions and cried out with the pain. Jean realized that a rescue party had arrived, probably headed by Mark, so there now was a chance of survival, if only the contractions would stop. The contractions became more severe as the gun battle raged for the next hour or so then with a feeling of being split in two, the water broke and she gave birth.

The baby was 'black.'

So the result of the 'fun sessions' with the head boy in the tool shed at the farm were confirmed and her attempt to pin the pregnancy onto Mark, by forcing herself onto him, had failed.

What now, God knows how Mark will react to the sight of a 'black baby'. How can I have been so stupid and let my lust control my actions?

The gun battle slowed down and fewer shots were being fired now. There were dead and dying Boers all round the table.

Spellman broke cover. He was shot in the stomach and his left hand was pressing on the wound with blood and entrails oozing through his fingers. He produced a revolver and started shooting wildly at Jean at point blank range. The first shot killed the baby and the second shot hit Jean in the upper chest. Spellman then collapsed and his death was imminent. Breathing was becoming difficult for Jean and she started to cough up blood. Each wracking cough seemed to be more painful than the last. Pain and loss of blood then took over and she just lay under the table and could feel the blood flowing out of the wound. A few Boers had run off to a rocky area and were still firing the odd shot till there was a loud explosion and then silence. Tad had used one of his home made grenades.

Mark broke cover and ran to Jean's side and started to check her wound. Then he spotted the 'black' baby. It was shot through the head and was very dead. Now he knew that he had been duped into thinking he was the father, but that could wait. Raymond appeared and said that all the Boers were accounted for, bar three who had been close to their horses and had been able to escape. Tad and Hassan were checking the corpses to be sure that there was not a repeat of Spellman's dying act. A couple of revolver shots rang out, so the area was secure, for now.

The other 'priest' was among the dead.

Raymond helped Mark to carry Jean to the nearest tent where they tried to make her comfortable. The coughing started again, but it was very feeble now. It was just a matter of time. The end came a few minutes later while Mark held her head and tried to comfort her.

Mark found himself in a state of shock mostly caused by the colour of the baby, he was angry, relieved and saddened all at the same time. Raymond and Tad wrapped Jean and her baby in canvas cut from one of the tents. Tad then blew on the cooking fire till it was burning brightly and started to cook a meal. Mark was too much in shock to eat and just sat with his head in his hands by the fire. They had a terrible night with only snatches of sleep because Mark insisted that they took it in turns to keep watch in case the surviving Boers came back with some of their friends in the night.

At first light, the Boer camp was systematically burnt and then the sad little party headed back to SATCO.

Sasha was getting ready to go out for her English and elocution class. She had made friends with a semi-retired governess who had come out from England with a wealthy family and then married a local man. The couple was very short of money so were glad of any opportunity to hold classes for anyone wanting to learn English. As Sasha went down the stairs, she heard the clatter of horses' hooves on the cobbles in the main entrance. Raymond opened the door into the office and then returned with a corpse wrapped in canvas and laid it on the table. For a moment she thought it was Mark. A terrible fear struck her, then she saw Mark standing by his horse still in a state of shock and not speaking. Sasha then saw that there was a small corpse as well. Mark turned to face Sasha and she went forward and held both his hands and looked into his tear stained face. Mark then put his head on Sasha's shoulder and told her the outline of what had happened. Sasha was appalled to think that Jean had tricked Mark into thinking it was his child and 'played on his honour' to find a father, when all the time she must have known that the father was a 'black' man. Mark gave Sasha a quick kiss and a hug, then Sasha said. "There is a cable marked URGENT from your brother Hugh upstairs

Mark hurried to his room and read the cable, his mother had been crushed by the wheel of a carriage when a motor car had back fired and the horses had bolted.

Agnes was on the danger list at the Chester infirmary. Sasha realized that Mark would have to go back to England as soon as possible.

"Sasha, please go and see that the men have a meal and get some rest, they are very tired and hungry. We must send a message to BHQ to let them know what has happened and advise them that there are still three Boers on the loose A message was quickly written and sent with a stable boy to BHQ.

Mark and Sasha were just sitting down to their evening meal when Frank arrived and wanted all the details from Mark. After listening carefully and making notes, Frank said.

"It is very good that you were able to follow their tracks and find their hideout. I am deeply sorry that you were not in time to save Miss McIntyre. Do not feel guilty for they would have killed her anyway, as they have with all the others. What are your plans now?"

"My plans are confused, because on top of all this, I have just learned that my mother was seriously injured in an accident and is on the danger list in hospital, so I must finish off here as soon as possible and then catch the next ship available.

George Bridgeman and Abdul arranged the funeral for Jean and the baby. Mark went through the motions in a state of shock and disbelief. The following day Mark developed a tremendous burst of energy and drove everyone at SATCO and the building site for twelve hours a day. Sasha did her best to comfort Mark and help him after the strain of the last few weeks. Late on the following Friday evening Frank rode into the SATCO. yard and asked to see Mark who was in his office with George and the company lawyer finalizing the details of the new construction company.

Sasha asked Frank to wait in a spare office till the meeting was finished.

"Mark, I have some good news for you, we have rounded up the last of the three Boers from Spellman's unit. One was shot, another fatally wounded and the third is in prison. After intensive questioning, the prisoner finally broke down and gave us a complete picture of how they operated. His story confirmed what we already suspected, but he also revealed a number of collaborators who are still helping the Boers, and they have all been rounded up. The list of brutal rapes, murders, pillaging, blowing up trains and vendetta attacks against loyal citizens, like your self, would fill a book. We have now completed nearly all the files on known enemy units

"That was very good work, Frank, I will always be in your debt for helping me in my hour of need. They shook hands and Mark asked Frank up to his sitting room for a quick drink to celebrate their success.

Frank then gave Mark a formal invitation to join the British officers for dinner in their mess that evening. It was well after midnight when Mark got back to SATCO, but Sasha was still up and insisted on making coffee for Mark before they went to bed. Just to have Sasha there to consult with and discuss all his plans was so very good. They used to lie in bed and discuss the day's events each night before making love and going to sleep. Gustav had arranged a passage on a ship in ten days time so Mark had to work even longer hours to finish off everything in time. On the day of Mark's departure, Sasha asked if they could say good by in the privacy of the sitting room before the formal farewell for all the staff arranged by Abdul. When they were in the sitting room Sasha said. "I love you darling Mark, and I will miss you terribly and will wait for your return. Please don't be away too long."

"I love you very much darling Sasha and now that we no longer have the threat of Jean's baby, I can ask you to marry me with a clear conscience. Will you marry me darling Sasha?" "Yes, oh yes, mon cheri, just as soon as you can return, we had better go down now for the formal farewells."

All the staff lined up in the main entrance and shook Mark's hand before he jumped into a spring cart and was driven to the station. A strong bond had developed between Mark and most of the staff which made it an emotional occasion. They all wished him a safe voyage and a speedy return to SATCO.

Gustav, Anna and the girls made Mark very welcome for the overnight stay before the ship sailed the next morning.

The girls had grown and were now becoming more mature. "Please can we come to stay with you in England when we are older." they pleaded.

"Don't be so forward girls." Said Anna.

"You are all very welcome, I would be delighted to see you anytime."

After the girls had gone to bed, Gustav gave Mark a few of the details of how the 'compensation' raid had been carried out.

Mark said. "Probably better that I don't know too much, but the cunning of the operation has never ceased to amaze me, the Cornishman just can't help following his ancestors."

Mark and Gustav sat up talking business till after midnight and Anna kept up the supply of coffee and brandy. The ship was due to sail with the tide at 0930 so they had an early breakfast and went on board early so that Gustav could formally introduce Mark to the captain and discuss future shipments of goods. Gustav explained that he spent time with the captains of the ships whenever possible to ensure that he got the best shipping rates available. The ship was a mixed cargo and passenger vessel and had sailed round southern Africa and was returning through de Lesseps' Suez Canal.

"You will be amazed to see the desert on both sides of the ship and the lakes at the Northern end, but you have seen it before, ja?"

The whole family were welcomed on board and shown to the captain's cabin. "This is Mr. Mark Oakhill who I do a lot of business with and you will please give him the special looking after. He has done much good work in beating the Boers."

"I am very pleased to meet you and you will have the freedom of my ship and I wish you a very comfortable voyage."

"Thank you Captain." After coffee in the captain's cabin there were fond farewells as Gustav's family went ashore.

Mark had been allocated a cabin on 'A' deck and everything looked set for a comfortable voyage. The purser was an old hand at match making and organized that there was a good supply of unattached females on the same table as Mark, but he found most of them of little interest.

The fond memory of Sasha was still uppermost in his mind.

Storms blew up as they entered the Mediterranean and most of the passengers retreated to their cabins suffering from 'la mal de mare', but Mark liked to stand on a lee deck and watch the big, green waves rushing towards the ship and crashing against the bows, straining every rivet in the hull.

Early one afternoon Mark was on the lee deck taking the air when a slightly built young woman came lurching out of the accommodation and made for the rail but she slipped and fell, hitting her head against the gunwale. She lay motionless in the scuppers. Mark ran forward and lifted her into a sitting position but there was no response so he picked her up and carried her through the nearest doorway. Once inside he put her down in a walkway in a sitting position leaning against a bulkhead. She slowly came round but was still partly concussed and dizzy. "How do you feel now?"

"I have a headache and still feel a bit dizzy, can you get me a brandy please."

"Yes of course, assuming the bar is open." She sipped the brandy and became more oriented and then asked. "Where am I? What is your name? I am Cynthia Marshall."

"You fell and hit your head on the gunwale, and you are now in a walkway on 'A' deck. My name is Mark Oakhill."

"Thank you so much Mr. Oakhill, please can you see me to my cabin, I still feel dizzy."

"Certainly, what is your cabin number?"

"B 27, but I can't remember how you get there."

"Don't worry, we can soon find it, the numbers are in the same pattern on each deck."

Mark had to half carry Cynthia to her cabin and unlock the door while still holding her. When inside, he put her on the bed and said. "Your clothes are wet through from when you fell into the scuppers, you had better change into something dry. Have you got a change of clothes some where?"

"Yes, I think so, over there, can you get a skirt and jumper and some underwear.

When he had found all the necessary clothes he turned and saw Cynthia standing by the bed in just her white satin underwear. She took the clothes from Mark and quite unashamedly removed her wet underwear and dried herself with a towel and slowly got dressed.

"Can I ask the purpose of your trip?"

"Yes, I am returning from a 'dig' near Cairo where I was helping my father catalogue some ancient ruins. What do you do?"

"I have a company in Johannesburg, and have been to sort out a few problems and then got mixed up in the war with the Boers. I am now on my way back to Cheshire to see my mother who is seriously ill in hospital."

"Let's send for some drinks, it is awfully naughty of me to entertain you in my cabin, you see I am to be married as soon as I get back to London."

Mark rang for the steward and ordered champagne. Two or three glasses of champagne later, Cynthia had lost all her inhibitions, if she ever had any, and was suggesting that Mark should spend the night with her. They had dinner sent to the cabin and helped it down with more champagne. Cynthia was to marry a young merchant banker, selected by her mother, the description of whom sounded awfully boring, they then planned to raise lots of children in the West end of London.

When the steward had cleared away the dinner trays, Cynthia became demanding and started to undress Mark with feverish haste and a new found lust in her eyes. The sight of the great scars and stitch marks on Mark's chest and leg made Cynthia gasp in horror.

"I have never seen wounds like that, and you say that you were only a civilian caught up in the Boer war, do they hurt?"

"Only if I exert my self too much, but generally I am as good as new thanks to a retired army doctor and his wife."

As Mark had suspected, Cynthia was still a virgin and the art of making love was a new experience for her, so he was able to get her fully aroused, before sliding into her. Cynthia responded with a lot of moans and convulsing and then she became uncontrollable and frenzied with excitement and came almost immediately.

Mark was invited to her cabin each evening till they arrived at Tilbury docks in London where they parted the best of friends and went on their separate ways.

CHAPTER 14

ENGLAND

Mark sent a cable to Hugh at Moregroves in Chester to let him know the arrival time of his train and then resigned himself to sleeping for most of the eight hour journey. Hugh, Margaret and Ted Moregrove met the train and they went immediately to the hospital.

Agnes was awake and partly sedated but still in a lot of pain. Pins had been put into the fractured pelvis and her ribs were just out of plaster. It was very distressing to see her looking so thin and gaunt and still in pain but she was well on the way to recovery and was very happy to see Mark and let him take over the responsibility of the property.

"I am so pleased to see you back and in one piece, even if it has needed a few stitches, I have tried to keep an eye on things from here and Hugh and Anne have been keeping me informed.

You must look after yourself and not do too much, just give the orders for the men to do what is necessary."

When they got back to the Moregrove's house, the Oakhill pony trap was waiting to take Mark home.

Anne was waiting when Mark arrived home and was keen to get the letter that Mark had brought from George. Mark then insisted that Phillips took him on a complete tour of the property, visiting every tenanted farm, and all of the home farm.

It was dark by the time that they finally drove into the stable yard. Over dinner Mark said to Anne. "It is very good to see the place looking so good, mother and both you and Hugh are to be congratulated on how well you have managed the estate while I was away. In spite of the foot and mouth plague, everything is blooming and the stock look healthy. The farm improvements and the overall picture is excellent."

"Thank you for your comments, we have all pulled together, especially after Mum's accident. That was terrible, we thought at one stage that we were going to loose her, she was in such a mess. She was just standing outside a shop when a motor car backfired and a carriage mounted the footpath and the wheel must have gone over her when the horses bolted.

Now we must think about your total recovery and get you up to Scotland away from the worry of the estate and get some shooting with Ghillie. You need a really good, complete break as soon as we have Mother home and settled but I hope that you will still be here for our wedding."

"Yes I would like that. I hear that Alice has TB. and is failing fast so I must go and see them all at Glencairn as soon as possible."

Some two weeks later Mark's mother was settled at home and he was in Scotland greeting Aunt Mary and uncle James.

Mark spent some time with Aunt Mary and Uncle James, then went to see Ghillie and asked. "How is Alice?"

"She is fading fast, especially in this cold, damp weather all the teme, but her spirit is as strong as ever. You must come over and see her. She's been fretting over your wounding and that operation you had in the bush, you're a very lucky mon, to be sure."

Mark followed Ghillie over to his cottage and was greeted by Sam in the garden. Alice came to the door and embraced Mark with sobs of joy at seeing him again and completely forgetting her weakened condition for the moment. Mark had great difficulty in not showing his shock at seeing Alice so thin and emaciated and with the usual high facial colour associated with TB.

Mark and Ghilllie then went over to the bothy for a serious talk and a 'wee dram.'

"Ghillie, what can we do for Alice, have you had her to a specialist?"

"Och ay, she's been to the city twice but all they say is that it is the Scottish weather that is killing her, she is much worse in winter."

"How would you like to live in a warm, dry climate on your own farm in Africa?" "If it would save her life, I would go anywhere, but how could that be possible?"

"Well, there is a farm that belonged to the late McIntyre family, before they were all murdered by the Boers, and I bought it from Jean, the last of the family to survive. She was the girl who was responsible for the early part of my recovery and escape.

I will have to do something with it soon. You can have it rent free for a few years if it will help Alice to recover. It is a bit run down after being pillaged by the Boers, but there is a very good native community who work the irrigation and they were devoted to Jean's family. Then there is John and May Ashcroft who live in there own shamba not far away. Talk it over with Alice and tell me what you would like to do. Oh yes, do not worry about any of the travel arrangements, we can let SATCO pick up the tab."

"You are too kind Mark, but I will have to clear the way with the estate here as well as talk Alice round, what can I say, it is a grand offer, are you sure now?"

"Your care in training me saved my life many times over and was a major contributor in saving the lives of many others as well, this is the least I can do."

"Can ye come over tomorrow evening so we can talk over the details, assuming that I can get Alice to agree."

"Yes that would be fine. I have to return to Cheshire in about two weeks, so we will need to arrange the travel plans quickly if you decide to go."

As Anne's wedding was a few weeks away, Mark now had time to relax a little and spent the next day driving round the home farm in a pony and trap with uncle James.

Ghillie must have done a very good job in presenting the idea of moving to a better climate, because Alice was already becoming enthusiastic and was looking better now that she had something positive to look forward to. Mark and Ghillie spent most of the next two weeks shooting on the moors and this gave Mark a chance to give Ghillie all the details of his exploits in Africa as they walked along. Mark left Glencairn some ten days before Ghillie and Alice were due to leave to catch the ship. He had cabled Sasha and Gustav asking them to meet Ghillie and Alice and make all the local arrangements to ensure that they had a comfortable transfer to the farm. Refreshed after his holiday in Scotland, Mark had renewed energy and drove all the men on the Oakhill property as hard as he had become used to doing in Africa.

He missed Sasha terribly and wrote a long letter to her every few days. It seemed an age before Sasha's letters started to come in reply to Mark's epistles.

All seemed to be going smoothly for a while on the property and home farm. The market garden project was going very well and John Bellis had two loads of fruit and vegetables going into Chester market almost every week. Just selling whole milk from the home farm gave a very poor return on the investment, so Mark decided that there had to be a better way. Some thing Gustav had said about the remote farms in Sweden being cut off by the snow in winter so they made cheese and then sold it after the thaw. This gave Mark the idea of making cheese on the home farm. A cheese making room was built and all the necessary vats and a boiler were installed as soon as possible, because the distinctive red coloured Cheshire cheese was becoming increasingly popular.

As the supply of milk from the home farm was limited, Mark bought milk from selected farms in the area to keep up cheese production at full capacity all the year round.

Now that Mark's mother was home she continued to recover rapidly and was soon moving round on crutches and taking an interest in everything again.

The last letter from Sasha said that Mr. Foster at the bank had been replaced by a much younger man and that he was an arrogant Frenchman. He keeps going through the books on the pretext of 'monitoring the mortgage risk'. He is very inquisitive and keeps coming and working in your office. He seems to want to know more about us than Mr. Foster and has tried to take 'liberties' with me, cochon.

That part of Sasha's letter really troubled Mark and he sent a cable immediately asking for more details. There was no reply from Sasha on the next ship. There were only the reports from Abdul and George.

Mark cabled Abdul and George asking for a full report on the new bank manager and his sudden interest in SATCO. and why there were no letters from Sasha. In due course replies arrived and it was George who gave the most information.

SATCO.

Dear Mark,

My report on the SATCO construction company is attached and as you will see we are getting a steady flow of work for the consulting, surveying and building and are starting to show a good return, I really appreciate the opportunity that you have given me to expand the business.

Now about the new bank Manager, a Frenchman called Claude Lambrier. He was sent out by their head office and is very close to some of the big mining companies. I think he has been told to check out SATCO for someone else who wants to take us over. On questioning Abdul and McKenzie, I find that Lambrier has tried to take liberties with Sasha on at least two occasions. Then late on a Saturday afternoon he appeared and wanted more information and got Sasha on her own in your office and tried to get her to take him up to your quarters.

Sasha explained that this area is for your exclusive use. Later, when the staff had gone home he tried to rape her. Sasha must have put up one hell of a fight because Lambrier was carted off to hospital with his family jewels damaged beyond repair, his testicles were nearly torn from his body. Within a week there was a solicitors letter demanding Sasha's instant dismissal and horrendous damages from SATCO. Doing a bit of snooping round, I find that Lambrier has been in court several times for his passionate advances and we sent a lawyer to give him a few counter claims while he was still in hospital. Unfortunately we have had 'to be seen to be taking action in dismissing Sasha' and have secretly sent her to stay with Ghillie to help at the McIntyre farm, where she is still being paid of course. As you will know, Ghillie and Alice are now established and Alice's health has already improved with the better climate.

I will take time off and go to see them soon. Ghillie tells me that Sasha is like a daughter to them and practically runs the place.

Kindest regards.

George.

Mark was furious with the trouble caused by Lambrier and cabled back instructing George and Abdul to change banks immediately and change the accounting system at SATCO so that any information obtained would be out of date. He then wrote a long letter to Sasha and another to Ghillie and Alice at the McIntyre farm. Some six weeks later there was a letter from Sasha giving Mark all the details of the encounter with Lambrier and the solicitors insistence that she was to be sacked.

There had been several discussions with Abdul, Sasha and George and it was decided that 'to be seen to be dismissing Sasha and loosing contact with her' was the only way to stop the solicitors demands, whereas in fact she was sent in secret to the McIntyre farm, escorted by Raymond for the journey. A letter from Ghillie arrived in the same mail.

McIntyre Farm.

Dear Mark,

Alice and I are eternally grateful for what you have done for us. We are very comfortable and in a way it seems familiar after being in the North West of India with your uncle.

Sasha is like the daughter that we never had. She is my 'Major Domo' with the natives and runs the farm with hardly a word from me.

Alice was very weak when we first arrived and it has been largely due to Sasha's care that she got over the worst times. Alice is now nearly fully recovered and we plan on a trip to see John Ashcroft again in two weeks time. I may even get in a bit of big game shooting while Alice is being looked after by John and May.

Sasha will travel with us in case Alice gets sick on the way. We now have a new boss boy who is reliable and very good with the stock and the irrigation crops. Time has just flown with the move and all the new things to be done here. Alice sends her regards and hopes that you will visit us soon.

Yours respectfully.

Ghillie and Alice.

Mark was delighted with the news about Alice's recovery and sent off a reply to Ghillie and another to Sasha as soon as possible. There was only a week before George would arrive in readiness for the wedding. Agnes was delighted to have mark home for Anne's wedding and was nearly fully recovered.

Anne was busy finalizing her arrangements and making numerous trips into Chester. The estate was now running smoothly and the market garden and the cheese making were 'putting the icing on the cake.'

Mark was missing Sasha and was becoming impatient to be back in Africa with her, but he had to wait for the wedding.

Mark said to his mother. "I can't very well travel on the same ship as the honeymooners but I will go on the very next available ship."

"Yes I see what you mean dear, how long do you expect to be away this time?"

"I am planning on about six months, there is still a lot to be done and this Lambrier affair is still not fully resolved. The new branch store will need a bit of a push and the new construction company is growing rapidly, thanks to George.

Then I must visit Ghillie and Alice as well as John and May. At least the railway is running now so that will save two weeks of travelling on horseback. The distances are so great and the communications are still very poor. I do hope that Sasha is alright after her encounter with Lambrier. She seems to have settled into life with Ghillie and Alice very well and virtually runs the farm according to Ghillie."

"You think a lot of Sasha, and from what I hear, she is a very capable girl and very good looking too, as shown in the photographs of the SATCO staff that you brought back."

"Yes Mother, she is a very wonderful girl and we have been in love for a long time."

The festivities for the wedding of George and Anne were now starting as guests began to arrive and stay in the area. Both sides of the family were pleased with the 'match' and the couple looked radiant and happy on the day.

Agnes was very tearful when it was time for the couple to leave and promised to visit in a year or two. "perhaps when the first child is due". "O Mother, that would be wonderful, we would love to see you anytime."

"You had better go now before I ball my eyes out, take care of each other."

And off they went to catch the train. The house seemed very empty and quiet when everyone had left and just Mark and Agnes sat down to a light supper later that evening.

Mark used the time waiting for the next ship to attended all the local agricultural shows and machinery agents to check on the new equipment available that might be of interest for SATCO or the home farm. He bought two pedigree bulls and some machines driven by the new combustion engines and picked up some machinery agencies for SATCO. in South Africa.

As soon as his passage was booked, Mark had cabled Sasha and Abdul giving details of his arrival and some of his plans for when he arrived.

Each day on the ship the purser ran a sweepstake on how many miles the ship had travelled in the 24 hours since the last 'noon fix'. Mark usually had a small bet and was always much too optimistic with his estimate in his desire to speed up the voyage and see Sasha again.

"Old Navy saying sir, once you pass through the Suez Canal, it is never long before you are through again," was the comment made by the steward as he cleaned Mark's cabin. "Certainly true in my case, it is only a few months since I last went through the canal."

Mark's thoughts went back to the encounter with Cynthia. Probably has a child by now, wonder if it is mine.

Mark's mind was too full of plans for SATCO and Sasha to take much interest in his fellow passengers. He worked in his cabin with plans for his time back in Africa while the ship crossed the Bay of Biscay and the Med. The familiar sounds and smells of Port Said had him up on deck taking note of all that was going on.

"I bet that stupid nigger in his little boat will loose everything he sends up in that basket on the rope that he has thrown up to the rail. Who is going to pay for that trash?"

The fat American was talking loudly to his wife so that others could hear. "Just look at those watches and ornaments, I bet they are stolen."

Mark said. "Excuse me, but the man in the little boat is an Arab trader, not a nigger as you call him, and I would suggest that you do not underestimate their business ability, they have been trading for thousands of years and are capable of outwitting most people."

"Gee, is that so mister, hey just look at that, somebody has bought that trash and sent the money down in the basket. You were right, pretty smart cookie that nigger in the boat, can't stand them myself."

Later in the evening Mark met the American couple in the bar who introduced themselves as Gus and Mary Louise Carter.

It came out, as they had a drink together, that Gus was a metallurgist going out to work for a gold mining consortium in Johannesburg. "The job offer was too good to pass up, three year contract, house and servants and a profit share with the French owned Colonial Mining Company, but the frogs get it ass up and call it the MCC. It is backed by some frog bank according to their annual report."

Mark's interest was aroused at the mention of MCC but tried not to show it. "What do they do in Johannesburg?" "They own several deep mines which are producing well, but they want to spread out and take advantage of the cheap nigger labour. Can't stand the niggers myself." A few more drinks later and Gus was boasting about the rich assay reports that he had seen on the MCC mines and the company's plans to become a monopoly in South Africa.

"Slowly buying shares in local companies before anyone wakes up, then 'Wham' and we walk in and take control. They have got some service companies already and many more in their sights."

The discussion was then steered by Mark onto lighter topics so that Gus would not realize that he had given away a lot of vital information.

So, the Lambrier affair would probably lead back to MCC and their plans to take over SATCO. Mark sent a cable from the ship's radio room to Abdul with a copy for George to get some investigation started.

> SATCO STOP
> JOHANNESBURG STOP
> ATTENTION SULIMAN/ BRIDGEMAN STOP
> BELIEVE LOVER BOY AFFAIR IS PART OF
> APETITE OF ABREVIATION
> FOR LORDS. STOP. PLEASE CHECK. STOP.
> BWANA ENDS.

It was necessary to disguise the message because of the 'open' nature of cables. The first part was easy and with George's love of cricket he would soon get the MCC worked out and start an investigation of the MCC mining group.

CHAPTER 15

SASHA

Mark was tired and hungry when he jumped out of the cab in the main entrance at SATCO and walked into the office. Abdul, McKenzie and all the staff welcomed him as a long lost friend, then Abdul said "You are probably tired and hungry after the journey and wanting a rest and some food so we have made everything ready for you in the quarters."

Mark was glad to take his leave and go up to the quarters. A pleasant smell of cooking greeted him at the top of the stairs and as he opened the door there was Sasha looking more beautiful than ever. He dropped his bag and ran over to embrace her passionately. That wonderful moment went on for a long time and they were both becoming aroused, when Sasha said. "We must wait till we have had a bath and dinner and then we can go to bed."

Dinner was simmering on the stove.

Sasha had the bath filled soon after dinner and they were relaxing in the warm water. It was just wonderful to be with Sasha again and feel her respond to his every touch.

Mark said. "I am always concerned that you will become pregnant when we make love, but so far nothing has happened, or has it?"

"My mother taught me how to not be with mtoto, just special herbs in my diet and in my love place every day is usually enough but that is what you want n'est pas?"

"Yes that is so but are you sure that we can have a mtoto when we are married?"

"Yes, just stop the herbs and wait two months, more jig y jig and voila!"

"That sounds too good to be true. Are you sure?"

"O yes, it has been used by my mother's ancestors for thousands of years. You see, because they lived in such a parched area they had to limit the number of people or some would have starved to death."

"How did you arrange to be back at SATCO when I arrived? I had a wonderful surprise."

"I have become very close to Ghillie and Alice and I am telling them everything and they are very happy for me and want to help me as a daughter, so they arranged for me to come back to SATCO one week ago so that I can make ready for you when you arrive."

"So, Ghillie and Alice are at the bottom of this wonderful surprise."

"But that is what you wanted, n'est pas?"

"Of course, darling Sasha, come, let us make love, I have missed you so much."

Sasha had matured in her manner and had picked up some Scottish sayings and pronunciation from Alice and Ghillie, which amused Mark.

There was a meeting the next morning for Mark, Sasha, George and Abdul to discuss the Lambrier affair and the M.C.C. threat.

George had deciphered the cable and had been doing some discreet detective work on the MCC group. "I have found that they are now owned by our original bank which was recently taken over by a big French bank and that they have a nondescript trading company, which they use as a "vehicle" to buy up anything that they find of interest. Rand Trading is the vehicle company which has already purchased Mining Supplies, who as you know, are trying to muscle in on our mining machinery and explosives business.

I can't get any more consulting or construction work from the MCC group and they also have all the Government officials eating out of their hands, thanks to bribes and provision of 'good time girls'.

One of my top level spies tells me that the French Bank will build up the MCC. group so it looks good on paper then sell it to local interests and make a huge profit without owning the group long enough to be there when the high risk phase cuts in. That certainly seem likely from the way that they are operating and the 'unrealistic' assay figures that they are carefully 'leaking' round the trade."

News of Mark's arrival travelled fast and pressure was increased by Rand Trading on company take-overs and cut price selling by Mining Supplies, almost immediately.

Mark could see SATCO being forced out of number one position to second or third place if nothing was done. A month of intensive work by Mark and the staff reduced the decline in sales but it needed something more to break the MCC group's monopoly in the market. Tad was very involved with Hassan and the mining business and was spending more and more time underground conducting demonstration blasting trials with all the new explosives and equipment becoming available.

George's spy was right about the French bank selling on a 'paper peak' for within two months a group of local Dutch miners and businessmen had bought out all of the bank's holdings in MCC, but there was no fanfare or change of name. The spy also reported that the local consortium had had to borrow very heavily to raise the cash to pay the French bank's very inflated price. By the third month SATCO sales to the mines had dropped to half of the former level in spite of renewed efforts by all at SATCO. Mark used to talk over his problems with Sasha in the evenings and she seemed to be very confident that there was a solution not far away.

The MCC deep mines were very close to some old workings that had been abandoned some years ago due to rock faults and fear of flooding from other old workings that were already flooded.

Mark met Gus Carter for a social drink and found him all steamed up about the latest excellent assay figures for the MCC deep mines. But on checking with George the next day, the actual weight of gold being produced had declined rapidly, so it would appear that their reef had run out and that the 'leaked assay figures', were just propaganda.

The new owners of MCC. soon found that they had been 'sold a pup' by the French bank and became enraged.

Lambrier was blamed personally for the inflated price paid for MCC, which had been based on false assay figures, and there were threats on his life. One day he was in his office and the next he was on a ship on his way back to France.

Gus and Mary Louise Carter were also targets of the new owners anger, and were glad to be on the same ship as Lambrier.

Anyone who has lived near to, or worked in a mine, knows the blood chilling sound of the steam siren which is sounded continuously when there is a major mine disaster. Each mine has its' own siren note which can be easily distinguished.

The MCC siren kept on sounding for over three hours and cage after cage of frightened, work stained miners came up to the surface. Finally the rescue teams went down to asses the damage and check for stragglers.

The telegraph rang and reports started to come in. "Lower levels already flooded and water is rising. Rock falls in middle levels and rock is unstable.

Abandon all levels—Abandon all levels".

The cages came up again and again and disgorged the rescue teams in their white helmets. They also brought up a few stragglers from the lower levels.

A mass meeting was held in the mine office to collate all the reports and make a decision on the cause of the disaster and the future of the mine. Apparently the thin wall of unstable rock separating the old workings had become weakened with the last blast, on the shift change, and had collapsed. At the same time, the water from the other old workings had started to pour into the lower levels causing the mine to flood slowly from the lower levels.

All the men were paid off and sent home. There were no reports of loss of life and only a few men had cuts and bruises from climbing over rock falls in their panic to get to the shafts. With the recent fall off in output, the flooded mine and the huge debt to pay off, the MCC. company was in imminent danger of collapse.

An attempt was made to raise new capital to buy machinery and dewater the mine, but the costs were out of all proportion and the bid failed. Within another month the whole MCC group was declared bankrupt and the assets were quickly auctioned off.

Mark was able to buy the whole of Mining Supplies for less than half the cost price of just the stock, which was then transferred to SATCO. The Mining Supplies business was closed down and the land and buildings sold for commercial development. A few days later Mark and Sasha were lying in bed talking over recent events when Mark said.

"It is hard to believe that the Lambrier affair and the MCC threat have been resolved so quickly. There was one stage when I thought that they would beat us."

"I was always confident that we would overcome the problems and that the MCC. would get into trouble."

"You seem very sure of the outcome, what do you know that I don't?"

"Perhaps you should ask Tad, ha ha."

"Do you mean to tell me that Tad had something to do with the rock fractures and the flooding?"

"Please do not make trouble. I am not supposed to tell you."

"I might have a quiet word with Tad and find out if all those trials for new types of explosives had a sinister purpose."

"The next morning Tad was called in on some minor pretext and then the big question was put to him.

"Tad, what do you know about the rock fractures and the flooding of the MCC deep mine?"

The corners of Tad's mouth twisted into a puckish grin and there was a sparkle in his eyes for a moment, then an impassive mask came over his face.

"What would I be knowing about the workings of a foreign owned mine, just careless I s'pose."

"You have been conducting trials for the new types of explosives that we have been sent and I have reason to think that you held some of these trials in the old workings of the deep mine alongside MCC."

"Yer, that be so."

"Anyway the outcome was very satisfactory from our point of view and there was no loss of life, so I can only say thank you."

"I will never say nuffink, but I did'na take any chances, yer see, the charges were all set in the abandoned mine all ready for me to link up the detonator wires with the MCC charges on that last day on the shift change when all the men were safe on a higher level. When she blew, all my charges and all their charges went off together and that broke the wall into the flooded mine. I had it all planned very careful like 'cos I knew them Frenchies were making trouble for you and their reef had run out anyway. They bin just bringing up rock for months. Good assay results my arse.

Got rid of that cock happy little Frog wot was bothering Miss Sasha too."

"Thank you Tad, but officially I don't know anything about what happened other than the official report of an accident in the bottom level of the MCC deep mine."

They shook hands and went up to Mark's sitting room to have a drink to seal their bond of silence.

Sasha was becoming worried that she had not seen Ghillie and Alice for too long and was keen for Mark to take her up to the McIntyre farm and the Ashcroft shamba. So arrangements were made and they headed off on the train two days later, accompanied by Raymond. The ride from Pietersburg to the farm, on horses hired from a new livery stable, was leisurely and it was then very good to be greeted by Ghillie and Alice and spend two days with them. Alice was full of energy and her recovery was almost complete. John Ashcroft had declared her 95% fit and still improving, which was amazing to see after the last time Mark had seen her so sick and weak in Scotland.

Ghillie's new boss boy and house girl had a hut close to the house and were becoming very reliable. The old native shamba had been completely rebuilt in a better location and the irrigation area had been nearly doubled in size. There was a lot of new machinery in use and the crops were all growing well. Mark and Ghillie walked round the farm and discussed every detail of the operation. Meanwhile, Alice fussed over

Sasha like a mother hen with a chick. "What are your plans with Mark?" Asked Alice. "We have always been very attracted to each other, as you know, and we are now in love and we discuss everything together, Mark has asked me to marry him but is just a bit hesitant about exactly when. He was very stressed after the wounding, but he is much better now. I hope that he will feel ready to get married very soon. How do you think that his family will accept my coloured skin?"

"Hopefully they will accept you as another person regardless of the colour of your skin, but there are always some prudish people who will not accept you and may even be rude to you. You see, there is so much prejudice from the pompous old men in the church who are afraid of loosing their power over the people, and also those men who are the government officials. You can only be yourself and be sure to always be better mannered than they are. I am sure that most people will accept you and that you will make a lot of new friends."

"There is usually no problem with the English people here, but the Boers are often rude or try to take liberties with me. They think that they are a superior race, but many of them have so little schooling that they can't read or add up money. We often get this type of ignorant Boer in SATCO and they start shouting about the bill being wrong and they can't even add up properly."

Mark and Ghillie returned in time for dinner and the plans to go on to the Ashcroft shamba were discussed. They decided to leave the day after next which gave Mark and Ghillie time to go on a quick hunting trip to shoot some waterbuck that could be left for the native's meat supply while they were away. The herds had moved away and they did not even find any fresh tracks at first. "Something has stirred up the herds in the last few weeks." Said Ghillie.

"I wonder if there have been any Boer patrols or hunters through here."

"I have not heard of any of either since we have been here, my natives go on their own hunting trips to spear a few impala or waterbuck about once a month so they have a good idea of what goes on, and of course they meet up with other natives and get the local gossip."

It was dark by the time that Mark and Ghillie rode into the yard with two water buck carcasses lashed onto the pack horses. The natives had seen them coming and appeared out of the gloom to carry off the meat supply to their shamba.

About an hour after dawn the next day, the party of five riders and two pack horses left the farm and headed Westwards. Raymond took the lead, followed by Ghillie and Alice while Mark and Sasha came in the rear with the pack horses. Sasha's supple body seemed to just flow with the horse's movements, even though riding was relatively new to her. Mark couldn't take his eyes off her and Sasha smiled and periodically reached out to touch his hand when they were close enough.

The journey went smoothly, and on the fourth evening when they were approaching John's shamba Raymond started signalling to the scouts hiding in the bush. John and his family were all on the veranda to greet them and there were hugs and kisses all round.

May prepared a wonderful meal for them and after a quick bath Mark and Sasha went into the main room and sat down to what John described as a bush banquet. There was a variety of roasted meat, a savoury liver and kidney dish, yams, beans, sauces, fruit of many kinds, cheese and fresh baked bread. Marcel had filled out and was now a mature looking young man and was very happy with his decision to stay and look after the cub and attend John's classes.

"Sally, Sarah and Marcel have all grown, how old are the girls now?" Asked Sasha.

"Yes they have all grown, the girls are now sixteen and fourteen

"Do you have any plans for their schooling?"

"Yes, we have talked about it and would like them to go to a college in Johannesburg but do not know of a suitable college. Our teaching facilities are so limited here and we do not have the right books that they need these days. Do you know of a suitable college?"

"No I do not, but we can make an enquiry for you. I think that there is a new college opening soon that might be suitable, we will let you know what we find."

John was very steamed up about a new coffee estate that was being established in a rich valley two miles away.

"We have had survey parties and many wagon loads of equipment through here in the last few months. They can't use the route that we use because it is too steep for the wagons so they go the long way round along the flatter country. There should be some benefits for us later on. I think they will grade a road through and have regular supply and mail wagons for the village that they plan to build soon.

They must be spending a fortune and it will be several years before they get any return. The Young manager that they have appointed, Mike Burgess, and his wife Sheila, called in here a few weeks ago. Sheila is a very frail little thing, poor girl, never been off a made road in her life before, and terrified of wild animals and black men. As you might expect, she is pregnant and scared stiff at the thought of having a baby with only witch doctors in attendance. Anyway, we have told them that Sheila can come here when she is near her time and that we will look after her. They were glad to accept our offer. The owners, British Coffee Estates, have been setting up plantations all over this part of Africa and train up young managers on each operating estate so that they can then go and start up another estate somewhere else. A good system but the young managers have to rough it and work very hard for the first few years. The Boers hate the idea and have made many threats and try to intimidate the workers so that they will not work for BCE.

As you know, the Boers reckon that they have divine rights to this land and will not accept anyone else setting up to make a living. My scouts tell me that they have seen several groups of Boers hanging round the BCE plantation and that the workers have been threatened that their villages would be burned down and the women raped and killed if they work for BCE.

The Boers also drove all the game away thinking that would make the workers follow the herds for food, but the game are coming back to where there is good grazing in the area where they have lived for hundreds, if not thousands of years.

We have told Mike and Sheila to let us know of the first signs of trouble. It is only half an hour's ride from their base camp to here. At this stage they have a native built hut similar to this, but later on when they get their first returns the company builds them wonderful colonial houses and put in better amenities as each crop is sold. Sort of incentive scheme you might call it. Young Marcel has been over and earned himself some pocket money helping to fix up their horses which were in a bad way after hauling all the heavy equipment through the bush from Pietersburg.

They now use the horses for clearing the land and cultivation ready for the coffee plants. They have a 'nursery' area protected by matting up on poles where they grow the young plants before planting them out in rows. The river has been partly damned up to divert some of the water onto the property and the first coffee bushes are growing already. Some of the young men from this shamba have been to work on the plantation. They say it is very heavy work but they get paid a good wage and are given all their food."

"Are there any problems with your new neighbours." Asked Ghillie.

"Yes there are two, there is the possibility of BCE taking a lot of the water from the river at some stage, and they attract Boer raiding parties to the area. We have had to start our system of native scouts again and keep on the alert all the time. Mike and Sheila keep two riding horses near their hut all the time so they can get over here quickly in an emergency.

They have no form of defence system and their workers huts are a long way from their hut."

Sasha asked. "Do they have any help in the house?"

"Oh yes, they have an elderly couple who came from one of the other plantations and live in a small hut alongside the main hut. It is all very exposed and they are very vulnerable.

Their workers are from many different tribes and are fairly new so they could not expect a cohesive response in the event of any trouble like we have here.

BCE. are sending out their area manager to check on the progress very soon. I think he is due to arrive in the next few days."

Mark recognized Sheeba's greeting call and a few minutes later she came padding onto the veranda to be met by Sally and Sarah but would not come into the hut because of all the strangers.

Mark went out onto the veranda and was greeted by Sheeba. She put her front paws onto his shoulders and licked his forehead with her rasping tongue. "Come out Sasha, and say hello to Sheeba again."

Sasha slowly moved onto the veranda while Mark stroked Sheeba's head and ears.

Sheeba smelt Sasha all over, then 'accepted' her again by licking her hand.

Sally said. "Can you see the cubs? They are over there on the edge of the lamplight waiting for their supper."

The two girls and Marcel then went off to feed the lions in their compound. The meat was then dragged down to the river bank to be eaten. John said. "Ghillie, you and Alice must be tired so do not stand on ceremony and just go to bed whenever you like. We can check on the patient in the morning."

"Come on lass, we had better get you into bed, goodnight everyone."

After Ghillie and Alice had gone to bed, May took Sasha into the kitchen on the pretext of planning the meals for the next few days, but when they were alone she said.

"What are your plans for the future? I can see that you and Mark are very much in love, do you plan to go back to England with him?" "Yes we love each other very much and I would like to go to where ever he wants to live, which is in England. He has asked me to marry him but is hesitating to confirm the date."

"As you know, John and I have been married for more than sixteen years and it is only recently that I have started to go into Pietersburg or Johannesburg with John. Even now there are some places that I can not go because of the colour bar. I do not think that they have the colour bar in England, so you should be all right there. It is the Boers who make all the trouble here. They are scared that the coloured people will push them out of power, so they try to keep us repressed and in poverty." "Yes, but they are quick enough to rape the coloured girls whenever they can and exploit the workers with very low wages."

"I will see if I can help Mark get over his sensitivity about your acceptance in England. I am sure that he is only holding back because he does not want to hurt you in any way. We got to know Mark very well when he was here with the wounding."

As the next day was Sunday, Mike and Sheila came to lunch and were introduced to the newcomers. Mike was a very fit and healthy looking young man of around 25, and Sheila was a frail slip of a girl with very fair hair and dark, surprised looking eyes. Her small body was becoming monopolized by her enlarged breasts and abdomen. The poor girl was terrified at the thought of Sheeba and the cubs coming into the house. It was obviously very good for Mike and Sheila to meet other 'settlers' and discuss common interests. Once the meal started, Sheila got into deep conversation with Sasha and May, who John had strategically placed sitting next to her. "So that they can have some women's talk." Mike was full of ideas for the plantation but was a little apprehensive about the pending visit by the area manager.

Mark and Sasha were invited to lunch the following day and were pleased to accept, partly because they felt sorry for the young couple and partly because they wanted to learn more about a coffee plantation. Mike and Sheila were also good, friendly people with similar interests. Even though Ghillie had also been invited, he said that he would stay to look after Alice and see that she rested.

The ride over to BCE did not take as long as expected, so Mark and Sasha stopped at the edge of the clearing and took time to have a good look at the whole plantation. A tremendous amount of back breaking work had been done. The trees cut down and the stumps removed, the soil cultivated and irrigation ditches dug, a small dam constructed, a small nursery area developed, the first coffee bushes planted out, a processing shed built and a workers living area established.

There was also a stable and servants quarters close to Mike and Sheila's large hut. The whole place was a hive of activity with some 40 workmen visible from where they sat on their horses. "This is a big operation, there must be a lot of money in coffee for BCE to outlay all this money to set up a plantation."

Sasha nodded and said. "Have you got any ideas of going into coffee?"

"I must admit that the thought did cross my mind. You read me like a book darling Sasha."

He leaned across and kissed her and then they slowly rode across to the house taking in all the details as they went. As they got close to the house a metal gong sounded and all the workers hurried to their mess hall for their midday meal.

Mike and Sheila greeted them at the door and were obviously pleased to see their new friends. Sheila had gone to a lot of trouble to make an excellent lunch. The house servants were good at their job and spoke good English. Mike said. "Would you like me to show you round after lunch while the girls have a chat?" "Yes, that would be most interesting, thank you."

When seated at the table, Mark said. "You seem to have a lot of men working on the plantation." "Yes there are over 50 at present, while we are still clearing new ground, but once that phase is finished, we will have a lot less most of the time. We will need to employ a lot of women to pick the beans at harvest time, and extra men to work the processing plant."

The meal was being cleared away and coffee was being served when Moses came in.

"Please master, the big boss is here and we have no more food What shall I do?"

"He will just have to wait while we prepare some more." Said Sheila and went into the kitchen to help Grace and Moses stretch the left-overs.

Moses was still muttering and wringing his hands with worry. Mike and Sheila went to the veranda to welcome the new arrivals while Mark and Sasha waited in the living room.

"How nice to see you again Mike and Shiela, this is my new assistant, Dennis Grant, he is an agronomist." They all shook hands very formally and came inside.

"Some neighbours have come to lunch, please meet Mark and Sasha. This is Mr. Brian Humphries and Mr. Dennis Grant."

Mark saw that Brian was not at all sure of what to make of Sasha who was wearing a low cut cotton dress and looked particularly attractive.

"Moses has gone to prepare your lunch while you have a wash and a drink. The bathroom is that way" Said Sheila.

Brian and Grant went to the bathroom and poor Sheila looked momentarily relieved and said. "What a time to arrive and expect a meal. I had better go and see how Moses is getting on at such short notice."

"Would you like us to leave?" Said Mark.

"Oh no, you are welcome to stay and you will help to soften the inquisition from Brian and Dennis."

Brian and Dennis reappeared looking refreshed and less travel stained and were given glasses of native beer which they drank thirstily. Their glasses were then refilled. Sheila appeared and said "Your lunch is ready. How was the journey?"

"We have had a difficult trip out because our usual porters would not come to this area, because of some sort of nonsense to do with threats from the Boers. The new boys that we got are so nervous that if they hear a twig snap, they practically wet themselves. I would not be surprised if they just vanish if there is any trouble."

"Come and sit down and enjoy your meal while we have our coffee."

Everyone was seated and the conversation was becoming more relaxed when a series of rifle shots rang out from the direction of the workers camp. Mark sprang to his feet, ran to his horse in the stable and grabbed his rifle and revolver from the saddle bag and returned to the living room. Mike was standing in the open doorway with a pair of field glasses trained on the workman's mess hall.

"There appears to be a number of Boers holding my men at gunpoint inside the mess hall. They appear to be trying to get the men to move out and have shot at least two already."

Mark said. "They are probably trying to intimidate the men into abandoning their jobs and going back to their villages. What weapons do you have?"

"There is a shotgun and an old rifle in that trunk under the bed and I have a revolver in the desk over there."

"Come on, get every weapon we can muster and make sure that they are all loaded with the safety catch on.

You had better get Moses in here and tell him what is going on and tell him and Grace to keep in the kitchen. Can I borrow your glasses please Mike."

Mark had a quick look and said. "I will go closer while one of you keeps me covered. Can anyone use that rifle with some accuracy?" "I can use it, but not with any accuracy." Said Mike.

"Perhaps Sasha can use that rifle and leave you free to defend the house with your revolver in case any Boers come up here from behind. Sasha, please can you keep me covered while I crawl down that row and get closer to see what the Boers are doing to the men. If you see any Boers in the open do not hesitate to shoot them. We have to think about the safety of all those men down there. Dennis and Brian, can you help to keep an eye on the Boers. It is a 'them or us' situation."

Mark then ran to the end of the nearest row of coffee plants and started to crawl towards the mess hall. Dennis and Brian just continued to eat their lunch. Mike helped Sasha up end a table by the window so that she could rest the rifle on the edge and keep Mark covered while he crawled down the row.

By this time Dennis and Brian had finished their first course and had started to take interest and stood in the open doorway, presenting a perfect target for the marksman in the stores shed alongside the mess hall.

Sasha said. "Get down, you may get shot there."

Within seconds, a shot rang out and Dennis collapsed with a cry and clutched his stomach.

Mike shoved Brian out of the way and dragged Dennis back into the room just as Sasha saw flashes of sunlight reflected off the field glasses being used by the Boer marksman in the stores shed. She took careful aim and fired. The rifle was not 'sighted in' and the bullet struck low left in the soft earth. Reloading, and allowing for the error, she fired again and this time she saw something that looked like field glasses fall out of a gap in the shed wall. The marksman was either wounded or dead, which would give Mark a better chance. Sasha then saw the shed door open for a moment and a man's arm come out to retrieve the glasses. So, there was at least one more in the shed. "How solid is that shed please Mike." Asked Sasha.

"We had to build it out of thick timber poles to stop the natives stealing the food stored in there, but there are small gaps between the poles so you have about a one in four chance of each bullet doing some damage inside. Sasha decided to work on the one in four chance of a bullet going inside and doing some damage and also to keep the Boers from being able to shoot at Mark, so she kept on shooting at the front of the shed. Mark must have heard the shooting because the bullets were going over his head and a bit to the left because he was now about half way down the first row. Dennis was making a lot of noise and appeared to be fatally wounded. Sheila and Grace had stopped the external bleeding but they could do nothing for the internal damage which was now beginning to prove fatal. Brian was called over to console has friend while Sheila and Grace cleaned up.

At Sasha's suggestion, Mike had been making a dummy out of a suit of clothes stuffed with pillows and rags The dummy had strings attached to it's shoulders and with the aid of Brian on the other side of the doorway it was held in the doorway in a lifelike position. It was not long before a bullet struck the dummy and it was allowed to collapse on the floor. This gave Sasha another chance to pinpoint where the marksman was hiding. The muzzle flashes were now coming from the other side of the shed, so she fired two shots and all was quiet.

When Sasha looked down the row, Mark had disappeared, he must have moved to a different row which was out of sight from the hut. There was a long silence and it was not possible to know what was happening down by the mess hall. Suddenly there were two rifle shots and several revolver shots and a lot of screaming. Within a few minutes, the workmen started to come out of the mess hall and up towards the house. Mark followed behind with two prisoners with their hands tied and guarded by the foreman. One prisoner had been shot in the shoulder and looked on the point of collapse. Mike asked the foreman what had happened. "Bwana, they kill three of my men when we go for chicoola. They was already hiding in the kitchen and came out with their banduki, some men not moving when they toll us to move so they was shot plenty dead. We was toll, no more Plantation work, go home, or our houses burnt and our wives raped and shot. Then more shooting and three Boers fall down dead, so I toll my men to hold the other two Boers. Then this Bwana came and toll us alright now and to come to the house."

By this time Mark had come up to the house and Sasha ran to him to see if he was alright.

"Yes, I am alright thank you Darling, just a bit dirty from crawling along the rows in the irrigation channels, but other wise I am fine. There appears to have been eight or nine Boers in the raiding party. Sasha, you got one in the shoulder and killed another in the store hut and I accounted for three more when I got in close, we have two prisoners, so one or two got away. There are three dead, and one wounded workman who is being looked after in the mess hall."

Mike then told the men that there was no more danger and that they must finish chicoola and go back to work. The men looked unconvinced and suspicious and slowly went down to the mess hall. When all the men had gone, Sheila said "Fresh coffee is poured for you."

Denis had died and his body had been dragged to the back veranda by Moses.

The group drank their coffee in silence for a while, then Mark said. "Have you thought about posting armed guards while you are still being troubled by the Boers?"

Brian said. "Never given that sort of thing any thought up till now. Never had to on other plantations, but they were not in areas as remote as this, so I suppose the Boers have picked this as an easy target. Mike, put some guards in the area if you find it necessary. We can not go on loosing men and having the crops put at risk because of some damned pirates. Now Mike, where are your accounts, I must get started immediately."

Brian then produced a large leather satchel and spread his papers over the dining room table and Mike brought in his books and papers.

Mark and Sasha went into the kitchen and there was poor Sheila sobbing quietly and being comforted by Grace. Moses had gone down with a first aid kit to attend to the wounded workman.

"An important visitor killed in my own house, and now all these threats of more violence, and me expecting, and all that bloody Brian can think of is his precious accounts."

"Careful, he might hear you, would you like to come back with us and stay at John's shamba till the baby is born?" Said Sasha.

"Yes, I think so, but I will have to talk it over with Mike first, ugh! That body on the veranda gives me the creeps."

Sasha stayed with Sheila while Mark went to find the foreman to organize a burial party. The foreman was at the end of the plantation and it took some time to organize the burials. Mark then wanted to know what had happened to the prisoners and was told that they were tied up in the stable close to the house, and hurried back to check on them. The prisoners were being guarded by the brother of one of the murdered men, who was dozing in the shade outside the stable. When they went inside they found that one of the prisoners had nearly cut through his bonds by rubbing them against the iron rim of a small cart wheel. The foreman spoke a few harsh words to the guard.

Mark supervised tying up the prisoners more securely and tried questioning them, but just got abuse, including. "We have heard of you, you are that bloody Oakhills that caused all the trouble on the railway, we will be remembering you, we will tell you nothing."

"We must send the prisoners back to Pietersburg with Mr. Humphries tomorrow under escort. We will need four very good men. Can you arrange that with Mr. Burgess?"

"Yes, that should be no problem as we have some Askari who have served in the army, they can take the prisoners."

Sheila got Mike and Brian to leave their accounts to have a cup of tea, and said that she would like to go back with Mark and Sasha and stay at the Ashcroft shamba till the baby was born in about a month's time.

Mike looked forlorn at the thought of being left on his own, but said. "What ever is best for you and the baby, dear."

"It was arranged that Brian would call into the Ashcroft Shamba and pick up a scout, who knew the best route to Pietersburg, on his way through in two days time, as his porter boys had fled as soon as the shooting started.

Darkness was only about an hour away when Mark, Sasha and Sheila rode up to John's hut. Mark quickly explained what had happened to John and May and that Shiela wanted to stay till the baby was born. Sheila was quickly taken inside and made to feel secure with the aid of one of John's stiff brandies. A few minutes later, Sheeba and the cubs arrived for their evening meal, but it was not till Sheeba came padding into the living room that Sheila realized what was happening. Sheeba was only about ten feet away when Sheila first saw her and tried to scream, but no sound came out. The only sound was the trickle of urine forming a puddle under her chair.

John said "You have nothing to fear, just sit still and let Sheeba get used to you, she is very friendly with us and our house guests. Sheeba, couja harpa."

Sheeba followed John to where Sheila was sitting and sniffed the puddle suspiciously and then put her head in Sheila's lap to be stroked and purred affectionately. Very slowly Sheila plucked up courage and started to fondle Sheeba's ears.

"There you see, there is nothing to it, she is just like a large domestic cat around the house. All right girls, feeding time."

Sheila watched as the girls took Sheeba to her compound.

"Look, over there, the cubs are sitting waiting for their mother to bring out the meat for their supper. They were born in the cellar under where you are sitting and we have watched them grow up to be nearly adult lions."

"Perhaps I can show you to your room?" said May, and led the rather embarrassed Sheila to her room in the guest wing of the rambling hut.

It was mid morning the next day when Brian and his party arrived with the prisoners tied on their horses. Mark considered sending Raymond as the scout, but on second thoughts decided that it was more important that Raymond should be available on the return journey in a few days time, in case there was any trouble. John sent two scouts with a shopping list of things to bring back for the baby and the household. John gave Sheila a thorough check up during the afternoon and said that all was well for an easy birth in about four weeks time, provided that she got plenty of exercise, particularly walking. "You can go with the girls when they take Sheeba for her walks."

Just before sunset on the next day, the usual evening gathering was under way on the veranda when John said." I could swear that I heard bag pipes just now, must be the drink affecting my judgment."

"Yes, I can hear the Scottish pipes." Said Sasha.

"I am sure that I can hear bag pipes, sounds like a lone piper and he plays very well." Said Mark.

All eyes were trained on the track running along the river bank and the sound of the pipes was getting louder and louder. A group of horsemen came into view at the end of the track and came on up to the hut followed by a number of incredulous children who were attracted by the strange sounds. John became very excited, and said. "Unless my eyes and ears are deceiving me, that is my 72 year old father, 'just dropping in for dinner', all the way from Scotland, Silly old bugger should have told us he was coming and we could have met him off the ship at Durban. Where would you like to put him up, May?" "He can have the spare room in our wing, there is a good bed in there and it is cooler on that side of the house because it faces South East."

The lone piper was playing 'Scotland the Brave' as he rode the last few yards up to the house.

John rushed forward to help his father down from his horse, but the old man jumped down with surprising agility and warmly greeted everyone.

"I would like you to meet my father, the reverend Angus Ashcroft from Edinburgh."

The children ran up to May with their eyes shining with delight at the new sound and pleaded with her for more of the wonderful music.

Sasha interpreted the request for Angus who said. "Not now, bit out of puff, but how about later in the evening, after a wee bit of supper?"

May explained this to the children and they ran off excitedly to tell their friends.

"Well Dad, what brings you to Africa?"

"It is now two years since your mother died and the Kirk has pensioned me off, so now I am free to go where ever the spirit moves me. Your letters have always fascinated me with stories of the African bush. Some of my parishioners had been in the Boer war and we ran a returned servicemen's group to look after the wounded and widows, so I decided that I would like to come and see the country for myself and spend some time with you and your new family. You have two very fine looking girls there John, not forgetting their charming mother."

"Thank you for your kind remarks about my family, we are delighted to have you with us, please stay just as long as you like, there is plenty of room, your porter boys have been put in the dormitory alongside the first aid hut. We are very nearly self sufficient and only have to go into Johannesburg for a few essentials every two or three months."

"That is very kind of you for making me so welcome, just tell me what I can do to help?"

"You can always help with our school in the mornings, and there will be the odd wedding service and baptism that you may wish to conduct."

Said John, giving Sasha a big wink.

May made the evening meal a memorable occasion to welcome Angus. Long before the meal was finished there was the sound of many small voices as the children came and sat in the clearing outside the hut waiting to hear more of the new music.

"Must not keep them waiting for too long."

Said Angus as he reached for his pipes and took up position on the veranda. While Angus played, John, Ghillie, Alice and sometimes Mark sang the words of the tunes that they knew.

Sasha noticed that the children had now been joined by many of the adults from the village. After about an hour Angus began to visibly tire and John thanked him and everyone clapped. May then said that she would organize an African dance and drum performance at another time.

Later that night as Mark and Sasha were about to get into bed, Mark said. "Darling Sasha, Will you marry me, as soon as possible now that the last obstacle has been resolved?" "Yes of course and I promise to be forever faithful to you and your family."

"Oh Sasha you make me so happy and I am delighted that I can at last ask you to marry me with a firm date now that the last obstacle has disappeared. I have always wanted to get married in Africa but could not work out how we were going to persuade some stuffy old vicar to perform a mixed marriage, but with Angus arriving out of the blue, and his offer to conduct a marriage, that makes everything different. Where would you like to get married?"

"I suppose my home is at SATCO, but Ghillie and Alice must be there, they have become very much part of my life and have treated me as their own daughter."

"All right that is what we will arrange. I am so happy, I love you Darling Sasha and promise to love and protect you always."

Everyone was settled down to breakfast the next morning, when Mark stood up and said that he had an announcement to make and called Sasha to his side.

"Sasha has accepted my proposal and we are now engaged and plan to get married as soon as possible in Johannesburg."

Cheers, congratulations, clapping and hugs all round made the two kitchen girls come out to check on the reason for the excitement and they then ran off to tell everyone in the village.

Angus said. "I would be privileged to have the opportunity to conduct your wedding service in Johannesburg and can arrange all the details for you." "We were just about to ask you, so yes we would be delighted if you can marry us, thank you so much."

Mark Sasha and Raymond rode over to the BCE. plantation to see how Mike was coping with the Boer threats. They found him doing his rounds with the foreman and noticed that two Askari had been equipped with two of the 7 mm Mauser rifles taken from the Boers and were patrolling the perimeter of the clearing. "Hello Mike, How are you?"

"Well thank you, how is Sheila?"

"Sheila is fine and has had a check up by John and all is well. Would you like to come over this evening?" "Yes."

"Sasha and I have some news for you! We have become engaged and plan to get married as soon as possible in Johannesburg."

"That is wonderful news, congratulations to you both, can I kiss the bride to be?"

Sasha stepped forward and kissed Mike firmly on the cheek. We are very pleased to see that you have the Askari on patrol, that must improve the confidence of the men. John and I have been discussing a system of scouts for the whole area. We have scouts out all the time now, mostly young boys from the village. They are happy to be involved and report back if they spot any Boer activity. They do not miss much and a lot of the time they are acting as herd boys for the cattle and horses. John can fill you in with the detail this evening. How did the discussions with Brian Humphries go?"

"He seemed pleased enough with the progress here and the way that I have kept costs down, but there is something troubling him, but he would not elaborate. I suspect that one or more of the other estates has had a crop failure or something like that. He was also very upset at the loss of Dennis because he was the expert sent out from England to ensure that all the crops are in perfect condition and free of pests." "If they run out of money at the development stage, where does that leave you?"

"Out in the bush without a job, but I hope that the problems are only temporary. We must not worry Sheila with any of this, poor dear has enough to worry about with the baby. I want her to have an easy time if at all possible."

"Yes we understand, we had better be getting back, see you tonight but do not travel alone, bring one man with you."

Angus had been sitting in on the school classes and had made a lot of notes and was rapidly becoming familiar with life at the shamba. At supper he said. "You have lived here for about sixteen years now John and have not given it a name yet. As I rode up the other evening I found myself playing 'Dream Valley of Glendarvel', so how does 'Glendarvel' sound, just to remind you of your Scottish heritage?" "Yes that sounds fine, so Glendarvel it is from now on." Said John.

"Sasha and I are so happy that you will conduct our wedding service. Thank you again. Finding a vicar to conduct the service was the one obstacle that was making me hesitate to formally announce our engagement, because I want Sasha to have a proper church wedding without any of the colour bar nonsense."

Sasha stepped forward and kissed Angus. "Thank you for saying that you will marry us, I am so happy now that we know that we can soon be man and wife."

"The pleasure is all mine dear Sasha. I am sure that you will be very happy together. I am becoming rapidly enchanted with life here at Glendarvel and may even consider staying on for a wee while now that I have no ties in Scotland."

May had arranged tribal dancing for that same evening and the villagers started to appear soon after noon to enlarge the clearing in front of John's house. There were several tribes represented and during the evening, each tribal group put on a show of their dancing, accompanied by an assortment of drums.

Mark, Sasha, Ghillie, Alice, Raymond and two Glendarvel scouts were ready to leave early the next morning. The journey back to the McIntyre farm was uneventful and after an overnight stop, the scouts started back to Glendarvel and Mark, Sasha and Raymond headed off for Pietersburg and Johannesburg.

Sasha's excitement was mounting as they left the station in a cab and approached SATCO "I am just so happy Darling Mark, I can't wait for Angus to come to Johannesburg and tell us where we can be married."

Abdul came out of the office to the entrance to greet them and was visibly excited when Mark told him of the pending wedding.

Mark spent most of the next week going over the new projects with Sasha, George and Anne.

Hassan was appointed manager of the new branch store, which had been built on the site of the kukri brandishing Indian's store, on the other side of the city. Angus arrived at the end of the second week and again stayed with the Bishop. He called in on his way through to say that he would be back with details of where the service was to be held, in a few days time. Two days later Angus came back and said that the service was to be held in a relatively new church on the way to Springs in four weeks time. Messages were sent quickly to Ghillie and John Ashcroft and wedding arrangements were put in top gear.

Ghillie and Alice must have left as soon as they got the message, because they arrived a week later and joined in the preparations just as though Sasha was their own daughter getting married. Ghillie made many visits to the Church and also visited BHQ to get the latest information on Boer activity in the city area. The day of the wedding finally arrived and Mark was pleased that nearly all of his friends had accepted the invitation.

John Ashcroft had delivered a beautiful baby daughter for Mike and Sheila the week before, so Mike and Sheila could not come to the wedding.

Sasha looked absolutely stunning in a long white satin dress, long white gloves and a white hat and veil. Ghillie did the honours and 'gave away' the bride. Alice wept with emotion and no body took particular notice when Ghillie walked to the back of the church rather than go and sit in the place allocated for him next to Alice.

The service proceeded with Angus officiating and obviously enjoying his duties. As the service drew to a close, the young couple went down the isle and took up position just inside the doorway for photographs. The guests were asked to stay inside the church. The photographer was getting set up when there was a series of explosions and some rifle fire around an old two storey warehouse diagonally opposite. Everyone ran back farther inside the church. One of the Glendarvel scouts appeared and handed a rifle to Mark and pointed to the stairs leading up to the bell tower. Mark took the rifle and mounted the steps two at a time with Sasha following with her dress held up to make it possible to go up the steps. Ghillie and Raymond were at the top and were firing at a number of Boers who had been exposed when the front of the old warehouse had been blown off. It appeared that there had been six or eight Boers in the old warehouse on the first floor waiting for an opportunity to shoot Mark and Sasha when Tad's charges had blown the front of the building out and left them exposed and trying to get to safety at the rear of the building and escape on their horses which were tied up in the back yard.

"Watch out for Tad, he is in that building on the left. The Army should have arrived before now, so we will have to keep the Boers pinned down till they arrive." Said Ghillie.

Angus had the congregation in one corner of the church and was talking to them over the back of a pew. "Just be patient and keep calm, the Army unit should be here in a wee while and will take care of the trouble makers. We got information just in time that there would be some reprisals and were able get the Army to send a unit, but they are a wee bit late coming."

Ghillie, Mark, Sasha and Raymond were all lying prone and shooting through the slit windows of the bell tower when Captain Fisher arrived at the top of the steps.

"Well, you 'irregulars' seem to have them well covered from here. How do you suggest that we flush them out of the warehouse?"

"Our man Tad, is in that building to the left of the warehouse and will start throwing grenades at the back of the warehouse when we give him a signal. We expect the Boers to break out of the back of the building any minute now and try to get to their horses."

"Give me five minutes to get my men in place and then give your signal for the grenades."

They both checked their watches. Captain Fisher hurried down to his men waiting in a side street and groups of troops moved quickly into position round the warehouse.

Ghillie reached over and gave the bell rope two sharp pulls and just after the second tone there was an explosion at the back of the warehouse which blew a hole in the rear wall. It was now possible for the troops in the road to see the Boers inside the hole in the wall waiting for an opportunity to get to their horses in the yard. Ghillie was able to shoot two of them as they tried to run across the yard.

A megaphone blared out. "This is a Company of British Infantrymen and you are surrounded. Come out into the street one at a time with your hands up or we will storm the building in five minutes!"

Very slowly, four Boers filed out into the street with their hands up and were tied up by the troops and led away. "At least two more inside." Shouted Ghillie.

Captain Fisher gave a hand signal and the troops stormed the building from the front. There were a few shots and two Boers were seen trying to escape into the yard only to be overcome by the troops waiting there.

Ten minutes later. Captain Fisher came into the church and said that all was secure.

"You and your men are very welcome to join us for the wedding reception back at SATCO." Said Mark.

"I would be very pleased to, but that depends on the colonel. Can we leave it open, and come later if possible?"

"Yes, that will be our pleasure."

All the wedding guests then started to slowly make their way back to SATCO.

Anne had excelled herself with the arrangements for the wedding breakfast. A new marquee had been put up in the yard and one of the warehouse buildings had been taken over by the caterer to prepare the food and drinks.

News of the 'fracas' at the church had attracted some journalists and photographers from local newspapers who were busy photographing the damaged warehouse and getting embellished 'eye witness' accounts from anyone still on the street, which included the verger, who was nearly stone deaf.

Finally the 'Press' arrived at SATCO and asked to be let in through the main gate for interviews and photographs. Abdul was summoned and after a brief discussion, Mark agreed to meet one senior reporter in the office with Ghillie and Angus. The reporter tried to insist that Mrs. Oakhill be photographed, but Mark would not consider putting Sasha at risk by having her photograph in the paper. Angus then took charge of the situation and made a formal statement. No mention was made of Tad or his contribution by placement of the charges and use of grenades, in fact Tad seemed to have just melted away when the church was declared secure. The reporter promised to publish a tasteful account in the Monday edition.

Mark returned to the marquee and looked for Sasha and found her talking to May and Alice. Everyone took their places at the beautifully decorated tables and Angus said grace in Swahili, and then in English. During the meal, Mark and Sasha went round the tables and spoke to as many people as possible.

A Glendarvel scout hurried up to Ghillie and said that there was a number of British Askari who wanted to come in. Ghillie went to the main gate and was pleasantly surprised to find Colonel Wilkinson, Captain Fisher and about twenty of his men and some BVC. friends waiting in the main entrance.

"Good evening Sor, Ex. Sergeant Major Mc Tavish, Highland Regiment, at your service. Please come in and I will introduce you to the other guests. This way please, Sor."

"Thank you Sergeant Major, Quite a crack unit you run here, should have more good men like you around, and especially when there is a bit of trouble, like now."

Mark came over and welcomed the Colonel and his men, and there were introductions all round. The Army personnel were seated among the other guests and the uniformed waiters quickly attended to their needs for food and drinks.

When the moment arrived, Angus stood up and there was a hushed silence.

"Mark, Sasha, Colonel Wilkinson, Army Personnel and wedding guests, it has given me great pleasure to conduct the service for such a fine couple and I am sure that you will join me in wishing them good health and happiness. Please be upstanding. Mark and Sasha, health and happiness, and may God bless them."

After Mark's brief response, Colonel Wilkinson stood up and there was another silence.

"Reverent Ashcroft, Mark, Sasha and wedding guests. It has been a privilege to receive reports of a small band of 'irregulars' who quite voluntarily, harassed the Boers, recovered a derelict train and reopened the line up to Pietersburg and then were responsible for the rounding up of more Boer units in the city. Unfortunately, their bravery and skill has made them the target of reprisals, as was demonstrated again today. We are deeply in your debt, and I have recommended that the 'Irregulars' be awarded suitable civilian honours. Now, let me congratulate Mark and his Beautiful bride on their marriage and ask them to accept this small gift from all of us at BHQ Johannesburg."

He handed a small package to Sasha. "Health and happiness to the Bride and Groom." "Health and happiness to

Mark and Sasha", echoed the guests. Mark stood up, and while Sasha opened the package, he responded.

"Thank you Colonel, and all the staff at BHQ. for your gift and good wishes, you are always welcome to visit us here or in England at any time.

However, much of the thanks should go to a very good friend and ex Indian Army Campaigner, Sergeant Major McTavish who was in my Uncle's regiment, and who carefully trained my brother and I and has played a vital role in our operations here. Ghillie, please step forward and let me formally thank you."

Ghillie came forward and Mark shook his hand and Sasha kissed him. Mark went on.

"I also have to thank Major John Ashcroft, who also served in India, for life saving surgery, and his wife, May, for nursing me back to health. Thank you John and May.

Our sincere thanks to each and every one of you for coming today to help us celebrate our marriage."

Now that the formal part of the evening was over, the guests started to move around and Mark found himself following Sasha to the table where Ghillie and Alice were sitting.

"Ghillie, how did you know that the Boers were planning a reprisal raid at the church?"

Ghillie paused a minute and then said. "It was the 'I' corps man, Frank, who tipped me off this morning. We did not have time to make any elaborate plans and did not want to spoil your wedding so we carefully checked out to see if it was safe if you stayed inside the church, and found that the line of fire from the warehouse could not enter the church doorway, so we ensured that everyone stayed inside when there was any threat. The sermon was shorter than expected, so the timing of the arrival of the Army unit was a bit late, and we had to keep the Boers pinned down till they arrived. Tad had had time to set a charge to stop the attack and keep them from rushing the church. We had Glendarvel scouts watching them all the time and reporting their every move."

"Thank you once again Ghillie, you have saved many lives today, and we are eternally grateful to you."

"Nay lad, it is Alice and I who are in your debt for giving us a new lease of life." Alice was crying with emotion and hugged Mark with the tears rolling down her cheeks.

George and Anne were looking radiant and happy while Mark and Sasha thanked them for making all the arrangements for the reception.

"George, how soon could you start the 'big house on Commando Hill?"

"The plans are prepared and the site is marked out, so we just need your approval to start."

"I will have to recheck the financial situation and will let you know as soon as possible."

Anne's eyes lit up and she said. "I can't wait to move into the new house designed by George, please make it soon."

Sasha came over and said. "Look what the BHQ staff has given us."

She reopened the package and there was a beautiful sterling silver tray engraved with a map of the Johannesburg to Pietersburg railway and the inscription.

To Mr. and Mrs. Mark Oakhill on the occasion of their Marriage.
With best wishes from
British HQ and Staff, Johannesburg.

They found Tad sitting with the Glendarvel scouts and some of Captain Fisher's men, but it was not the right time to thank him for his part in the day's events. Tad preferred to remain a 'mystery man' in the background, which suited Mark.

There had been another letter from Tad's wife to say that she had sold the house and that the family was booked on the next ship.

"That is wonderful news Tad, you know that there is a new cottage booked for you on Commando Hill, which should be ready in about three months, if that is what you want?"

"Yer, that would be wonderful, thank 'ee, can I take time off to meet the ship, cos they aint used to foreign travel yer,' knows."

"That will be fine, just let Abdul know when you want to go so that he can make the arrangements at this end for you."

Two days later, Mark and Sasha were on a ship heading up towards the Suez Canal having had an overnight stop in Durban with Gustav's family.

At first, Sasha got some odd looks from some of the other passengers, but her sincere and friendly nature soon started to win friends and gain acceptance. Mark enjoyed having Sasha as a constant companion and carefully explained all the new sights as they unfolded along the way. They arrived in London early in the morning so they were in time to catch a train going North and pick up a connection to Chester via Crew Junction.

Sasha started to become apprehensive about the reception awaiting her at Oakhill Hall.

Mark tried to assure her that there was nothing to worry about.

"You were quickly accepted by the people on the ship. Just be yourself. I will protect you if there is any unpleasantness, but I don't think that there will be any, all of the people that we will meet today are local country people, many of whom have at least one member of the family who has served overseas and is used to people from other parts of the world. I am sure that Mother will just accept you as another daughter."

"How about the servants, what do I expect them to think of a coloured girl coming into the house and giving the orders for the running of the house?"

"I am sure that Mother will gradually release her position and help you to take up the rains. The staff will naturally be curious at first but they have always accepted all the members of the family without question.

Oh yes, there is an old English custom that when the Squire brings home a new Bride that they all line up at the door to welcome her and there is a sort of welcoming party for all the tenants and the staff. There may be a few impromptu speeches, but do not worry, you are not expected to say anything. Just be your charming self. The formal welcome will be a good way of meeting everyone, and then you can get to know them better in time. The wire that we sent from London will probably mean that we are met at Chester station by Hugh and Margaret and possibly Ted Moregrove. Mother will probably stay at home to supervise the welcoming arrangements."

Hugh, Margaret and Ted Moregrove were on the platform to meet the train and Sasha was introduced.

They then went to the station restaurant for a quick cup of tea before meeting Phillips, who had the family carriage waiting in the station yard.

"Very pleased to meet you Ma—am, we have put some rugs inside in case you feel cold after being in Africa." Said Phillips.

"I am pleased to meet you and thank you for the rugs, that is most thoughtful of you."

Mark pointed out all the landmarks as they drove through the city and then out on the main road heading South East.

Sasha was fascinated by how old all the buildings were and how small all the fields were compared with the farms in Africa.

It had been dark for the last part of the journey, and when they started up the drive to Oakhill Hall, there was an assortment of carriages and traps, with their lamps lit, lining the last few hundred yards which made an impressive sight. Phillips drove right up to the front door through the throng of people and as Sasha stepped out there was a cheer.

"Welcome home, long live the bride and groom."

John potter, a tenant farmer, stood on the top step and said. "I 'ave been asked to say a few words. Welcome back, Mr. Mark, and a special welcome for your new bride, we all 'ope that you will be very 'appy. We would also like to thank you for 'elping us through the foot and mouth. You and Mrs. Oakhill are always welcome in all our 'omes and we 'ope that you will visit us soon."

Mark responded. "Thank you John for those kind words. Sasha and I look forward to calling on each of you very soon. A special thank you for coming tonight, to make Sasha so welcome.

My mother has arranged some refreshments in the dining room so please come in and join us."

While the throng of people was going through the front door, Mark took Sasha into the library where Agnes was waiting to greet the couple.

"Mother, please meet Sasha."

Agnes kissed Sasha on the cheek and said. "I am delighted to meet you. You are much more beautiful than your photograph. You are so tall and graceful. I am sure that you and Mark will be very happy together and I am delighted to have you in the family. We had better go through now and meet the guests. Are you ready Dear?"

Mark and Sasha held hands as they walked into the dining room with Agnes following. There was silence and John Potter raised his glass and said. "Welcome to the Bride and Groom."

Which was echoed by the throng.

Sasha squeezed Mark's hand to attract his attention and said.

"May I say a few words?" "Yes of course darling, are you sure?." Sasha nodded.

Mark raised his hand and said. "Sasha would like to say a few words."

"Ladies and Gentlemen, I am honoured to have you all here to make a special welcome for Mark and me. I expect that you would like to know something about me. My father was a French engineer working on the Suez Canal. My mother's father was English and my mother's mother came from the Sudan.

It is nearly three years since I started working for Mark's company in Johannesburg and I have seen Mark overcome terrible wounding and many of the problems with the Boer war.

I am looking forward to getting to know you all, very soon. Thank you again for your welcome."

There was loud clapping and then the hum of conversation started up again.

"You were wonderful Darling. That little speech has broken the ice and I am sure that you are going to be very happy here."

They kissed and went to mingle with the guests.